COMPASS ROSE

ANNA BURKE

Bywater
BOOKS

Ann Arbor

Bywater Books

Copyright © 2018 Anna Burke

Print ISBN: 978-1-61294-119-6

Bywater Books First Edition: July 2018

Printed in the United States of America on acid-free paper.

Cover designer: Ann McMan, TreeHouse Studio

Bywater Books
PO Box 3671
Ann Arbor MI 48106-3671
www.bywaterbooks.com

for Tiffany

Foreword

On November 7th, 2015, I lost my wife, and the world lost a talented writer and learned scholar. Sandra Moran cared deeply, not just about her own fiction, but about lesbian-centric fiction in general.

The Golden Crown Literary Society, an organization about which Sandra also cared deeply, approached me about establishing a scholarship to their writing academy in her memory. As Sandra was an instructor at the Academy and believed strongly in mentorship, I agreed this would be one of the most impactful ways to honor Sandra's memory. Thus came into being the Golden Crown Literary Society Writing Academy's Sandra Moran Scholarship.

Sandra would be so honored to know that she was the impetus for creating an opportunity for up-and-coming writers to be mentored and to succeed in their own right.

It is a privilege to introduce to you the work of Anna Burke, the inaugural recipient of the Sandra Moran Scholarship. Anna's talent is profound, and Sandra would be so proud of this, Anna's first published novel.

Enjoy reading this book, and the many to follow from this gifted writer.

Cheryl Pletcher
Asheville, NC
July 2018

East

Captain's Log
Admiral Josephine Comita
North Star, Polarian Fleet
June 15, 2513
37.1, -58.2°

As Admiral of Polaris Station and acting captain of her flagship, the *North Star*, it is with growing frustration that I record yet another log without decisive naval action. We are now seeing increased raids on outlying stations and supply lines, and despite repeated reports to the Council, no action has been taken to address the growing pirate threat. If things continue in this vein, we are at risk of losing the coastal mines, and without the mines our entire way of life will collapse into anarchy.

I have found myself revisiting Andrea Shang's canonical text, *A History of the North Atlantic Archipelago*. Her study of societal collapse is especially relevant in light of the pirate Ching Shih's growing influence in the Atlantic.

Like the collapse of Western civilization, we are at risk of failing to act until it is much too late, despite the clear warnings provided by myself and others. Now, it is not the threat of rising seas and warming temperatures that will destroy us, as we have learned to live in this altered world, but a bitter struggle for the last of the resources left that will drive us over the edge.

Unlike the collapse of the West, however, there is still time to avoid disaster, provided the Council remembers its duties to all

3

Archipelago stations instead of sinking deeper and deeper into corruption and complacency.

I will end this log with a passage from our history:

The North Atlantic Archipelago is still perhaps the greatest feat of human engineering in our impressive history as a species. Today, the Archipelago stands as a testament to the courage, resilience, and adaptability of the human race—and as a reminder of our failures. Shang, 2503.

We will not repeat these failures on my watch.

Chapter One

I was born facing due north. By the time I was three, I could pick the North Star out of the heavens with the unerring certainty with which other children picked their mothers' faces out of a crowd, and the constellations burned against my eyelids even in the darkness beneath the waves. My mother used to tell me I could be anything I wanted, except lost.

She was a literal sort of woman. My name was proof of that.

I checked our direction out of habit, tuning out the sounds around me. We were sailing east. The ship was subbed beneath the surface, keeping out of the way of the fractious wind, and down in the training room the crew burned off steam while the whitecaps mounted somewhere far above us and the night shift navigator charted a course over the deeps.

"North, south, east, west."

I named the cardinal directions softly to myself as I worked the punching bag, a little frustration boiling over into my combination each time I came back to north.

I had perilous straits of my own to navigate, and not even a compass for a brain was going to get me out of this one. Ship life was tight. It made it hard to breathe, sometimes, and even harder to avoid people like Maddox.

"Hey, jelly."

I paused mid-punch, wiping the sweat from my brow with an equally sweaty forearm. The ship's training yard was always packed after the shift change, and it took me a moment to isolate the taunt from amid the sweaty throng of people boxing, grunting, cursing, and lifting in the long, echoing room.

I didn't have to look far. Maddox's large bulk towered over me, a bead of sweat dripping from his crooked nose to the floor. His nose had been broken several times, unfortunately not by me, and it ruined his otherwise handsome face. I took an involuntary step back into the punching bag.

"What, Maddox?" I said, trying to make up for my lost ground with a bolder tone.

"We don't let drifters use the gym here," he said with a smirk.

I clenched my jaw and bit back a sharp reply. Maddox's chiseled chest glistened in the light of the bioluminescence, the genetically modified algae that flowed through the light tubes of the ship casting blue shadows over his brown skin. I entertained myself with a fantasy of plunging several sharp objects into his over-developed pectorals, but kept my mouth shut. If I didn't rise to his bait, he usually left me alone after a few rounds of verbal abuse.

"Your yellow-eyed father must have been a real noodle," he said, his lip curling in disgust. "Raised the fever flag for your mum all right, though, didn't he?"

My jaw clenched tighter, threatening to crack a few molars.

Pure-bred Archipelago citizens viewed drifters as little more than vectors for disease, their small, boxy vessels bobbing around the Archipelago ships and stations like toxic flotsam, and little better than parasites. In fairness, disease was an issue on drifter tubs, but I had a suspicion Maddox was not referring to the flag drifters raised to warn each other about contamination.

"At least he had something to raise, you—"

"If anyone deserves yellow fever, it's you, Maddox," said Harper Comita, coming to my rescue before I could finish the insult. Her arms were folded menacingly over her generous chest, and I didn't bother trying to hide my smile as she stepped between me and Maddox. Harper was shorter than me, but nobody on the *North Star* messed with my best friend. We called her "Right Cross" for her signature knockout punch.

6

"Careful who you hang with, Harper," Maddox said, his leer slipping. "Only place she's going is Davy Jones's. I'd like to see you navigate your way out of that, Compass fucking Rose."

His fists flexed impotently as he glared at me.

There were two reasons no one messed with Harper. One was her killer punch, and the other was her mother. Admiral Comita didn't play favorites, but she also wasn't about to let her crew members tangle with her only daughter.

"Go screw a barnacle," I said to his retreating back. He stiffened, but fear of retribution kept his feet moving in the other direction.

"Screw a barnacle? Really, Rose?" Harper shook her head and grinned, showing off her dimples.

"I thought it was pretty clever," I said.

"You would." She knocked my shoulder with hers, then wrinkled her nose. "You're sweaty."

"You're about to be," I pointed out, nodding toward the mats.

Harper was dressed in her Fleet-issued training clothes, her tank top and shorts clinging to her curves in a way that mine decidedly did not. Where I was tall and narrow, Harper was a bundle of muscle and feminine overtones that would have been hard not to drool over if she weren't my only friend.

"I don't know what his deal is with you," she said, narrowing her eyes in the direction Maddox had departed. "It's not like he was on the navigational track before you got here. The only thing keeping him out of the bilges is his daddy."

"He's just jealous that my nose is straighter than his," I said.

Harper laughed, her dark curls bouncing cheerfully around her head.

"Spar with me?" she asked. "I promise I'll go easy on you."

"I don't know. I had a pretty tough bout with this bag right here." I made to sidle past her and sprint for the showers, but she grabbed my wrist and hauled me over to an empty mat.

"You owe me. Maddox would totally have kicked your ass."

"Friends don't owe friends." I lectured her as she did a few warm-ups. "But if we're keeping score, then maybe we should talk about all of the things I haven't reported you for."

"Like what?"

She threw a few punches at the air. I winced as the blue light from the bioluminescent ceiling tubes blurred under the speed of her practice blows, and reached for my own gloves with exaggerated slowness.

"Like how last week you helped Jonah set up a new still, Miss Chief of Engineering."

"Whatever. I'm not Chief yet. I can do what I want."

She assumed a fighting stance, forcing me to follow suit.

"I'll remind you of that when you are Chief and you can't figure out why your staff is always drunk. There was a reason they shut Jonah down. His shit is too strong."

"For you, maybe," she said with a smirk, then lunged.

It was a short bout. They usually were with Harper. I managed to block her and she refrained from breaking my face, which by my standards was the measure of a strong friendship. Harper liked to hit things.

We sparred until we were both dripping sweat and I refused to continue.

"I need to shower," I said, wiping down the mat while Harper stretched.

"Noodle," she said.

I rolled my eyes at her. I hadn't heard the insult until I joined the Polarian Fleet. I also hadn't eaten a noodle before leaving my home station, Cassiopeia, either, which might have explained a few things.

The ocean was the soup, a sagely twelve-year-old Harper had explained to me when I first arrived, and if you couldn't handle the heat, you noodled.

The showers were not as crowded as the gym, which was a relief, and the water was pleasantly warm. It had been a sunny day and the solar heat lingered in the whole three minutes of water I was allotted.

"You're an engineer," I grumbled to Harper as I toweled off and reached for my clean uniform. "Why can't we have longer showers? There is literally water all around us."

"The rate of passive desalination is fixed, you mollusk. If everyone took the kind of showers you like, we'd die of thirst. And you'd hog all of the hot water. If you want to soak, go to the pools when we get back to Polaris."

I pictured the soaking pools on Polaris Station, with their trailing willow trees and stands of bamboo—heat from the surface sunlight keeping the water temperature toeing the fine line between refreshing and comfortable.

It was pointless. We didn't have station leave for another month.

"Does your mom have an override or something for her shower?" I asked.

"That is an obscene abuse of power," Harper said, pointing a finger at me in mock outrage. "Besides. Does it look like she ever relaxes?"

I had to give her that. Comita was the hardest woman I knew. With her steel gray hair and steelier eyes, she kept Polaris's fleet in military order. The *North Star* was the Polarian flagship, and we operated on Comita time.

"Oh. She wants to see you, by the way," Harper added. "I forgot to tell you."

I groaned and shoved my legs through my soft hemp trousers. My damp toes caught on the hem and I danced around for a few steps trying to keep my balance.

"Why? My shift is over." Dreams of my bunk faded into obscurity.

"She didn't say. She also didn't say it was urgent. Have you eaten yet?"

Harper winked at me as she shimmied into the close-fitting shirts favored by engineers and mechanics. Getting pulled into the ship's mechanisms was a risk nobody wanted to take. I pulled on my much looser shirt, enjoying the freedom. Navigators didn't have to worry about getting sucked into equipment, just the occasional hurricane.

"No," I said, not bothering to hide the despair in my voice.

"Then come get some food with me and tell the Admiral that I couldn't find you. Or that I forgot to tell you. Or whatever." She eyed me warily. "You're a beast when you're hungry. If my mother thought about it, she'd thank me for sparing her the effort of dealing with you on an empty stomach."

"I should have told you to screw a barnacle," I said. "You just don't want to sit by yourself. I'll eat as long as we make it quick. She's not my mother. I can't be late."

"You already are."

Harper smiled sweetly and led the way to the dining hall. The bio-lights were stronger, here, and the tables were full of *North Star's* finest. Laughter and the low rumble of hungry sailors filled the long room.

Dinner was fish and greens. I wolfed mine down while Harper chattered on about the latest gossip from engineering. It slipped in one ear and out of the other.

I had never been called before Comita like this. If it had been an emergency, she wouldn't have sent someone as unreliable as Harper to find me, and if it had something to do with my mother or Cassiopeia Station, then Harper wouldn't look so cheerful.

"Get out of here," Harper said, interrupting my thoughts. "I'll clear your tray, since you're not listening to anything I say anyway. My mom is in her quarters."

"Her quarters?" My voice squeaked a little. The Admiral didn't summon crew to her quarters.

"Yeah." Harper seemed unfazed by this breach in protocol, but then again, she had lived in the Admiral's suite most of her life.

"Is this about the pirates?" I asked in a hushed voice.

"She didn't say. Why don't you go find out and tell me all about it later? I have some of Jonah's brew in my bunk, if you can stomach it." She made a shooing gesture and I fled the dining hall, my mind whirling.

I dodged Maddox on the way out. I would never live it down if he knew I'd been summoned to the Admiral's personal quarters. It was bad enough that he had somehow figured out that my father was a drifter. A special summons would confirm his suspicions that I got special treatment, deepening his distrust and his unwavering belief that I didn't belong, not just on the *North Star* or Polaris, but in the Archipelago itself.

It wouldn't have bothered me if it had only been Maddox. He was just the loudest among the Fleet Prep kids I'd grown up with.

Sometimes, I wished my mother had never requested my transfer off of tiny, run-down Cassiopeia Station. Life on the edge of the Archipelago was far less glamorous, and Cassiopeia's fleet was a joke compared to the Polarian Fleet, but no one blinked twice at my parentage at home.

I ducked my head as I passed a group of sailors around my age. As a navigator, avoiding trouble was my job description.

Things were different on the smaller stations. We didn't have the resources of Polaris or Orion, two of the most influential stations in the Archipelago. We lacked the bioplastic algae farms that dominated production elsewhere, and our plastic reclamation plant relied on a handful of trawlers instead of a full fleet. As Maddox liked to remind me, we depended on trade with the drifters to keep our plant operational. There were a lot of drifter children on the smaller stations. I hadn't realized there was a stigma to it until I left.

Being a drifter had seemed exciting to me as a child. They got to go wherever they wanted, floating free of Archipelago rules, trading with the outlying stations and whoever else they pleased, but my mother had pursed her lips in silent disapproval whenever she caught me playing Drifter, Pirate, Fleet with my friends.

In retrospect, losing my father to the ocean's malice had probably sucked the romance right out of drifter culture for her, if it had ever been there in the first place.

Malnutrition and disease are rarely sexy.

I shook off thoughts of my mother. It had been a long time since I'd been back to Cassiopeia, and I was overdue for a visit. Of course, that would mean sacrificing station leave on Polaris to make the trip to Cassiopeia, a prospect that filled me with guilty reluctance.

11

Then again, I reminded myself, if I had stayed on Cassiopeia, I would not be a navigator on Polaris's flagship, serving under the greatest Admiral of our time. I could deal with anything, so long as I had that.

I repeated the cardinal points as I walked, my anxiety temporarily soothed by the repetitive chant. North, northeast, east. Southeast, south, southwest. West, northwest, and north again.

North was my point.

My mother said I scared the midwife, floating like a compass needle in the birthing bath with my infant eyes wide open. She named me Compass Rose, because, as she liked to joke, there was no other possible course. I could find my cardinal points while tied upside down in a spinning sack, which was how I'd gained an early and unprecedented acceptance into Polaris Fleet Preparatory, the most elite military sailing academy in the Archipelago.

Now that I was one of the official quartermasters under the second mate, our chief navigator, I understood why Comita had been so eager to see me enrolled. My uncanny sense of direction was useful. The ocean never stayed the same. Each minute brought new hazards, and the unpredictable winds and shifting currents obeyed mandates that even the best navigators failed to understand. It was different for me. The sea was in my blood.

I took the steep stairs to the upper decks, listening for the sound of approaching sailors. A tiny jellyfish pulsed in the biolight tube nearest my head. I paused to examine it, wondering how it had escaped the filters. Maybe, I reasoned, Comita had caught wind of a jelly swarm and wanted my advice about the best course to avoid it—except that she had a perfectly qualified night shift navigator on deck who was more than capable of avoiding a swarm.

I wiped my sweaty palms on my thighs.

I'd been to Comita's quarters a few times, but several years had passed since it was appropriate for Harper to take me to visit her mother. Time hadn't dimmed my memory of the rooms. Comita's office commanded a port side view of the bow, and her desk was a sweeping curve that faced the brilliance of the window and the waves beyond. It was an imposing room. Comita didn't believe in creature comforts.

I knocked twice on the gray door. The smooth plastic rapped hollowly under my knuckles. My mouth was dry as I straightened my uniform, and I regretted stopping for dinner with Harper. The lateness of the hour impressed itself upon me with the silence coming from the corridor.

Comita opened the door, still dressed with the military efficiency expected of a fleet Admiral. I had asked Harper, once, if her mother owned anything other than that uniform. It was impossible to picture her in civilian clothes, no matter how hard I tried. Harper had offered to show me her mother's wardrobe, but when we got to the door of her bedroom I panicked. All I could think about was Comita's eyes, boring into the back of my head.

"Compass Rose," Comita said, greeting me with her firm, measured voice. Her gray eyes took in my clean uniform with approval, and she stepped back to allow me into her quarters. Bio-light revealed the familiar entry room with its hard bench. The door beyond was open, and I could see the starlight pouring in through the window. Comita led the way, passing through her office and into the smaller, more intimate living room.

"Sit," she said, indicating one of the two low armchairs by the window.

I sat, tucking my hands between my knees.

I heard the tinkle of liquid hitting glass and hid my surprise as Comita poured me a small measure of rum. She set her own glass on the small side table and let out a deep sigh as she joined me. I tried to observe her surreptitiously. Her eyes closed, briefly, and the bio-light cast dark shadows over their hollows. She looked old.

"Forgive the informality," she said after a moment, straightening her cuffs. "I wanted to speak with you privately."

I was pretty sure I twitched visibly at her words.

"Of course, Admiral." I was proud that my voice held steady. I swirled the rum in the glass, wondering if it would be polite to drink before she did.

"How are you liking navigation?" she asked.

I blinked at her words.

"Very much."

"Walker is treating you well?"

"Yes, Admiral. Second Mate Walker is very patient with me," I said, thinking of Walker's kind eyes, so different from Comita's flinty ones.

Comita gave a little snort of un-admiral-like laughter.

"It would be easy to be patient with you, I hear. Walker swears we've never had a navigator of your caliber on this fleet, or possibly in the entire Archipelago."

"Admiral?" I said, my voice cracking at the unexpected praise.

"You are a very valuable commodity, Rose. Walker says you can calculate direction to the nearest degree without consulting any of his instruments. You know when a storm is coming before our barometers, and you can read the currents better than the ship's instruments. Walker tells me it is thanks to you we haven't hit a swarm in weeks. Whatever it is you can do, it's uncanny."

I stiffened at her last words.

"You have a gift, Rose. Uncanny or not, it is nothing to be ashamed of." She gave me a small smile. "I am not blind to the difficulties of your position. Harper lets on more than she knows, and I am not surprised. Shipboard life is cruel. Only discipline can overcome it. All that you need to know is that the fleet needs you. The fleet needs twenty of you, seas save us."

She shook her head and glanced out the window at the constellations. A small cloudbank scudded over Orion's Belt.

"Do you know why our stations are named after constellations?" she asked, continuing before I could answer. "Ancient navigators had nothing else to go by. The North Star and the sun were the only fixed points, and the constellations marked the seasons. When we learned how to navigate without them, we stopped looking up. A great deal might be different, if we hadn't. Our names are a reminder. You don't need a reminder, though. You're the kind of navigator who remembers to give the stars their due."

"Thank you, Captain."

I didn't know what else to say. Her praise undid all of Maddox's bullying, washing away the years of uncertainty in an instant. My captain needed me. My fleet needed me. She wished she had more of me, placing value on the instinct that had labeled me a freak. Little bubbles of joy burst in my chest.

"Don't thank me yet."

Her voice held a wryness I hadn't heard before, but then again I had never been summoned to her private quarters for a quiet drink. The bubbles continued their celebration, undeterred.

"Remember this, Rose. Always question whenever someone offers you praise, even when it is deserved."

She took a sip of her rum. I followed suit, grateful for a chance to hide my joy and confusion behind the glass.

It was far superior to Jonah's brew. I savored it for a moment before its potency forced me to swallow or spit it out. I held on to the glass tightly as the warmth trickled down my chest.

"I am going to offer you an unusual position for advancement," she said, meeting my eyes with the full strength of her command. I held on to the warm feeling. I had a sudden premonition it wasn't going to last much longer.

"Advancement?" I asked.

"Of a sort. There are those who might see it as something else. I won't lie to you, Rose. I am taking a risk with you. You may refuse the position, but if you refuse, I will require your complete silence and cooperation. Even from Harper."

"Of course, Admiral Comita." I took another sip of rum to wet my throat.

"You are aware that pirate raids have been increasing in frequency."

I nodded. Part of my job was mapping out safe routes for our transport subs to and from the offshore mines. We'd been losing more ships than usual.

15

"What you are not aware of is that we are at risk of losing the mines entirely."

I almost dropped my glass. Losing the mines was unthinkable. We depended on them for the raw materials necessary for ship and station repair, and they also provided the minerals that powered food, biofuel, and bioplastic production.

"Why isn't the Council doing anything?" I asked.

"You're a navigator, Rose. You see several possible courses and you take the one that makes the most sense. Politics are different. The Council's choices do not always make sense to people like you and me. Our ships can't navigate in coastal waters as well as the pirate vessels. Some council members fear we would expose the Archipelago to a direct attack from the pirates if we launched a full-frontal assault. They are willing to try to deal with the ringleader on her terms, something that anyone familiar with her tactics knows is a recipe for disaster. Which brings us to why you are here.

"I have hired a mercenary named Miranda to find out more about the threat we face. She needs a navigator who can travel undetected, and who can guide a ship through the hazards of the coast."

I choked on my next inhale. The implications of Comita's words reverberated through my buzzing skull, bouncing off the limited architecture of my rum-soaked mind. Comita had hired a mercenary? And unless I was mistaken, she wanted me to leave the *North Star* to navigate for a woman who was little more than a pirate herself, through waters infested with pirates and practically designed to swallow unwary sailors. I swallowed harshly, stifling the cough, and stared out the window to avoid meeting Comita's eyes.

The cloud had moved on from Orion, and I followed the invisible curve of his bow, longing to be topside with the wind stripping the sound of Comita's voice from my ears.

Comita's earlier praise felt hollow now. She had warned me it would, in her brusque way. The bubbles of joy in my chest were gone. Popped, like foam on a whitecap.

16

The hush grew between me and Comita as I watched the stars blink in and out of the reaching clouds. I wished I had Harper beside me. Instead, I had a small sip of rum remaining and my silent captain.

Navigating along the coasts was the stuff of legend. Boiling storms and toxic seas were the norm, and then there was the occasional methane burst. Near active fault lines, those could catch fire, burning up oxygen topside and detonating with the force of a small meteorite strike. These days, we avoided the coastal surface as best we could by using only subs to access the mines, but the pirates managed to operate both above and below water, giving them the advantage. Navigating along the coast took more than skill. It had to be in your blood.

No one else could do the job Comita was offering as well as I could. A slight thrill raced through me as I realized that there would be no Walker on that ship, no one following behind to check my calculations, nobody hoping for the inevitable slip that would prove that I was just as fallible as they were.

Of course, there would be no Harper, either, and no Comita to protect me. I felt a current catch at the wave turbines, and a minute shifting of the vessel's bulk. If I accepted, I would be alone, a ship without anchor or port.

"Are you offering me a position on this ship?" I asked, just to be sure I hadn't misunderstood.

"I am," Comita said, with a look on her face that might have resembled pity on someone else. "It will be very dangerous, Rose. You're a navigator, not a fighter. There are worse things than rough seas out there. I can't guarantee your safety."

"With all due respect, Admiral," I said softly, "nobody knows that better than a navigator."

Comita toasted me with her glass. Her mouth twisted with the bitterness of my words, and I would have bet almost anything that her thoughts were on the vessel we'd lost a few months ago to a raid.

"It won't just be jelly swarms and algae blooms. You can handle methane burps and storms. It's people I'm worried about. Harper tells me you're not much of a boxer."

I looked down at my hands and shook my head.

"Will there be fighting?" I asked.

"On a Merc ship?" Comita laughed humorlessly. "Miranda has given me her word that you won't come to harm. It is one of our conditions." She scowled, as if remembering something unpleasant, and I jumped a little in my seat as she leaned forward. Her gray eyes speared mine.

"You are to do exactly as she says, no matter what happens and no matter what you see. Your safety depends on that. If she reneges on our parley, she reneges. She's a mercenary. You, though, are a valuable tool. Pirates and mercenaries don't just throw tools away, not if they think they can use them. Obey Miranda as you would me, and even if the worst comes to pass you'll have a place on a ship. It's a bitter bargain. I wouldn't ask it of any of my crew if it wasn't absolutely necessary."

"How long would I be gone?" I turned the word "renege" over in my mind. It sent out ripples with each rotation.

"I can't give you a time frame. I will, however, give you a few days to think it over." She ran a hand through her cropped hair. It fell back into perfect military precision.

The stars swirled slightly as I tried to clear my head. The rum and the unrealness of the conversation made it hard to think.

I remembered the first time I sensed a jellyfish swarm. I was six or so, swimming in one of the filter pools on Cassiopeia with a few other children. I loved swimming close to the edge, where deep ocean hung beneath the catchment in all its murky glory. I was diving when I felt the shift in the current, as if the ocean were taking a deep breath.

The jellyfish appeared a few moments later. I heard my mother yelling my name from the upper walk, and I swam toward her, hardly able to contain my excitement. I knew with the certainty of a child that I had felt the jellyfish coming.

Later I learned the reason for this queer prescience. The languid motions of the giant swarms pulled cooler water up from the depths, circulating where the weakened winds had failed. That was the thing about the swarms. They always left cooler water behind, even as their presence clogged the filters of our submerged cities and warned of warmer waters and the toxic algae blooms to come.

"You can't feel jellies coming," my mother had scolded.

I wondered at the tiny jelly I had seen today, trapped in the bio-light, and tried not to feel it had been a warning.

"I'll do it," I told Comita.

"Think about it," she cautioned me. "Speak to me before the end of your shift tomorrow. And remember, Rose, not a word of this to the rest of the crew. Or my daughter."

Chapter Two

"So what did she want?" Harper asked when I slipped into her room later on that evening.

I had decided it would look more suspicious to Harper if I stayed away. I knew from experience that it was much better to feed her a white lie early on than to try and cover my tracks later.

"I'm not supposed to tell you," I said, collapsing into my usual chair.

Her quarters could have fit into Comita's closet. Her bunk took up one wall, and the folding table and two chairs filled the space in between. There was a small sink with a washbasin at the far end. Like me, she used the bathroom down the hall, and we ate all of our meals in the ship's cafeteria. Being the admiral's daughter had precious few perks. Her quarters, in short, were identical to mine, with one glaring exception: a jug of Jonah's brew lurked evilly on the small table, glowing an unhealthy orange in the greenish cast of Harper's bio-lights. Jonah Juice, he called it. I averted my eyes before my head started to pound in sympathetic memory of the last time I'd encountered it.

"Come on. I tell you everything that happens in engineering," she pleaded.

"That's because nothing happens in engineering. Except that." I pointed at the foul liquid.

"Let me get you a glass then," she said with an impish grin. She leaned across me to grab two cups from the tiny cabinet, which was tucked neatly into the recess behind the folding table. I held my breath and hoped she didn't catch a whiff of her mother's rum on my lips. With a sickening lurch of my stomach, I realized that there was only one possible way I could evade Harper's nose—masking the rum with the liquid fumes in the jar before me.

"This is rank, Harp," I said as I choked down a sip.

"What did you expect? It's Jonah's finest. And in case you wondered, it only gets worse with age, so drink up." She tossed back her glass to illustrate her statement, wrinkling her nose as it went down.

"If you won't tell me," she said, narrowing her eyes at me, "I'll have to guess."

"Why don't you ask your mother?" I suggested, holding the alcohol as far away from my nose as possible.

"And get sent to the bilges for insubordination? No thank you!"

I had a brief vision of Harper in the bilges, wearing the waders and high boots of a bilge hand while she slaved away in the bowels of the ship, operating the pumps that allowed the fleet ships to submerge in unfavorable seas.

Harper raised her glass in a mock toast. The gesture reminded me of her mother's an hour and several lifetimes ago. For a split second the similarities between them shone through, despite Harper's infectious charm. Her eyes were brown, unlike Comita's gray, and her hair curled sleekly around her shoulders in dark waves, but the steel lay just beneath the veneer of youth. The steel, and the discipline. Harper would turn out all right.

The morbidity of the thought shook me, as I faced a future where I might not get to see Harper come into her own. Something on my face must have shown the tenor of my thoughts, because Harper's voice lost a little of its playful edge.

"It can't be that bad. What, is she sending you to the bilges instead?"

"Hardly," I said, trying to force a smile.

"Okay. So it's not a punishment, but you're not excited, and she wanted to speak with you privately about it. That can only mean one thing." She gave me a grin. "You're getting promoted and you're worried I'll be jealous."

I laughed, shaking my head at her. "I can't keep anything a secret from you," I said in mock surrender.

"Okay," she said, rolling her eyes, "not a promotion then. So, if she didn't promote you, why did my mother have me send you to her private lair?"

That was an excellent question, I realized. Comita knew I was close with Harper, and she had to know that Harper would try to pry the truth out of me. Either she had been distracted by the prospect of war with the pirates, or it was a test to see if I really could keep my mouth shut. My brain spun, and I regretted drinking both the rum and the Jonah Juice. I needed a story that would pass inspection if Comita followed up with Harper. I didn't think Harper would rat me out, but I didn't fancy her chances against Comita's iron will, either.

"She wanted to see how I was liking being second to the Second Mate," I said. It was partially true. "Walker must have given her a report recently, because she sat me down and asked me a bunch of questions about my skills and how I was handling the pressure of being a quartermaster."

"She *is* going to promote you!" Harper said with a gasp and a toss of her head. The toast she gave me this time had none of Comita's reserve.

"Maybe," I allowed, "but Harp, think about it. She's not going to give me Walker's position. What if she wants to move me off ship?"

It was so close to the truth that it hurt. Harper's hair swung around her face as she settled back in her seat to consider this possibility. A lump formed unexpectedly in my throat, and I took another sip to fight back the onslaught of unspoken words.

The *North Star* was my home, for all that I sometimes felt out of place. Harper's friendship more than made up for people like Maddox, and I liked serving under Comita. Walker, too, had always been kind to me. His bright smile thawed the ice in the other sailors' glares, and he managed to discourage the low muttering of the other quartermasters without picking favorites. In another few years, I promised myself, their resentment would fade. They would forget about the young upstart from Cassiopeia who bypassed the training protocols and slipped into the helm.

All I had to do was stay.

Or, I could risk everything on a mission that Comita didn't dare share with the rest of her crew, including her own daughter. I wished I could spill the truth to Harper. I wanted someone else to tell me which was the right decision.

"She wouldn't," Harper said. "You're too valuable. You're practically magic." She grinned at me.

"If she did offer me a position off ship, though, what would I do? I can't leave the *North Star*."

I ran a finger around the rim of the glass. My quarters had plastic cups. Perhaps there was some merit in being the admiral's daughter after all.

"Sure you could. If you could be a navigator in your own right, wouldn't that be worth it?" Harper's eyes avoided mine.

"Only if you were my Chief of Engineering," I said, reaching out to give her shoulder a playful punch.

"The way you steer, you'd need me." She smacked my hand away and scowled.

"I thought you said I was magic."

"I said you were practically magic, not magic. Otherwise you would have seen this coming." She leapt to her feet and dragged me out of my chair, play wrestling me onto the ground and forcing another foul mouthful into my throat.

I choked on the bootlegged liquor and my own laughter.

Harper. Comita. Miranda.

I let the last name roll around in my mouth, tasting it as if I could learn something about the mercenary by repeating her name. The weight of the decision before me made my bed all the more appealing, and I curled up beneath the sheet for a few more moments as anxiety flooded me like water into a bulkhead.

The hiss of the showers slowed, marking the dwindling passage of time before I had to report to the dining hall for breakfast. I crawled out of my bunk, shouldering the weight of my dread, and splashed some water onto my face. It tasted vaguely salinated, as always, and I ran my wet hands through my hair before glancing into the mirror.

I frowned at my reflection. I kept my black hair short, although not as short as Comita's. Disobedient curls stuck up at odd angles and I splashed more water on them, following up with a comb. I didn't know why I bothered, really. It would dry however it liked. I would have to get it cut before I left.

If I left, I corrected myself. I hadn't made up my mind yet. Comita had been right to give me more time, despite my hasty words the night before. I rubbed my eyes, wondering if their color would mark me as an outcast on a mercenary vessel the same way they did on the *North Star*.

Against my dark hair and brown skin, my eyes burned with a strange amber unlike anyone else I had met in the Archipelago. The dark ring at the edge of the iris only emphasized the feral gold at the center.

I didn't like looking at them.

"Yellow-eyed drifter," Maddox called me. I had never seen a case of yellow fever, but I knew that it was the whites that turned yellow, not the irises. None of the drifters who came to Cassiopeia would dare bring an infected person close to a station.

Drifters, with their tiny trawlers and family sized vessels, operated under the radar. They were technically not part of the Archipelago, and owed our city stations no allegiance, but they depended on trade with the outlying stations for seeds and medical supplies. None would risk exile by bringing an infection to our floating ports. They raised the yellow flag of fever and drifted by themselves until the sickness passed. A black flag meant the whole vessel was contaminated, either by one of the ocean's many fevers or the bleeding sickness that hemorrhaged life out of every orifice. I shuddered, glad of the contamination protocols that kept the stations quarantined in the event of an outbreak.

I hoped the mercenary vessel had similar protocols.

I pulled on my uniform, rolling the sleeves up past my elbows, then took a deep breath and checked our direction. The light filtering through my ceiling was bright, and we were headed northeast. I felt a sudden urge to be on deck, assuming we were in clean waters, letting the sunlight and wind burn away the vestiges of the night before. The rum and the bootlegged liquor had left a gummy film over my body, like the slippery, burning flesh of a jellyfish. Maybe there would be a swarm on the horizon. Then I would have a day's work ahead of me, plotting coordinates and helping Walker run risk analysis. It was not the sort of thing I would normally wish for, but there was nothing normal about my thoughts this morning.

Breakfast was rice pudding. I toyed with it until Harper's raised eyebrow forced me to shovel the bites into my mouth with mechanical precision. At least Harper wasn't chatty, I told myself. The dining hall was packed with the rest of the day shift. I glanced around me, trying not to feel like I was saying goodbye.

"What's gotten into you?" Harper asked as she cleared her tray.

"Just a little hung over," I lied.

"Lightweight."

She pushed back from the bench and took her tray up to the compost, leaving me alone with my rice pudding. I prodded the remains of the gelatinous mass, picturing the rice paddies of Polaris and the freshwater fish that swam through the shallows. I might never see them again.

Perhaps, I thought, I should have gone into aquaculture or hydroponics, instead of navigation.

My internal compass twitched. Sunlight streamed through the windows, but to the east the winds were shifting. I could feel it in the currents. A storm was coming. I abandoned the last few bites of my breakfast and cleared my tray, avoiding the eyes of the other sailors on my way to the compost chute, which smelled strongly of last night's fish.

Harper met me at the cafeteria's noxious yellow door with a yawn.

"See you tonight?" she asked, preparing to descend the tight stairs to the lower levels where she spent her days. I nodded mutely, suddenly unable to force words out of my tight throat. She rolled her eyes at me and turned to leave.

"Harp," I called after her. She stopped and I took a hesitant step forward.

"You're being weird, Rose."

I pulled her to me in a tight hug, squeezing some of the breath out of both of us. Her head barely came up to my chin, and I rested my cheek against her sleek hair, trying to make sense of my tumbling world. Harper tolerated this for a few seconds before pulling away.

"Sorry," I mumbled, letting my arms drop to my sides. They hung there limply while Harper stared at me.

"Are you sure you're okay?"

"Yeah," I said. "Storm's coming. I have to get to the helm."

I could feel her eyes on my back the entire length of the narrow hallway.

Walker was waiting.

Sunlight drenched the helm, which jutted out from the submerged body of the ship like a knife handle to give us 360 degrees of unobstructed ocean. Charts covered the table in the center and the ship's computer hummed quietly, salt water coursing through the conduit wires to the wave-generated battery in the ship's belly. I could feel the pulses. The computer reminded me of a giant octopus, with its tentacles hooked into every system onboard. The electrical impulses sometimes interfered with my inner compass.

"There's too much water in you," one of the fortune tellers on Cassiopeia had told me as a child. I was inclined to believe her.

"Rose," Walker said in his gently authoritative tone. I stood to attention, noting the presence of my two fellow quartermasters. Neither glanced my way. As always, their resentment was palpable.

I wondered if Walker knew about Comita's secret request. His warm eyes met mine, revealing nothing.

"At ease. Take a look at this." He beckoned me over to the central table.

"Are the barometers getting any low pressure readings?" I asked him, eying the computer's glossy screen.

"Not yet, no. You picking up on something they're not?"

"Might be a storm headed our way," I said, glancing out at the peerless blue sky.

"Storms I can handle. This is more concerning." He pointed a thick finger at a chart. "One of our scouts reported some unusual activity."

"What kind of activity?" I examined the chart. It was of an area of ocean some fifty miles east, between us and the Gulf of Mexico.

"A transport vessel reported something tonal. It wasn't like our sonar, but it was definitely code. Whatever it is, it is closer than usual, and we didn't get a good sighting."

"Could just be drifters," a quartermaster named Marjory offered.

"Or pirates," suggested Sam, the other quartermaster.

"Could very well be pirates," Walker repeated, looking up at me. "Pirates that are subbed deeper than we thought possible, and far too close for comfort. Rose, I need an estimated trajectory based on these coordinates, and I will keep you up to date on anything our scout can send in."

"What about that storm, sir?" I asked.

"I'll have someone report it to Polaris and have the ship prepped to sub," Walker said. "In the meantime, I need you on this, Rose."

"Yes, sir," I said. I took a seat at the table and pulled the charts closer, running my hands along the printed plastic maps.

Deep-subbing pirate ships were bad news. It almost eclipsed Comita's request, and I spent the morning charting possible courses and trying to determine how long it would take the pirate vessels to make contact with our supply line. The trouble was, if they had technology we didn't know about, then I had no way of calculating their knots, which meant that at best I had a vague window of their arrival—if they meant to attack at all.

I looked up from the chart in time to catch a glare from Marjory that I wasn't supposed to see. I ignored her. Marjory had been forced to split her duties with me when I graduated, and I couldn't blame her for her resentment, even though it stung. At least she had a good reason for disliking me, unlike Maddox.

I rubbed the web between my forefinger and thumb, feeling for the shift in currents that indicated the shape of the coming storm.

There was a slight tug to the east, a catch in the currents that suggested the beginnings of a hurricane. Out here in the soup, monster storms formed overnight, turning the summer seas into boiling cauldrons. Even subbed there were still risks. A storm might delay a pirate attack, even if their vessels could sub as deeply as ours. On the other hand, it would also provide ideal cover for their movements. Comita was right. We needed more intel. I bit my lip in frustration.

"You're a navigator, Rose. You see several possible courses and you take the one that makes the most sense." Comita's voice echoed in my ears, shadowing the bright sunshine with the memory of our conversation the night before. Nervous sweat pricked my armpits.

There was only one possible course.

Chapter Three

Comita was an active admiral.

Technically her office was below the upper helm, in a circular suite that commanded almost the same view as Navigation, but in practice she roamed the ship, acting as both captain and admiral as she kept tabs on her subordinates and made sure everything operated as it should. Tracking her down was easy enough. She left a trail of hyperefficient sailors in her wake, all of whom cast the occasional anxious glance over their shoulders.

I found her on the upper deck, examining the hydrofarms.

Most of our staple provisions were grown on Polaris, but the ship produced fresh greens, fish, and edible algae for its crew. Unlike the gardens on Polaris, this hydrofarm was built for function, not form, and the uniform lines of plants did little to soothe my anxiety. I passed through rows of green until I was within earshot of the admiral and the technician making his report.

". . . trace elements of toxicity in the first purification cycle, but we get it all out by the third," the tech said. Comita looked up as I rustled past an army of collards.

"Thank you, Jerome," she said to the tech. "Compass Rose."

"Admiral," I said.

"Excuse me, Jerome. I look forward to reading your report."

Jerome gave her a salute as Comita strode out of the garden. I nodded at the tech and followed, breathing in the humid air. Comita's short stature was less evident here among the many rows of lettuce, spinach, and kale, and I followed her with my pulse pounding in my ears. She led me out of the greenhouse and through the ship's less traveled passageways. These narrow hallways were usually reserved for the maintenance crews, and they were full of exposed pipes and the hiss of water and recycled air. I was out of breath by the time we returned to the lower helm.

"Let's take a walk on deck," Comita suggested. "We are far from any reported dead zones, and air toxicity levels are normal."

We would be in full view of Navigation from the small deck at the base of the helm, which made me uneasy. I blinked into the harsh sunlight as she flung open the hatch. The deck was damp with spray, although the textured surface gripped the soles of my boots firmly, and the wind caught at my clothes and buffeted them around my legs and waist. Comita's short cropped hair barely stirred as she beckoned me over to the starboard side.

The first traces of clouds floated on the horizon, gathering strength in thin wisps. Sunlight gleamed off the smooth surface of the water, refracting on the glass of the helm at our backs and the roofs of the hydrofarms ahead. Comita leaned against the starboard rail and looked out over the quiet sea.

"There is nothing unusual about a captain consulting a navigator on a clear day," she said in a measured tone. "And no one will hear us here."

The implication that someone might be listening made my skin itch.

"It won't be clear for long," I told her, pointing at the sky.

"It never is." She smiled thinly. "So, Rose, do you have an answer for me?"

"I do," I said. The next words caught in my throat and my hand clenched the rail. "I will do it. Anything for the fleet, and the Archipelago."

"I am glad you feel that way. Not many would, in your position." She met my eyes. "There is something else you should know. I will have no way of communicating with you directly while you are with Miranda. All communication will have to go through her, so watch what you say."

"You don't trust her, Captain?"

"She is a mercenary. I don't trust anyone off of my ship, let alone a mercenary, and neither should you. Do your job, play it safe, and keep your eyes and ears open. Miranda has too much riding on this to renege, but there is always something beneath the surface. War is an iceberg. Remember that."

"Yes, Admiral," I said, not bothering to point out that neither she nor I had ever seen an iceberg.

"There is one more thing. You will no longer be under Polarian Fleet protection once you leave this ship. If word gets out that Polaris has undermined council authority, things will get complicated. For all intents and purposes, you must act as a member of her crew. If you are captured by another fleet, you will be on your own. Don't let that happen. If it does, do whatever is necessary to escape, and we will deal with the consequences later. There is no need for you to lose your life at the hands of your own people. Don't make me say this twice, Compass Rose. You are a rare sailor. I would not see you drowned."

She turned away from me before I could see her face, leaving me speechless. "You leave within the hour. Pack your things."

"Within the hour?" My voice squeaked. I had assumed that I would not leave until tomorrow at the earliest, if not a week from now.

"This storm and Walker's intel changes things. I want you safely to the parley point and my vessel back to the *North Star* before this hits. You won't have time to say goodbye to anyone, and the fewer people who know where you are, the better. Do you understand?"

"No," I answered truthfully. I didn't see how telling Harper my whereabouts would put Comita at risk. Harper was her own daughter, and was hardly likely to betray her mother to the council. A slight frown creased Comita's forehead.

"What did I tell you about politics last night?"

"That they don't make much sense to people like you and me," I repeated.

"The same can be said of certain orders from your admiral."

31

There was no mistaking her meaning. I clicked my teeth shut on my questions, stinging slightly from the reprimand.

"Report to the helm as soon as you are packed. Take clothes, and nothing more. I will have a scouting vessel ready for you, and all that you will need to serve under Miranda."

My bunk had never looked so bleak. I stood in the doorway for a moment, then grabbed my fleet-issued hemp duffel and shoved my training clothes into it. There was plenty of space left over. I paused. The only other clothes I owned were fleet uniforms. Somehow, I didn't think that would go over well on a Merc ship. I fingered the soft hemp trousers and the loose shirts in my drawer, then left them there. Instead, I picked up the small, crude carving Harper had given me one year for my birthday. It was supposed to be a jellyfish, but looked more like a drowned mushroom.

They called me "jelly" because my father was a drifter, and jellyfish ride the currents, unwanted wherever they go. Harper was the only one to soften the nickname.

"He calls you jelly because he's jealous. Get it? Jelly?"

"Please, never abbreviate your words again. I get enough of that in the helm," I'd said, but I'd been unable to hide the smile that followed me around the rest of that day.

I smiled again at the memory. Harper would be furious with me for leaving without saying goodbye. I could leave her a note, but that would be in direct defiance of Comita's orders. I chewed my lip. Comita would tell Harper something, but would it be the truth?

There was nothing else to pack, except a few toiletries. I straightened the sheets on my bed and hoisted my bag. It was depressingly light.

My head felt tight as I ascended the stairs to the helm for what might be the last time. I clutched the duffel tightly in my fist and hoped nobody would ask me any questions. For once in my life, Maddox didn't appear to torment me when I wanted it least, disproving my theory that he could smell my misery from across the ship. The only people I passed were sailors about their business. I avoided their eyes and walked more quickly.

I took the back passageways again. The bio-lights illuminated the tubes and pipes twining around each other like the eels in the salt pools on Cassiopeia. I didn't see any more captive jelly-fish, although the water in the light tubes was slightly clouded. The storm was going to be massive.

After the dimness of the hallways, the light in the helm was blinding. My eyes watered, and I blinked the false tears away. Comita was waiting with a handful of burly sailors I recognized by their uniforms if not by name.

"Fair seas, Compass Rose," Comita said.

Her stern tone was at odds with a roughness that disarmed me. She cleared her throat, and for several moments I was afraid I might actually cry. Comita had shown more emotion toward me in the past twenty-four hours than in my entire time onboard the *North Star*.

"This way, navigator," the largest of the sailors said. He had a flat face with a flatter nose, and his dark hair was slightly gray at the temple. The woman beside him was only slightly less intim-idating, with biceps that were at least as thick as my thighs. The third sailor was another man, unremarkable except for a livid scar that ran the length of his face and neck.

These were no ordinary crew members. These were SHARKs, the Archipelago Fleet elite. I felt very small and fragile standing before them.

The woman held a thick binder, which I assumed enclosed copies of the charts I'd need to navigate for Miranda. It looked tiny next to her Amazonian figure. She tossed it to me, and I caught it awkwardly with one hand and packed it in with my clothes.

"All right, people, let's move," said the woman.

I was jostled between the two men as we exited the helm, and my stomach clenched as I realized where we were going.

The vessel bay was accessible by several routes. There were stairs and passages within the ship, and then there was the

Ladder. I hated the Ladder. It was, more accurately, several ladders, but they all plunged down the side of the ship, pausing occasionally to allow room for a maintenance hatch. The fact that the ladder was fully encased in clear plastic several inches thick did not diminish the terror of descent. With a long drop below me and the pressure of the ocean all around, it was, in short, a thing of nightmare.

Rung after rung passed beneath my hands. One of the maintenance hatches had been used recently, and the maintenance tech had not bothered to take the time to wipe the water from her boots. My hands slipped on the wet rungs.

I lost my grip twice, catching myself both times just before one of the SHARKs could reach out and steady me. I was shaking by the time we reached the door that led to the vessel bay level. It opened into a tight tunnel, which did not ease my growing claustrophobia, and we had to pass through several more hatches as we navigated in between the bulkheads. The muscles on the female SHARK bulged as she turned the hatch wheels. I tried not to stare, but she caught my gaze and winked.

Despite everything, I blushed.

The last hatch led to the vessel bay. Here, the scouting subs bobbed in a pool of salt water, charging their batteries, along with some flotsam and the inevitable rogue jellyfish. Each vessel was sleek, designed for speed beneath the waves, and thick cables bobbed along the surface. I was reminded yet again of the sinuous eels of my childhood. Like some of the eels, these cables were also electric.

One of the subs was fully charged and disconnected, and a few techs were busy putting the finishing launch preparations together as we entered. The bio-lights were dimmer down here. I wondered how they were able to see what they were doing.

Maybe they would make a mistake, I hoped, and I would be forced to delay my departure.

My eyes found the doorway to the inner decks at the top of a long flight of stairs. I stared at it, willing Harper or Comita to step out and tell me that this was all a misunderstanding, or in

34

Harper's case a prank that had lost its humor. I was prepared to forgive her, as long as she emerged soon.

The seconds ticked by and the SHARKs joked with the techs, making their own operational sweep of the vessel.

"Come on, navigator," the woman called out. "We've got coordinates to catch before this motherfucker blows."

I tore my eyes away from the doorway and clambered awkwardly into the sub. Inside, the bio-light was even dimmer, if possible. I waited for my eyes to adjust before finding a low bench on the far wall alongside the instrument panels. There was a small window there, and I sought out the dwindling doorway again as the SHARKs piled in and the sub dropped through the first level. I heard the dock seal up, and then the gate below us opened into deep ocean. The sub whirred away and slipped easily into the nearest current.

"Make yourself useful, navigator," the woman suggested.

I stumbled to my feet and approached the navigation panel. Coordinates mapped themselves onto the computer screen, glowing with the same blue green light as the bioluminescence in the bio-lights around us.

I hadn't navigated for a sub before. It took me a few minutes to orient myself, which the tightness in my head impeded. It wasn't the pressure change, although that took some time to adjust to as well. I missed the *North Star* already.

The blinking lights on the screen were no match for the sun or stars. I tried to block out the morbid jests of the SHARKs and concentrate on the currents, feeling the way they nudged at the sub. The female SHARK even let me take the wheel, which momentarily dispelled all of my fears and misgivings. The sub handled more lightly than a fleet vessel, and the power mechanisms were slightly different. I glanced around at the various instruments, trying to make sense of things.

"How does it work?" I asked.

"Are you a navigator or an engineer?" Flat Nose said with a sneer. "There's a manual in here somewhere. A little light reading for you."

I shut up after that.

The parley point was two hours away, past the range of Fleet sonar, which would give the vessel just enough time to return to the *North Star* before things hit the soup topside and docking grew difficult even beneath the waves. The SHARKs gradually fell silent, hulking in the small space like their namesake. My thoughts turned toward Miranda.

Miranda the mercenary. Mercenary Miranda. It had a nice ring to it, if a slightly ominous one. How had Comita made contact with her? What exactly was I supposed to be doing onboard her illegitimate vessel?

Miranda was the mercenary spy, I tried to reassure myself. I was just the navigator. My lip twitched in bleak amusement. I had been on a ship long enough to know a shifting current when I felt one. Things were never quite that simple. Few roles were as important as a navigator's. The captain called the shots, but the navigators told the captain where to sail.

If Miranda sank, I sank with her.

"We're almost there," I said, keeping my voice flat.

"Alright, kiddo," the SHARK woman said. "Here's how this is gonna go down. We'll breach and dock against their vessel. It should be a small one, an intermediary, if they follow the rules of parley."

"Which they never do," the scarred SHARK added.

"We hand you over," the woman continued, "unless things look soupy, and then we'll try to bail."

"With or without you," the scarred SHARK promised.

"We bail with you. You are the mission priority as long as you're on this sub." The woman ignored the other man's comment. "All you have to do is sit tight, look pretty, and try not to piss off the Mercs."

She winked at me again, bringing on another blush. I hoped it didn't show in the half dark.

"All right then." Flat Nose stood and cracked his knuckles, stretching out his trunkish forearms. "Let's get wet."

My stomach plummeted as the vessel rose. The water was definitely getting murkier outside the window, and I resumed my seat while the pros took over. I felt the vibration of a water horn through the sub's wall, and knew that we'd been hailed by the other vessel.

Panic tightened my throat. This was not how things were supposed to be. I was going to be second mate one day, and Harper was destined to be chief of engineering of the *North Star*. This was wrong. It was all wrong. I didn't care about supply lines or politics. Comita could find someone else to wage her war on the sea and on the pirates. Politics were above my pay grade, and espionage was nowhere in my job description.

That wasn't true, I thought with another wave of dread. It was in there, with firm warnings about how dabbling in intrigue would end up with me taking a long walk off a short pier.

I whimpered deep in my throat as the surf frothed against the window.

"Looks like your ride is here, kid." There was a thump as a line hit the roof of the sub, and the SHARKs piled cautiously out of the hatch. It was only after the last one vanished that I noticed how heavily armed they were. My teeth began to chatter.

"Hey-oh," a strange woman's voice called.

"Parley," said the female SHARK.

"You got the navigator?" The stranger asked.

"You got any manners?" The SHARK shot back. "We'll need some proof before we hand her over to you."

"Here—signed and sealed by Miranda herself." There was the sound of someone spitting, and the bump of two vessels docking.

"No need to tie us on. We won't be staying for a drink," said the female SHARK.

"Too bad. There's a big old cocktail all around you, and you look a little thirsty," said the mercenary. I didn't like her tone at all.

"I've got orders not to kill you, scum, so shut your mouth before I make my admiral wish she'd drowned my mother before I was born," said the SHARK woman.

The mercenary laughed before replying.

"Your mother was too ugly to drown. Ocean spat her right back out."

"Ain't that the truth. Sounds like you've met her, seas save you." The SHARK woman laughed along with the mercenary. "Anyway, looks like this checks out. Hey kid!" She leaned down the hatch. "You've got some new friends out here anxious to meet you."

I didn't piss myself, which is all I could say about my courage as I climbed the ladder. The clouds were mounting heavily now, and the waves had turned into swells. A small vessel bobbed alongside our sub, its battered hull more rust than steel.

On it stood a group of people I could happily have gone a lifetime without meeting up close. Tattoos covered most of their available skin, and there was a leanness to their bodies that suggested hunger more than discipline. None of them looked happy to see me in my clean fleet uniform. I counted six sets of scowls, each unique in its expression of distaste.

"Good luck, kiddo," said the female SHARK. She squeezed my shoulder. "You'll make Admiral Comita proud."

Flat Nose thrust a rope ladder in my hands and tossed my duffel to the other deck. A huge, dark-skinned man caught it, with a smile that turned my blood to algae.

"Can you find your way, navigator?" Flat Nose asked.

I met his eyes. Beneath the cruel humor was a touch of pity. I nodded and swung out on the ladder. There was a dizzying feeling of weightlessness before the ladder caught, and then I had to focus all my energy on scaling the swinging thing and not slipping into the Atlantic. The water was darkening to match the clouds, and the spray wet the crude rungs as I dangled against the rusted hull. Large flakes of rust fell into the water as my boots scraped the side, revealing darker layers of corrosion beneath.

"I've had enough ladders for one day," I whispered to myself as I climbed. Wind assaulted me in little gusts, and the spray from the surf drenched my trousers from the knee down within seconds. The rope ladder was made of tough hemp, and the fibers dug into my palms and slipped beneath my feet, making for a clumsy climb.

I was glad I couldn't see the faces of the crew above me, or the derisive pity of the crew leaving me behind.

The top of the ladder came too soon. With an effortless motion, the dark-skinned man reached out and hauled me over the rail. I wasn't ready for it. One of my boots tangled in the last rung and tugged free with a painful wrench. It wobbled unsteadily beneath me as he set me down, forcing me to grab onto his forearm for support. My pride wilted beneath the snort of laughter I heard from one of his crewmates.

In the unwanted proximity, I realized that his skin was actually brown, like mine. The black tone came from the grotesque kraken inked all across his chest and arms, resplendent in its glory only inches from my nose. Tattooed tentacles curled around his body with disturbingly lifelike suckers. The worst part was his face. Around his mouth, some twisted tattoo artist had detailed a kraken's beak, and his real eyes were lost in the inky pupils of the massive squid-like orbs the artist had obviously seen in a nightmare before rendering onto flesh. I stifled a small scream.

"Welcome aboard, fleet scum," he said cheerfully.

I stiffened my knees to prevent them from collapsing and tried not to wince at the pain in my ankle. Behind me, I heard the familiar gurgle of a fleet vessel subbing, lost to me now beneath the waves, just a dark shape beneath a darker sea.

Chapter Four

"All useless hands below," a woman shouted, and the tattooed man shoved me gently toward the less-than-sturdy stairs below the helm.

"We're not subbing?" I asked, hesitating as a large wave rocked the deck.

"Only way this tub will sub is if you put a hole in her," he said in the same cheerful tone.

I didn't find the thought cheerful at all.

"Don't worry, kid, we'll be back to the big ship before you can spit."

I cast a frantic glance around at the empty ocean. There wasn't a single ship on the horizon, only the massive thunderheads boiling into a hurricane above us.

It was almost pitch black below deck. The only light came from a huge jar of bio-light screwed into the table against one wall.

"Annie, at the helm. I'll be right up."

The woman's voice was the same one that had jested with the SHARKs. I struggled to make out her features as she approached me in the gloom. She was shorter than the man, and wore her hair pulled back into a hundred small braids threaded through with shells. They clinked with her impatience as she placed a hand on the short sword at her hip. Her fingers tapped on the hilt as she stared at me.

"You're the Polarian Fleet's best navigator?" She eyed me up and down.

The scrutiny raised my hackles. It was too familiar.

"I am," I said, straightening my spine.

"How old are you, five? No wonder Comita is desperate." She shook her head, making the shells sing.

"Who the hell are you?" I said, trying to ignore the jab.

A few of the other mercenaries whooped their approval at my abrasive words. I steadied myself on my injured ankle as the woman took a step closer to me. The half-light revealed the orcas tattooed around her biceps. Their eyes were blood red, even in the gloom.

"I am Orca, Miranda's First Mate. And you are nobody until I tell you something different, so listen to me carefully. Miranda wants you alive and ready to work, but she didn't say anything about delivering you untouched. Do you understand me?"

I refused to nod.

"We have another hour before we reach the *Man o' War*. That's Miranda's ship. Don't speak. Don't move."

She leaned in a little closer. I could smell the salt air on her skin.

"And if you are not the best fucking navigator that your fleet has ever seen, I will drink rum out of your skull and flog you with strips of your own hide."

She smiled, then turned on her heel and ascended the stairs to the helm to battle the waves. I looked around me at the faces of my new crew. I wondered what they would do to me if I vomited all over their patched and salt-stained clothes. My stomach lurched threateningly.

Fleet ships were stable. They subbed beneath the worst of the waves during storms, which made for smooth sailing 99.9 percent of the time. The mercenary parley ship was a whole other kettle of fish. Sick fish. I sank to the ground and fought the urge to throw up for as long as I could.

"We got a greenie," one of the mercenaries announced, curling his lip at me as I fought down the impulse to retch.

"Someone get her a bucket," the giant ordered from his seat at the table. He was carving something with a sharp knife and acting like the entire world wasn't rocking up and down.

I thanked the bucket deliverer by not getting sick on her shoes. It seemed polite under the circumstances.

I was sick for an eternity. Eventually, the kraken knelt next to me with a jug of water and a dirty-looking handkerchief.

"Hey, Fleeter. You'll be wanting to drink this, now. *Man o' War* is ready for us."

I wiped my streaming eyes with the handkerchief before pouring water into my mouth. I spat the first mouthful out, then choked down half of the jug.

"Easy, now," he said, and patted me with a giant hand. "I'm Kraken. This here is Jeanine," he pointed at a lanky woman with her hair shaved on the left side to reveal a decidedly hungry shark tattooed on her scalp.

"And this over here is Barney the Barnacle and Hammerhead Harry." The two men grinned as he named them, revealing enough teeth between them for a complete set. "Up top is Annie. She's the skipper of this tub, and Orca, who you've already gotten yourself acquainted with." He stood up and offered a hand.

I took it reluctantly and rose shakily to my feet.

"We're Miranda's most reliable," he added, eliciting a round of appreciative laughter, "and now we're going to deliver you to the good captain."

I braced myself against the wall as the seas bucked against us.

"She's going to be sick again," Jeanine said.

"No, she's not," Kraken said, looking at me. "She's going to pull her little fleeter ass together, unless she wants a baptism." This brought more laughter. None of it was friendly.

"And you can keep that," he said as I offered him the handkerchief.

"She'll need it when she cries herself to sleep tonight." The woman with the shark tattoo smiled at me.

I decided I didn't like Jeanine.

"Does the *Man o' War* sub?" I asked in a weak voice.

"Sinks like a stone. Come up top now and see for yourself."

Kraken stood up, filling the room, and I forced myself to follow him up the steep stairs despite the waves that slammed me into either side of the stairwell. He threw open the hatch door, and through the beginnings of the storm I saw my new ship breaching through the waves. Water cascaded off her in rivulets, revealing a hull that gleamed a steely silver through the sheets of rain. I blinked drops of blowing rain out of my eyes and tried to keep my jaw shut on both vomit and awe.

The *Man o' War* was smaller than the *North Star*, but what it lacked in size and sophistication it made up for with its strangeness. It had none of a fleet ship's narrow grace. The hull was rounder, blunter, built for handling waves on top of the water as well as beneath, and rust and weather damage had left its mark on every surface.

Directly ahead of us, a sea door opened, and our boat bobbed toward it like an errant cork. I could hear Annie cursing the wind and waves from the helm as she struggled to keep us on course through the swells. The sea door grew larger as we approached, and someone lit a torch in the darkness to guide us in.

My earlier confidence in my ability to navigate the coasts wavered as Annie forced the boat through the opening by sheer force of will, riding on top of a particularly rambunctious swell. A dozen hands rushed to catch the ropes thrown out by the crew of the parley vessel, and I braced myself for an impact that never came. Kraken, Orca, Annie, and the others shouted out commands while the sea door creaked shut behind us, blocking out the last of the light.

"Let's get her back under," Kraken bellowed. It echoed in the large chamber, and I wondered how many other leaky vessels lurked in the bay. The ship groaned all around me as the pumps started their reverse, and I heard the familiar rush of water into the bulkheads.

At least some things remained the same.

The crew's chatter was full of unfamiliar slang, and it beat at my ears until I stopped trying to decipher it. Instead, I stood on the deck, clutching my duffel and a filthy handkerchief, while my eyes adjusted to the bio-light. It was greener than what I was used to, and the large porthole over the sea door needed a good scrubbing. The light it let in was tainted by dust and filth. I watched the waves foam up around it as we subbed.

"Are you deaf? Fleeter!"

I jumped as Orca shouted into my face.

"What?" I said.

"Follow me. The captain wants to see you, though once she gets a look at you she might change her mind." Orca smirked.

She had full lips and high cheekbones, but I would drown myself before I admitted that someone who looked at me like I had recently crawled out of the sewage tank was beautiful.

I stiffened in indignation, but Orca didn't wait to hear if I had a response. She leapt over the railing and to the dock below, leaving me standing alone. My ankle throbbed preemptively as I glanced over the side. It was a long way down.

"Please don't let me fall," I whispered, sending a brief prayer to the cardinal directions.

It was an awkward jump and a clumsy landing, but I didn't lose my balance. Orca was waiting for me with the same little smirk on her lips. I made a silent vow to wipe it off one day, preferably with my fist.

Kraken peeled away from the docking crew and loomed above me. I took an involuntary step toward Orca.

"Put this on her, Kraken," she said, tossing a length of cloth past my left ear.

Kraken caught it in a massive fist. It took me a moment too long to register that it was a hood.

"Try to keep up," Orca said to me, in a voice that suggested she didn't care if I fell into the compost chute.

Kraken looped a thin cord around my wrists before dropping the rough sack over my head. It smelled like salt and stale breath. I bit my lip to fight back a surge of panic and followed them, struggling to hide my limp as my boots stumbled blindly over unfamiliar ground.

Light pulsed and faded through the sacking. That was the only indication I had of my progress through the bowels of the ship. I tripped up stairs and scraped against walls, listening for the quick tread of Orca's boots ahead of me and the thud of Kraken's heavier step behind. Orca held the rope that bound me. She didn't jerk it, but she didn't slow to accommodate my cautious steps, either.

I was shaking by the time I stumbled into Orca. She gave an irritated sigh, then ripped the hood from my head, along with several strands of hair. I blinked at the blinding light.

We were in a round room. Worn red carpets covered the floor, and the wood paneling on the walls gleamed in the light of a huge chandelier. Paintings leapt out at me, some of ships, others of landscapes that were as alien to me as the surface of the moon. Everything in the room was a direct contradiction to the aesthetics of fleet command, and I wondered, with a surge in my heart rate, where in all seven seas Admiral Comita had sent me.

"Compass Rose."

The voice cut into my panic. I turned, briefly noticing the long table covered with maps before I saw the woman leaning against the end of it. Her toned, bared arms were crossed over her chest and a thick, dark braid hung over one shoulder, gleaming warmly in the firelight.

My mouth went a little drier. I knew her eyes were blue before I met them, and the sudden chill that shook my body had nothing to do with my lengthy bout of sea sickness.

"Welcome aboard," she said.

I didn't need an introduction. This was Miranda. I could tell by the reverent looks on the faces of Orca and Kraken, and by the dangerous heat that radiated from the woman like the light from the lamps above her.

She nodded at Orca, who undid my wrists with significantly more courtesy than she'd previously shown me. I rubbed the mark where the cord had cut into my skin and tried to calm my rapid heartbeat as I stole another glance at the mercenary captain. She couldn't have been that much older than me, mid-twenties maybe, and I thought twenty-five was pushing it.

Blue eyes met mine with all the unexpected force of a rogue wave. My breath caught, and for a split second I was back on the parley vessel, plunging down into the trough of a passing swell with the ocean opening beneath me.

North, east, south, west. I clung to my cardinal points and tried not to drown.

"Rough seas?" Miranda asked, holding out her hand.

I reached for it, still reeling. Her grip was firm and warm and I felt an unusual callus on her palm as she withdrew, almost like a scar.

"Nothing Annie couldn't handle." Orca's voice held none of its earlier contempt. It was almost pleasant. "Gave Rose here a little upset, though."

Miranda raised an eyebrow.

"We prefer to avoid waves, where I'm from," I said.

"No surprise there," said Orca under her breath.

"You'll adapt." Miranda's words held no room for alternatives.

She reached below the table and pulled out a flagon of what looked alarmingly like rum. My stomach flopped. More rum was the last thing I needed after a sail like that.

I was in the process of preparing a polite refusal when Miranda laid a slender knife and a clean bandage by the bottle. I traced the blade with my eyes. It was old, and carved from the bone of some ancient sea creature with a blade that had been honed so often that it was barely more than a sliver.

"So," Miranda said, running a finger along the blade. "This is a rare opportunity. The Polarian Fleet's most promising navigator aboard a mercenary vessel."

I saw Orca smirk out of the corner of my eye.

"I run a tight ship. It might not look like much to you, but we follow a code, and with that code comes rules. You, however, pose an interesting dilemma. I have a deal with your captain, but deals at sea are rarely weather-tight. If you are going to serve on my ship, then you and I need to come to an agreement."

"Admiral Comita," I began, but Miranda cut me off.

"Admiral Comita is a long ways away. I need your word, not your admiral's."

I looked at the blade on the table again, wondering what would happen if I refused. Comita had bid me to do whatever Miranda ordered, no matter how strange it might seem to me.

"What kind of agreement did you have in mind?" I asked.

She unstoppered the rum bottle and let two drops run down either side of the knife blade. I watched them drip off the tip and onto the stained wood table. In the silence, I heard them hit the surface with a faint plop that sounded disturbingly like dripping blood.

Comita better make me second mate for this when I get back, I thought.

"This is how we seal a contract." Miranda placed her right hand on the table next to mine, palm up. A curious scar marked the surface, interrupting what Cassiopeia's fortune tellers called the life line, the heart line, and the head line. I tried not to dwell on the superstitious significance.

A curved line underscored her fingers, and three squiggly lines branched out from beneath it. The name of the ship suddenly made sense. The scar resembled a simplified jellyfish, rather like a man o' war. I felt my eyes widen and tried to stop them. The scars were deep, as was the irony. I would never escape the nickname now. I looked at my own smooth palm, and back to Miranda's, then to the knife.

There was no mercy in Miranda's eyes.

"Give me your hand," she said.

In the light of the burning lamps, I noticed a thin tracery of scars covering her face. They stood out from her suntanned skin in ghostly lines, and continued down her neck. I looked at her hands, and her bare arms, and saw the faint scars there, too.

I knew better than to ask. Instead, I stuck out my right hand and tried not to tremble. My little finger quaked traitorously. When she offered me a drink of the rum, I took a long swig.

47

"You have strong hands," Miranda said, running her thumb across my palm. "Orca, read her the articles."

"The whole thing?"

"The important parts." Miranda kept my hand trapped in hers while Orca's voice recited the ship's articles from memory.

"One. Every crew member has a vote, which you may cast as you see fit whenever a vote is called. Any crew can call for a vote at any time, provided they are seconded by another crew member.

"Two. Every crew member is issued two sets of clothes, one pair of boots, a ration of rum, and two meals a day, plus pay. If you steal from a crew member, you will be punished according to the severity of your theft. If you steal twice, you shall be lashed. Steal thrice, and the captain reserves the right to maroon or walk you, as she chooses.

"Three. Don't gamble. Just don't. Especially you, fleeter. You'll lose. Four. Deserters will be killed. So will spies. Five. You will be ready at all times to defend your ship, your captain, and your fellow crew, and you will keep your weapons sharp and close at hand. Six. Any and all disputes between crew members will be settled on the deck at the hour of the First Mate's choosing. Brawling shipside is punishable by three lashes. Seven. In exchange for loyal service, the captain will care for you and your family. Since you don't have a family, I'll skip this part with your leave, Captain." Miranda nodded.

"Eight. You will suffer no rat to live upon this ship and you will treat ship cats as crew, knowing that at all times they are more essential to your captain than you are. Nine. You will perform your duties with pride and efficiency. Ten. Rape is punishable by death or castration, at the discretion of the captain. Murder is punishable by death. All crimes will be tried by random jury, and you vow now to uphold their verdict."

I struggled to digest Orca's words.

"Comita has something similar, I understand," Miranda said. I thought about the contract I'd signed when I joined the Polarian Fleet.

"Something similar," I said in a voice that lacked conviction. It was vaguely similar to the *North Star's* contract, in an abstract way. Minus the lashes, the death penalty, and the part about the cats, it upheld discipline and a loose interpretation of democratic principles.

It was hard to think with Miranda's grip on my hand.

"What happens if I don't take your oath?"

Miranda paused before she answered. I watched her blue eyes and regretted my question as they visibly cooled.

"Then we have no contract with Comita."

My stomach wobbled. Comita hadn't prepared me for this. I needed a moment to think, and that was impossible in this strange, windowless room with its red carpets, ancient paintings, and the three mercenaries waiting to hear my response. A refusal would please Orca, I guessed, and I suspected that something that pleased her would not be good for me.

If I agreed to Miranda's articles, I was bound to her service as surely as I was bound to Comita, at least where her laws were concerned. That would protect me on her ship just as my position in the fleet had protected me on the *North Star*. It also meant that I would be violating Miranda's Code if I went against her orders, with far steeper consequences than I was used to.

My mind chased itself in circles for another moment before coming to the only possible conclusion. As had been happening all too frequently of late, there was only one possible course that didn't involve heavy bailing and turbulent seas.

I repeated the articles after Orca, stumbling over the unfamiliar language and trying hard not to look at the knife lying next to the bottle. I was shaking when I finished the recitation.

"This mark will protect you on this ship," she told me as she picked up the blade.

The unspoken words echoed in my head. Protect me, maybe, but I'd heard enough stories about pirates and mercenaries to know the mark was more than a gesture of protection.

It was a brand.

Once marked, I would be hers. I glanced at the door, where

Kraken stood with his arms crossed over his inked chest. There was no way out.

The first cut was bearable. It barely stung, and I stared in fascinated horror as the knife slid through my skin. Blood didn't well up immediately, as if my vessels were too surprised at the violation to react.

The second cut hurt like a bitch. I bit my lip and clenched my teeth as sweat sprung up on my forehead. The blood followed, dripping down my wrist. I instinctively jerked away as she raised the knife for the third slice, but Miranda's grip tightened as she made the final two cuts.

They were by far the worst. Bile rose in the back of my throat and a bead of sweat dripped from my nose onto the table. My jaw ached from clenching, and a mewling whimper fought to get out past my front teeth. Had Comita known what Miranda would do to me?

Breath hissed out of me as Miranda splashed a measure of rum over the fresh cuts. It burned like nothing I had ever experienced. It was still burning as she wrapped a length of bandage around my hand, and spots danced around the corners of my vision.

"Take her to her new quarters," Miranda said, cleaning the knife off with a practiced flip of her wrist.

She glanced up at me, once, as Kraken and Orca gripped my arms.

I blamed the slow burning spreading through my body on the rum, and the lingering relief from pain.

South

Captain's Log
Captain Miranda
Man o' War
June 16, 2513
34, -66.7°

I don't know what Comita is playing at.

The promised navigator arrived today, looking like something Kraken pulled out of the bilge water. If it wasn't for her eyes I might have tossed her back. They are as golden as the center of the compass, and strangely compelling.

She tolerated the signing better than I anticipated. Marking her, I admit, could prove to be a mistake, but she won't last a day without it, even with Orca keeping an eye on her.

On the other hand, she would not be the first Archipelago castoff to make a name for herself on this ship.

Let's just hope she's stronger than she looks.

Chapter Five

I woke with a dull ache in the front of my skull and a sick feeling in the pit of my stomach. My mouth was dry and tasted like several rats had died in it, and my right hand throbbed menacingly. I tried to block the memories before they washed over me. I might as well have tried to stop a wave.

One of the downfalls of my unerring sense of direction was that I always knew exactly where I was, even when ignorance might have been preferable. It helped, of course, that Orca was shouting at me.

"Get up, fleet scum. If you make me miss breakfast, I will drown you myself."

I blinked at my surroundings, trying to get my eyes used to the sickly green light. Miranda's vessel, it appeared, did not have the genetically modified bio-luminescent organisms in their light tubes that I had taken for granted on the fleet. These looked like they had been harvested from some murky region of the ocean where respectable boats knew better than to sail.

I took stock of my situation.

My wounded hand curled protectively against my chest and the other hung limply from the coarse hammock where Orca and Kraken had deposited me the evening before. The hammock, I remembered, hung in Orca's private quarters. Miranda was afraid her crew would harass me if I bunked with the rest of them in the common hold. I wondered if that might have been preferable to sharing close quarters with her irascible first mate.

My tongue stuck dryly to the roof of my mouth as I sat up. The world spun into focus in time for me to see Orca standing over my open duffel, rummaging through the contents.

"Hey," I protested. It came out in a rasp.

"Put these on. You stink worse than a bilge rat." She tossed a clean pair of training clothes at me, then paused. I cringed as she scooped up the jellyfish. "What's this?"

"Nothing," I said.

Orca hefted it experimentally.

"Do I even want to know why you have this?"

"It's not important."

Orca raised the carving to eye level. "Looks like a jellyfish. Did your boyfriend make this for you when he was high?"

"I don't have a boyfriend," I said in another rasp.

"Why does that not surprise me?" Orca asked herself. "There's water in the corner for you. You wouldn't last a minute in the showers." She grinned. It was not a friendly expression.

I stepped gingerly out of the hammock, unused to the way it swung underneath me. The floor was cold and slightly uneven, as if it had been pieced together at different times by different builders, all of them falling down drunk. It was impossible to see clearly in the light, so I stopped trying and stumbled to the washbasin. A stained but presumably clean rag lay next to the large bucket of water. I scooped a handful up to drink and retched it back up.

"It's seawater," I said, my nose burning.

"Yeah, well, beggars can't be choosers."

Orca was still tossing the jellyfish from hand to hand. I splashed my face with the briny water and dampened the rag. I didn't feel comfortable stripping with Orca watching, but I was acutely aware of the lingering smell of vomit on my skin. I shucked off my shirt and folded it neatly at my side, keeping my back to her. The cold water felt good, despite the slight burn of the salt. I scrubbed my chest, neck, arms, and stomach, but couldn't bring myself to strip down to my underwear. My lower half would have to wait.

I shuffled awkwardly over to my clothes and pulled a clean shirt over my head, breathing in the familiar smell of the fleet laundry. It stung deeper than the salt, and I willed a presumptuous tear back into its duct. If this was what Comita needed me to do, then however strange and painful it was, I was determined to do it.

"You eat well on the fleet, don't you?"

There was an undercurrent of resentment to Orca's taunt. I glanced down at my bare legs as I hopped into my pants. They were slender and well-muscled. Fleet life was not soft, but compared to Orca I was plump.

"You said something about breakfast," I said, ignoring her comment.

"Not that you need it." She dropped the jellyfish back into the bag.

I let out a small sigh of relief as it nestled back into my clothes.

"Do I get to walk on my own this time, or are you going to put that thing back over my head?" The more I talked, the thirstier I became.

Orca eyed me up and down.

"The hood was just a precaution. You only need to know your way around four parts of the ship. This room, unfortunately, the mess hall, the head, and navigation. Just don't get lost."

"I'm a navigator," I said before I could stop myself. "I don't get lost."

"Good. Nobody on this ship likes fleeters. You get lost, you're not my responsibility."

She turned and made for the door. It had a crude bar across it for security and I noticed a shadow above the doorway.

"You like it?" Orca asked, noticing my stare.

"What is it?"

"All your fancy tech, and you can't identify a sea wolf? It's the skull of an orca."

I strained my eyes to see in the light, forgetting my thirst for a moment. A whale skull. A real whale skull. I wanted to ask Orca where she'd gotten it, but the smirk on her face shut me up.

I decided she had to be around my age as I trailed after her and down the hallway. She walked with the arrogance of someone who knew how to beat the shit out of others, but her skin was still fresh beneath the scars and tattoos.

The hallway was a mockery of fleet order. Curtains of shells, bones, and ragged cloth hung across doorways, and I glanced into several large rooms full of hammocks that looked like a crude version of the common bunk where I had spent my nights in fleet prep school. Merc crew members were up and moving, shouting at one another and emitting a distinct odor that made me doubt the efficacy of the showers.

Like Orca's room, the floor was composed of patchwork plastic. Here and there, grates spanned several feet of flooring, and I caught a glimpse of the lower levels and the tops of hurrying heads. The walls of the hallway writhed with pipes, which snaked haphazardly around doorways and hatches, casting sinuous shadows in the eerie glow of the dubious bio-light tubes.

The hallway ended with a catwalk and a flight of open stairs. I swayed as we passed the landing, noting the long drop into the poorly lit darkness that extended below. Above, bright sunlight flared in the distance, forcing its way into the bowels of the ship. I shuddered as I realized I must have passed this way the night before with my face covered. The walk was narrow and the railings looked like they would give way if a cat brushed against them.

There were cats, too. More cats than I had ever seen on a fleet ship. We only kept a symbolic few, as the mice and rat populations were carefully restricted to the elite ranks of rodents who had survived a rigorous campaign of baiting, trapping, poisoning, and predation. A black and white tom stared at me from the shadows, and a ginger twined her narrow body between the railing's supports, unfazed by the drop beneath her.

Orca mounted the stairs lightly. Her feet moved surely up the flights while I struggled to keep up on my sore ankle. I kept my left hand on the rail, as my right ached, and tried to make sense of the ship's organization as we climbed. It was impossible, which unnerved me more than the dark looks my new crew shot me.

"Rumor's true, Orca?" someone asked.

"Fleet's finest," Orca said with a shrug. Measuring eyes weighed me, and I wished I were taller, stronger, and significantly more intimidating.

I kept my eyes on Orca's back and followed her up.

The mess hall was more organized than I'd anticipated. The lighting was better, for one thing, and the tables were laid out with familiar structure. The round captain's table was on the far side of the room and long tables with benches filled the rest of the space. Orca made her way to the captain's table and gave me a sidelong look.

"Don't get used to it," she said as she pointed at a chair. "One wrong move, and you'll be sitting with them." I followed her pointing finger to the nearest table, where a group of sailors stared at me with open dislike.

So far, this was turning out to be more like the fleet than I'd expected. I forced myself to meet their eyes before I turned away. Fleet Prep had taught me many things, among them that showing weakness was a sure way to get beat up in a dark corner.

The tray Orca handed me was battered and old, but clean, and I stood beside her in line for the kitchen window. A bowl of some sort of grain mash plopped onto my tray when my turn came, along with a tall glass of lemon water. My stomach dropped. Lemon water was a scurvy ration, which we reserved for long missions. It didn't bode well for the cuisine.

Orca saw my face and laughed.

"Used to better?"

"It's fine," I said, wondering if I could manage to hold my tray and down the water at the same time.

The mash was tasteless. I missed the rice pudding I had toyed with only yesterday, and wondered what Harper was doing. I concentrated on that thought as I spooned the stuff into my mouth. At least the mash was warm.

The captain's table filled up during the course of the meal.

Kraken joined us, seating himself on my other side. I eyed his tattoos. They were even more lifelike in the brighter light. I thought about asking him what his position was, until a tentacle rippled over his bicep.

We were sailing southwest, away from the fleet, and the sunshine I'd noticed in the stairwell meant we'd outdistanced the storm during the night. The memory of the waves made my stomach clench.

More crew sat at the table. They greeted Orca and Kraken and ignored me. None of them wore a uniform or any signifier of rank, but each moved with the self-assurance of authority. One man carried a whip at his belt. The coiled lashes had a pinkish tint that I told myself couldn't possibly be blood.

I finished my food quickly, afraid to ask for more, and sipped at the last of the water in my glass. Orca was talking with a tall, dark haired woman about people I didn't know, and Kraken sat in stoic silence. I didn't think he was much of a morning person. I gently probed my bandaged hand beneath the table. It stung and throbbed, but I felt significantly better with food and water in my system.

"Captain on deck," someone called out from the far end of the mess hall.

The grain mash made a bid for freedom in my belly. My back was to the door and I didn't dare turn to stare as Miranda entered the mess hall, but I could hear.

The initial respectful hush was replaced with the kind of banter Comita didn't stand for. I couldn't make out her words through the strange buzzing in my ears. She laughed at something someone said, and the sound sent a chill down my spine. I squeezed my bandaged hand to clear my head.

She passed very close by my chair. The wind from her passage left a hint of fragrance—salt, sweat, and a floral scent I couldn't identify. It reminded me of the gardens on Polaris in full bloom. Orca straightened beside me, and even Kraken looked up from his bowl.

Miranda stood at her chair for a moment, glancing around the table. Her scars were more apparent in the light, but they didn't detract from the striking beauty of her face.

Beauty? I asked myself. The last thing I needed was to start thinking about Miranda as anything other than a mercenary captain.

I wished there was more water in my glass.

"Looks like fair weather today," Miranda said, spooning up an unappetizing mouthful of the same slop the rest of us were eating.

My eyes were torn between the drippy, grayish-brown mash and the fullness of her lips. The contrast was disorienting.

"Annie must have had a rough time coming in last night," a tall man with long dreadlocks said.

"Annie? Nah. She knows what she's doing," said Kraken.

"Any sailor would have struggled out in that soup."

"Not Annie." Kraken's voice brooked no arguments, but the man persisted.

"It was risky, bringing a boat in like that."

I felt Kraken stiffen next to me. The rest of the table glanced at Miranda. She took another bite of mash, apparently unconcerned.

"Just because you couldn't handle it doesn't mean the rest of us can't," Orca said with a smile. Something about the set of her jaw reminded me of the skull hanging above her door.

"Has nothing to do with what I can and can't handle. It's risky, taking a boat in like that for something so . . ."

He trailed off and looked at me. I willed myself not to flush. I was used to this, I reminded myself, and met his dark eyes.

"If you have something to say, Andre, spit it out."

Kraken's voice sank another octave, which I would not have thought possible. I could have sailed across the tension at the table. Miranda pushed her tray away slowly, and ran a hand over her tightly braided hair where it lay heavily against her hemp shirt. Andre glanced at his captain. A vein in his forehead pulsed.

"It just seems like a big risk for one girl."

Around the table, the subtle shift in postures suggested a few others shared his opinion.

"You think I risked a vessel on a girl?" Miranda said. Her voice was low and calm. Andre's forehead vein jumped again. "If you wish to call a vote, I can see you have some support." Miranda looked slowly around the table. Her eyes passed over me without stopping.

"We just want to know," he began, but at the sudden withdrawal of interest he amended his speech. "I just want to know, as your Chief Mechanic, that the risk to one of my boats was worth it."

"One of your boats?"

"Our boats, Captain. Yours to command, mine to keep afloat."

Miranda smiled at his words. Like Orca, her smile had teeth.

"Compass Rose," she said, catching me off guard.

Her eyes harpooned mine, and my breath caught in my throat. I didn't want to swim in these waters. I was pretty sure there were sharks.

"Captain," I said. The word burned in my mouth like the brand on my hand.

"Which direction are we sailing?"

"South southwest."

"What direction is the major current?"

"Northeast."

"What are our coordinates?"

I glanced around the table, my mind running through the calculations and barely seeing the faces of Miranda's crew.

"Between 23.6, -40.7 and 24.2, -40.9," I said after a moment.

"Annie." Miranda raised her voice loud enough that the mess hall quieted.

Annie appeared a few moments later. I recognized her from the night before. Her black hair was graying and her dark skin had seen plenty of weather, but there was nothing fragile about her wiry frame.

"What are our coordinates?" Miranda asked her.

"23.7, -40.7," Annie said.

I was startled at my own accuracy. Even for me that was a good guess. The storm could have knocked us much further off course than I'd allowed for.

"Compass Rose, what would you say the wind direction was?"

"West, between 15 and 20 knots," I said, feeling for the slight pull that indicated a misalignment with the current.

"How far are we from your fleet?"

"That depends on their trajectory, the storm, and whether or not they changed course, but they can't be more than 50 miles in any direction, and only 45 due east if they have to fight wind and current." The answers spilled out of me.

"And that," Miranda said to the table, "is why I risked one of Andre's boats in a hurricane. Thank you, Rose. Annie."

Annie frowned slightly at me as she left. It was the friendliest look I'd received so far.

The familiar feeling of suspicious eyes raked over me from elsewhere around the table. Orca was staring at me with a mixture of surprise and distrust. Andre's vein pulsed in double-time. Kraken glanced at me out of the corner of his eye, which was unsettling in itself, considering the larger eye tattooed around it.

Miranda, I realized with a leap of my pulse, looked more than pleased. A satisfied smile tugged at the corners of her lips as she observed the reaction my words had stirred.

"She's got eyes like a Sea Wolf," someone said under their breath. Miranda spoke before I could identify the whisperer.

"Orca, Compass Rose, with me," she said, standing. "The rest of you get back to work. Unless anyone else has any more questions?" Silence met her words, and her eyes simmered with controlled anger as she looked squarely into all of their faces. I was glad her eyes avoided mine.

"Come on, fleet scum," Orca said, rising to follow her captain. Kraken stood as well, a giant shadow looming on my right.

I could feel the eyes of the entire mess hall on me as we walked out. I kept my own eyes straight ahead, glued to Miranda's back. It was certainly distracting enough. Her shoulders were broad and muscular, and she walked with a confidence that made Orca's swagger look like a posturing kitten. I was already thirsty again by the time the doors swung shut behind us.

Orca glanced at me with a frown, then at Miranda.

"Do you want me to hood her, Captain?"

"No. I don't think a hood can confuse our new compass."

Kraken laughed behind me. The sound was so low that for a moment I thought it was the ship's machinery. Orca flushed and glared at me.

I kept my mouth shut.

We followed the same corridor Orca had taken me through that morning. I braced myself for the catwalks and the stairs and tried not to let my limp show.

We climbed right into the sun. I blinked as the light grew brighter and brighter and kept one hand on the rail for guidance. The top of the stairs branched into six possible directions, each leading to a door. The roof was composed of a liquid level, judging by the watery brilliance, and I guessed that it was a part of their passive desalination system. Even with the liquid barrier, the heat from the concentrated sunlight made beads of sweat break out on my forehead.

The door Miranda chose opened into another bright room. I tripped in surprise as my eyes traveled upward. A tower jutted out of the roof, encased in thick, clear plastic. The bow side of the tower narrowed to a point, allowing it to cut through water and wind, and a ladder was mounted on the stern side opposite.

I eyed the ladder where it descended into the middle of the room with an unpleasant suspicion. The rest of the room was devoted to shelves and small tables with charts and maps, but Miranda walked straight up to the ladder and began to climb. I tore my eyes away from the muscles in her arms and followed, vowing not to glance up.

That turned out to be easy.

The clear wall commanded my full attention. Beyond it hung empty air and the choppy sea, still frothing from yesterday's storm. The effect was dizzying, but at least there was no wind buffeting me or spray slicking the rungs. The top of Orca's head rushed my feet and I climbed faster. The tower had to be at least twenty feet tall. I couldn't see the top past Miranda, and looking up was far too distracting. I hadn't realized how form-fitting her loose trousers were.

The top took me by surprise. Miranda offered me a hand up, and I reached out unthinkingly with my right. The pressure of her grip on the bandage made me wince.

Orca swung herself up without assistance, and Kraken emerged like something out of a watery nightmare. I thought instantly of the jellyfish trapped in the light tube.

We were in a small room, no more than fifteen feet wide at the stern and fifteen feet long where it narrowed into a point at the prow. The walls were clear, but the ceiling had a smoky tint to it that kept the room from cooking.

"Captain," said a voice from the prow. A man swiveled around in a chair. I did a double take, and glanced from the ladder back to his legs. They ended at the knee.

"I've got arms, girlie," he said, noticing my stare. He flexed his biceps at me. They were as thick as my thighs, if not thicker.

"Crow's Eye, this is Compass Rose, our new navigator."

"Huh," he said, his dark mustache twitching. Gray streaked his beard. "Guess we got something in common. It's a curse, getting named for your job. Means you can never get away from it." He grinned, revealing crooked teeth. "But I bet you know that, don't you?"

"Yes sir," I said.

"Sir!" His laughter broke into a fit of coughing. "I could get used to that. The mercury settled nicely in you. She'll do just fine," he said, nodding at Miranda.

Orca crossed her arms over her chest, clearly irritated at Crow's Eye's reception.

"Not much gets past Crow's Eye, above or below water," Miranda said to me.

"That's very impressive."

I regretted the words as soon as they left my mouth. I saw Orca shake her head out of the corner of my eye. Crow's Eye's laugh was less kindly this time.

"Impressive? That's a high compliment, coming from a fleeter. Tell me, little navigator, what else do you think of our ship?" There was a warning glint in his eyes.

"I didn't mean to offend," I said, feeling my face burn.

"We don't have fancy toys here like you're used to. No lush stations to run home to. This ship, here, is our home and harbor. If you ask me, I'd say that's a bit more impressive than anything you can do with your computers and your hydraulics and your antibiotics."

He emphasized the last word harshly, and my eyes flicked again to his legs, wondering.

"Keep your hand clean, fleeter, or you'll lose it before you get to use it."

With that, he swiveled back around to stare at the open ocean. I could have fried a fish on my cheeks.

"You'll work up here and below," Miranda said. Her blue eyes masked her emotions.

I nodded.

"Keep a weather eye out," she told Crow's Eye as she descended the ladder. Orca followed, but I hung back for a moment, staring at the back of Crow's Eye's head.

"Spit it out, fleeter," he said without turning around.

"I said it's impressive because I know."

Kraken waited by the ladder and Crow's Eye swung slowly toward me, one bushy eyebrow raised. I took a deep breath and gambled.

"Most sailors need the instruments. There aren't many who can do what we do."

"Huh," he said, leaning forward. "Come a little closer."

I took a step towards him, hoping he wasn't about to spit in my face. He stared into my eyes for a few long seconds.

"You ever heard of the Sea Wolves?" he asked. Kraken grew very still behind me.

"Orca has a skull in her quarters. She said it belonged to a sea wolf, but we call them orca on the Polarian Fleet."

"I see," he said. His tone suggested that whatever it was he saw,

I did not. "Don't keep the captain waiting. She's not a patient woman."

I bolted down the ladder as fast as my sore ankle and sliced hand could manage.

Chapter Six

I was exhausted by the time dinner rolled around. Miranda's articles hadn't mentioned lunch, which had escaped my notice at the time, and my stomach growled ominously as I followed Orca to the dining hall. My mind reeled with the effects of prolonged stimulation. If someone had asked me to find due north right then I would have given them a blank stare.

I had spent several hours going over charts with Miranda while Orca paced the room, scowling, until Miranda ordered her to explain some of the more obscure shorthand used by the *Man o' War* crew. Talking about the ship eased the irritation from Orca's voice, and there was a fierce joy in her eyes as she laid out the ship's systems for me. She even forgot to mock my ignorance of life outside of the fleet.

When Miranda was satisfied that I could read the charts, she explained what she wanted me to do for the next week. As I turned the list over in my mind, I found myself agreeing with what Orca had said earlier. I only needed to know the way to the mess hall, my room, navigation, and the head, because those were the only places I was going to have time to go. If I wanted to explore the rest of the ship, I would have to forgo sleep, and wandering the ship by night didn't strike me as the wisest course of action.

After we'd left the charts, Orca took me to pick up a blanket and a change of clothes and get me on the ship's books. I repressed a vivid memory of the woman in charge of supplies. Her tattoos had put Kraken's to shame.

"Here," Orca said, shoving a tray into my hands and snapping my attention back to the unfortunate present. On closer inspection, some of the shells in her narrow braids turned out to be fish skulls. Gray eyes glared at me from beneath dark brows. If it weren't for the orca tattoos on her arms she would have fit right in on Polaris.

The noise in the hall was much rowdier than what I was used to. Meals on *North Star* were orderly and taken in the presence of officers who never quite let you forget you were beneath them.

A limp fish steak flopped onto my plate through the buffet window, followed by a wet lump of what I assumed were stewed greens and sprouts. I filled up my new water flask at the filter station and took my place beside Orca at the captain's table. Maybe if I ate slowly, I reasoned, I could make the small serving last longer. Orca spoke with the woman on her other side, leaving me to eat in silence.

I remembered my first days on Polaris, waiting to take the Fleet Prep entry exam and too scared to leave the tiny room my mother had rented for me, and then the first few months onboard *North Star* before Harper befriended me. No one had spoken a kind word to me for weeks. I didn't mind the brusqueness of my instructors, because they were that way with everyone, but I'd had friends on Cassiopeia before I left and had fully expected to make new ones on Polaris. Harper ended my solitude one morning with a yawn, plopping down on the bench next to me.

"Hi, I'm Harper. I like your eyes," she'd said, and just like that we were best friends.

This was different, I told myself. I was not expecting a warm reception from the mercenaries and, if anything, I was the one looking down on them. I didn't need to make a place for myself here. It meant nothing to me if Orca chose to judge me before getting to know me. Miranda, at least, seemed impressed.

Thinking about Miranda sent a thrill through my body. The mercenary captain was a few years older than me, but, I remembered involuntarily, age hadn't stopped Harper from hooking up with one of the more attractive techs from the greenhouse. Not, of course, that I had any interest in Miranda.

I didn't typically fall for blue-eyed women, anyway. For starters, there weren't many of them around, and as a navigator I spent way too much time already staring out over blue sky and blue water. Blue was a dangerous color.

I am not falling for anyone, I reminded myself, *least of all a mercenary captain with a penchant for slicing up her sailors' palms.*

I finished my last bite of fish and looked at her empty seat, feeling an unwarranted wave of disappointment wash over me.

Kraken, I noticed, was also absent. His empty seat opened me up to scrutiny from the rest of the table. I tried not to sink lower in my chair.

"Hey, fleeter," said a woman's voice. I started as a hand touched my shoulder. Orca glanced over and frowned.

I looked up to find Annie standing behind me. I opened my mouth and thought of nothing to say, so I shut it again.

"What's up, Annie?" Orca asked.

"Miranda's finest are a little curious about what we hauled in. Mind if we borrow her?"

Orca raised an eyebrow and shrugged.

"If you like bad company, sure, she's all yours. Just don't lose her."

"I hear she doesn't get lost." Annie offered me a hint of a smile and stepped back.

"Clear your tray, fleeter. We pick up after ourselves here." Orca didn't even bother looking at me as she spoke.

My ears burned, and I carried my tray to its stack amid a low chorus of laughter.

Annie had made room on her bench by the time I made it back. The group around her was as motley a bunch as I had ever seen. I recognized the woman with the shark tattoo from the parley vessel. Jeanine, the one who had handed me the bucket.

"Feeling any better?" Jeanine asked. I met her eyes, feeling a flash of irritation burning through my embarrassment.

"Come sit next to me and find out."

Jeanine's eyes widened at my reply, and then she laughed.

"Got some spit in you when you're not spitting up."

"Here," Annie said, saving me the effort of coming up with a response. She poured a small measure of amber liquid from a flask into a tiny cup. This time I was ready for it, and knocked it back.

"You drink a lot of rum here, don't you?" I said.

"Sugar beets are the only thing that grows reliably," said Annie. "Something got into the rice and we've had trouble with seed, so rum it is." She poured a glass for herself.

"Orca didn't give you your rum measure yet?" Jeanine asked. There was a gleam of mischief in her eyes.

"No."

"We'll have to fix that. You're one of us now, I hear."

"What's that?" asked the man sitting beside Jeanine. He had waves shaved into his short, dark hair, chasing themselves around his head in an endless wake.

"Finnegan, this is Compass Rose. Show us your hand, fleeter." Jeanine tapped the table top pointedly.

I placed my bandaged hand on the surface.

"Miranda marked an Archipelago sailor?" Finnegan narrowed his eyes at me. "I don't believe it."

I unwrapped the bandage carefully, feeling the rum going to my head. The red lines were still raw on my palm, and one broke open as the cloth came unstuck.

"Well, shit," Finnegan said, leaning back to give me another look. "There's a first for everything. I thought she hated the fleets."

"Apparently this one is special." Jeanine's voice implied that she had some serious doubts.

"You should clean that," Annie said quietly. "And get a fresh bandage."

"I don't know where to find one."

"I can get you some supplies if Orca hasn't already. They're not far from here. All crew have access to the ship's doctor, especially at first signing. We don't like losing people to infection if we can help it."

"Thank you," I said, meaning it.

"It's what I'd do for anyone on this ship," Annie said, raising her voice so that Jeanine could hear her. "Once Miranda marks you, you're crew for life."

"I thought we could leave at the end of the contract," I said, rewrapping my hand.

"Oh, you can leave," Jeanine said. "But unless you cut off your hand, no other ship will sign you on. You're Miranda's now, kid. Didn't anyone tell you?"

I looked at my hand with a sinking feeling in my stomach.

"Maybe she was planning on going back to the fleet," Finnegan suggested. I didn't like his tone.

"The fleet doesn't take in pirates," said Jeanine. "And if you wash up on one of your stations with that mark, they'll hang you before you can say 'parley.'"

Comita had said she would have me back no matter what happened, I reminded myself. Jeanine's words registered with a jolt.

"Pirates?"

"Pirates, mercenaries, it's all the same to the Archipelago, isn't it? Why are you here, anyway?"

"If Miranda didn't tell you, then you don't need to know." Annie's voice cut through Jeanine's like fins through water.

"So you're either a traitor or a spy."

I met Jeanine's eyes as I realized with a plunging feeling that whatever I said here would make its way around the ship by the end of the night. I clung to due north as I struggled to think of the right words to say. I could put an end to speculation now, if I played my cards right, or I could set myself up for months of misery. I looked around the table, trying to read their faces. Everyone was thinner than I was used to, and there was a haunted, hunted look in some of the eyes that met mine. I remembered how Polaris had looked to me when I first arrived, overflowing with abundance and full of happy, healthy people. My mother had had the same look as these sailors when she said goodbye. She'd bought me a one-way ticket off of Cassiopeia, but there was no room on Polaris for an aging eel farmer.

"You know what they called me on the Polarian Fleet?" I said, flexing my sliced hand. "Jelly. My father was a drifter."

"Trawling scum," Finnegan agreed.

I ignored him. It was nothing I hadn't heard before.

"I'm not a traitor, and I'm not a spy. I'm a navigator. I don't have time for politics."

"I don't care much about your politics. It's who you'd choose, when push came to shove, that concerns me. Never met an Archipelagean who wouldn't choose their own skin over mine."

"I'm a drifter half-breed," I said. "You think they'd choose me, either?"

"But you got their fancy vaccines and good food, didn't you?"

"I did. And if Miranda has her way, you will too, am I right?"

Annie watched me with a faint trace of approval in her scowl. I was guessing here, but my gut told me I was right just as surely as it knew north. I didn't know the whole of Comita's bargain with Miranda, but if I were a mercenary captain in a position to make demands of a fleet admiral, I would ask for seeds, drugs, and whatever else my crew needed that was outside my reach.

"You gave her too much rum, Annie," Jeanine said. "I liked her better when she was too busy puking to talk."

"So, drifter," Finnegan said. "Who would you choose? Me, or you?"

"If it was just the two of us?" I said, leveling what I hoped was an impenetrable look at him. "Me. But if it was a choice between my hide or my ship, I'd choose my ship. You just better hope you're on it."

Jeanine choked on her rum and spluttered out what sounded suspiciously like a laugh.

"Well said." Annie nodded. "That's good enough for me, and she was good enough for Miranda. Does that satisfy you?" she asked Jeanine and Finnegan.

"Only one thing satisfies me." Jeanine took another swig of rum, kissing her flask when she finished. "What about you, Finn?"

"You know what satisfies me." He leaned toward her, puckering his lips. She shoved him away.

I relaxed very slightly as I tried to gauge the shift in the conversational current. Real currents were much easier.

"Now there's a thought," Jeanine said, throwing me a wink as she held Finnegan at bay. "Maybe Miranda is looking for a little satisfaction herself. I hear they do it differently on the Archipelago."

I blushed to the roots of my hair.

Am I that fucking obvious? I thought, wishing a whirlpool would open up beneath me. Several vivid images overpowered me at once, and all of them involved Miranda.

"Oh, and by the way, kid, you should never have told me people call you jelly."

"Wake up, jelly."

I groaned and burrowed underneath the blanket and deeper into the hammock. The familiar insult overrode my sense of direction, and for a moment I thought I was back on the *North Star*. Then someone shook my hammock and reality came rushing back in.

"How long do I have to bunk with you?" I asked Orca as I sat up to meet her glare. It had been five days now since I'd arrived, and I was ready to strangle her in her sleep.

"Until Miranda stops punishing me. Good news, though. You're on your own today. You get to spend the day in navigation all by yourself."

"And here I was just getting used to you holding my hand." I reached for my shirt.

Orca pulled on her boots and stretched before answering.

"Listen up. Maybe you've gotten the wrong idea, with me running around with you all over the damn ship, but I'm Miranda's first mate. The only reason you are even speaking to me right now is because Miranda was worried you'd get eaten alive without my protection. Does that make sense to you? Miranda didn't trust you to Annie, who you seem so cozy with, or any of the other people who should have been stuck with you.

73

No. She gave you to me, because I'm the only one she trusts to make sure you're still breathing at the end of the day.

"The crew doesn't care that you're special. All they know is that they grew up hungry and you didn't. Most of them were pirates before they jumped ship. Do you know what pirates think about your precious Archipelago? I thought so. So don't you dare complain about bunking with me. I don't like you, but as long as Miranda wants you alive, I'll make sure you stay that way. Now get your ass up."

I obeyed, fuming. I could think of nothing to say in response. She had pulled rank on me, and it rankled. I also didn't like the implication of her words. If Miranda's crew felt that way, why was Miranda working with Comita?

Mercenaries needed division, I reminded myself. As much as this crew apparently hated the Archipelago, they would be hard-pressed to find work without us. The Archipelago produced the products that kept ships floating, and the pirates, drifters, and other unsavory sorts depended on those things just as surely as we did. Plus, they needed a market for their less reputable hemp byproducts.

That didn't explain why Comita had sought out Miranda, of all people, especially if she hated the fleet as much as her crew seemed to think she did. I wished Comita had given me more information.

More than that, I wished I could punch Orca in the face. Habit and a coordinate roundup kept my temper in check, but a pounding pressure rose behind my eyes and narrowed my vision for a moment down to her twisted smirk. She met my glare with her own, which sent a different sort of thrill through my body than the sort Miranda summoned. My hatred for Maddox was nothing compared to what I was currently feeling for Orca.

Miranda wasn't at breakfast, again. My eyes kept wandering to her empty chair, and I spent another meal in silence with only Orca's back for company, her shoulders managing to convey her disdain. She continued to ignore me on the walk to the chart room, although I noticed that she kept a watchful eye on the crew members we passed. I wanted to tell her that I didn't need her protection, and that I'd managed to make a place for myself on the *North Star* without help, but the looks some of the mercenaries sent my way stilled the words in my throat. By the end of the walk I was seriously regretting the hours I'd wasted with Harper. Instead of concentrating on avoiding her punches, I should have asked Harper to show me how to throw my own.

"Don't leave until I come to get you unless Miranda herself shows up," Orca said as the guards opened the doors to the chart room. The bright light blinded me again, but this time I was ready for it. I waited until the doors shut behind me to let out a silent scream of frustration. When that didn't help, I pounded my thigh a few times with my fist.

The room was deserted. I knew there had to be others who used the charts, but the only person nearby was Crow's Eye in the crow's nest. I glanced up the ladder, wondering if he had observed my tantrum. The crow's nest seemed very far away.

I pulled out the stack of charts Comita had sent with me and laid them on one of the tables. Finding the corresponding charts from Miranda's records didn't take as long as I'd anticipated. The room was surprisingly organized, with an assortment of charts and maps that clearly came from many different places. Some were in different languages, and a few were so old I didn't dare remove them from their shelves.

Solitude and work restored my temper. I counted out the cardinal points to dispel the last of my anger. It was a trick I had taught myself when I was in the Fleet Prep. Navigators couldn't afford distractions.

I traced the line of the coasts on the chart with a finger. I had never been within sight of land, and had never wanted to be, but now here I was, planning the best route to pass along the coast undetected, dodging pirates, methane, dead zones, and hurricanes, not to mention fleet supply ships and the mining stations themselves.

The mines were a distant reality that none of us really thought about. They had to be closer to the coasts in order for our rigs to reach the mineral and ore deposits on the ocean floor. I had never met a miner, and could not imagine spending my life that far beneath the waves, living in the total darkness of the deeps.

We had mines all up and down the east coast of the North American continent, but the majority were clustered in the Gulf of Mexico, a location conspicuously easy to control, thanks to the shape of the continent and the outlying islands. All the pirates had to do was restrict access to and from the Gulf and, barring that, keep our patrol ships too busy fighting off raiders to defend supply lines.

The tricky part for me was getting us into the Gulf undetected by either pirates or Archipelago forces, both of whom would be on the lookout for any suspicious ships, and who might be tempted to shoot first and ask questions later—or never.

My hand was cramped from marking coordinates by mid-afternoon. I stood up and stretched, looking around the empty room. I needed to see water.

The ocean spilled out around me as I climbed to the crow's nest. I paused halfway up. Clouds were building into a light squall in the west, and rain fell over the water in sheets. We would pass it on our current course, but I found myself wishing for a storm to settle the electricity sending sparks through my frustration. Ahead of the rain danced several water spouts. The funnel clouds spun down like slender threads, gathering sea water like fibers onto a spindle.

Crow's Eye was watching them when I hauled myself into the crow's nest.

"Funnel weather," he said. "Is that what brings you up here?"

"I just wanted to see the water."

"Why do you think I never leave?" He gestured at a bottle in the corner. It contained a yellow liquid. "Don't even come down to piss. I might miss something."

I recoiled from the jar.

"It's nice up here," I said, changing the subject before he shared anything else about his bodily functions.

"That it is. I leave the charts to people like you." His eyes remained fixed on the water spouts.

76

"How long has Miranda been captain?" I asked. "You must have been here before her."

"I've been sailing under Miranda for three years. She was first mate under my former captain when we first met, but it was clear she was headed for a ship of her own."

I thought of Orca and wondered if Crow's Eye saw the same potential there. I didn't ask, just in case. The thought of Orca captaining anything other than a sinking sub made my blood boil.

"Who did you sail with before that?"

"You've got a lot of questions today. I don't like questions."

"Sorry." I stared out at the distant rain. "Have you ever been to the Gulf?"

Crow's Eye cleared his throat and swiveled in his chair to face me.

"Wouldn't be worth my salt if I hadn't, now would I?"

"Those charts down there have a lot of variability in the dead zones. I was wondering if you could tell me what it was like to sail there," I said, hoping he would forget that he didn't like questions.

"This time of year, the whole Gulf is a dead zone. If you're on the surface, you better hope you keep the vents shut, or hydrogen sulfide will wipe out the crew. The good water is down deep, where you want to be anyway. Too much algae, jellyfish, and hurricanes up top. It's a hellhole, and there's things in the water there that you haven't even had nightmares about, girl."

"Like what?"

"Squid, right below the shelf, and octopus as big as small boats. Makes Kraken look friendly, doesn't it?"

"I guess so."

"But that's where the mines are, girl, so that's where we're going. And you're gonna get us there." He tapped on the stumps of his legs with thick fingers.

"That's the idea," I said, feeling, if possible, even less confident than I had a few moments ago about the prospect.

"Well, I tell you what. You can do it. There's more to you than meets the eye. Your only problem is that you don't know how to think like a pirate yet."

"How do I think like a pirate?"

"For starters, you're gonna have to drink a lot more rum. Gives you big ideas, especially if rum's all you got. The captain don't hold with smoking the pirate weed." His smile revealed a few missing teeth. "Then, you gotta get lean. Live from one meal to the next. It gets you thinking about doing things you can't imagine, hunger does. Thirst too. No port to turn to, just ships to raid for food and parts. Once you can make that your reality, the rest comes easy."

"Sounds like you have some experience."

"I've sailed under a lot of captains and a lot of flags. Only made one rule for myself, and that was that I'm done sailing in the Gulf." He grimaced. "Fat lot of good that did me, eh? The poles, on the other hand, are something I would still like to see."

"What do you think is there?" I asked.

"Ocean isn't dead at the poles, they say. Yet. I'd like to see that before I die. Schools of fish. Maybe even a whale, or a shark."

"Why not go?"

"Need a captain willing to take me. So far, the spoils are here." One of the spouts receded into the cloud, only to be replaced by another. "Now I have a question for you. Where did you come by those eyes of yours?"

"I was born with them," I said.

"You didn't get those eyes from the fleet."

"My father was a drifter."

"Is that what your mother told you?" He stroked his beard. "I suppose he could have been. Blood thins."

"What are you talking about?" I didn't like the turn the conversation was taking.

"Just that I've heard of eyes like yours before."

"Maybe you ran into a plague ship," I said, regretting my climb.

"It wasn't yellow fever."

"Then maybe you should speak clearly, Crow's Eye." Anger slipped into my voice and I steadied myself on due north.

"Or maybe you should learn to read the deeper currents. Now get out of here. You're distracting me."

I glared at the back of his head as I descended. The only thing unusual about my eyes was their color. Fleet blood was relatively homogenous. Our eyes were mostly brown, after so many generations of interbreeding, with the occasional blues, grays, and greens popping up in unexpected places, and hair color tended toward brown or black as well.

Most of the genetic variations happened on the outlying stations, like Cassiopeia, where outsiders occasionally mingled their blood with the Archipelago's. My eyes hadn't set me apart on Cassiopeia. It had been my sense of direction and my mother's pride that did that.

Whatever Crow's Eye thought I was, he was wrong. My father was just like any other man before he vanished. Average height, weather-beaten skin, and my curly dark hair. His eyes were brown, like my mother's, and he trawled for plastic in exchange for seeds, supplies, and medicine. He was a drifter, nothing more, and my mother cultivated seaweed in the eel beds.

I pulled out a chart at random from the shelf, for the moment too angry to plot coordinates. It detailed a small patch of sea near the Gulf and showed absolutely nothing of interest. I shoved it back on the shelf in disgust.

"You've made a surprising amount of headway on these charts."

I jumped a foot in the air and whirled around. Miranda was sitting at the table I'd vacated, watching me. There was nobody else in the room.

"Um," I said, searching for words that failed to appear.

"Did I startle you?"

"No," I lied.

She raised an eyebrow at me.

"A little, Captain."

"You shouldn't let your guard down like that. Now. Come show me what you have so far."

I sat opposite her, my heart still racing.

"Our options are limited. There are only a few ways in, and you can bet both sides have them tightly patrolled. The way I see it, we have two options. We sneak in, or we don't."

"Explain," she said.

"A lot of my plan is dependent on variables outside of our control, and I also need more information." I took a deep breath and met her eyes. "I need to know more about your trading relationships with the pirates, and I need to know what kind of small craft you have in the hold."

"I suppose that is fair," she said. "Assuming I tell you, what do you have in mind?"

"Well, if we only had to hide from the Archipelago on our way in, that would make things a lot easier. I have an idea of their patrol patterns, and I am pretty sure I can avoid them. I plotted them here with a margin of error." I pointed to one of the charts. "But I don't know much about pirate patrols. I was thinking that once we're in, you could pick up a contract with the pirates, and we could send out a small craft to get a feel for what is going on. I can keep a smaller boat off of the sonar, I think, but we need to get *Man o' War* into the Gulf and the best way to do that is to have a valid reason for being there."

Miranda leaned forward on her elbows, examining my notes.

I couldn't keep my eyes on the chart. The scars on her skin were unusual. They weren't raised, like ordinary scars, but looked like someone had brushed them on as an afterthought. Some were small, others were long, but all were narrow in diameter and curved almost lazily over her body.

"That could work," she said, nodding. "What kind of small craft would you need?"

"Nobody looks twice at drifter trawlers. They're not fast, but if we're careful, we won't need to worry about moving quickly."

"You want a drifter trawler?"

"Yes," I said. So far it was the only plan I had thought of that held water.

"Done. You'll have it. As for trade, that might be more difficult." She lapsed into a thoughtful silence. "I'd need something going in, and I don't have anything to spare in my hold. Mercenaries trade in three things, Rose: supplies, fighting power, and information."

80

I swallowed, realizing with a sinking feeling where this was going.

"I don't have supplies, and I have no desire to shed unnecessary blood. That leaves information, and the only information that will interest these particular captains is Archipelago intelligence. Intelligence," she said, tapping the fleet patrol patterns I had mapped out, "that you happen to have."

"We can't give them that," I said, reaching out to snatch the chart away from her. She caught my wrist in her hand and gently placed it back down on the table.

"If you can come up with another plan, we won't need to."

"What if we fed them false coordinates?" I said.

"Then we would be dead. They would find us, and even if we managed to escape, my reputation would be ruined and there would be no going back. If we do this, we do it right, and hope the gain outweighs the risk."

I stared at the charts, searching for another option. My eyes lighted on a familiar patch of sea.

"Do you know anything about these coordinates here?" I asked, pointing to the place on the map where I'd approximated the location of the unknown ship I'd investigated for Walker.

Miranda frowned slightly, then glanced up at me.

"Why do you want to know?"

I opened my mouth, then shut it, unsure of how to answer. Comita had told me to obey Miranda. She hadn't said anything about confidentiality.

"There was an anomaly recorded from this quadrant. It could be important."

"Anomalies usually are," Miranda said, giving me a look I couldn't interpret. I told her about the sonar readings *North Star* had picked up, and what it implied about the pirate force's capacity to sub. Miranda's eyebrows raised throughout my story, until they were almost lost in her hairline.

"Comita didn't tell you who was leading the pirates, did she?" she asked.

81

"No." Comita had not told me very much at all, I reflected, and I hadn't thought to ask.

"I can see why the Archipelago wants to keep that particular piece of information to themselves," Miranda said, shaking her head. "Panic isn't a good strategy."

"Who is it?" I asked.

"Ching Shih."

My hands balled into involuntary fists, muscles, and tendons contracting in fear as everything I had ever heard about Ching Shih ripped through my brain like a hurricane.

For starters, nobody knew her real name, or her origins. She had taken the name of a long dead Chinese pirate queen, and she matched the legendary queen in strength, ruthlessness, and cunning. Ching came out of the South Atlantic in a red tide, binding unassociated pirates to her infamous Red Flag Fleet and organizing the pirate drug cartels for the first time in decades. If she had set her sights on the Archipelago mines, we were in much deeper waters than I realized.

"No," I said, "Comita did not tell me that."

"Your *North Star* probably picked up one of Ching's scouts, which means we have less time than I thought. If Ching is scoping out the stations, then she's planning to do a lot more than just cut off the Archipelago from the mines." Miranda didn't look nearly as concerned about this as I felt she should. "Either way, I have a new task for you. There are some rumors on my ship that you're an Archipelago spy, and I need to give my crew something else to stew over. I can't have them second-guessing my navigator's choices."

Chapter Seven

"This is fucking ridiculous," Orca said as she shoved through the door to the *Man o' War's* training room. I couldn't have agreed more. The room was smaller than the one I was used to, the mats looked like they hadn't been washed in years, and the lighting was just as bad. "First she wants me to babysit your ass, and now I'm supposed to train with you?"

"First mate comes with all sorts of responsibilities," I snapped back. "Maybe you should call for a vote."

Orca whirled and grabbed my shirt at the collar.

"I won't need to call a vote if I break your fucking neck."

"And here I thought you were supposed to keep me alive." This close, I noticed that Orca had unusually long eyelashes. I imagined plucking them out, one by one.

"'Alive' is open to interpretation."

Miranda's plan to simultaneously distract the crew from the rumor mill and make them respect me had several flaws, in my opinion. The first was definitely Orca, who had taken to sharpening her belt knife before we fell asleep each night. I had no doubt about the implied threat, and the sound was highly irritating. In retaliation, I made a habit of coughing loudly just as her breathing deepened into sleep. The result was that she was even more irritable than usual, but I felt better.

I didn't see how a public beating at Orca's hands was going to improve my standing. If anything, it should make things worse for me. If the mercenaries already saw me as soft and weak, watching me fight was certainly not going to disprove their suspicions.

The second flaw was also Orca. The first mate and the navigator didn't operate in the same sphere, but our paths would certainly overlap. Orca's hatred was going to be an issue, and more time spent in her company only seemed to fuel it.

"Take these," Orca said, shoving some wraps at me. There were a few other sailors in the room, but my vision was focused very narrowly. If I could land just one punch on Orca's perfectly straight nose, I would be satisfied. I wrapped my hands carefully, wondering how much damage my healing right hand would suffer, and grateful that my ankle, at least, had stabilized.

"No head shots," Orca said in a voice that suggested a head shot was exactly what she wanted to do, too. "Let's see what you're made of, jelly."

She sounded too much like Maddox. The pulsing feeling behind my eyes grew.

Orca stood loosely, rocking back and forth on the balls of her feet while she weighed me. We were of a height, which meant she didn't have much reach on me, but I had no illusions about my chances. I didn't think even Harper would have been able to hold her own against Orca.

Her first swing hit me in the ribs. Breath whistled through my teeth even as I sensed the control in her punch. I would be bruised, but nothing was broken.

I managed to block her second. She didn't leave me much time to celebrate. Her kick knocked my legs out from under me and I gasped like a fish out of water for a few moments, letting the laughter from the onlookers fan my anger.

Orca looked amused when I struggled to my feet.

"Who taught you to fight? Your grandma?"

I feinted and aimed for her stomach. She blocked my punch easily and lashed out at my face with one of her own. I ducked just in time.

So much for no head shots.

"I wonder what will happen if I knock your compass right out of your ass," she said.

I gritted my teeth and kicked.

She grabbed my leg and threw me to the ground as my heel collided with her thigh. This time, I was almost ready for it, and rolled into the fall, reaching for Orca's legs. She sidestepped and aimed a kick at my ribs. I blocked it with my forearm, feeling the impact up into my shoulder.

"On your feet. You wanna learn how to fight? Then show me what you've got."

I lunged for her. It was a rookie mistake, and she sidestepped again, landing a blow on my back. I turned, breathing heavily. Her smile soothed my bruises with a balm of rage. Orca was everyone who had ever hurt me, all rolled into one slim package. I would bring her to her knees.

Although, I reflected as I landed on the ground again, maybe not today.

Orca stood over me, smirking as she offered me a hand up. I stared at the jellyfish brand on her palm, then grabbed hold of her wrist and kicked out with my legs. She fell on top of me, whipping my arm around behind my back and looping her leg around my throat.

I smiled into the crook of her knee, tasting blood. It was a dirty move, and she had come out on top, but it had worked. *One point to Compass Rose*, I told myself.

Orca released me slowly. This time she didn't offer me a hand.

"You want to fight dirty?"

She launched herself at me, and I shielded my face with my arms as blow after blow landed on my body.

"First mate," said a deep, male voice.

I lay on the ground without moving. Every part of my body hurt. I could hear Orca breathing heavily.

"I expected better from you."

It was Kraken.

"Neptune's balls, Kraken, are you defending her?"

"I'm defending you."

Orca had nothing to say to that. Kraken knelt down beside me and placed a massive hand on my shoulder. "Can you breathe?"

"Yes," I wheezed.

"She's fine," Orca said, but there was a touch of panic in her voice.

"She's about as fine as you were, the first time Miranda gave you a taste of her fist in the ring. Only you grew up brawling and raiding, instead of looking at charts."

"I'm fine," I said. The wheeze worsened.

"See, she's fine." Orca sounded defensive.

"On your feet, fleeter." Kraken helped me rise.

I stared at him out of one eye. The other was swelling shut. I squared my shoulders, which produced a painful grating sensation that definitely hadn't been there a few moments ago. Kraken patted my back, which emphasized the pain. I raised my fists and assumed a fighting stance.

"Now," I said to Orca, with more self-control then I was aware I possessed, "why don't you show me how to block myself from assholes like you?"

I heard the gurgle of the bio-lights in the silence that filled the room after my words. Nobody cheered, but nobody was laughing anymore, either.

"Maybe tomorrow," Orca said with scorn. I met her eyes with my good one, and was gratified to see the tiniest bit of discomfort on her face.

The watching crew stepped out of my way as I limped off the mat. Kraken's frown followed me, and he whispered something to Orca that I didn't catch.

"Yeah, Rose," someone called out from the back of the room. I squinted in the dim light. Jeanine. I felt a sliver of hope worm its way into my chest. Jeanine's solitary clapping echoed in the silence. I would take it.

"Did I break any of your precious bones?" Orca asked as she walked with me to the showers. I ignored her. "I was speaking to you, fleeter."

I turned and faced her, blocking hallway traffic, and held up my palm. The half-healed wounds glared angrily from the puckered flesh.

"I'm not a fleeter." I registered interested looks from the onlookers, but couldn't focus on their faces.

"Once a fleeter, always a fleeter," she hissed back.

"Watch yourself, Orca," said a low voice from behind her. I squinted, but could not make out the face. The voice sounded like Annie. "You're forgetting where our captain came from."

If my jaw hadn't been swollen mostly shut, it would have fallen open. Miranda? From the Archipelago? It wasn't possible.

"Careful, Annie. We don't want to give your pet navigator any ideas."

"I think you've given her plenty." There was disgust in Annie's voice. "I expected better from you."

It was exactly what Kraken had said.

"Why?" I asked. "Why did you expect better?"

Annie didn't answer, and Orca grabbed my wrist and pulled me along after her.

"Strip," she ordered when we arrived at the showers.

"Over my dead body." It came out in a slur.

"Look, fleeter. I'm not sorry for kicking your ass. But you're not tracking blood all over my room."

Her hands were surprisingly gentle as she tugged at the hem of my shirt. I tried to glare at her, but the effort made my skull throb.

"Come on," she said as I pulled away.

"No."

"You're in no shape to take care of yourself."

"Your fault," I pointed out.

"Suit yourself. But I'm staying. Leave it to a fleeter to pass out and drown in the shower instead of the ocean."

"Fuck you," I said.

Orca stepped away from me without comment. I struggled with my shirt, managing to work it up over my head despite my bruised ribs. My bra was more difficult. I fumbled with the strap until Orca let out a disgusted sound and unsnapped it for me.

"Don't touch me."

The look on Orca's face as she assessed the damage she'd inflicted said more about my physical state than my personal inventory of aches and pains.

"Shit," she said, looking genuinely surprised.

I shucked myself out of my pants and shivered in my underwear. "You can leave that on if you want," she said, "but I'm not going to try anything. It's nothing either of us haven't seen before."

I stepped out of my underwear.

"All right," she said, yanking the curtain shut around us. "I'm going to turn the water on. It's going to sting. Are you ready?"

"Sure." I refused to flinch as the water hit my body. Most of the cuts were on my face. My lips were busted and my nose felt pulpy, and there was a scrape above one eye that stung horribly in the salty water.

"I'm sorry, fleeter."

For a moment I thought the sound of the shower had altered her words.

"What?" I asked through swollen lips.

"I'm sorry, okay? Don't make me say it again."

I stared at her. *You're not sorry now*, I thought, *but you will be.* I would make her pay for this. I was not a mess she could just clean up and wash away. The beating she'd given me today would be returned, no matter how hard I had to work to perform the honors.

I ignored Orca that night and huddled as best I could into my hammock. Nothing was broken, only bruised, but it hurt to breathe and I had a pounding headache. Orca paced the room and finally left, leaving me in blissful silence. I was asleep by the time she came back in, but not before I'd engaged in several detailed fantasies where I kicked her skinny ass into next week in front of Miranda and the entire crew of the *Man o' War*. Then

I allowed myself the brief illusion that Miranda would see the state I was in and order Orca flogged or, better yet, beat her up herself.

I knew the reality would be quite different. Shame and anger warred within me as I stared into the green-tinged dark. Miranda would see that I was as weak as her crew thought I was, and I would die of some strange disease far from the Archipelago and everyone I knew. Worse, Comita wouldn't tell anyone what had happened to me, and I would never get to see Harper or my mother again.

Comita had sent me here to suffer, I decided. This wasn't a pact to save the Archipelago; it was a personal punishment for rising too quickly through her ranks. Maddox was right. I didn't belong there, and I sure as hell didn't belong here.

The only difference, I comforted myself as I fell asleep, was that here at least I might get to take out a little bit of my frustration. Miranda had given me the perfect opportunity for revenge, as long as I was allowed to continue training with Orca. Even if she beat me senseless every day, there would eventually come a round where my fist could collide with her face, relieving her of her teeth and good looks.

Breakfast the next morning was a nightmare. Silence met my arrival, and even Orca seemed a little subdued. I didn't wait to see if Miranda would show up. I took my tray and sat by Annie, who moved over with one of her frowns.

"Neptune's big ol' blue balls," Finnegan said appreciatively. "What the hell happened to you?"

"Something that isn't going to happen twice." I ate my mash carefully, grateful for its mushy consistency.

"Tonight," Annie said without any preamble. "Meet me in the training yard after dinner. Before you spar with that one." She jerked her head in Orca's direction. "Eat light."

As if dinner here could be anything but light. My stomach grumbled.

"Captain's coming," Finnegan said.

I kept my face averted from Miranda's view. It was just my

luck that today she decided to show up for breakfast when she hadn't been present in almost a week.

"Must be back from a raid," said Jeanine. "Hide your face, little fishy," she added for my benefit, making a fish face at me with her lips.

"A raid?" That got my attention.

"Life out here isn't free, chica. Someone's got to pay for it, and our captain makes sure it isn't us."

"She leaves the ship?" This was counter to everything I'd ever learned about captaincy.

"Not for very long. If I were her, though, I'd pick someone prettier than Kraken to go with me."

"Anytime you wanna take a private boat ride, I'm all yours," Finnegan said around a mouthful of food.

"Like I said. Someone prettier. That rules you out, Finn."

Finnegan pretended to look upset, but the surprised look on Jeanine's face and the slap she gave him a few seconds later suggested his hand had wandered beneath the table. I smiled, cracking my lips open again.

"What are we going to do?" I asked Annie.

"I'm going to show you a few things Orca doesn't know. Has she let you off your leash yet?"

The smile that split her wrinkled face sent a shiver of vengeful hope down my spine. I decided I wouldn't bet against Annie in a fight.

"No. Miranda's orders. Apparently I can't protect myself."

"You're not in a position to change her mind about that," Annie pointed out. "How is your hand healing up?"

I glanced at the bandage. I'd been doing my best to keep it clean, but the skin had a puckered, angry look beneath the cloth.

"Healing."

"Good. We've lost crew members before to infection."

"Where did Miranda get her scars?"

Annie met my question with a shrewd look.

"You mean you haven't heard of Miranda?"

I shook my head.

90

"Jelly," Orca said, interrupting. "It's time to get to work."

I stood slowly and glared at her, shouldering past her with my tray. Her gray eyes snapped back, showing none of the guilt they'd been full of last night.

There were new charts waiting for me, along with a note from Miranda.

Fleet patrol coordinates. 2506-2515.

The dates surprised me. Each chart corresponded with one of the years, and I leafed through the pages in the binder in confusion. The charts were not drawn using the fleet shorthand, and it was disconcerting to think that our movements had been tracked so meticulously.

There was something here that Miranda wanted me to see. I put a hand over my bruised eye to block out the light and spread the charts across the table.

Fleet territory shifted from year to year as the stations floated with the currents. There was nothing unusual about the drift. It followed the same pattern. North in the summer and south in the winter, tracking the optimal temperature. I had seen these charts before, back on the *North Star*, and had plotted a few myself.

My stomach rumbled. I glanced at the sky, noting the passage of time in the sun's zenith. What would be lunchtime on the *North Star* had come and gone, leaving me hungry, bruised, and with a headache that made it difficult to focus. My eyes swam a little as I stared at the charts spread before me in chronological order. The charts blurred, the lines waving back and forth like seaweed, expanding and contracting with my pulse.

Only the lines weren't expanding, I realized with a start. They were contracting, yes, a few miles each year, but while the coordinates shifted as expected, the range decreased. The Archipelago was losing water.

I leaned closer to the charts, transfixed. The smaller stations were drifting inward, and there were little divots in their range.

Something was nibbling away at it, like fish at a carcass. Some of the loss, I recalled from memory, was due to huge swaths of dead sea. That did not explain the slow recession, or the fact that the biggest fleets lost the least ground while stations with a smaller naval presence lost more.

"How long has this been going on?" I asked Miranda when she swung by an hour later. Miranda didn't even seem to notice my face, or the bruises on my arms.

"These are all the records I have," she said. "I am sure if you compared all of the fleet logbooks for the past fifty years you'd see something similar."

"Why?"

Her eyebrows raised at my question.

"You really have no idea, do you?" She shook her head in genuine surprise, and braced her elbows on the table to rest her chin in her hands. "You can find north from the belly of a whale, but you can't see a shark five feet away from you, can you?"

Seeing as the only thing five feet away from me at the moment was Miranda herself, this statement was a little unsettling.

"The Archipelago," she continued, "is like a school of fish. Lose a few here and there, and none of the other fish notice. Lose too many fish at once and the school weakens. Now," she said, reaching out and taking my left hand. She turned the palm over and drew a firm circle on the unbroken skin. "Pirates are like sharks. They circle, taking a few fish as needed. You following?"

I nodded.

"Imagine that school of fish in a tank. That's the ocean. Then put a leak in it. As the water drains, there is less and less territory for both the fish and the sharks." Her finger drew a smaller circle. "What do you think happens to the fish?"

"Maybe you should ask me a different question," I said, struggling to keep my cool. Her touch was doing far more than illustrating her point. At her raised eyebrow, I continued. "What happens to the sharks after they eat all of the fish?"

Miranda's laughter startled me, as did the friendly squeeze to my hand.

"You're so much more entertaining than an ordinary compass. Has anyone ever told you that?" She grinned at me.

"Maybe. I don't remember them using exactly those words."

"You'll make a good second mate one day, once you figure out how to avoid catching fists with your face."

She stood to go, but paused by my bench on her way out and raised a warm hand to my swollen jaw.

"That's the difference between fish and sharks," she said, running her thumb along the worst of the bruise. "Schooling fish will stick together until the bitter end. Sharks, though. They'll turn on each other."

I leaned into her hand, the pain from the bruise clearing my thoughts.

"Which are you?" I gazed up at her.

"Which are we, my Compass Rose," she corrected. Her thumb traced my lower lip, and then she patted my cheek with just the slightest measure of force.

I had nothing to say in response, and watched her leave with a dry mouth and a racing heart.

I chafed the rest of the afternoon. The chart room was a quiet, lonely place, made all the more so by the knowledge of Crow's Eye sitting far above me, the ship's permanent lookout. I longed to be on the navigation bridge, doing more than shuffling paper.

I also had to figure out how to escape Orca after dinner. I could always pretend to go to the head, or try to lose her on the way out of the dining hall, but there was a small part of me that was more than a little afraid of angering the first mate further. I still wanted to knock her into Davy Jones's locker, but my body ached as the day lengthened and I was hesitant to give her any more reason to beat me than she already had.

Dinner was its usual sorry self, and I ate too quickly, wishing there was more. Miranda met my eye as she sliced into her fish. It was a very shark-like thing to do, I reflected.

"When do we hit Red Flag territory?" asked one of Miranda's officers.

"Tonight. Have a watch ready. Orca, I need you to make sure all shifts are covered."

I suppressed a shudder. If my calculations were correct, we were well out of the way of Archipelago fleet patrols, but that did not make the prospect of a run-in with a pirate any less horrifying, especially now that I knew they sailed under Ching Shih and her Red Flag fleet.

"Sorry, fleeter. Looks like we'll have to put off our lesson for tonight," Orca said.

I looked away from her, clutching my anger to prevent the small seed of relief from sprouting.

"I'd be happy to take her for you," Annie said from behind me. "If that's all right with you, Captain."

Miranda's smile brought a wicked shaft of sunlight into the room.

"Give her all you've got, skipper."

Annie nodded and gestured at me to follow her. I wanted to stay at the table to try and glean some more information, but Miranda dismissed me with a wave. I remembered the feel of her hand on my cheek and met her eyes for a moment too long. Something must have shown in my face, because Miranda's look changed from distraction to speculation. I hurried to clear my tray.

Annie's face was wary as she led me down the mostly empty corridors to the training yard. I followed her wiry shoulders, sticking close to her heels and trying not to dwell on Orca's threats about the rest of the crew.

The yard was deserted, save for a few stalwart souls, and the low ceiling seemed loftier in the emptiness.

"Now. I'm going to show you everything you did wrong with Orca, beginning with your temper," she said, stretching her muscles.

"I don't have a temper."

"Oh yes you do." Annie smiled grimly at me. "You just don't know it yet. How many times have you bit back your tongue, girl? It must be bloody scarred by now."

I opened my mouth to protest, then shut it.

"Ship life isn't easy, especially when half the crew hates you and the other half is scared of you. Tell me, have you ever had any gut feelings about anything else, or is it just direction?"

"Just direction."

Annie assumed a sparring stance.

"We'll go through simple blocks and strikes, real slow. You've got too many bruises for anything else today."

I tried not to show my relief.

"I bet your friends on the fleet won't admit they're scared of you, Compass Rose, so I'll let you in on the secret. When you know something other people don't, they expect you to know other things, too. Your eyes don't help much either."

She demonstrated a few strike and block combos, and I relaxed into the motions.

"Fighting isn't easy. Your mind will try and trip you up, so your body needs to know what your brain will forget. Repetition. Now. Let me know once you feel comfortable and I'll show you what I mean."

I nodded, getting the hang of it.

"You good, then? All right. Now I'm going to tell you a little bit about yourself, and you're going to concentrate on your rhythm. Let's start with this temper of yours. You keep it in check, and I'd bet you're one to back down instead of fighting, usually. Maybe that's how it works on the Archipelago. Here, though, you're going to need that anger. You need to learn how to use it, and how to control it when you do."

I struggled to focus on Annie's words as well as the drill. She had increased the speed and I found myself sweating.

"Controlled anger is energy you can draw on. Uncontrolled anger is a drain, and it leads you to make poor choices, like letting a little fleet navigator get under your skin. Orca didn't do herself any favors by beating the shit out of you. She's earned this crew's respect, but we don't favor uneven odds unless we're the underdogs. Keep your core tight."

I tightened my core and grunted with pain as my bruised ribs protested.

"You're not a fighter."

I wasn't so sure about that. My feelings at the moment were anything but peaceful.

"You don't need to have it in you, though, to hold your own. If you can accept that, you'll do fine. Bend your knees a little more. There. Very good. Now switch. Left hand strike, right hand block. You'll never beat Orca in a fight on skill alone. She's got natural talent and experience, so I'm going to tell you something you're not going to like very much. Don't try to beat her. If you can hold your own against her, you'll earn her respect and the respect of the rest of the crew. That temper of yours will try to get in the way, but don't let it. Show them you're not some soft rice-fed Archipelagean and they'll leave you alone. That's the only victory you can hope for."

"Okay," I said, renewing my vow to break Orca's face wide open. Annie might mean well, but I couldn't let Orca walk around with that smug smile, not if I wanted to stay on this ship. If I wanted to stay on this ship. A burst of homesickness made me falter, and Annie's strike connected with my shoulder.

"Don't let your mind wander."

"Were you born on this ship?" I asked, trying to regain my rhythm.

"I followed Miranda. I was born on a raiding ship in the South Atlantic."

I faltered again.

"You're a pirate?"

"Born and bred."

"Then why are you helping me?"

"I'm not helping you, girl. I'm helping my captain. If she wants to keep you alive, then you got a whole lot of work to do."

"Oh." I allowed myself a small measure of self-pity. I should have known better than to assume someone liked me for my own sake.

"And I like you well enough, for a fleet brat." She smiled and dropped her arms. "That's enough for now. You'll get the hang of it, although I've lost a little respect for fleet discipline."

I thought of Harper and the other sailors who had proved their worth in and out of the ring.

"There's nothing wrong with fleet discipline. I just never took it seriously, I guess. I never thought I'd actually need hand-to-hand combat skills. Plus, I wasn't very good at it."

"Didn't like that, did you?" Annie guessed a little too shrewdly.

My cheeks burned as I realized Annie might be right.

I was sweating and sore, but the movement seemed to have loosened my stiff muscles. I glanced around the training yard, wondering what I was supposed to do next. I didn't have Orca looming over my shoulder, and the thought of going back to the horrible little room we shared was enough to set my teeth on edge.

"Annie," I asked with a little hesitation. "What does the rest of the crew do after dinner?"

"Depends. Some are on watch. Some stay in their quarters. Most drink, and those that have partners fuck, I suppose."

"What do you do?"

"Fish," Annie said with the first real smile I'd seen. "Care to join me?" I nodded, more curious than anything else.

I followed Annie down to the shipyard and through a side door into a small room with a hatch in the floor. Diving equipment hung on the walls. It was late summer, and I judged that the sun would just be setting outside.

"Grab an O2 pack," Annie said. "And put a suit on while you're at it."

We stripped out of our clothes and into the wet suits. I grimaced as I wrestled my way into the neoprene, impressed that Miranda's ship had such high-quality gear. Then I saw the scuff marks where the logo had been scraped away, and paused.

"Where did these suits come from?"

"Hmm? Oh. I'm sure they were bought fairly. And if not, well, if you can't hold on to it, maybe you don't deserve to keep it."

Her low voice sounded so reasonable that the thieves' logic almost made sense.

"What are we fishing for? I didn't think there was anything left."

"Grab a spear and find out."

I finished suiting up, grabbed flippers, goggles, and an O2 tank and waited by the hatch. It sprung open with a slight pop as Annie crouched to turn it.

Dark water splashed against the sides of the opening.

"Follow me, Compass Rose."

Annie slid into the hole, pausing long enough to place the O2 mask before vanishing with her spear. I stared at the water and clutched my spear carefully, not wanting to stab myself or Annie, whom I could no longer see in the black water. I snapped the headlamp into place and dove.

Annie waited for me at the bottom of the dive shoot with a harness and line. Hers was already snapped into place, and I immediately understood the necessity. The ship was topside and making good time. It would be very easy to get left behind.

The shadow of the ship hung heavily above us, and the water pressure pressed against my eardrums. Sunlight beckoned past the murk. Annie gave me a questioning thumbs up, then swam towards the stern with an expert flip of her flippers. I followed, more glad than I would have thought possible to be out of the dank holds of the *Man o' War*.

The last of the daylight streaked through the surface in striated columns, and I waved my hand through the light experimentally. I hadn't spent that much time in the underwater observatories on the *North Star*. They reminded me too much of home. Station sleeping quarters on Cassiopeia always bordered the ocean, with thick, clear walls separating the chambers from the sea. The proximity of the water maintained a cooler sleeping temperature. I used to love waking in the morning and watching the light break through the waves like a thousand reaching fingers.

Something disturbed the water at the stern, and Annie paused to beckon me closer. It took me a moment to recognize the effluence that constantly trickled out as sewage.

That, I registered, was why their hydroponics were unsuccessful. The nitrogen and other nutrients in the waste bled out into the ocean instead of recycling back into the system. Either their hydrofarmer was an idiot, or there was a serious problem with their waste management system.

Something bumped my leg, and I instinctively thrust my spear at the shape as it darted past.

I missed.

I narrowed my eyes. There were a lot more fish here than I had expected. Something had survived the collapse of the fisheries after all. Then again, we were closer to the coast than I was used to, and I didn't spend much time swimming beneath boats.

Annie was poised between the border of sunlight and shadow, which also coincided with the end of our lines. I felt the slack take up and the pull of the ship nudge the harness. It was a comforting weight.

There were jellyfish, too, but these were free floating instead of swarming, and I avoided their tentacles with ease. Most of the fish were small. Annie watched them as she treaded water but didn't appear overeager to strike. I wondered if she ever ate the fish she caught. My mother had drilled the risks of wildcaught fish into me from a young age. The neurotoxins in the algae blooms infected most of the fish that floated in the top zone of the ocean. Only drifters fished, which helped explain the high mortality rate among their tiny vessels.

Annie's anxious hand signal caught my attention. I looked over my shoulder in time to see a large, dark shape moving in the shadows, and swam toward her as quickly as I could. Annie raised her spear in front of her.

It was a small shark, scarred and swimming with a slightly erratic pattern that reminded me of a staggering drunk. It looked more sick than deadly, and it swam past us without interest into a small school of silver fish. They scattered, and the shark swam on. The daylight faded as the O2 in my tank slowly dwindled, and I was glad of the headlamp.

In the growing dark, I could see shapes rising from the deeps. Annie hefted her spear and launched it.

There was a slight yank on my line, and then a feeling of weightlessness. I looked up in time to see Annie retrieve her spear as I drifted past her, and then panic set in as the reality of my situation burst around the corners of my vision in a spray of stars.

The line that connected me like an umbilical cord to the ship had been severed. I kicked out, making for the belly of the ship in the hopes that I might find something to grab on to. The wake fought me as I swam, spitting my progress back in my face. I was pulling up too much O2 with my exertions, but I didn't care. If I slipped away, I would never be found.

My legs were burning, and my chest was on fire with pain from my lungs and my bruised ribs by the time I made it to the shadow of the boat, which by this point was barely distinguishable from the greater darkness. I couldn't see Annie and, at any rate, her harness didn't reach this far out. My fingers scraped along the smooth hull for purchase, finding none.

The protuberant eye beside me saved my life. The shock of seeing the living, breathing relative of Kraken's namesake swimming alongside me sent me scrabbling sideways, and my hand latched onto the rung of a service ladder with an instinctive spasm that almost jerked my arm from its socket as the momentum of the ship caught up with me.

Now that I was still, I could see Annie far away, waving at me frantically. I didn't dare remove a hand to wave back. Annie would go for help. In the meantime, the O2 in my tank was almost gone, and I needed to get to fresh air. Assuming, of course, that the air was actually fresh, and not laced with hydrogen sulfide.

The service ladder curved around the stern, and I stared up through my partially fogged mask at the frothing wake. Last I had checked, the air was clean, and I was lucky the ship was close enough to the surface for me to reach. Tightening my grip on the ladder, I took what I hoped wasn't the last breath of air in my tank and forced my way through the surface of the water.

The force of the ship's passage almost ripped me from the rung. I clung on, the strain threatening to break my fingers, and hauled myself back in. I had survived Fleet Preparatory. I could survive this.

Far above me, up a ladder slick with spray and half-rotted in places, was a service door. Ripping the O2 mask off my face, I wrapped one arm around the ladder and used the other to haul in the remains of my line. I tied it off on the rung, hoping it would be enough to get me to the door. I didn't like the look of the ladder.

Real stars pricked against the sky, crisp and clear between the scudding clouds. The roar of the wake rushed beneath me as I grabbed for another rung, then another, occasionally skipping to the one above it if it looked particularly weak. My arms, already tired from their swim, trembled uncontrollably, and my feet fumbled for purchase. I stopped to free them from their flippers and climbed on.

There was no landing outside the service door. I hung on the last rung, limply, using my chin as a third arm in case the other two gave out. A hot tear slipped down my cheek. The door had no handle. I reached up with one hand and knocked. The sound echoed dully in the airlock beyond, and I knew with a grim certainty that it would go unanswered.

North, east, south, west. The stars burned my eyes.

I hung for a long time. The sound of the surf faded, blending with the roar of my heartbeat, and the stars blazed with unbearable brightness. I was alone beneath them. As far as the eye could see, I was the only pair of eyes looking upward.

Me and Crow's Eye.

My heart gave a little lurch, offering a trickle of adrenaline. Crow's Eye, who never left the crow's nest, beautiful, grumpy, cryptic Crow's Eye, who just might see me out here if I could get his attention.

My headlamp was gone, but the diving suit came with an

emergency flashlight. I pried it out of the belt and prayed with all my heart to whatever might be listening that it was charged.

Blue light bathed my face like a kiss. My breath caught in a sob of relief, and I shone the light down the ladder toward the black water. Crow's Eye would not be able to see my signal from the back of the ship. I would have to trust that my line would hold a second time, and swim out far enough into the ship's wake to enter his line of vision, regardless of how weak my arms already felt and the ache in my bruised ribs. Securing the flashlight in my teeth, I started my descent.

I was halfway down when the rung snapped beneath my foot. I had the sense to snatch the flashlight from my teeth as I fell, and my heart pounded for three terrified beats before I hit the surface.

The wake washed over me in a dark tumult and I struggled to resurface, gasping. The line took up slack quickly, but not before the ship had dwindled significantly against the stars. I kicked out, working my way over the wake and into a direct line of sight to the crow's nest. I could just make out the thin spire against the sky.

Treading water forcefully against the pull of the current and mourning the loss of my flippers, I waved one hand over the light in the SOS sequence, pausing now and then to give my legs a break. I wasn't sure what to expect in response, or even if I would get a response. Water rushed past my ears, and I slowed my kicks, taking deep breaths and holding them to stay afloat while my legs rested.

Someone or something had cut my line. I remembered Annie, launching her spear at a squid seconds before I was cut loose. It could have been a coincidence. In the aftermath of adrenaline, my body told me otherwise. There was an ache deep in my stomach that I had felt before.

"You don't belong here," whispered the stars.

I glanced up at them, feeling as hollow as an empty shell. Something blinked from the corner of my eye. I looked at the crow's nest, where a small light pulsed back. I repeated my signal, the hollow feeling momentarily dispelled. He had seen me. I reeled myself back into the shelter of the boat and hung, half in and half out of the water while I waited. I was not climbing that ladder until I was sure there was someone on the other side of the door to haul me in.

A creak and a groan sounded far away.

"Rose," Annie shouted down to me from the service door. I looked up to see her silhouetted against the light from the hatch. She was alone.

The ache in my stomach deepened, and my compass quivered, looking for another course. Through the deepening haze of exhaustion, I could tell things weren't adding up. Annie should have gone immediately for help, instead of racing to the service hatch at the back of the ship like someone covering her tracks. For that matter, my O2 tank should have lasted a lot longer than it had, even with my struggle.

I climbed up a few rungs, determined not to show her how tired I was. I wanted to believe that I was wrong. I also wanted to live, and I stood a better chance of that if I could keep her talking.

"I can't make the rest of the climb," I said, double-checking that my line was still securely tied to my diving suit with one hand.

"Are you hurt?" she asked.

"Yeah. My right arm. I think it's dislocated," I lied, letting it hang limp. I had lost my spear, but the suit came with a diving knife. My right hand closed around it out of her sight.

"I'll help you," she said, glancing over her shoulder.

"The ladder is half rotted. Can you go and get a rope?" I waited to hear what she would say to that.

"I can't leave you here, Rose," she said.

"I'll be fine. I just can't climb. I think someone cut my line. They must have followed us down." Silence met my words. "I think it was Orca," I said, crossing my fingers. If I was right about Annie, then the minute she found out I suspected her, I was dead.

103

"No. It's not Orca. She'd die before she went against Miranda's orders. Orca, whatever her faults, is the best friend you have on this ship."

"Then maybe it was someone else," I said. "Andre. He doesn't like me." Annie watched me. I couldn't see her face, but I could almost hear the decisions tumbling through her head. *Come on, Crow's Eye*, I thought. I wasn't going to be able to buy myself much more time.

And if Crow's Eye was in on it, then I would have to coax Annie down the ladder to finish me off, stab her, and hope there was nobody else waiting.

"Skipper," said a familiar voice. I rested my head against the bars, not sure whether to laugh or to cry at the arrival of my unlikely savior.

"Orca."

"Captain's coming, Annie," Orca said. "She'll be wanting a report. What the hell is going on?"

I couldn't see her, but I could hear the note of warning in her voice.

"Rose is down there," Annie said. Her voice didn't waver.

"I can see that. How did she get there, and why is she still there?"

"I took her squidding. Something, or someone, cut her line, and she's too hurt to make the climb."

"Typical," Orca said. She leaned out to stare down at me, and then put one foot on the top rung.

"Wait," I said, startling her. "The ladder. It's half rotted at the top." She froze, then slowly swung herself back into the hatch.

"If you can't climb, how do you know it's rotted?" she asked.

I heard Annie suck in her breath. I don't know what would have happened if Miranda hadn't shoved her way between them a second later.

"Why is my navigator clinging to my stern like a fucking barnacle?" she asked. Her voice was dead calm.

"There was an accident, Captain," Annie said.

"Kraken, secure the skipper before there are any more accidents on her watch. Orca, make sure that lifeline is secure."

So there was a rope up there, after all.

"Captain, I can—," Orca said.

"Secure it, Orca. Rose," she called down to me. "Can you climb?"

"Yes," I said. The ladder would not withstand the weight of a rescuer. Even if I had been hurt, I would have had no choice.

"Rose, I'm tossing you a line. Tie it to your harness."

The light from the hatch flickered in and out of sight, and I heard the slither of the lifeline tumbling down the ladder. I fumbled for it and tied it around my waist, then began the longest climb of my life—which had included more than its fair share of ladders, recently.

Miranda waited at the other end, and her firm grip closed around my forearms and pulled me to safety.

"Are you all right, Rose?" she asked.

"Yes, Captain."

I squared my shoulders and met Annie's eyes. They gave nothing away.

"I thought you were hurt," Orca asked as I cut the diving line that still secured me to the boat.

I slid the diving knife slowly back in the sheath. She met my eyes, and beneath her general dislike I saw a flicker of respect.

"Kraken, get the skipper to the brig and under guard. I'll question her later. Rose," Miranda said, taking my hand to pull me out of Annie's reach, "you're coming with me."

Chapter Eight

"Let's get you out of that," she said, when Kraken, Annie, and Orca had left.

I let her pull the suit off of me, shivering from cold and shock in the dark hallway. My clothes were damp with water and sweat.

"Leave your gear there. You need a drink and a blanket."

I trailed after her down the winding, narrow corridors of the *Man o' War*. We passed several crew members enjoying their off hours. Some toasted Miranda; others stared at me with open distrust. Miranda demanded a blanket from one of them and wrapped it securely around my shoulders.

Her route eventually led us to a common room, where she made a point of offering me a seat on a low couch in a corner. The bartender rushed to deliver us two glasses of rum, diluted only slightly with some sort of juice. The brief hush that had settled over the room in Miranda's wake passed, and the tide of voices rose again, punctuated here and there by an outbreak of laughter or an angry shout. Miranda sipped her drink with a thoughtful expression as she surveyed the room, then tossed back the rest of the rum in a fluid motion. A second appeared at her elbow almost instantaneously.

I stared into the murky depths of my glass. A shadowy reflection stared back, eyes wide beneath frazzled hair. My curls had been confined beneath a wetsuit, exposed to salt water, and now were drying mutinously however they pleased. I needed to see a barber or, barring that, a comb. I ran a hand over my hair and tried to finger comb my topknot back into a semblance of order, wishing a haircut was my biggest concern.

"You keep your hair short," Miranda said. "Like your captain."

"A lot of women have short hair where I'm from," I pointed out, tracing her sleek braid with my eyes.

"Yes, well, you also have higher-quality soap." She raised her glass and clinked it against mine. I took a nervous swallow. "Braids are easier to manage here, although I draw the line at dreads, myself. Too heavy."

"Oh," I said. I was proving to be a less than scintillating conversationalist, but I allowed myself some slack, considering that someone had just tried to kill me.

"You can call me Miranda."

I choked on my drink. Calling a captain by their first name was unthinkable. Nobody called Admiral Comita anything but "Admiral" to her face, and we stuck with her last name behind her back, just to be safe.

"Are you sure, Captain?"

"Do you always question your superiors, Compass Rose?" She was grinning now, revealing a dimple in her left cheek.

Of course she has a dimple, I thought. *I should have just drowned.*

"No, Captain."

"Say it."

I gave her a look that must have revealed the depth of my discomfort and exasperation, because she laughed out loud, causing quite a few heads to turn our way.

"Or say it after a drink, I don't care, but we're not leaving this table until we're on first-name terms."

"All right," I said, taking a gulp.

"Do you go by Compass or Rose? I assumed Rose, and I'm usually right about my assumptions, so think carefully before answering."

"Rose. Compass is a little too utilitarian, even for a navigator."

Although if you say my name one more time, I'll call you whatever you want, Captain. I tightened my hold on my drink, wondering why my inner voice sounded so much like Harper.

"I had a cat named Compass," she said, toying with her glass. "He used to get lost all the time. Never understood it. I don't think I'll have that problem with you."

"Should I be flattered or offended that you think I have more potential than a cat?" I took another sip of rum. I was not accustomed to the continual drinking that seemed to be the norm on this ship, and the alcohol was loosening too many things at once.

"Flattered. I loved that cat."

"In that case, I'm honored," I said, toasting her and draining the glass with exaggerated respect. Maybe it would drown out Harper's commentary.

"Feeling braver?" she asked.

"Why?"

"Address me properly."

"Captain Miranda."

"I could have you flogged for insubordination, you know." Her smile assured me that this time, at least, she was joking.

"Well then." I took a deep breath and met her eyes. "Miranda. Thank you for the drink." *And saving my life.* I tried not to savor the taste of her name.

"My generosity is renowned across the seven seas. Just ask Nasrin."

The bartender had arrived with more drinks. I gave the glass a suspicious glance. With the exception of Harper, the only people who had offered me a drink in the past two weeks had wanted something from me.

The rum hummed through my veins.

"Whatever you say, Captain," Nasrin said with a smirk. Her biceps could have crushed several windpipes at once, and I suspected she played bouncer as well as tender at this bar.

Focus, Rose.

"Hear that, Rose? 'Whatever I say.' Those are the house rules."

Nasrin laughed as she strolled away.

"Whatever you say?" I repeated, hoping she didn't notice my slightly slurred speech.

"Yep. Although not everybody believes, me. Isn't that right, Nasrin?"

Nasrin made a rude hand gesture from behind the bar, which looked as if it had been salvaged from the deck of an ancient fishing vessel. I looked back to find Miranda watching me out of half-lidded eyes. She smiled at my startled expression.

"So," she said. "Let's get the hard questions out of the way then, shall we?"

"Yes, Captain." The rum made sense, now. This wasn't about soothing my nerves. This was about information, the only currency that never lost its value.

"Miranda."

"Miranda," I repeated. I would have happily said it another time, if she'd asked.

"Annie took you squidding?"

"Yes." Miranda, I noticed, had a habit of twirling the ring on her thumb as she spoke.

"Why?"

"I asked her what the crew did when their shifts were over. She told me most of them drank and fucked." I blushed slightly. "So I asked her what she did."

What do you do, Captain? I needed to stop drinking.

"She lied to you if she said she didn't drink or fuck. Annie's as bad as they come."

"She told me she fished."

"I'll give her that. Annie's got a way with the squid, and I've never seen someone so enthusiastic about squid ink in their cooking. She's a good cook, too. Our food isn't usually quite this terrible." She grimaced at the memory of dinner. "So she didn't ask you to go with her; you asked her?"

"Yes."

Miranda tapped her fingers on the table.

"You like Annie, don't you?" she said.

I nodded.

"I do, too," Miranda continued. "I don't want to believe that she set you up."

"She couldn't have." Hearing Miranda voice my suspicions out loud set off a domino effect of denial.

"She very easily could have. Only your line was cut."

My breath caught at the memory of that feeling of sudden weightlessness, and the belly of the ship rushing past me.

"It doesn't make any sense, though. Why would she do that, after helping me?" Annie had been the first person on the ship to reach out to me. Now that I was no longer dangling off the side of the boat, my suspicions seemed ill-founded. It could have been an accident.

"We elect our captains, outside of the Archipelago. The chain of command is fluid. Not everyone agrees with my actions, and there are a good many sailors who prefer slitting Archipelagean throats to working with them. If it makes you feel any better, it wasn't personal."

It did not make me feel better.

"Maybe it was an accident," I said.

Miranda turned cold eyes on me.

"Annie's first mistake was putting you in a position where an accident was possible. She did not have my leave to take you off the ship."

"It was my fault."

"And you paid the price." Her look softened. "Drink. It will take the edge off the shock."

I obeyed.

"What are you going to do to Annie?"

"Question her." Miranda's face hardened, erasing any memory of softness, dimples, and friendly banter.

I was glad I wasn't Annie. I didn't think she would be getting a blanket and a stiff drink. I remembered the spear streaking through the water from Annie's hand.

After a squid, or my line?

"I don't understand," I said, not meaning to say the words out loud. Miranda set her glass down on the table.

110

"Don't you?"

I thought back to what Annie had told me earlier that evening while we were sparring. *"Show them you're not some soft rice-fed fleeter and they'll leave you alone. That's the only victory you can hope for."* An odd thing to say, to someone you were planning to kill.

Unless she hadn't planned on it. She was a self-professed pirate and a mercenary skipper—in other words, an opportunist. You had to be, to survive the waters outside of the protection of the Archipelago. What had Annie tried to prove out there, and to whom? Why hadn't she gone for help? What would have happened if she had climbed down that ladder after me?

No, I thought, knowing better than to say it again. *I don't want to understand.*

"You look like you're dead on your feet," Miranda said, rising.

"I'm fine, Miranda."

"I'm sure you will be after a few hours of sleep. Let's get you to a bed."

She didn't take my hand again. I briefly thought about tripping, then shook myself, appalled. I was a Polarian Fleet navigator, now a mercenary navigator, and I had a small helping of self-respect on top of that. I didn't swoon.

I gritted my teeth and kept pace with Miranda, holding my bruised head as high as it would comfortably go. Miranda laughed low in her throat at my efforts, and I forgot myself enough to glare at her.

Her look cut through me like a hot knife, and there was nothing feigned about the sudden weakness in my knees.

Shit, I thought fervently. *Shit, shit, shit.* Attempted murder was the least of my problems. I needed to get off this ship and far away from Miranda.

Instead, I went with her to her quarters, legs shaking.

Her rooms were disturbingly close to Orca's. I hoped the walls were soundproof and that she hadn't heard some of the nastier fights I'd had with her first mate or, worse, touched the web of my dreams with hers.

The first room in her suite was wider than it was long, and the

111

walls were hung with antique remnants of a long dead ocean. A whaling harpoon framed a low couch, and a pair of tridents threatened whoever might be brave enough to sit in the armchair beneath their crossed tines. I almost caught my foot on a braided rope rug as I followed Miranda through into the second room, still glancing behind me at the other unfamiliar objects on the walls.

The second room in her suite had a tiny kitchen. I thought of all the meals Miranda missed and forgave her instantly. The lowest bilge drudge could have cooked a finer meal than the slop I'd consumed since my arrival, and Miranda's kitchen showed the marks of frequent use. There was a small table with two chairs, but the second chair was laden with a pile of books. I blinked and took an involuntary step toward the chair. Real books were a rarity, even in the Archipelago. These, tossed almost carelessly, would have given an Archipelago librarian a fit of apoplexy.

"There's fresh water in the tap if you're thirsty, and feel free to help yourself to some fruit."

My eyes darted eagerly to the basket of fruit on the counter. I resisted the urge to snatch a bunch for later. Miranda pushed through a curtain of tiny shells into the third room, and I hesitated at the door.

Miranda didn't sleep in a hammock. Her bunk filled one half of the small room. It had been made with military precision, which was slightly spoiled by the fat orange cat lying sprawled in the center of the mattress. Green eyes were slitted suspiciously at me. The walls of the room were bare of all ornamentation, save for an ugly painting, and the only personal item in sight was the captain herself.

That was unsettling enough.

"Make yourself useful, Seamus." The cat blinked slowly at Miranda and refused to move. "This is Seamus, my personal ratter. He makes sure nothing creeps or crawls in here."

The sight of the bed, even with the cat in it, was too distracting. I looked around the rest of the room for something else to focus on.

The painting caught my eye. It was little more than an irregularly shaped canvas, painted with what I assumed was squid ink. Nothing else had that dark gray, almost blue-black, tint. Her room had decent lights, and the crude representation of a Portuguese man o' war jellyfish loomed larger than life before me, a mass of swirling strokes that had a vaguely hypnotic and violent effect on the viewer.

"Ugly as sin, isn't it? They're actually quite beautiful up close. I had a limited color palette."

"You painted that?" I asked.

She ran a hand over her hair, and I ached to touch the curve of her lips.

"Have you ever been in a swarm?"

There was a faraway look to her eyes that stopped me from answering the odd question.

"It's incredible." She shook her head. "Of course, if you'd ever been in a swarm, I'd have to question your credentials."

I tried to imagine Admiral Comita showing me her bedroom, and failed. Nothing about this followed protocol.

"Anyway, these are the captain's quarters. I'm going to lock you in for the night. There's a shower there, next to the head, and I have a spare shirt you can borrow."

She rummaged through a set of drawers by the bed. The cat's tail twitched in annoyance at the disturbance as Miranda pulled out an oversize shirt that looked like it belonged to a man twice her size.

Maybe it did. That would serve me right. I remembered Jeanine's comment about Miranda and Kraken. The idea of Miranda touching Kraken's tattooed skin burned more fiercely than the rum.

"I won't be back for hours, so you might as well sleep here if Seamus will let you. We'll figure something else out later. I might put you back with Orca after I flog a few sailors. The last thing I need is to find out that your body got shoved down the head."

"It would be the last thing I want, too," I said with feeling.

"Quite literally. A shitty situation for everyone involved." Miranda

113

laughed at my startled face. "What, Comita doesn't have a sense of humor?"

"No, not really."

"Well, she's old. She's earned the right to be an iron bitch."

"She's not that old," I protested.

"How long do you think the average person lives, off of the Archipelago?"

I did a brief tally of the number of gray heads I'd seen on the *Man o' War* or among the drifters on Cassiopeia. It was a very small percentage.

"Fair enough, I guess. But if she's old, what does that make you?" I asked.

"Same thing it makes both of us—in the prime of our short lives, which are slipping away as we speak. You'll be asleep when I get back. If anyone knocks on the door, ignore it. No one will be able to touch you here."

She toyed with the collar of her white shirt for a moment, scanning the room for invisible threats.

"Thank you," I said in a quiet voice.

Her eyes snapped back to mine.

"I'd do the same for any of my crew."

The coldness in her voice caught me by surprise. I watched her leave, stunned by the sudden change in her demeanor.

"And that," I said to the cat, "is why you never address your captain by her first name."

I glanced around the rooms warily and tried the handle of the door. It didn't budge. Not only was no one getting in, but I wasn't getting out, either. I sat at the table and peeled myself an orange, absorbing the silence moment by moment.

Someone had tried to kill me today. Yesterday, Orca had beaten me to a pulp, rather like the red flesh of the blood orange in my hands. A few days before that, Admiral Comita had turned my world upside down and sent me on a mission that hadn't gotten any clearer, into the hands of a moody captain who, I reluctantly acknowledged, I was drooling after like a lovesick teenager. I got up abruptly, shoving the remaining orange segments into my mouth and stripping down out of my clothes.

Since I wasn't dead, I might as well be clean.

The water in the shower wasn't hot, but it was fresh. I closed my eyes and let it wash away a week's worth of salt from my face, hair, and body. I scrubbed at my skin with my hands until I felt raw and my bruises ached from the abuse.

Half-drunk, half-drowned, and half-asleep, I stepped out of the shower and slipped into the clean shirt.

It didn't smell like a man. I shivered as Miranda's scent washed over me and sat on the bed to steady myself. It gave beneath me gratifyingly and I leaned back, resting my damp head on the pillows. The light dimmed around me, and as I sank into sleep I registered the presence of the cat as he settled himself in the crook of my arm and began to purr.

A lump welled in my sleepy throat at the contact. I tentatively stroked the soft head and body, my fingers clumsily responding to the cat's insistent purr. The lump grew.

What was the point in showering, I thought bitterly, *if I was just going to drown myself in tears?* I held back the sobs, not wanting to disturb my new friend, and fell asleep to the sound of my ragged breathing.

"Wake up."

I nestled instinctively deeper into the covers, not wanting to deal with Orca.

"That's an order."

I opened my eyes, expecting to see the surly first mate, and found Miranda standing in the doorway instead. She was wearing an undershirt that clung to the firm lines of her body. I shut my eyes and opened them again, willing myself to wake up somewhere else as yesterday crashed over me. Miranda's face was closed and distant, and the bed appeared untouched save for where I'd lain. I didn't dare ask her where she'd slept.

"Yes, Captain," I said, my mouth thick with sleep and last night's unshed tears.

I pulled back the blanket and slipped out of bed, the shirt thankfully falling to my knees. I avoided meeting Miranda's eye as I made a beeline for the clothes I'd left crumpled on the bathroom floor. They were gone.

"Looking for these?" Miranda held up my shirt on her finger. It was clean.

I ran a hand nervously through my hair, feeling the nightshirt take a leap toward my upper thigh. I pulled it down again. She tossed my clothes toward me, and I caught them awkwardly, trying to keep the collar of the shirt from slipping off one shoulder.

Miranda's eyebrow arched very slightly, and I turned away to hide my face.

You were nearly killed yesterday, I reminded myself. *You could be killed today. This woman is not your friend. She is your only chance of survival, and she will never be anything more.*

I pulled my pants on as quickly as I could. My heel caught at the hem and I jumped around for a step or two, feeling the color in my cheeks flare brighter. I pulled the nightshirt over my head, yanked my own, clean shirt over the top, and took several steadying breaths. Not looking at Miranda, I escaped to her small bathroom and splashed some water on my face.

My reflection was not promising. I finger combed my hair, but I couldn't get the unnatural glaze out of my eyes or the spots of flaming color out of my cheeks. I looked feverish. I felt crazy. Too many things were happening at once. I missed Harper. I needed her frankness and her affectionate physicality.

I had worried, once, that I might develop feelings for Harper. Now I realized how ridiculous that was. What I felt for Harper was love, but it was pure. *Pure-ish,* I corrected. I was only human.

"You like dangerous girls," she'd told me once, after she caught me nursing a crush on an officer named Natalia. Natalia had short black hair and a jawline that could have made Poseidon weep. She also terrified the Fleet Prep, and was one of the reasons why my combat skills were subpar. She had been our instructor, and I had never really been able to concentrate properly, despite Harper's well-aimed jabs to my side.

This was different. This was actually dangerous. I splashed a little more water on my face for good measure. Miranda was a mercenary, and I was far from home. My healing palm itched in remembrance. Getting distracted wasn't an option.

Then, of course, there was the fact that Miranda had bigger fish to fry than one little navigator. The only reason she gave me the time of day was because I had a skill she needed.

I concentrated on that. I was good at what I did. I was the best at what I did. *North. South. East. West.* I could find the North Star from the bottom of the Mariana Trench, and I'd been born with the ocean's currents running through my veins.

Only now my compass had found a new pole. I felt it twitch as Miranda moved around the room, and I ducked hurriedly out of the head.

Miranda's naked back was to me. I stopped mid-stride and grabbed the wall for support while Miranda bent to pull a clean shirt from the drawers nested underneath the bed. Her muscular shoulders tapered into a narrow waist, and the lithe muscles of her back moved beneath the thin tracery of scars. Her pants rode low, revealing the slight curve of her hip, and the belt dipped under the weight of the thin whip coiled at her side.

The sight of the weapon clicked my jaw shut. I dropped my eyes and turned to face the kitchen, fear and something else spurring my heartbeat in a brutal race to the finish line.

"Ready?"

I nodded mutely as Miranda stalked past me, dressed in the white hemp shirt that was her particular brand of uniform.

"Where are we going, Captain?"

She shot me a look that crippled my voice halfway through my last word.

"Stay close to me, navigator, and you'll find out."

My stomach rumbled in protest as we bypassed the cafeteria, but Miranda's silence kept my hunger at bay. The ship was oddly deserted. A few cats scattered from our path, but I didn't see a single human as we wound our way up the catwalks toward the sun and the upper deck. My heart still beat uncomfortably in my throat, and the length of Miranda's strides wasn't helping matters. The few inches she had on me in height were clearly all located in her legs.

My sense of unease rose with every flight of stairs. The lines of Miranda's back stiffened the higher we climbed, and something about the severity of her expression reminded me of Comita.

At the hatch to the upper deck, she turned. One hand clenched the handle of the door and the other rubbed the top of the whip handle. I forced myself to meet her eyes.

A chill washed over me that had nothing to do with desire. Her eyes were blue, cold, and far away. Warmth drained from my face, and my internal compass swiveled, then settled, aligned in trembling certainty with due north as I realized what was about to happen.

The ship was topside.

"You can't," I said, reaching out to grab her arm. Her eyes locked with mine. They were no longer far away, and the icy cold settled into my bones.

"Nobody tells me what I can and can't do. Not on this ship."

"She—." I struggled to find words to describe my protest. Somehow simply stating Annie had shown me kindness didn't seem like enough. "Do you have proof?"

Something moved behind her eyes, like a deep swell that hasn't yet stirred the surface of the water. She didn't answer.

"It is as much my fault for going with her as hers. Take me instead. Your crew would like that." I'd always wondered what drove the heroes in stories to utter such foolish words. It was hasty stupidity, I reflected as they left my lips.

Miranda's eyebrow twitched upward, and something very much like the ghost of a smile flitted across her lips.

"I could take you any way I wanted you."

My heart hammered once, then stopped as I struggled to stay standing. My hand was still on her arm, and her skin burned beneath my fingers. I pulled my hand away and clamped both hands safely beneath my armpits.

"Then do it. Wait until after the trial to punish her."

Miranda shook her head.

"Rose. If I wait, if I show even a moment of weakness, my crew will tear you to pieces. Too much is riding on you. I don't have time for this bullshit. I said she could train you, not take you underneath the goddamn boat." Her eyes blazed. "From now on, you train with Orca and nobody else. You talk to Orca. You sit with Orca. You follow her around like a remora, unless you are with me. Do you understand?"

"Yes, Captain."

"What are you?"

"A remora, Captain."

Miranda grabbed the front of my shirt and pulled me toward her. I had time to notice a fleck of green in one eye before she broke into my stunned reverie.

"I don't want to have to flog any more of my crew, Compass Rose. Start acting like a pretty little sucker fish, or you and your entire Archipelago will sink to the bottom of the fucking ocean."

"Yes, Miranda." Our eyes locked again. Anger warred with desire and won, and I straightened as best I could. "Whatever you say, Miranda." The venom in my voice surprised me.

"Watch your tone, navigator."

I took a step toward her. She didn't back down, and I found myself glaring directly into her eyes. Her gaze flickered down to my lips and then back up, and all of the nerves in my body leapt to attention.

"I think I've figured you out, Captain," I said, my voice catching.

Her eyelids lowered ever so slightly at my words.

"You're not a fish. You're not a shark. You're the hole in this goddamn tank."

Silence stretched between us in a tight bubble. Miranda's chest rose and fell twice before she spoke.

"And you're about to be a fish out of water."

Her fingers tightened on my shirt front, bringing me another millimeter closer to her full lips. I forgot about Annie. I forgot about Miranda's crew. I forgot about everything except the feeling of the charged air between us.

"Is it draining, always getting the last word? Or is it just that you're a drain?" I said as sweetly as I could to keep myself afloat.

"I should make punning punishable by flogging." Her voice was as husky as mine. "Then you'd get your wish."

"You'd like that, wouldn't you?" I tilted my head, daring her to break the tension between us.

"As a rule, I don't enjoy disciplining my crew, fleeter, but for you I could make an exception."

"If you keep calling me fleeter, does that mean I'm exempt from your rules?"

"My crew knows better than to question their captain."

"As your navigator, it's my job to tell you when I think you're sailing into troubled waters."

"The only thing troubling these waters right now is you."

I glanced at her lips, unable to control myself. There was something wrong with me. My muscles refused to obey my orders, and I was acutely aware of my pounding heartbeat. There was no way Miranda could miss it, either, with her hand so close to my chest. There were too many ways to take her words.

The hatch door opened, forcing us both to jump back. Orca stood in the doorway with a stony expression on her face.

"She's ready for you, Captain."

"I doubt that," Miranda said quietly, releasing me. "Remember what I said, Rose. Remora. Orca, don't let her out of your sight."

"Follow me, little jellyfish." Orca's tone had a forced lightness to it, and the look she sent my way by all rights should have killed me.

Miranda set off up the stairs, leaving me out of breath and very, very confused.

The top deck was thronged with people, most of whom could have used a bath. I was grateful for the stiff breeze blowing in my face and followed Orca with what could only be described as sucker fish-like devotion. My bruises ached at the sight of her fists, but I was also aware that her fists were the only things keeping me safe from the agitated mercenaries.

Dangerous women were a problem.

The crowd parted for Miranda, and as we followed the captain Orca grabbed my arm and shoved me in front of her, keeping a grip on my elbow and a snarl on her lips. The crew kept their distance.

Annie and Kraken waited in a clear space at the center of the deck. The glass tower of the crow's nest jutted above them, and I wondered if Crow's Eye was watching from his lofty perch.

"Anemone Dive," Miranda said into the sudden silence. "I charge you with neglect of yourself and ship property. Do you have anything to say in your defense?"

Annie shook her head and straightened her wiry shoulders.

"Then let me say this." Miranda turned away from Annie and faced the assembled crew. The wind whipped her words around the deck, slicing into the listeners. Her face was as hard as an October sky.

Orca shoved me toward her, and I stumbled into the cleared space to a muted hiss of disapproval. Miranda pointed at me and addressed the crowd.

"This is a tool. Like many of our tools, she comes from the Archipelago. There is no difference between her and the seeds we grow, trade fairly for, or the engines we raid, which is a fairer trade still." The crew laughed appreciatively. "So much of our ship comes from fleet vessels. Do you want to stab a few holes in our hydroponics? Do you want to rip open the bulkheads and go back to pumping by hand, up to your throats in water in the bilges?"

Silence met her words.

"This is my tool." She grabbed my half-healed hand and held it in the air. "With her help, I will fulfill my promises to you, and if any harm befalls her, I will flog each and every one of you until I find the source of the mutiny." She stared around at the rows of tattooed mercenaries with a grim light in her eyes. "Are there any objections?"

121

Nobody spoke.

"Kraken."

Kraken nodded at the command and seized Annie by the arms, his huge bulk acting as a whipping post. Her ankles were bound, and I could not see her face, only her back, her shoulders taut with anticipatory pain.

Miranda uncoiled the whip at her belt and raised her arm.

"Wait."

I held out a hand to stop the fall of the whip. The tip lashed out and caught me across the stomach, doubling me over in a red haze of pain.

"Learn your place, Compass," Miranda said in a cruelly careless voice.

I looked up at her through a veil of tears and watched her arm fall once, twice, and three times across Annie's back, blood welling in the bright red stripes the blows left behind.

"You fucking idiot," Orca hissed in my ear. "Annie was the one trying to kill you. She confessed it last night."

Pain is as limitless as the sky, I reflected, soaring to new and unbearable heights. Orca's grip on my shoulder was the only thing that kept me on my feet.

Chapter Nine

"Block. Strike. Block. Jesus, why am I even trying?"

Orca blocked my strike and turned away from me, clutching her hair in frustration. Air hissed out from between my teeth and I leaned toward the ground, bracing myself on my knees and wondering if I could manage to break my neck if I fell at the right angle. The mat was certainly hard enough.

I was tired, I was hungry, and I was sick of listening to Orca list my many faults in a voice that could have cut through steel.

The training yard was predictably full, mostly with sailors eager to watch Orca repeatedly annihilate my attempts to measure up to whatever diabolical standards she expected me to meet. My popularity was on the rise since my ill-fated adventure, and occasionally a voice from the crowd would offer a word of encouragement.

Right now, they were silent. I watched a bead of sweat drip off my nose and splatter on the mat, counting the seconds before she hauled me back up by the collar of my shirt.

The bruises she'd given me that first day had long since been replaced by new ones. I woke up sore and went to bed aching, the hours in-between passing in a blur of maps and coordinates as I charted out possible points of entry into the Gulf.

The time for planning was almost at an end; we were close now, and the strain of waiting for Miranda's signal grated. Every passing day took me farther and farther from the waters I knew, and each evening Orca lectured me about the dangers of lassitude and weakness, two qualities that I apparently possessed in abundance, while my mind reeled from hunger and confusion and the weal on my stomach healed.

The memory of Miranda's cruelty wiped away the last of my reserves of strength.

It was too much, coming hard on the wake of today's events. My head lolled as Orca jerked me upright, disgust written all over her face.

"You're not done."

I met her eyes, waiting for another insult. She couldn't hurt me any more today.

Annie's trial had been short, the evidence overwhelming. This morning, Miranda had sent her to see Davy Jones for her final judgment. I blocked the sound of that distant splash. Annie had chosen the plank, despite Miranda's offer of a more civilized ending, and the defiance in her eyes had carried a message that I hadn't understood.

Her death did not lessen the pain of betrayal; if anything, it had made it worse.

Orca brought her practice knife up with exaggerated slowness. I blocked it clumsily. There was a stir by the door that I ignored, keeping a wary eye on the plastic knife. Orca grew less predictable the more frustrated she became with my efforts, and I wasn't so sunk in despair that I was willing to suffer a blade to the ribs if I could avoid it.

I felt the footstep on the mat behind me before I saw Orca's eyes widen in surprise. I whipped around, my right arm deflecting the knife thrust and bringing me into my attacker's guard. She blocked my punch and I barely had time to twist out of the way of the knife as it came back toward me. The mouth, twisted in amusement, was achingly familiar.

Miranda.

She didn't waste time taking advantage of my hesitation. My twist had brought me up hard against her body, and her elbow whipped around my throat, pulling me closer still as I struggled to fend off her knife. Stars burst in the corners of my vision, accompanied by a swarming haze of gray.

"The legs," she whispered encouragingly into my ear. "Go for the legs."

I threw my weight to the right and kicked at the back of her knee with my own knee, a move Orca had illustrated for me with concussive force several days ago. Miranda stumbled, and I pulled free long enough to snatch a breath of air before I was thrown to the ground.

I froze, feeling the weight of her body on top of mine and the prick of a knife at my throat. Strong thighs gripped my hips, doing more to my heart rate than terror allowed, and I closed my eyes as the knife point pressed its advantage.

"You're making progress," Miranda said, leaning over me.

I opened my eyes to see her face a foot away, that damned crooked smile still on her lips.

"Nice work, Orca."

She sat back, resting her full weight on me as she wiped a bead of blood off of the tip of her knife. The heat from her body burned against me with destructive urgency, drying my mouth, and the silence in the training hall was deafening. I lay as still as I could, not daring to look away from the captain.

Orca, for once, had nothing to say. I could see her out of the corner of my eye, standing with her arms crossed over her chest and an expression on her face I couldn't identify. Miranda glanced around at the assembled crew.

"If she'd had a knife on her, I might be dead, wouldn't I, Orca?"

Orca, who was clearly torn between the thrill of insulting me and the thrill of Miranda's praise at her teaching, nodded in agreement.

"She's making some progress," Orca said.

"Have you showed her how to use a knife?"

I didn't give Orca time to answer. I hadn't entirely bombed my combat courses in Fleet Prep, and Miranda had left my hands free when she pinned me.

I slammed the side of my palm into the wrist that held the

knife. It sprang from her fingers and I caught it, resting the blade against her inner thigh. I could almost feel the pulse of her femoral artery through the knife handle. The silence in the room deepened further.

"You tell me, Captain," I said.

In my mind's eye, I saw the rise of the whip, and my hand trembled.

Miranda flinched.

I stared at where the knife had nicked through the cloth to the skin beneath. Blood welled from the tiny cut.

And now I've marked you, Captain.

"Kraken." Miranda held out her hand, her eyes locked on mine, and caught a heavy object inches from my face.

I blinked up at the sharp tip of a second knife. Miranda tossed it in the air and caught it by the blade. The hilt faced me, and there, embossed in the butt of the handle, I saw the compass rose.

"It's yours," Miranda said in a voice so low only Orca could have heard it.

I let the other knife fall to the mat, and propped myself up on one elbow to accept the offered blade. The motion sent her hips sliding over mine. My body reacted before I could reign in its wayward impulses, pressing against her.

Orca cleared her throat pointedly, and I felt a flush creep up my neck. I avoided looking at Miranda as she stood, rising off my body in a fluid motion that displayed the strength of her thighs and the weakness of my resolve. Again, I saw the flash of the whip, and willed my body to cooperate with my mind.

I had spent the better part of the last week convincing myself that Miranda was dangerous, unpredictable, and a terrible human being. I needed to rid myself of the attraction I felt for her before it got me killed.

I rose, determined to keep a level head. Her back was toward me, and all I could see of her face was what was reflected in Orca's angry eyes. That was enough to send another shiver down my spine.

126

"Orca, Rose, with me," Miranda ordered.

I tucked the knife into the waist of my pants. The hilt was carved out of a smooth ivory-colored material that did not feel like plastic. I ran a thumb along it as I trailed after Miranda. *Ivory.* It wasn't just ivory-colored, it was ivory. I stumbled at the realization, which Orca took as an invitation to shove me roughly in the kidney.

"Watch where you're going," she hissed at me.

I glanced back at her and almost stumbled again at the depth of hatred in her eyes.

Hatred, I wondered as I turned back around, *or jealousy?*

Miranda led the way out of the dark training yard, ignoring the buzz of conversation that followed our departure. Her public display had been planned, I gathered, judging by the thoughtful expressions on the faces of the sailors we passed, but I didn't understand the purpose of it.

I kept my thumb on the hilt, tracing the cardinal points. North. Back to Polaris and *North Star.* Back to order and routine and three square meals a day, provided by a captain whose cruelest act didn't even begin to measure up to what Miranda had done to Annie. Annie, who I had foolishly trusted without question. I would have killed even to hear Maddox mock me from across the hall.

"All right, mates, it's business time."

Miranda's words interrupted my thoughts. We were back in the round room with the red rugs, and the table at the center was covered with familiar charts. Orca's frown melted and Kraken made a grumbling sound deep in his chest that I interpreted as a laugh. The muscles in my stomach tightened. I did not share their enthusiasm. I reached across the table and pulled the charts toward me, looking over the maps I'd committed to memory and biting my lip hard enough to break the skin.

There were two ways into the Gulf of Mexico: the Straits of Florida and the Caribbean Sea, past the Yucatan peninsula. Both passages were narrow by ocean standards, and easy to control. The straits were our best bet, as the low-lying islands offered protection from sonar in a pinch, compared to the relative openness of the Caribbean Sea. It was also more direct, and up until a few months ago, more heavily patrolled by Archipelago fleet ships.

My plan was simple. We would weave through the islands, avoiding fleet patrols by sticking to the more dangerous shallows, weather dependent. Avoiding the pirates was going to be more difficult, which was where things got tricky.

"Explain our strategy," Miranda ordered.

I avoided her eyes and laid out the first part of my plan to Kraken and Orca.

"The shallows?" Orca asked, and I could have sworn there was a note of fear in her voice.

"Fleet ships are designed for deep water. Their sonar will weaken the closer we get to the coasts, which decreases our odds of detection. If the pirates have control over these waters, they'll be looking for fleet ships, not pirate or mercenary vessels, and if a patrol does pick us up it will just look like we're avoiding the fleet, not them," I said.

"And once we're through the straits? How are we going to hide in the Gulf?" Orca tapped the open water on the map.

"The same way the pirates are hiding from the Archipelago," I said. Miranda's breath caught in her throat, and I could feel the sharpness of her gaze.

I had worked it out a few days ago, when my mind had wandered back to Walker's anomaly, and the pirate ship sending out sonar pings without appearing on our sonar. It was the name of Miranda's ship that had triggered the epiphany, and I laid out the second part of my plan with her eyes glued to my face. I hadn't had time to run it by her, and now it was too late. She would find out at the same time as Kraken and Orca, for better or for worse.

"We find a low-level swarm of siphonophores," I said, "and stay beneath it."

"Siphonophores?" Orca asked.

"They are like jellyfish," I explained. "Some float on the surface, like—"

"Portuguese man o' war."

Miranda bit off the words, venom tipping her tongue. The look she gave me burned, and then vanished, replaced by her usual, cool blue gaze.

Kraken and Orca exchanged glances.

"Yes," I said, wondering what I was missing. "Man o' war stay on the surface, but there are others that live deeper, perfect for hiding submarines. They're not actually jellyfish, more like a colony of—"

"You didn't mention this." Miranda cut me off again.

"I'm your navigator," I said. "You asked for a course. This is the only way in."

"*Man o' War* can't stay subbed that deeply for long periods of time."

"She won't have to." I took a deep breath. "*Man o' War* only needs to hide long enough to get past both patrols. Once she's in, she'll look for someone to trade with. Information for materials."

Miranda nodded slowly, and I swallowed my guilt. I would trade information for safe passage, if it would help the Archipelago in the end. Comita would understand.

"This is why you wanted a trawler," she said.

"Yes. While *Man o' War* is picking up contracts, a trawler, hidden by swarms, will take the measure of their forces. If we're careful, we should be able to pass undetected and, if not, drifters trawl the Gulf all the time. Nobody will think twice about it, as long as we don't make too many appearances. Between two ships, we should be able to find out what we need to know."

Miranda examined the charts.

"Well done, Compass Rose. Orca, brief the crew. Kraken, have the trawler prepped and ready. Rose, with me. We'll hit the outer islands in a few hours."

"You want to navigate the islands at night?" Fear rose in me like a tide. Miranda's smile was far from reassuring.

"With the Polarian Fleet's best navigator at the helm, I'm sure we'll manage."

In a way, it didn't matter if it was daylight or pitch black; the majority of the islands that made up what was once known as the Bahamas were under water. You couldn't see them any more than you could see the dangers they posed, just the occasional swirl or eddy hinting at sharp shallows and submerged rocks, low hills that had sunk to join the rest of the mountains they had once been, broken finger joints dug into the ocean floor in a tectonic grasping and resettling.

I stared at the dark waters outside the helm and wiped my forehead with my sleeve, feeling the first prick of nervous sweat break my skin. *North, south, east, west.* Peril lay in every direction.

This was not the first time I'd been on Miranda's bridge, but it was the first time I'd been there as acting navigator. It was much smaller than the *North Star's* command center, housing the ship's wheel, the control panel, and the window that looked out over water or sky, depending on how deeply we were subbed. Right now, we were fully topside, keeping our draft as shallow as possible for a ship this size. Miranda dismissed the other shift, barking out a few terse orders.

"Bring Finnegan," was one of them.

I tore my gaze away from the water, glancing at the stars before focusing on the faint sonar readings on the screen. Miranda leaned over my shoulder, her eyes intent on the landscape painted for us by the sound waves while her hand kept a firm grip on the wheel.

I closed my eyes and reached out to the waters, feeling for treacherous currents, rip tides, and the myriad other dangers that awaited vessels in the islands, all the while keeping fleet patrol pattern coordinates firmly in my mind's eye.

"Why are her eyes closed, Captain?" Finn asked as he entered the bridge.

"Hard to port," I said, ignoring him. Miranda cranked the wheel, avoiding a rough patch of water that would have sent us hard up against a shoal.

"I need you on surveillance, Finn," Miranda said. "You pick up anything—sonar, radio waves—you let me know."

"Aye aye, Capitan," he said, affecting an accent as he settled himself into a pair of headphones.

"Straight ahead." I reached out and grabbed Miranda's arm. "Port again." The boat moved, painfully slowly.

"How the hell is she doing that?"

Finn was not the first person to ask that question, nor would he be the last, unless he distracted me and killed us all. I ignored him. I didn't have an answer for him, any more than I had for anyone else. I could feel the ocean in my veins, shifting around me even through the walls of the ship. Through it all spun the earth's magnetic field, pulling at the filaments in my blood and pointing me always toward true north. As the currents and my compass aligned and misaligned, the shape of the ocean unfolded, an uncomprehendingly complex system of action and reaction, displacement creating a wave there and a trough here, and all of it humming through me.

I was born facing due north, and I would die that way, too, strung between the poles like a vibrating harp string.

It took us three days of night sailing to get through the islands. We subbed in shallow coves by day, our hull scraping dangerously close to the ocean floor, but protected by sonar from the rocky arms of the islands. Miranda didn't dare sail during the day, when a lookout might see us stark against the horizon, and her faith in my ability to keep us out of trouble left no room for other options. We scuttled over the water like a ghost ship, crabbing between the islands in a drunken pattern that I hoped would discredit us in the eyes of any potential watchers.

Sleeping during the day was harder than sailing at night. Orca, who was on the day shift, was not around, and the silence was oddly disquieting. I would never let her know that I had grown so used to her presence that I could not sleep without her, and I comforted myself with pleasant fantasies involving sharp objects and her face. If I missed the sound of her breathing, I still hated the sound of her voice, and I had not forgotten the beating she had given me. The truce we'd come to the night Annie tried to kill me was fragile, at best.

I woke up in the early afternoon after my second night navigating, unable to fall back asleep. A tug to the southeast had pulled me awake, faint, but enough of a disturbance that it warranted watching. Even a small storm would be enough to throw my plan off kilter and smash us against the very rocks we were depending on for shelter.

Wandering the ship alone was still inadvisable; remaining in Orca's room was intolerable. I ran a hand through my tousled hair, checked that my new knife was at my hip, and slipped out the door. I doubted Crow's Eye would take it upon himself to kill me, and I wanted to look over the charts one more time.

A sailor, lounging at the end of the hallway, stood with a yawn and took off at a brisk pace in the opposite direction. I frowned after him. Annie was dead, but I was not naive enough to believe that she was alone in her sentiments.

Footsteps behind me brought me up short, and I turned, knife concealed by my sleeve, ready to fight.

"Easy there, killer jelly."

I glared at Orca.

"I'm heading to the chart room," I said, annoyed that I felt like I had to explain myself to her.

"No you're not. Miranda wanted to see you if you woke up before your shift." She started walking, forcing me to follow her.

"How did you know I was awake?" I asked, a suspicion creeping over me.

"Are you really that dumb?" Orca rolled her eyes at me.

"You put a watch on the door." That explained the sailor.

"You're lucky I didn't just lock you in. It's this way." She led me to an unfamiliar part of the ship and down a long hallway. At the end was a door.

"Well?" I asked.

Orca looked around us, then moved closer to me, her eyes murderous.

"Watch yourself with the captain, fleeter."

"What's that supposed to mean?"

Orca's braids moved around her face, the shells whispering things I was glad I couldn't hear. She raised a hand toward my cheek, and I braced myself for whatever new harm she intended.

Miranda opened the door.

"She's awake," Orca said, a little unnecessarily in my opinion.

"Good." Her eyes flickered over Orca, once, and then she smiled, clapping the first mate affectionately on the back.

I reminded myself that I had no right to be jealous, and kept the memory of Miranda's cruel justice at the forefront of my mind.

The door shut behind me with a click, a sound I echoed when I realized my jaw was hanging open. The room faced out over the stern, with reinforced plastic giving an unrestricted view of sea, sky, and a few low lines of rocks. Grass and stone covered the floor, and a narrow pathway led to a circular courtyard with a low table and two chairs.

Around the courtyard bloomed a collection of flowers, more than I had seen even in the botanical gardens on Polaris. I recognized the faint floral scent that clung to Miranda immediately. It was coming from a flowering bush directly beside the door. More of them bordered the walls, framing the room in a riot of red blossoms.

"Hibiscus," Miranda said, noticing my interest.

A green and yellow shape swooped past my face. I jumped again, feeling foolish when the bird landed on Miranda's shoulder. It was almost as tall as her head, and had a curved, black beak that looked far too sharp for comfort. I had only ever seen a bird in photographs, and once from a distance. They didn't fly over the open ocean we called home.

"What is that?" I asked.

"Blue skies," croaked the bird.

Miranda's lips quirked at my expression.

"It's a parrot."

"It can talk."

"Yes, although the conversation is a little limited. His mate is nesting over there. Don't go near her, unless you want to lose an eye."

I scanned the bushes where she'd pointed, but saw nothing beyond the impossible display of color. Then I noticed the trees.

Lemons, limes, oranges, and other fruits grew in pots, shading the sitting area with fragrant shadows.

"What is this place?" I asked, my voice a little shaky.

"A reminder. Here, let me show you something."

The bird turned its head around to watch me. I kept a healthy distance between us, noting a distinctly unfriendly gleam in his beady little eyes. At the end of a short pathway was a small pond, fed by a trickle from the evaporator on the roof.

Beside the pond rested a creature the size of a large cat. It had a dark shell with reddish spots, a bizarrely long neck, and stubby legs.

"This is Starbuck," she said, kneeling by the animal. It turned its head toward her slowly as she broke off a nearby blossom and fed it to the animal. "A friend of mine found him on an island south of here. She gave him to me, when we parted ways."

"What is he?"

"A tortoise."

I had never seen a terrestrial animal in my life, aside from cats and rats, and the sight simultaneously took my breath away and filled me with a deep-seated anxiety that bordered on longing. Miranda stroked Starbuck's shell affectionately.

"May I?" I asked, unsure of the protocol for touching a captain's tortoise.

At her nod, I knelt and reached out a hand, letting it hover over his shell, suddenly hesitant. The tortoise turned his head to look at me, blinking reptilian eyes.

Miranda placed her hand over mind and gently pressed it down.

The shell was warm, and the tortoise shifted beneath the sudden weight, startling me into a laugh that shattered a tightness I had not known was inside me, and I glanced up at Miranda with a stupid smile on my face.

She squeezed my hand and let it go, leaving me to trace the bumps on the tortoise's shell.

I had spent my entire life at sea, as had generations of my family. I had no words for the affinity I felt for this strange creature, forced to share an exodus I had never truly thought about until now. My heart clenched in unexpected sorrow for my forebears, bundled onto ships and sent to live on half-constructed stations in the middle of the Atlantic, away from the one thing they had taken for granted since time immemorial—solid ground.

"Why did you show me this place?"

"I come here to think. It's a good place for it, kind of like the gardens on your stations. Starbuck is something, isn't he? Maybe one day we'll visit his island, see if we can't find him a lady friend," she said, speaking half to me and half to the tortoise. "First, though, there is something I need to discuss with you."

She moved to one of the low chairs, gesturing for me to join her.

I sat, trying to take in everything at once. I disagreed with the captain. This was nothing like the gardens on Polaris.

There, trees lined the wider hallways, and the grove at the heart of the station took ten minutes to walk across. The gardens were carefully cultivated, each species labeled and maintained with a precision that bordered on obsession. You could spend hours wandering the largest of the garden grounds, lost behind hedges and flowers and occasionally encountering small swaths of grassy lawn. Each garden had a theme, modeled after a distant climate zone.

My favorite had been what we called the North Garden. At the center of the grove stood one lone pine. Smaller pines bordered the edges, but there at the heart, next to a large, lichen covered boulder, was only the pine and a few scrubby bushes. It was austere to the extreme and, more importantly to me, rarely occupied.

If there was order here, it was haphazard, and as far as I could tell the only plants of practical value were the fruit trees. Miranda reached up and plucked an orange from the nearest one and tossed it to me. I caught it, cupping it in my hands.

"You're better than advertised," she said, plucking an orange for herself and sprawling in the chair. The bird flew off to perch on a branch.

"Blue skies," it croaked again.

"Thank you," I said, the thrill of the tortoise wearing off.

Sunlight broke through the shade of the trees, casting a bar of light across her eyes. I toyed with the orange peel in my hand as Comita's warning about flattery came back to me.

"Where we're going, I am going to need more than a borrowed fleet navigator. I need a navigator I can trust, and who does not question my decisions." She stared at me until I met her eyes. "I need your loyalty."

"You have it." I held up my scarred hand.

Miranda gave a short laugh and looked out over the water.

"Loyalty taken at knife point is treachery in waiting, they say. How is your stomach?"

My hand went to the tender weal without thinking.

"Healing, captain."

"You don't agree with my treatment of Anemone Dive."

I shuddered, trying to suppress the memory of the flogging and subsequent trial and execution.

"You are the captain," I said.

"Exactly. But that was not enough for you, was it? I don't typically explain myself to crew, but since you're new here, I'll cut you a little slack. This is not the Archipelago. I am not a fleet captain. I do what I have to do to keep my ship afloat and my crew behind me. I have sailed in the Gulf, and I have sailed with the pirates we are up against. There will be no time for me to justify my actions to my navigator. For better or for worse, you and I are on the same side, and if you can't take orders from me, I will have you off this ship faster than you can say 'Davy Jones.'"

The cardinal points blew out of my head. Long practice kept my mouth shut while protests boiled into steam inside my skull. She was right, of course. I would never have dared challenge Admiral Comita, even if I had disagreed with her. I had let personal feelings, in more ways than one, come between me and my sense of duty. Comita would be ashamed.

"Captain," I said, my voice as raw as my pride. "It won't be a problem."

"Good."

I focused on peeling my orange to hide my shame, and to avoid looking at her face. *Remember this moment, Compass Rose*, I told myself. *Do not make the mistake again of forgetting that she is your captain.*

I remembered the tension between us in the few moments before Annie's public flogging and bit my lip. Maybe Miranda hadn't felt it after all, and so what if she had? She was the captain. She made the rules. There was only one way this could end for me, and it held a thousand variations of pain. Only, unlike my previous experiences with unrequited love, this one could actually get me killed. A distracted navigator was a liability to everyone she sailed with.

It was better this way, even if it hurt.

"We'll be in the straits tomorrow," Miranda said, moving to the next order of business.

I gathered myself together. *North, south, east, west.*

"I want to launch the trawler then, just in case *Man o' War* gets caught in the crossing. And if she gets held up by pirates, it might be best if I were off the ship."

There were several problems with that strategy. In this, at least, it was my place to question her, and I did.

"The trawler won't hold many of us, not if it has to stay subbed in the Gulf. If *Man o' War* doesn't make it, then it's game over. We're better off staying together and trying again."

"Spoken like someone who has never trawled," she said, shooting me a small smile to soften her words. "You need to get in touch with that drifter heritage of yours. The trawler won't need to support many of us. I want you on it at all times, and I will be there too, whenever possible."

The prospect of sharing the confines of a trawler with Miranda did not bode well for my self-control.

"Won't the pirates wonder where you are, when *Man o' War* begs parley?" I asked.

"They can treat with Orca." She glanced out the window.

"You said you sailed with them before. They know you. With all due respect, Captain—"

"If they refuse to treat with *Man o' War*, she'll have to leave the Gulf. If that happens, you will need me on that trawler with you, or you are as good as dead."

I didn't much like the prospect of death.

"We need to move now, then," I said, wishing I'd remained asleep. "There's a storm coming up behind us. We can still catch a swarm if we're lucky."

There were a few hours until sunset, plenty of time to prep a trawler and track down the nearest swarm. Getting there undetected would be something else. I didn't like the idea of leaving *Man o' War* to fend for herself, not with a storm on the horizon. The currents would rip at her, throwing her off my carefully plotted course, unless she wanted to sub one hundred meters or more.

Navigating a trawler in a storm, on the other hand, was a prospect I didn't even want to consider.

"One more thing."

Miranda, who had stood at my words, paused to listen. I knew the question was out of line, especially coming so close on the heels of her reprimand, but I had to know.

"Why are you helping the Archipelago? I would have thought a mercenary would be on the other side."

Miranda ate the last segment of her orange slowly, watching me. Several emotions flickered across her face, among them irritation, but in the end she answered.

"If we lose the mines, we lose everything. I may not like the Archipelago, but I like the idea of the ocean's lifeblood in the hands of Ching Shih even less. I'd rather steal from you than her."

The wink she gave me was positively roguish, and any resemblance between her sense of propriety and Comita's vanished.

"Come on, Compass Rose," she said. "Let's make some wake."

Chapter Ten

"Now would be a good time to confess any inadequacies you think I should be aware of," Miranda said to me as we stood on the dry dock in the landing bay with Kraken.

The boat waiting in the dock was the ugliest trawler I had ever seen. Algae dripped from the retractable trawl, and the narrow hull was more patch than bow. The windows needed a good scrubbing, and looking at the engine compartment made me glad I wasn't a mechanic. I would be lucky if it even had sonar. It looked hardly big enough to house a family, let alone the extended family that usually occupied drifter vessels.

"Who is the skipper?" I asked, shifting my weight from foot to foot as the water flooded the dock beneath the boat. I hadn't thought to ask, and I didn't want to think about Annie.

"That would be me, for now," Miranda said. She looked at the boat like a cat stalking a rat, daring it to challenge her. "Can't exactly bring Annie aboard, now can we?"

No, I thought, *I suppose we can't, since she is moldering at the bottom of the ocean.*

"The mechanic?"

"Jeanine."

The shark tattoo on her shaved scalp grinning even in the dim light of the hold, Jeanine leapt aboard the deck of the ship and slipped into the hatch. I watched Kraken run a hand fondly over the trawl beam and swallowed, not entirely sure I wanted to ask what his role was. Finn sauntered down the dock, whistling something out of tune and shattering my concentration.

"Evening, Captain," he said, breaking off his tune to eye the ship. "She's a real beauty. What are we calling her?"

"*Sea Cat*," Kraken said, patting the ship the same way he might have patted a woman's backside.

Miranda shook her head at him.

"We're not calling her anything yet," she said, turning back to me. "Finn will be our sonar and systems specialist."

"Does this ship have a system?"

"Of sorts," Miranda said.

Finn winked at me as he followed Jeanine into the bowels of the trawler. I jumped a little, surprised at the friendly overture after the isolation of the past few days. "But there are plenty of other ships in the soup to keep him occupied." She took hold of my elbow and steered me towards the edge of the dock. The deck of the boat was slightly green and encrusted with patches of optimistic barnacles.

"Watch your step," Miranda said. "It's slippery when it's wet."

"Just like our goddamn captain," Kraken called up from the hatch.

Miranda's laugh haunted my burning cheeks as I clambered up the slope of the deck and down the ladder into the ship's belly.

I really, really wished they would stop saying things like that.

The inside of the rig smelled strongly of fish. Portholes let in the dim light of the docking bay, illuminating cramped and dingy living quarters. Something brushed against my ankle and I jumped backward, bumping into Miranda as she descended the ladder.

"Easy there," she said, placing a steadying hand on my waist.

The thing brushed against me again, and I recognized Seamus's bushy tail as it flicked out of the shadows on his way to investigate any rodent stowaways.

The boat lurched as the water filled the dry dock, and Miranda stepped around me on her way to the helm. Her fingers trailed absently across the small of my back. I willed myself to ignore it, her reprimand still ringing in my ears, while my body informed me unequivocally that it had every intention of betraying me.

She paused at the doorway and looked back.

"This tub isn't going to navigate herself."

The hallway leading to the bridge was tiny. I couldn't imagine Kraken fitting through it, let alone what would happen if two people tried to pass each other at the same time. At one point, windows opened into the greenhouse as we wound up toward the bow, and I had my first look at a drifter hydrofarm. My stomach rumbled preemptively, not impressed with the messy rows of plants in dilapidated trays and the vat of stinking nutrient soup that I imagined I could almost smell through the heavy plastic. It wouldn't do us much good anyway if we subbed as deeply as I planned.

A second door led down into the ship's intestines by way of a dank hole and ladder that made me glad of Seamus's presence. The storage hold farther on, at least, looked dry, and I was comforted to see bags of provisions that bore the stamp of the Archipelago on them.

"Where did this ship come from?" I asked Miranda as I ducked below the low door frame and climbed the short stairs to the helm, just in time to see the door to the ship's bay open into the evening.

Miranda dropped into the chair behind the wheel and swung around to face me.

"Think of it as a recent recruit."

I glanced around the small room. The front wall was made of thick, clear plastic, blurred here and there from the heat of a repair torch. The bio-light was no worse than what I'd gotten used to on the *Man o' War*, and I noticed a few personal touches left by the drifter family who had lived here. A tiny doll was shoved in a corner behind Miranda's chair, no more than a bundle of rags with beads for eyes. My seat had a badly frayed cover over the lumpy frame, stitched all over with tiny waves. I ran my hand over the raised, blue shapes with a finger.

The back of the seat had a dark stain on it. I touched it tentatively. It looked and felt like dried blood.

"This wasn't a plague ship, was it?"

"No." Miranda raised an eyebrow at me. "Unless you count family as a sickness. There were ten adults on this ship and six children. Maybe someone got tired of it." She nodded at the bloodstain and I jerked my hand away.

"With my recent track record, I'm not sure I should sit in a chair where someone else got stabbed," I said.

"Suit yourself, but you're not sitting on my lap." Miranda waved her hand around the cramped room. There were no other chairs.

I sat a little more heavily than I'd planned, trying to get that particular image out of my mind. I could still feel the place on my waist where her hand had rested.

Pirates, hurricanes, and jellyfish, I reminded myself. *Oh, and most likely death and the destruction of all you love.*

Miranda seized the wheel and waited expectantly. The mouth of the docking hatch opened, revealing the sun-streaked shallows. The shoal blocked most of the ocean, and I couldn't get a reading.

"Take us out," I said, feeling panic like a band across my chest.

We were headed into the straits and, beyond that, the largest dead zone in Archipelago territory. Toxic waters and violent weather lay ahead, and swarms of jellyfish that clogged filters and blocked visibility, concealing us from enemy ships—and enemy ships from us.

Fleet Preparatory had not prepared me for this.

The distant storm had picked up strength since I'd last checked, and the evening water was cloudy in anticipation as I checked the sonar against my inner compass and the coordinates I knew by heart.

"Once we're under cover, I want you to look for a decent current. We need to get the trawl out," Miranda said.

"We're actually trawling?"

"Damn straight. We can't be floating around in a drifter tub without something to trade. The wrong people might get the right idea."

"My father was a drifter," I said. "But I've never trawled for anything in my life."

"Ask Kraken how it's done. He knows a thing or two." She paused, looking me up and down. "Any chance he's your daddy?"

The idea was horrifying.

"He's a good-looking man, once you get past the tattoos and the scars. I can see a little family resemblance."

I stared at her to make sure she was joking. She put on an earnest expression. "No, really. Ink a kraken on you and you could pass for twins."

"Over my dead body."

"Careful, he might like that."

I shook my head slowly, unsure of how to respond to her playful banter. This was not the same woman who had given me an ultimatum a few hours ago.

"How fast does this thing move?" I asked, steering back into familiar waters.

"That depends on Jeanine. It's a split engine system. These rigs burn methane like you wouldn't believe, and the solar cells do the rest, not that they are in great shape. Luckily for us, we have an override. We gutted an old fleet-issue W5000 and installed her engines along with the rest, just in case we need to move quickly."

"Where did you get a fleet W5000?" The W5000 was an older model of the ships the Archipelago used in combat maneuvers. Small, fast, and hard to detect on sonar. Harper had gone to great length one afternoon to explain the inner workings of the engine to me. I hadn't listened to the details, but her tone of voice suggested that the appropriate response was awe.

"A previous contract."

"With who?"

"You're not very good at unquestioning obedience, are you?" She swiveled toward me slowly, tapping long fingers on the wheel.

"I'm sorry, Captain."

We lapsed into silence and I felt the tug of the currents. We were headed for a large surface swarm, which would do for now until I could locate something deeper. It would be difficult; the swarm would block our sonar, which would leave us entirely reliant on my instincts. It was a gamble no fleet captain would have made.

"There's a swarm ahead. Not deep enough for us to follow for long, but it will give us cover." I peered out through the darkening water, feeling for the current shift that heralded miles and miles of jellyfish ahead.

Miranda had a peculiar expression on her face as she stared out into the black sea. The light played across her profile, casting shadows beneath her brows. Her knuckles were white where they clenched the wheel, and I could see the muscles in her shoulders tense.

"Captain?"

"Do me a favor, will you? Find something to put in this." She tossed me a flask, not bothering to meet my eyes. "Course is clear enough."

I turned the slender flask over in my hands, noting the man o' war engraved on the front. My palm itched in sympathy. There were too many jellyfish around for comfort.

I ducked out into the hallway and into the storage room, where bags of rice and tins of salted fish towered over me on the shelves. Seamus was here, patrolling the corners with a vigilance that made me uneasy. Rodents on a drifter ship were vectors for disease.

"Get them all, Seamus," I encouraged as I rummaged through the small room. The grain had the Archipelago stamp on it, and on closer inspection I saw the smaller stamp—Ursa Minor, with one point emphasized. Polaris. I ran a hand over it and tried to fight off the sudden constriction in my chest.

"Need something?" Kraken's deep voice startled me.

I held up the flask defensively, and he chuckled.

"You might make a decent mate after all. We keep the rum down here."

He removed his bulk from the doorway, allowing it to breathe again, and led me back to the common room. There was a plastic barrel lashed to one end of the galley kitchen, and he held the flask out beneath the spigot.

"You can help yourself, as long as you stay sober." He winked. "And just remember that you have the captain to answer to if this runs dry."

He patted the barrel affectionately, and turned back to the kitchen.

I watched for a moment as he pulled pans down from the hanging rack.

"You're the cook?" I asked, feeling a little incredulous.

"Calamari, rice, and beans. It will be on the stove. Bring some to Miranda when you can, and make sure she eats it."

"Oh," I said.

My view of Kraken had taken a shift I was not prepared for. He grinned at my confusion.

"Don't worry," he said, hauling a small squid out of a bucket of brine. "We're not related."

It took me a moment to realize he was referring to the squid, after Miranda's teasing, and my laughter surprised me.

"You sure it's not a distant cousin?"

"Trust me. If I ever catch a little kraken, I'll release it."

"Release the kraken," Finn intoned dramatically as he popped into the room. "Smells good in here. Jeanine's about ready to blow this cork. When you installed the new pump on the bilge, did you notice it catching on anything?"

"Nothing wrong with the gears."

"Something is jamming it."

"Well," Kraken said, bringing the knife down on the squid decisively. "Looks like one of you has to go in."

"You're small," Finn said, looking at me. "Feel like spelunking?"

I waved the flask around and backed out of the room, mumbling something about the captain's orders.

The captain in question had her head in her hands when I returned bearing the rum. I paused in the doorway. Miranda's

146

broad shoulders were hunched, the muscles bunched and knotted beneath her thin shirt. Her hands had a death grip on her hair, and I watched her take several steadying breaths before I cleared my throat.

"Miranda," I said as softly as I could.

She sat up slowly and held out a hand. I placed the flask in it, mesmerized by the curve of her throat as she took a long pull of the alcohol.

"That's a little better," she said, licking her lower lip.

"It sounds like they'll have the ship ready to sub soon, assuming we can find a deep water swarm."

"Good."

I sat down, watching her out of the corner of my eye. The rum didn't do much to relax her. Blue eyes scanned the water ahead.

"Can you tell what kind they are?" she asked.

"The swarm?"

"Yes."

"Not really. I can tell if it is a big swarm or a smaller one, but that's about it."

The ocean was swarming with jellies, more varieties than I could count.

"Have you ever been stung?" Her voice was so low I had to lean in to hear.

"Once or twice, when I was a kid."

Miranda passed me the flask and I drank obediently. She leaned back slowly in her chair. I could feel the swarm getting closer as the minutes ticked by.

"Dammit," Miranda muttered, taking another drink as the first jellyfish appeared, dark shapes floating at the surface and brushing against the partially submerged window of the low-riding vessel. "Of course they're man o' war."

Above us, the blue bladders of the jellyfish floated on the surface of the water, lit by the last light of the setting sun, while their long tentacles trailed down to tangle and part in front of us. Man o' war follow the current. I hoped this current continued on its course, and I prayed the coordinates I'd left with Orca got the rest of the crew into the Gulf.

As much as I disliked her, I didn't want anything happening to the first mate. Orca was mine to destroy.

The rum burned in my belly. Drinking while navigating was a punishable offense on the *North Star*, but this captain didn't seem to care.

I had never seen her this agitated. Her blue eyes were feral, and the nervous energy radiating from her body could have powered a small engine as the jellyfish grew thicker around us. Long tentacles brushed against the ship, and I shuddered slightly at the residual charge. Miranda's hand hovered over the lever that triggered the subbing mechanism, shaking like an addict's.

"We'll be here for a while," I said. "We need to get out into deeper water before we sub to another swarm. I can relieve you if you want to get some food, Captain."

Miranda let out a short breath, and the tension abated as she visibly pulled herself together.

"Why don't you grab some, and bring me a plate on your way back. Can't leave you to fend for yourself in these waters yet."

I double-checked our course, well aware that Miranda had just dismissed me twice in the span of a few minutes, and followed the smell of frying squid to the common area.

"I don't understand," I said to Kraken as I heaped food onto my plate. "She named her ship *Man o' War*. Why would she do that if she hates them?"

"Did she say she hates them?" Kraken said, not rising to my bait.

"Not exactly, but she looks like she'd rather chew off her own hand than sail through this swarm."

Kraken's mouth twitched in a smile at my words, and I took a mouthful of food, hoping to offset the effects of the rum. The rest of Miranda's crew might drink like fish, but I was not yet immune to its effects.

"Every sailor has something she—or he—hates. It's the nature of the business. We're not meant to be out here, and some part of us remembers that. Isn't there something that unsettles you, Compass Rose?"

"Yeah," I said, my tongue too quick to respond. "Your captain."

Kraken dangled a tentacle in his tongs. "You're smarter than you look, then."

"We got problems." Finn popped his head into the common room, catching my eye. "Fleet ship, coming in hot."

My squid turned to rubber in my mouth and I bolted back to the helm.

"Ship," I said by way of explanation to Miranda. Finn was right on my heels.

"We've been pinged," he said, "but I don't think they've noticed us yet."

"They've noticed something." I stared out through the mass of man o' war. This route didn't make sense for patrol, and I couldn't see anything on the sonar. Just reflected sound waves, bouncing back off the jellies.

"You got a course, Compass Rose?" Miranda's voice cut through my calculations.

"Take us out of gear and keep us in the swarm. If they've seen us, there's nothing we can do, and if they haven't, then they'll try to avoid the swarm for the sake of visibility."

My words sounded a lot more confident than I felt. Man o' war might fool sonar from a distance, but they were surface jellies, which did not offer us much protection from close quarters. It was a small comfort, at least, that the sun had set, shielding us from watching eyes.

"And shutter the windows," I added.

Miranda flipped off the lights in the helm, casting us into an almost total darkness, broken only by the dim lights of the dash and the murky light of the stars filtering through the water.

We drifted in silence for several minutes, waiting for the fleet ship to pass in the night or hail us. I closed my eyes, feeling for any hint of events to come in the currents.

149

"Rose," Miranda said, touching my arm. I opened my eyes. There was a break in the jellyfish ahead, and the sonar readings coming in were definite. There was not one ship out there, but two. I recognized the telltale shape of the fleet ship in the reading. The other ship was smaller, unfamiliar, and headed straight toward it.

"Shit." Finn ducked out of the helm and ran toward the common area, bellowing for Jeanine and Kraken. Miranda's eyes widened, and she brought the trawler back into gear.

"What are you doing?" I asked. "They'll see us."

"No they won't," she said. "And we need to get the hell out of here."

"Why—." My question strangled itself in my throat.

A bright light lit the water, a red flash that turned the Portuguese man o' war into blue-red blood vessels, pulsing above us.

"Get down!"

Miranda dragged me out of my chair and onto the ground, throwing herself on top of me. A wave hit the trawler, for all that it was impossible for a wave to hit us underwater, tossing the trawler into a jumbled mass of lights and floor and walls. Miranda had one arm wrapped around my head, and I heard the sharp crack of her elbow striking a solid surface. The impact reverberated through my skull, and I had a brief and terrible moment of clarity where I realized what might have happened had her arm not been there, and then the world turned back into chaos.

North, west, east, south. The directions made no sense.

There was something heavy on top of me, a dead weight that made it hard to breathe.

My ears popped, and my eyes felt tight.

We were in a downward spiral, the trawler hurtling toward the deeps much faster than was survivable.

"Miranda?"

There was no response from the warm body on top of me. The trawler still spun, although not as quickly, and our bodies had come to rest pressed up against the foot space of the dash. My tumbled compass picked up on the most pressing direction in my world—down. If we kept up this pace without pressurizing, we would all be very dead very soon.

Miranda groaned faintly, and I wriggled out from under her, resisting the urge to check her vital signs. I had been trained for situations like this, and I appreciated the drills now as muscle memory and conditioning took over. The ship was the priority, and I had to get her righted, because if I didn't, Miranda would die, along with me and everybody else onboard.

Hauling myself up the dash was disorienting to the point of nausea. I groped around for the wheel and nearly wrenched my arm out of the socket in the process. It spun freely, and I braced my lower half beneath the dash and grabbed on to it as firmly as I could before groping around for the sub clutch.

The ship bucked under me, shuddering as the pressure around us grew greater and greater. I wrenched the wheel up and back toward the surface, thanking the cardinal directions for their presence in my bloodstream, because what I could see of the instrument panel was totally shot, and every direction looks the same at night below the waves.

When a vessel is deeply subbed, it has to rise slowly, or else the pressure change will be lethal. I resisted the urge to throttle back to the surface and instead brought us up to a place where my ears no longer felt like rupturing, and let the trawler stabilize with a series of loud hisses and a distant, metallic screech. The sudden stillness knocked me off balance, and I slid down the wheel like a deflated life raft, feeling around in the dark for Miranda.

I encountered her hand, first, warm and limp, and felt my way up her arm until I found her face.

"Miranda?"

Her pulse beat steadily under my searching fingers, but she didn't respond.

"Miranda."

I patted her face, gently, not daring to move her in case something was broken. I needed light.

The switch for the bio-lights was back up by the wheel, and I fumbled around in the dark, turning on the ship's bow lights as well. I left them on, too worried about Miranda to bother hunting for the off switch.

Miranda lay crumpled on the floor, her chest rising and falling evenly. A large lump above her left eye was already bruising, but all her limbs lay at the right angles. I remembered the sound of her elbow hitting something hard, and gently worked her sleeve up her arm. There was bruising there, too, and a little bit of blood, but the joint moved fluidly and nothing pulled, snapped, or ground.

I didn't have a pocket light to check her pupils, but I prayed the worst she would suffer was a mild concussion. The clarity of my thoughts surprised me, and with that realization the clarity shattered, and I curled up around Miranda, stroking her hair and fighting the ball of panic knocking around in my chest.

"Captain," I said, my face close enough to feel her breath. "Captain, wake up." I wrapped my hand around hers, hoping for some sign of life. Without Miranda, it was game over, for me and for any hope of gaining access to the pirates. Without Miranda . . . The ball of panic expanded, stealing my breath and choking me with an unexpected sob.

"You're hurt."

The blackness around the corners of my vision contracted, bringing me down to a narrow corridor that ended in a pair of blue eyes.

"Captain?"

With a wince, she reached up and touched my cheek. Her fingers felt wet, and when I looked at them they were black in the half-light with my blood.

"I'm fine," I said. "You hit your head."

"Is that why I feel like squid shit?" Her fingers, still covered in my blood, probed the knot on her forehead gingerly.

"Yeah, that's about right." The events of the past few minutes came back to me. A bright light, Miranda throwing herself over me to protect me, and then chaos. "You shouldn't move," I added as she tried to sit up.

"Neptune's balls," she swore, the hand still wrapped in mine squeezing my fingers so hard they creaked. "Help me up, then."

"You really should stay down, just in case—"

"Just help me sit up." She leaned against me and I helped her into a sitting position, her head resting against mine.

"Does anything else hurt?" I asked.

"Nothing serious. Just don't let me fall asleep, okay? The way my head feels, I might not wake up."

"Of course, Miranda." A slight pause followed my slip in protocol.

"I like the way you say my name." Her face was very close to mine.

"Captain," I said, hating myself for voicing the truth, "I think you have a serious concussion."

Something bumped into the ship. I glanced up, and Miranda swore as she turned her head, both in pain and at the sight illuminated by the bow lights.

Bodies floated past the helm. Bodies, wearing Archipelago fleet uniforms, accompanied by a flotilla of debris.

Chapter Eleven

My hands shook as I brought the trawler up to the surface. Waves broke over the helm, the froth matching the overcast sky. My storm was coming, and there was no sign of *Man o' War* on the sonar or the horizon. I double-checked our coordinates. This was definitely the rendezvous, but we were the only ship for miles, unless you counted the ghost ship I carried in my mind's eye.

There was no way for me to know the name of the vessel I'd watched sink around me as Miranda and I had borne witness to the destruction, any more than I could have known the names of the dead sailors who bumped up against the helm, unnaturally pale in our bow lights, even for corpses.

Someone had blown a hole in their ship. We never saw the bulk of the vessel; it was possible, even, that some of the crew survived, clinging to the wreckage, but I doubted it. I had seen the size of the flash, and felt the force of the detonation.

"Give them time, Rose," Miranda said, keeping one eye on the sonar and the other on the sea.

For a moment I wasn't sure who she meant—the dead sailors, or *Man o' War*.

"Of course, Captain."

The cut on my cheek was deeper than I'd realized. I had no idea how I had gotten it, and as I touched the tender flesh I wondered just how many scars I would rack up in Miranda's service.

Miranda, who had been kept awake by the rest of us in turns, looked exhausted, and Kraken, Finn, and Jeanine had all sustained minor injuries. The trawler itself was fine.

"Death is easier when it's a statistic, navigator." Miranda's voice didn't betray any emotion. "Seeing it up close makes it personal. If it's any comfort, you get used to it, and we learned something useful."

"What did we learn?" I asked, staring at her in horror. She met my eyes with a grim smile.

"We now know that they are more heavily armed than we realized, and that they can destroy fleet battleships. And we know that we really, really don't want to piss them off."

And I learned that you care enough about me to put my life before yours, Captain, and that you like the way I say your name.

"How long should we wait for *Man o' War*?" I asked instead.

"A day. After that, she'll get here or she won't. If Orca got wind of the blast, she'll keep her distance for a little while to make sure it's safe. We'll keep an ear out for her frequency and get a feel for the area until then."

She yawned.

"Wake me up in a few hours. At this point, I don't care if I die in my sleep, and if Kraken says anything about it, tell him he can stick to doctoring dinner."

She strung the tattered hammock that had come with the vessel across the small helm and climbed in, sounding more like Orca than my captain. Her breathing slowed immediately, and I had the disconcerting sensation of being alone in the helm, waiting for a ship in a cemetery and listening to Miranda dream behind me.

"It's time for a christening," Finn announced the next morning.

I glanced up from breakfast with my mouth stuffed with a surprisingly delicious helping of stewed greens. Kraken, it appeared, knew his way around a galley kitchen. Miranda raised a bruised eyebrow and took a sip of bitter tea, which was another specialty of Kraken's. Her tall frame lounged in the rickety chair at the head of the table, and only the knot on her head suggested that she had been anything but cool and collected for the past twenty-four hours.

"Don't you think maybe you're taking things one step too far, Finn?" Miranda asked.

"Nothing is too far for our glorious captain."

"Flatterer," Jeanine said, reaching across the table for the carafe of tea. "Too bad she already knows you're full of hot air."

"That's not what you said last night," Finn said with an exaggerated leer. I choked on my greens, horrified that they could even think about sex after the carnage we'd witnessed and the looming absence of *Man o' War*.

"Captain, do I have your leave to discipline this man?" Jeanine raised a threatening hand.

Miranda waved away their bickering with her mug. After a full day and a half of idle waiting, I'd had a little time to explore all three square feet of the ship. The kitchen also served as the dining area, living quarters, and sleeping room. Bunks were built into the walls, one on top of the other, and aside from their lack of tact I sincerely hoped that Finn and Jeanine were joking. The thought of lying there listening to them coupling in the stifling darkness made me cringe.

It was bad enough that Miranda's bunk was directly above mine. The curtains that draped the shallow recess of my thin mattress didn't do much to block the steady sound of her soft breathing or, for that matter, Finn's snoring.

It almost made me miss Orca.

"Shall we hold a vote, then?" Finn dodged Jeanine's swipe.

"If it's that or a mutiny, I guess I have no choice." Miranda took another sip of tea and glanced at the keg of rum in the corner.

Kraken shook his head at her pointedly. He had forbidden her access to alcohol until she felt one hundred percent. I chewed down another mouthful, eying the platter hungrily. Rum was secondary. This was the first time in weeks I'd had the opportunity to go back for a second helping of food, and I had no intention of letting it pass me by.

"*Miranda's Pussycat* has a nice ring to it," Finn said.

"I am glad that references to my genitalia occupy so much of your limited brain space, Finn, but, unlike you, I think with the head on my shoulders."

"Captain, I'm hurt. You know I was only thinking of your deep and abiding love for Seamus," Finn said, affecting an injured expression and pointing at the cat in question, who was sniffing hopefully up at the counter.

"Which is why *Sea Cat* is in much better taste."

"You should have heard his first idea," Jeanine said, aiming another slap in Finn's direction.

"I did." Miranda pressed a hand to her temple. "Which is why I still have a headache."

I tried to picture Admiral Comita joking around with her crew like this and failed. This level of insubordination was inconceivable, but then again, most of Miranda's crew were from questionable backgrounds. I had no idea what passed for respect on a mercenary vessel or a pirate ship.

"Let's get this over with, then." Miranda cleared her plate, and the rest of us piled ours in the washbasin while Finn, who had wash duty, muttered something under his breath and curled his lip at the full sink as he passed.

"What are we doing?" I asked Jeanine.

"Christening this little beauty. We survived our first sub, so now she needs a name."

"Rose was the one who saved our asses," Finn added. "Maybe we should call her *Rosie's*—"

"Enough." Miranda cut him off. "Rose, let's bring her up."

"Up?" I said, feeling the first stirrings of panic. You didn't surface in the Gulf, not unless you absolutely had to, and not with a storm building.

"Up," Miranda repeated, vanishing around the corner toward the helm.

"Shit." I bit down firmly on my lip and followed Miranda.

The nose of the trawler rose through the murky waters, sunlight filtering oddly through the thick soup of the Gulf of Mexico. I repeated our coordinates to myself, watching Miranda's hands on the controls and wondering where in all seven hells *Man o' War* was at this moment. I looked up at one point to see a half smile on her face, and I tried to wipe my obvious anxiety from my expression.

Conditions topside had deadly potential. The storm that had chased us into the straits had yet to follow, but I could feel it building strength over the Atlantic. It could still turn into a hurricane, and even without wind and waves the probability of a toxic algae bloom in the vicinity was much higher than any sailor would risk, not to mention the fact that the Gulf was notorious for its dead zones. Breathe too much of that air, and any question of the ship's name would be moot.

Only the most desperate drifters trawled the Gulf, raking in microplastics in their sweeping nets. The rest of the ocean's occupants avoided the dead zones like the plagues they were. I didn't see any atmospheric instruments on the dash, which meant that we would be in for a nasty surprise if there were heavy levels of hydrogen sulfide at the surface. I shuddered at the memory of the putrid smell. Fleet Prep required their students to identify the odorous toxin by scent, an experience I could happily have done without. Born on Cassiopeia, I'd seen enough drifters and trawlers return to the Archipelago suffering from the side effects of the gas to keep my curiosity more than satisfied.

The thick soup parted, and we nosed past the remnants of ancient trash rendered unrecognizable by years of sunlight and salt.

"Ready?" Miranda breached the trawler and I felt the rumble of the bulkheads emptying their contents back into the sea.

"Is it safe?"

"You tell me, navigator."

I stared out at the overcast sky. The ocean was a flat, calm gray that showed no outward signs of contamination. Nothing bloomed across the surface, and the water was unusually still. If there was a layer of poisonous gas hovering above the smooth, rippling waves, it was past my ability to judge. It looked about as peaceful as I'd ever seen the sea.

"It looks calm," I said, "but we should send up a canary."

"A canary?" Miranda's eyebrows contracted slightly.

"A sniffer, someone to check for gas."

"Why the hell don't you just call it a sniffer, then?" She engaged the stabilizer and leaned back, grinning.

"I don't make the rules," I said, shrugging and blushing under her scrutiny.

"I never understood why the Archipelago clings to archaic terminology. Do you even know what a canary is?"

"No." I had never stopped to think about it. A canary was what you called the unlucky person who got sent topside first in the event of a system failure.

"It's a bird. They sent them down into mines. Land mines, obviously, not the ones we have on the ocean floor." She shook her head.

"They don't like to explain themselves too much on the fleet," I said.

Miranda considered me for a moment, and I wondered if she was remembering the little chat we'd had in her garden.

"Do you miss your fleet ship?"

"Parts of it," I admitted. "But not all of it. The food, I guess." I shifted in my chair, plucking at a loose thread in the knee of my pants.

Miranda didn't say anything as she flicked a few more knobs. There was another rumbling, this time from the trawling mechanisms engaging.

"All right," she said, stretching. "Let's get this over with."

"Would it matter?" I asked, standing beside her in the cramped space.

"Would what matter?"

She was very close to me. I could feel the warmth of her body and the shift in the air between us, and I had an overwhelming desire to tell her that I was glad she wasn't dead. I couldn't think about the sight of her unconscious face without feeling like Orca had punched me in the gut.

"If I missed the fleet," I said.

She tilted her head slightly, her eyes scanning my face.

"It would mean you had bad taste in company."

"Do you know many fleeters?"

"Enough to know you're not like most of them. Come on," she said, giving me a gentle push. "Let's get some fresh air."

Fresh was not the word I would have used to describe the air in the Gulf. There was a strange quality to it. It wasn't sulfurous, but it lacked something. The salt wind was limpid and listless against my face, the tiny deck was slick with water and debris, and the ocean was murky with plastic sediment while the clouds hung hard and gray above us, rippled like folded steel. Kraken and Miranda stood at the bow, fiddling with their flasks. Jeanine, Finnegan, and I stood closer to the stern, the low rail of the top deck pressing into my calf.

"To the *Sea Cat*. She floats," Miranda said, raising one flask in the air. She took a sip and passed it to Kraken, who took a sip and passed it to me. I hesitated only a second before following suit, surprised at the taste of fresh water.

"May she pass unnoticed over the deeps."

Kraken's voice rumbled over the water as the next flask came around. This one was rum, and I noticed that Miranda took only a small sip.

"We place our lives in the safety of her hold."

Miranda emptied what was left in both flasks onto the deck. The liquid mingled with the brine, and I thought there were a few barnacles who'd wake up with a hangover tomorrow.

I glanced around the assembled crew, wondering what was next. It seemed like an awfully simple ceremony, lacking the long-winded speeches and self-congratulatory back-patting that accompanied christenings on the Archipelago.

The flat sky pressed down on us, casting a dull light over our little assembly. Miranda's shirt moved with the slow breeze, and Kraken's smooth skull gleamed under the clouds. Behind us, the horizon was empty, with no sign of life, hostile or otherwise.

"All right." Miranda pocketed the flasks and gave a cursory surveillance of the ocean. "Rose, stay topside. The rest of you, back to work."

I scuffed a toe across some barnacles and waited for the others to descend. Miranda waved me closer.

"Captain?" I asked.

"What do you see?"

"Nothing." It was true. The weather was quiet, and the swarm had long since moved on.

"Look again."

I obeyed. "Still nothing."

"You're looking at the lifeblood of every ship on the ocean."

"It looks a little weak."

In truth, I had pictured the Gulf differently. Floating islands of trash, desperate marine life still clinging to the flotsam, while our miners sucked out minerals and ore from the ocean floor.

"Do you know what I've learned, since being captain?" Miranda's eyes were bright blue against the gray of the sky and the water. Her full mouth curved in a bitter smile. "Futility."

"That's a little bleak," I said.

"That's command for you." Her smile lost its edge. "Really, though. What are we going to do when we lose the surface? Can you imagine spending your entire life beneath the waves? We're fighting to keep a world we've already lost."

"Why do you bother, then?" I crossed my arms over my chest. Miranda toyed with the end of her braid. The gold ring on her thumb glinted.

"I'm very selfish," she said after a moment.

I found myself at a loss for words and unable to look away from her eyes. I had the sense, as I usually did whenever Miranda spoke to me, that there was a deeper meaning behind her words.

Her eyes narrowed and she took a step toward me, reaching for my arm with an intensity I wasn't prepared for. I braced

161

myself and nearly sent us both into the ocean as she pulled me behind her, and I caught myself at the last second with a hand on her belt.

"Captain?"

"Shhhh."

My grip on her belt tightened and I took an involuntary step closer to her as the source of her alarm breached through the murk, water running in rivulets off the narrow hull of another ship.

"Don't move," Miranda said as the other boat finished surfacing. Its hull narrowed into a knife's edge at the prow, and while it was roughly the same size as *Man o' War*, there was an air of menace to its sharp lines and the abundance of armed sailors that appeared on the deck. Miranda pulled me closer. I could feel the tension radiating from every muscle on her body.

I tried not to enjoy it.

The hatch popped open with a hiss behind us, and Finn's voice carried over the rumble of the other ship's bulkheads.

"Vessel approaching, Captain. I couldn't get the damn sonar in the W5000 . . ." He trailed off, then ducked back below.

I could feel the reverberation of his running footsteps and the boom of Kraken's voice calling out orders from the hold. The other ship inched closer. There were jagged fins welded to the side, with rusted teeth like a saw. If they came into contact with our hull, they would rend right through it, which, I realized with a shudder of fear, was exactly their purpose.

There was only one class of ships that employed that sort of violence. Pirates. I thought of the destroyed fleet ship and a wave of hatred rolled over me.

"Don't, Rose," Miranda said, stopping me from pushing past her.

The ship inched closer until there was a real risk of it slicing through our trawler.

"Prepare to be boarded," one of the pirates shouted.

There were footsteps behind me, and then Kraken's bulk towered comfortingly to my left. Finn appeared at my right. Jeanine had remained below, where I hoped that she was prepping the hidden W5000 engine for an expedient escape. Our trawler was not equipped for combat, and, despite the red rage swamping my vision, I knew this was not a battle we would win.

The boarding ramp slid out from their top deck like an eel. We were outnumbered at least three to one, and I didn't think that I really counted as a fighter compared to the two pirates making their way down the gang plank.

The man landed first, his dreadlocks swinging behind him like tangled sea snakes. The woman's head was as bald as Kraken's, shaved smooth to display the complex geometric shapes tattooed on her scalp. Both stepped off the plank deliberately, surveying us with interest.

Miranda broke the silence.

"I thought it seemed a little quiet around here," she said. She let go of my arm deliberately and placed her hand on her hip, a casual inch above the long knife she carried there.

"What's in your hold?" asked the man.

"Nothing yet," said Miranda.

"Small crew you've got." The female pirate stepped forward, the swagger in her step rivaling Orca's.

"Had a touch of fever a few months back," Miranda lied.

The male pirate tapped a finger on the butt of his sword, looking a little uneasy. Kraken shifted his weight from one foot to the other, emphasizing the advantage his size gave him over the rest of us.

"Mind if we take a look?" the male pirate asked, apparently overcoming any fears about lingering contagion. He took a step forward without waiting for a response.

Miranda was quicker. Her hand shot out, catching his in a gesture of greeting that brought her up into his guard. The look on his face might have made me laugh if I had not been suppressing an urge to hurl my knife at his throat.

"I do mind," she said, keeping her voice level. "I've got orders."

"What the fuck, Jeremiah," the female pirate said, frowning at her crewmate's sudden hesitation.

"My mistake," Jeremiah said to Miranda as he backed up. "They're Miranda's, Kira."

"An easy misunderstanding." Miranda shrugged.

"Neptune's balls. What are you doing out here?" Kira asked.

"Right now? Trawling. Later, who can say?"

I couldn't see Miranda's face, but I heard the grin in her voice and hated her for it, even as I understood its necessity.

"What about you?"

"Well," Jeremiah nodded at his ship, "we're not exactly equipped to trawl, so we've been, ah, relieving a few vessels of their haul. Mostly fleet." He spat. "Cut off the body, and the head dies."

I felt the heat in my glare as I watched Jeremiah. He had not admitted to destroying the fleet warship, but the pleasure in his voice boiled my blood.

"Shit," he said, catching my glance. "What the hell is that?"

Miranda reached behind her and placed a warning hand on mine.

"One of Miranda's crew," Miranda said.

Kira elbowed her way past Jeremiah and walked up to us, stopping a few inches from where we stood. She raked her eyes over me, then settled them on my face.

"Who are you, wolf pup?" she asked me.

"One of Miranda's," Miranda repeated.

Her hand squeezed mine, more warning than reassurance.

I kept my lips sealed.

"She treat you right?" The woman smiled at me. "We could make you an offer. Sea wolves are always welcome on my crew."

"She's not open to negotiation." Miranda's voice was low.

"I could make you an offer then," the woman said, smiling at Miranda now.

"She's not for sale, and her contract isn't up." Miranda stepped to the side, pulling my right hand forward.

My palm lay face to the sky, the fresh scar red and puckered.

"That's too bad," the pirate said, shaking her head. "If you change your mind," she told me, "look for *Mercy*."

"Who are you sailing with?" Miranda asked, resuming her position in front of me.

"Black Daniel's working the southern quadrant with *Fever*, and Iris and *Jonesy* are in the north. Last I heard, we were all taking orders from Ching Shih, but you know how she is."

The woman rolled her eyes and a chill passed over me that had nothing to do with the coming storm.

"She's something, all right." Miranda agreed. "The woman's got balls bigger than Neptune."

"So does your captain, from what I hear," said Jeremiah. "It takes real cahones to tell Ching to fuck off."

"I'm sure she'll be glad to hear you have a healthy respect for her gentlemanly bits," Miranda said.

I felt Kraken's laugh through the soles of my boots.

"Who captains *Mercy*?" Miranda asked.

"Serafina Lopez."

"Well," Miranda said, shifting her weight, "do we have your leave to trawl?"

The pirates exchanged significant looks.

"We'll give you two days, and I can't make any promises about Daniel and Iris." The woman's eyes flicked back to me one last time. "If you change your mind, puppy, come find us."

I shivered.

"Leave off," Jeremiah said to her, narrowing his eyes at Miranda with the look of someone who had just put two and two together. "That's Miranda fucking Stillwater."

Mercy disengaged, leaving me alone with my crew and staring at Miranda in confusion. Miranda Stillwater. The name was familiar. The memory tugged at me, anchorless and aggravating.

"Do we trawl?" Kraken asked.

"Not much of a choice now, and it will buy Orca some time to get here." Miranda scanned the flat horizon.

"The debris blocked that ship from the sonar," Finn said. "We need to get clear of it."

"Or we can hope that it will block us." Miranda glanced at me for confirmation.

The thought of staying in the debris field turned my stomach, but Miranda was right. I nodded.

"It will buy us a little time, but if you want to trawl, we'll need to break free of the worst of it," I said.

"Not quite." Kraken glanced out at the water. "This is a trawler's dream, minus the bodies. *Man o' War* could use a few replacement parts, and fleet supply capsules float."

Kraken was right, of course. Nothing in the ocean went to waste, and ship parts were too precious to let sink, which was why most were constructed to float in the event of a catastrophe. Comita would have done the same thing. Sure, she would have held a short service and said a few words for the dead, but in the end the fleet trawlers would launch either way. That thin veil of humanity was the only difference.

An important difference.

"Why did they try and recruit me?" I asked. Kraken, Finn, and Miranda exchanged glances.

"They think you're something you're not," Miranda said.

"What do they think I am, then?" Adrenaline from the unexpected boarding strung out my voice into a reedy breath.

Miranda sighed. "Kraken, get our nets in order. Finn, see what you can do about that radar. Rose, come with me. I'll explain once we're below."

"There's no reason why you would know about the sea wolves on the Archipelago. They're an old buccaneer legend, with a few grains of truth."

She winked conspiratorially and adopted a storyteller's exaggerated tones.

"It is said that the blood of Neptune himself flows in their veins, appearing now and then in old pirate bloodlines."

I hovered on the edge of my chair with a pit in my stomach. I knew what her next words were going to be before she spoke. Crow's Eye had asked me something similar, and I did not think it was a coincidence.

"Where was your father's family from?" she asked.

I wished I knew. He had sailed in and out of my young life like all of his kind, and in the years that had passed since he vanished, I had left Cassiopeia and thoughts of him and my mother behind. Guilt, ever-present in any thought of my home station, urged me to look forward. Looking back was pointless. There was nothing I could do for my mother now.

You might have asked her what it was like, to lose both lover and daughter.

But I hadn't.

Next time I get home leave, I will, I vowed. If I got to go home.

"I don't know. He was a drifter, that's all my mother told me. Why?"

"The sea wolves are ruthless, elusive, and unnaturally good sailors. They also, according to superstition, have one distinguishing characteristic."

I waited, feeling the blood rise to my face.

"It's your eyes, Rose. That's what gives people the wrong idea."

She twisted the ring around her thumb. There was something engraved in it that I couldn't make out. It might have been the roman numeral two. She looked at me.

"They give me the wrong idea sometimes, too."

"They're just eyes," I said, willing my heart to resume its normal pace and failing. Miranda's eyes were far more interesting. I couldn't have looked away from them any more than I could have sprouted gills and breathed water.

"Comita had no idea what she had in you."

She leaned forward until her knees brushed my thigh. Whoever had designed the rig had anticipated the pilot and co-pilot getting along. There wasn't room for discord.

"I don't care if you have sea wolf in you. I don't give two shits who your dad was, or your mother. You've got a gift and it doesn't matter how you came by it, as long as you stay on my ship."

"You don't think I actually considered signing on to *Mercy* for a second, do you?" I said.

Miranda's eyes narrowed, and the corner of her lip twitched in what might have been a suppressed grin.

"Why not? Seemed like a decent offer, to me."

"Because they're pirates."

Miranda's lips curved in a cruel smile, and she took my hand and turned over my palm. She traced the scars she'd left there with her forefinger, her eyes never leaving mine.

"Honey, what exactly do you think a mercenary is?"

My brain clumsily tried decipher the meaning behind her words. Her voice was husky, and my pulse leapt at her touch like a sail in the wind.

"You're not a pirate," I said.

"Not today, no." She continued tracing the scar, following the middle line down my wrist and up my thundering vein. "But last year? Tomorrow? Who knows. That's the beauty of being a mercenary. You get to choose."

I wanted to snatch back my hand, but my body betrayed me.

"Why are you working with the Archipelago now, then?" I asked.

Her finger slid back down my wrist and to my palm, where she drew a slow circle.

"Because I know what I want, and I know how to get it. For the moment, that means working with Comita."

"*If she reneges, she reneges,*" Comita had said. I hadn't thought about the consequences of those words at the time. I thought about them now.

"What do you want?" I asked.

Her smile hit me like a rogue wave. My ship capsized, flooded, and sank before my lookout could sound the slightest warning.

"Now that," she said, lightly tapping the calluses on my palm, "is something a smart player doesn't reveal until she's sure of her hand."

"Who are you, Miranda?" I asked.

I hardly recognized my voice. It had dropped an octave and acquired a throaty timber that sent a chill down my back. The raw desire lacing it was unmistakable. *Miranda Stillwater.* The familiarity of the name ached like a loose tooth.

Miranda's smile deepened, and she leaned in until her lips brushed my ear. Her braid slipped over her shoulder and fell against my breast, and the heat of her body overrode any remaining sense I had managed to cling to.

"I'm your goddamn captain," she said.

Her voice vibrated in my eardrum, sending a jolt through my body that arched my back as my breath caught. I reached up, grabbing her braid and turning her face to mine. Her blue eyes widened with surprise and a flash of something deeper, and her lips parted slightly as she braced herself against my chair. I held her gaze for as long as I could without pulling her lips to mine, and with my last shred of dignity forced my vocal cords into submission.

"And I'm your fucking navigator. I don't like sailing blind."

Miranda's pulse beat rapidly against my wrist. My fingers tightened around her hair in answer, and her eyes closed at the sudden prick of pain. Her sharp exhale rippled over every nerve on my body. When her eyes opened, I was blindsided by the naked need reflected there.

"Careful," she said, her voice as raw as mine. "You might not like what you see."

"Captain." Finn's voice echoed down the hallway, followed by his footsteps. "I need you to take a look at something."

She pulled away, leaving me limp as a wet rag and shaking.

Chapter Twelve

"How do you know how much is in the nets?" I asked Kraken as he cranked open the doors to the airlock above the lower hold.

"You don't always," he said. The tendons in his neck bulged as he worked the handle. If the squawks and shrieks coming from the joint were any indication, it was in desperate need of serious lubrication.

"So how do you know when to pull it in?"

"Every twelve hours. That way if the net needs repairs, you haven't lost too many days' worth of cargo, and when it's full it can be even more of a drag on the engine than it already is."

That much I knew. The weight of the trawl was throwing off my calculations badly. The sheer reach of the nets allowed for any wandering current to pluck at its edges, altering our course. The past day had been brutal. The trawler had bucked and wriggled under my guidance, and Finn's news had not been comforting. *Man o' War* was in the Gulf, but she was steering clear of our rendezvous the way any sane sailor steered clear of a plague ship.

There were several plausible explanations for this. The most likely was that *Man o' War* was being watched, but I had a secret theory: mutiny. It made sense. Without Miranda, the captain's seat might start to look pretty tempting to the people who had wanted me dead. At least Annie wasn't around to stir things up.

Kraken's hideous tattoos were oddly comforting in the light of these dark thoughts. He was shirtless as usual, and the tentacles rippled with the muscles of his back. I noticed a few ships locked in their grasp, floundering between his shoulder blades. The sight was darkly comical and I bit back a grin, wondering if I would see tiny, inked figures flailing in the surf if I looked closely.

"How did you end up on *Man o' War*?" I asked.

The outer airlock doors clanged open with a bang, and he engaged the switch that raised the trawl, starting the laborious process of hauling in the nets. I felt the ship groan beneath me at the strain.

"I got tired of trawling," he said, "right around the same time our boat came down with yellow fever."

"Oh." It didn't seem appropriate to ask if any of his family survived.

"I trawled alone for a year after that. Then I signed on with a raider, for the company. That was when I met Miranda."

He walked along the edge of the holding tank, inspecting it for flaws I couldn't see.

"Who did you trade with when you trawled?"

I pictured a younger Kraken, all alone on a trawler for a year with the shades of his family haunting every empty day. In my mental image, his skin was smooth and free of the tattoos that now defined him.

"Gemini," he said.

The mention of the station sent a nasty jolt through me. Gemini, site of the recent rebellion that had weakened our defenses and distracted our fleets from the threat in the Gulf. The leader of the rebellion had been young, I remembered. A Gemini Fleet captain, top of her class, a rising star that took a spectacular fall straight into Davy Jones's locker.

"Were you around during the rebellion?" I asked.

Kraken paused his inspection. "You have a lot of questions today."

"Sorry. How much do you think we'll haul in?" I changed tactics quickly, not wanting him to retreat behind his tattooed mask.

"With luck, enough to get the hell out of here. Miranda doesn't like drifting and she can be a real bitch in close quarters. Figure that out yet?"

He winked at me. The inked eye remained open, though, which gave the gesture a grotesque effect.

The mention of close quarters with Miranda sent a wave of heat to my cheeks. I mumbled something incoherent and focused on the floor by my feet.

Miranda was a problem. The fleet had strict rules about fraternizing with officers. It was only permitted if you served outside of their jurisdiction, and the rules probably had something to do with why the officers were always irritable. It was hard to get laid if everyone around you was off-limits.

Comita would have a few choice words to say to me if she could see inside my head. Not only was Miranda my commanding officer, but she was a valuable asset to the fleet. I couldn't do anything to jeopardize that.

Harper's impish grin rose before my mind's eye. "Or you could really seal the deal," said my phantom friend. "Maybe she talks in her sleep."

Somehow, though, I wasn't sure even Harper would approve of my most recent wayward tendency. I closed my eyes against the memory of Miranda's indrawn breath as my hand had closed on her hair.

Shit, I thought, as heat pooled between my thighs. *Shit, shit, shit.*

"You all right, Rose?"

Miranda's voice did not help things. I jumped, nearly tumbling over the railing, and avoided looking at her as she caught my arm, only too aware that my emotions were written all over my face.

"Yeah, I'm fine," I said.

"You sure? You seem a little jumpy." She smirked.

She knows exactly what she's doing to me, I realized. *And she's enjoying every fucking second of it.*

It was too much. I stepped away from her, mentally berating

my body for its delayed response. Moving away from Miranda was the last thing it seemed to want to do, but I was done being toyed with. I'd spent the better part of my life at the mercy of someone else's game.

I was a Polarian Fleet navigator. I had self-respect.

"Water's too calm," I said, glaring at her.

"I thought you liked calm seas." She tilted her head.

I felt Kraken's covert observation as he adjusted a few knobs. "Calm never lasts for long."

"So you prefer a challenge?" Her smirk deepened.

"I prefer to know what I'm dealing with."

I want you, Captain, and I think you like that just a little too much. The thought rang with an unpleasant truth.

I was an idiot. I'd trusted Annie, and look how that had turned out. I was a tool to Miranda, and just because we would both enjoy it if she used me didn't make me any less disposable when this was all over.

"I'm not judging. I like storms, myself. All this waiting around drives me crazy. Got anything for me, Kraken?"

"Patience, woman," he said with a grumble. "I'm only on the first net. You'll know as soon as I do."

"You might want to step back," Miranda said to me as the net spilled its contents into the ship.

I stumbled into her as a wall of spray soaked my clothes. She caught me about the waist. I felt the vibrations of her laugh against my back and I yanked away from her, my insides writhing with self-loathing and desire.

Absurdly, I missed Orca. She, at least, was honest.

I distracted myself with the contents of the hold. The nets had been full, and their close-knit fibers glistened wetly in the sunlight and cast strange shadows over the murky soup slopping around the hold. Seaweed floated to the top, looking gray and diseased, and sure enough, there were several fleet supply capsules amid the sludge. I didn't look too closely at some of the other, fleshy looking objects. If there were bodies, I didn't want to know about them.

"How does that turn into something like this?" I asked, tapping the plastic railing.

The idea of the briny plastic sludge fueling our 3-D printers was as remote as the idea of solid earth beneath my feet. I knew it existed, but I couldn't imagine it.

"Beats the shit out of me," Kraken said. "I just deliver."

"We'll do another haul overnight, but I want to get out of here in the morning before Ching Shih gets wind of us. If she's got someone following Orca, she'll send out another scout, and I don't like the idea of *Mercy* knowing we're here."

"You sure you don't want to be found?" Kraken said. His tone was slightly suggestive.

I glanced at Miranda, who was watching me. I wanted to suture her eyebrow back down to a normal position. Something about the way she arched it made my stomach perform acrobatics.

"Once was enough," Miranda said.

Kraken's snort of laughter echoed in the hold.

His words drove home something else. Miranda knew the enemy. Knew her well enough that random pirates like Kira and Jeremiah associated Miranda with Ching Shih.

Then there was the disconcerting matter of Miranda's mark, which was infamous enough that it had given Jeremiah pause, even though the pirates had outnumbered our tiny crew ten to one.

The line between Miranda and the pirates blurred still further, and I hated myself for being so blind.

Miranda Stillwater. Her name sent alarm bells off in a distant part of my skull.

"Excuse me, Captain," I said, deciding I needed a break from her blue eyes and her mocking smile.

"You're not dismissed."

I froze. Anger won out over desire, finally clearing my head.

"What do you need, Captain?" I said, remembering her earlier threat to throw me overboard if I did not follow orders.

"Miranda." Kraken's voice was quiet, calm, and with a hint of warning.

"From you? Obedience. Come with me." The look she gave Kraken was defiant.

He shook his bald head as she left the hold, leaving me fuming and confused.

"I told you. She can be a real bitch when she's drifting." His eyes measured me and for a moment I thought he was about to say more. He didn't.

"Compass Rose. Now," Miranda ordered.

I followed, holding on to a sharp reply by the skin of my teeth.

Clouds built like ancient empires on the horizon as the sun set over the Gulf. The sound of the hatch sealing behind me severed any feelings of connection with the rest of the ship, along with any hope of escaping my captain. She walked to the prow and stood against the sun, her hair burning a deep, dark red in the light. I crossed my arms over my chest and refused to be drawn in by the sight.

"Someone should be at the helm," I said.

"The trawler will be fine for a few fucking minutes." Miranda's voice carried the same edge as it had before the swarm, a restless cocktail of danger and uncertainty.

"Do you need a drink, Captain?"

The poorly concealed mockery in my voice made her back stiffen. She turned slowly, her face not nearly shadowed enough to hide her anger.

"Do you have a problem, navigator?"

"I do, actually," I said. I had a lot of problems. *I am far from home, surrounded by pirates, and in serious danger of falling in love with you.*

The ring on her thumb sent a flash of reflected fire into my eyes. Roman numeral two. The symbol of Gemini station.

The pieces fell into place, filling me with a disconsolate rush of betrayal.

The leader of the Gemini mutiny had been a young Gemini Fleet captain. Her name came to me in the soft rush of twilight. Stillwater. *Miranda Stillwater.*

I was subordinate to a traitor.

Worse than that, worse than the knowledge of the blood on her hands, was the knowledge that there was a part of me that didn't care who she was or what she had done, which made me just as much a traitor.

I had thought I felt the pain of betrayal, hanging from the ladder with Annie above me, plotting how best to finish me off. I had thought I'd known loneliness, too drifter for Polaris, and too Polarian for the mercenaries.

I knew nothing.

The wide sky and the purpling clouds filled me with an incomprehensibly bloated sense of loss.

"Name your complaint, Rose."

She was so beautiful, and so arrogant, standing with her boots sure on the slick deck and her body equally sure of her position beneath the heavens while I spun like a compass needle, seeking north and finding nothing.

"You're Miranda Stillwater, leader of the Gemini rebellion," I said, throwing the words at her like knives.

She plucked them out of the air.

"That's what this is about?" Her face registered genuine surprise.

I took a step back. My ankle hit the railing as she moved closer.

"You're a traitor."

"And you took my oath," she said, her own anger warming to mine. "What does that make you?"

"An idiot," I said, shaking with rage. A bead of sweat ran down my throat and between my breasts.

"And I am your captain. Will you serve?"

I lunged. There was no thought behind it, only blind pain and weeks of Orca's conditioning. She grabbed my wrists and held them above my head, the muscles in her arms rippling with strain.

"Will you serve?" she repeated.

I struggled in her grasp, the feeling of helplessness fueling my anger, and refused to respond.

"Does Comita know?" I asked, wondering if I had just given Ching Shih the keys to the Gulf.

176

Miranda knew more about fleet patrol patterns at this point than most fleet patrollers, thanks to me, and if she was Miranda Stillwater, then she was capable of anything. For all I knew, she had been communicating with Ching Shih this whole time.

"Of course. It's a simple concept, Rose. Captains call it leverage."

She let me go, and I rubbed my wrists. Red marks stood out on my skin from her fingers.

"Comita is blackmailing you?" I asked as I backed away from her, trying to catch my breath.

"Not exactly."

She pressed her advantage, backing me closer to the edge.

I tried to dodge out of her way, but her foot snaked out to hook mine. I landed hard, several barnacles gouging tracks down my back. Miranda stood over me with that infuriating smile.

I had never hated anyone as much as I hated her right then. Nor, despite everything, had I wanted anyone or anything more.

"Done?" she asked as she offered me a hand.

I decided to try the trick that had worked with Orca. I took her hand and pulled, bringing my foot up into the back of her knee and collapsing it. She fell onto me, catching her palm on the barnacled deck and letting out a colorful curse.

I could smell her, brine and hibiscus and the underlying scent of sailor's sweat and Miranda herself. Her braid slid off her shoulder, hanging over me like a lifeline. I had an absurd recollection of the children's story about the princess in her tall tower, letting down her hair for her prince—only Miranda was the sort of woman who would have chopped off that braid and propelled herself down the wall at its expense, and I was no prince.

You should have let yourself drown, I told myself.

My heart pounded with leftover adrenaline and the intoxicating effects of the weight of her body on top of mine. The evening sky blazed behind her, setting fire to the distant banks of clouds. I listened to the sound of her breathing slowing. Mine remained ragged, drowning out the slow lap of the waves against the hull. Neither of us moved.

My captain was Miranda Stillwater, and I was a drifter half-breed out of her depth.

The sunset bled into Miranda's eyes, bathing the blue with the same fire that washed the horizon, and her slightly parted lips looked almost innocent, stripped of arrogance by her landing.

Looking into her eyes was a mistake.

The current that leapt between us was paralyzing. The boat dropped away from me, and I hurtled into blue at a speed that ripped the breath from my throat. *Falling*. That was what they called this.

The sky faded, its brilliance nothing more than a backdrop as the moment stretched out between us. I tried to control my breathing and failed. My chest rose and fell at its own rapid pace, brushing against her with each inhale. Miranda would have to be blind and deaf not to notice. Out of the corner of my eye I saw the pulse in her throat quicken.

"Rose," she said, her voice rough and lower than normal. "There are things I can't tell you, but you have to trust that I am on your side."

My inner compass quivered and settled, discarding true north to point at the place in her chest where I could feel her heartbeat racing mine. I couldn't answer. I felt as if I'd swum three miles. There wasn't enough air in the world to fill the space inside of me, and I felt as empty and limitless as the fading sky.

I bit my lip, hoping that the prick of pain would bring me back to earth. Miranda glanced down at my mouth. Her eyes turned a darker shade of blue, and a flush rose along her skin, making the scars stand out in stark testimony to her emotions. When she raised her eyes back to mine, the look she gave me sent a deep tremor through my body. My heart kicked things up another notch as I reeled from the aftershock.

I don't care who you are. If you don't kiss me, I will die. The certainty of the thought eroded any last shred of reason.

Her name spilled from my mouth, and she caught it with her lips, sealing it between us as she kissed me. She tasted like salt air and something far sweeter, soft and fierce and real.

She started off gently, her restraint evident in the way her breath caught and her body shook. Her hair brushed my neck, sending another shiver through me. I wanted to wrap her braid around my fist. I wanted to feel her full weight along the length of me, heat and muscle and skin. More than that, I wanted to forget about who she was or who she had been, and I really didn't want to think about what either of those things could mean to me.

She took my lower lip between her teeth, and my resolve broke with a low moan. It was a sound I had never heard myself make before, and it was as startling as it was thrilling. I pulled her face closer to mine, barnacles biting into my shoulder blades as I charted a determined course into oblivion, taking my captain with me.

Miranda cast off her restraint and with it any doubt I might have had about how this woman could command a ship of surly mercenaries with a single look. The wind tugged at my curls and she collected my surrender with her mouth while the pollution of past centuries swirled around us.

"We have to stop," Miranda said, rolling off me. I blinked at the stars overhead, feeling dizzy. The sky had lost the last bit of light, and the waves lapping against the ship's hull were swiftly losing the tranquility of twilight. *Sea Cat* had strayed slightly from her course, thanks to the nets that were once again flung out behind us, and my mind hazily set about running the corrections.

My lips felt bruised and swollen. It was past time to start searching for *Man o' War*, and far past time to sub. Any number of things could have killed us while we lingered topside, from hydrogen sulfide to methane bursts and giant squid.

I lay still, pinioned between the desire to lie like this forever and the dread of what would happen next. Something had to happen. We couldn't stay here, and returning to the ship carried consequences I wasn't ready to think about. If my hair looked anything like Miranda's, it wasn't something I would be able to hide, either.

Miranda Stillwater. Gemini's most infamous captain, and a name the Archipelago had done its best to wipe from the maps. How in Neptune's seven seas had she survived, and what the hell was I doing in her arms?

Miranda straightened her clothes and grimaced as her hands explored her hair. My body ached with unreleased longing as I watched her fingers quickly establish order. My own curls required more vigorous attention, and I knew my efforts fell short.

"Captain," I said, rising unsteadily to my feet.

Miranda's face looked different in the darkness, but I could feel the distance opening up between us.

"'Captain' again already?" she said, a smile playing with her swollen lips.

I looked away. "What happens now?"

Miranda placed her scarred hand under my chin and tilted my head up. She kissed me gently, pulling out any last vestiges of resistance.

"Nothing happens. We sail. You navigate. Right now, we eat. Later, we find my ship."

"But what about this?" I ran my hand down her side, feeling the curve of her hip. There would be consequences on a fleet ship for fraternizing with your commanding officer.

"I only have one real rule on my ship, navigator," she said, turning toward the hatch. "I don't care who my crew fucks, as long as it doesn't distract them from their duties."

Well, I thought as I watched her leave, *with an attitude like that, you'll be lucky if you get fucked anytime soon, Captain.*

"How was that fresh air?" Kraken asked as we entered the common area. Finn and Jeanine were at the table playing cards while Kraken flipped fish over the small stove.

"Very . . . refreshing," Miranda said.

I bolted for the helm, mumbling something about correcting our course on the way out. I was not ready to face the gauntlet of *Sea Cat's* crew.

I found Seamus nestled in Miranda's chair. I stroked his chin, eliciting a contented purr from the huge tom. The corrections were minor, and I updated the autopilot for the evening with half of my brain still on the upper deck. My lips ached, and there was a deeper ache in the center of my chest.

"North, east, south, west," I told Seamus, plopping into my chair. I clutched my head in my hands and let out a frustrated sigh. "Life used to be a lot less complicated."

Only a few weeks ago, my biggest concern had been Maddox. Now, I had pirates, traitors, and the fate of the Archipelago itself on my plate, and I didn't have much of an appetite for the next course.

Tomorrow we would leave the rendezvous, keeping *Man o' War* at a safe distance as we skirted the first of the mines. Tomorrow, dawning with a promise of toxic waters and gathering storms. I needed my wits about me. I thought about the way Miranda's lips had felt on my neck and shivered. There was little hope for that now.

I took a few more deep breaths and stood, giving Seamus another pat on my way out. I stepped quietly, not wanting to break into the bright sphere of the common room just yet.

"The main crew isn't going to like it." Kraken's voice rumbled from the storage room. I froze, pressing myself against the wall. "I don't care what you do, but you need to be more careful, Miranda."

"I am careful." Miranda's tone was stubborn.

"You're not, Mere." Kraken sighed, and I wondered at the tenderness in his voice. "She's dangerous."

"It's harmless, and I could use a break, don't you think?"

"There's only one thing that girl is going to break. You need to concentrate on Ching right now, not a pretty pair of eyes and a nice ass."

"Watch it, Kraken."

"She's not my type."

There was a pause.

"It doesn't mean anything. She's fleet. We have to give her

back at the end of this, remember? I have no plans on getting attached."

Her words stung, and I recoiled at the force behind them. Recoiled, and wondered at their vehemence.

"I hope so, Mere. Go get something to eat. I'll get Rose. I don't want to lose you for another two hours. And Mere—"

There was a pause.

"Don't even say it."

"You owe me your rum ration."

"Like hell I do."

"Then next time, Captain, keep your eyes on the pot and off the honey."

Were they betting on me and Miranda? I bolted back to the helm, fuming and confused. Kraken appeared a few minutes later.

"Hungry?" he asked mildly. I looked up at him, searching his face for remnants of the conversation I'd overheard. I found none. If he truly thought I was dangerous, his face didn't show it, and I wasn't about to ask him where the other bets had lain.

"Always," I said, standing. "I was just finishing up."

We walked to the common area in silence. Finn and Jeanine were still playing cards, and Finn dealt Miranda in as we entered.

"Loser cleans up," Finn said.

"I thought you didn't gamble," I said, taking a seat far away from Miranda.

"Of course we gamble. Why do you think there is a rule about it?" Finn said. "Just don't tell the captain." He winked at Miranda.

"Shut up and deal," Miranda said. "You want in, Rose?"

"I don't know how to play," I admitted.

"You don't play poker on the Archipelago?" Finn looked scandalized. "What the hell do you do, then?"

I thought about the officer's lounge, and the card tables and games that went on behind closed doors.

"Well," I said, recalling late nights in the commons with Harper, "there's always dice, darts, and drinking on a fleet ship." I smiled at his shocked expression. "I was never good at cards, and I don't like losing." I could feel Miranda's eyes on me and looked studiously away.

"Deal her in," said Jeanine. "Maybe you'll stand a better chance of winning with some new blood, Finn."

"It's not my fault you cheat," Finn said, slapping the cards down on the table. "Here, I'll show you the rules."

Finn patted the bench next to him and I scooted over, across the table now from Miranda.

"I hope you like scrubbing pots," Jeanine said. "Finn can't play to save his life."

"The trick," Finn explained, ignoring Jeanine, "is your poker face. You've got to keep these jackasses from reading your mind. Think you can do that?"

I looked up at Miranda and blushed.

"Sure," I said.

Miranda smirked.

"Maybe you better stick to dice," said Jeanine.

We played through dinner. I wolfed down my food quickly, glancing surreptitiously at the pot to see if there was anything left.

"I hope you hide your hand better than you hide your appetite," Miranda said.

I glared at her and placed a card face up on the table. Her eyes narrowed and she consulted her own hand.

"And I hope you can keep up," I said.

Kraken coughed on a burst of laughter as he settled down to join us.

"That's never been a problem before." Jeanine's voice was laden with double meaning. "You want in, Kraken?"

"No. But I've got a pair of dice that have been gathering dust."

"You all need to be flogged," Miranda said, laying down her cards. I smiled smugly at my higher hand.

"She always enforces the rules when she's losing," Kraken said. "It's a serious character flaw."

Jeanine's hand trumped mine and Miranda's. Finn sighed and played his, shaking his head as Jeanine collected the chips.

"On second thought," he said, "dice seems like a better idea."

"What's the game?" Jeanine asked, looking from me to Kraken.

"Crown and anchor." Kraken cast the dice on the table, the crude symbols spinning in the dim light.

"Now that," Miranda said, crossing her arms, "is definitely against the Code."

"My apologies, Captain. I'll return them to the bilge swill who gave them to me."

"Bilge swill?" Miranda repeated.

"That's the nicest name I could think of off the top of my head."

The top of his head, which loomed far above the rest of ours, gleamed.

"She must have a rough reputation, this bilge swill of yours," Miranda said.

"Too rough," Kraken agreed. "It got her into trouble."

"Cut the crap," Jeanine said. "Rose, Miranda gave Kraken those dice years ago. She's the worst gambler on her goddamn boat, which is why she won't let the rest of us play."

Miranda gave Jeanine a tolerant grin.

I thought about the conversation I'd overheard, and wondered who Miranda had put her money on.

"If by worst you mean best, then yes. But crown and anchor is definitely out. I should remind you it was a gamble that won me *Man o' War* in the first place."

"Craps, then," Kraken said, pulling out another set of dice from his pocket.

I stared at him.

"How many dice do you carry with you?" I asked.

"This set is lucky," he said, collecting the crown and anchor die from the table.

"You mean rigged." Finn shuffled the cards and put the deck back in a little drawer beneath the table.

"All right, Rose, let's see what you've got," Miranda said.

"Yes, Rose, we're all anxious to see what you've got." Jeanine rolled her eyes and ignored the warning look Finn sent her. "Especially the captain."

Miranda's knife landed between Jeanine's fingers, quivering in the table. Jeanine froze, her mouth hanging slightly open.

"Oops. Must have slipped out of my hand." Miranda smiled and casually plucked the knife out of the wood, running a finger down the blade.

Jeanine swallowed and flexed her fingers. My mouth went dry.

It was a good thing dice required very little skill.

The next morning didn't so much dawn as glower. The clouds from the night before had multiplied, and the water above the trawler frothed and foamed, lashed by wind and rain. Even at our cruising depth the waves rocked the boat. I rolled out of my bunk feeling queasy and wishing I had held off on the rum. The rest of the crew slept fitfully, their inner clocks promising a few more minutes of sleep while mine lurched ahead of schedule.

Miranda stirred in her bunk. I froze, my heart beating much faster than it had any right to this early in the morning. Her breathing evened out again, and I leaned against the bunk, resting my head against the wall to listen. Despite Miranda's dismissive comment last night, a smile launched a successful coup against my doubts, and I grinned like an idiot in the predawn light. Miranda wanted me.

We were leaving the debris zone today, and I couldn't wait to get out of it. There was a cloying feel to the water here, a reminder of failure and death that clung to everything. On the other hand, there was also comfort in the knowledge that debris did not fight back.

Today we were hunting pirates.

I splashed water on my face in the tiny head, grimacing at my reflection in the mirror. I needed a haircut. My hair grew quickly, and already it was creeping past my ears in a dark profusion of tangled curls. I finger combed my forelock into submission as best I could, frowning.

"I like it messy."

I jumped, nearly hitting my head on the low ceiling. Miranda leaned against the doorway with her arms folded across her chest. She hadn't gotten fully dressed yet, and the thin tank top and baggy sleep shorts left little to the imagination.

"Um," I said, ever articulate.

"Try this." She stepped behind me, running her fingers through my hair. I watched our reflections. Miranda was only an inch or so taller than me, and she had to lean around my head to see what she was doing. Her own hair hung loose about her shoulders. She'd taken it out of its braid, and it gave her face a softer look. The effect was unsettling in more ways than one as it brushed against me.

She combed my hair forward, reaching past me to wet her fingers in the faucet. I shivered at the contact.

"Salt is the best hair product around," she said, arranging my curls in a decidedly edgy sprawl. "It has real staying power."

"There is only so much styling can fix. I need a haircut."

"Kraken will fix you up." She stepped back to admire her handiwork.

I raised an eyebrow at her.

"I'd like to keep some of it," I said, thinking about Kraken's bald pate.

"Tell him to take off the sides and leave the top."

"Captain," I said, holding her eyes in the mirror. "Was that an order?"

"Of course not. You can wear your hair however you want." She trailed a finger down my neck. "It is just a preference."

I turned around to face her in the tiny space, completely awake. The knowing smile was back on her lips, and I had the sense that she was fully conscious of what she was doing to my pulse. I reached out, hating the way my hand shook, and touched the thick fall of unbound hair. She closed her hand gently around my wrist.

I tightened my grip on her hair before she could pull my hand away. Miranda might be in control of this ship, and she certainly had a few strings on me, but I hadn't forgotten the look in her eyes as she said my name the evening before.

Miranda shook her head at me, a silent warning not to take things further. I wrapped her hair around my fingers and pulled.

It was like a switch. Miranda's eyes closed, and when they opened again, the look that had nearly undone me on the deck hit me again.

"You're a real problem," she said, pressing me up against the sink.

I chose to respond by pulling her lips to mine. Miranda let out a low groan and reached out to yank the door shut, locking us in the tiny space. I wrapped my other hand in her hair, soaking up the way it felt as she lifted me up onto the sink with a practiced ease I decided not to dwell on. My legs tightened around her involuntarily and Miranda proceeded to return disorder to my appearance with a determination that wiped all thoughts of pirates from my mind.

"Seriously, hurry the fuck up in there."

Jeanine's voice, paired with a barrage of knocking, broke us apart.

Miranda opened the door with a curse and glared at Jeanine, who held her ground.

"Go piss in the ocean," Miranda said, shoving past her.

That left me face to face with Jeanine. I ran my hands through my disheveled hair.

Jeanine had a curious expression on her face. She tilted her head, showing off the shark tattoo on the shaved side of her skull.

"You're in deep, aren't you?" she said.

I shrugged and made to step past her. She flung out an arm and stopped me, leaning in to whisper in my ear.

"For what it's worth, I had a full ration on Orca, but I'm not a sore loser. Be careful with the captain. You hurt her, we'll kill you."

She dropped her arm and stepped into the head, slamming the door in the face of my questions.

I didn't have much time for contemplation, either of Jeanine's motives or Miranda's. Finn cornered me over breakfast with the latest findings on the sonar. There were several large ships in the area, and it was my job to chart a course that would take us close enough to identify them without attracting their attention. Our last encounter with piratical forces had been unpleasant enough to satisfy my curiosity for a lifetime.

The storm gathered and grew into midday, threatening to split the seas asunder with its force. Navigating beneath the waves at our depth didn't pose a problem, but it did interfere with my line of sight. Murky water greeted me every time I raised my eyes, and scattered swarms of jellyfish shot past the helm. I trusted that Finn was interpreting the sonar and did my best to keep our course as unobtrusive as possible, just a little drifter ship making its way toward the mines in hopes of trade.

Miranda paced the hallway between the helm and Finn's lair, her braid twitching like a cat's tail. Now and then she cursed the sonar, keeping an eye on *Man o' War*. We'd had a confusing ping from them shortly after breakfast, urging us to stay away a little while longer.

I was soaked in nervous sweat by the time dinner rolled around.

"You look like you need a drink," Finn said, tossing me his flask as I slumped onto the bench next to him. I drank deeply. Harper would be proud of my new vice.

"Captain said something about a haircut," Kraken said, setting a platter of food on the table.

I rolled my eyes at Finn and took another swig of rum.

"Seas save us, will you please let him do something interesting? You look like a mop. It honestly hurts me to look at you sometimes." Jeanine emphasized her point by averting her eyes in disgust.

"Go easy on her. She can't help the fact that she's been surrounded by a bunch of people with eels up their asses for her entire life. Have you seen those fleet uniforms?" Kraken shook his head disparagingly. "And they call us criminals."

"I was thinking just a trim," I said, inching away from Finn's enthusiasm.

"Miranda, knock some sense into the poor thing," Finn said.

"She looks just fine." Miranda silenced their protests with a look. "If she wants her mop, let her keep her mop." Her eyes challenged mine. "On the other hand, you are free from fleet constraints. It might not be a bad idea to blend in with my crew."

"Define 'blend in,'" I said, with a feeling I was about to regret my decision.

The face staring out of the mirror was mine, but the hair was not. Kraken had taken the sides down to stubble, leaving the curls on top to fend for themselves. They fell almost into my eyes, a tousled look that would have given Comita a serious case of indigestion.

"Holy shit," I said, looking back at Kraken.

"It suits you, wolf pup," he said, roughing up his handiwork in a gesture that felt suspiciously like affection.

"Let us see," Jeanine said, leaning into the head.

I stepped out and faced the rest of the assembled crew.

"Hot damn." Finn nodded in approval. "Now you look like a proper Merc. We just need to get you a few tattoos, and—"

"One step at a time there, Finn; you don't want to scare the girl," Jeanine said, looking me up and down. "Definite improvement. Unless you want a tattoo?"

"I think I'll pass on that for now, thanks," I said, thinking about dirty needles.

"What about an earring? I have a spare hoop somewhere." Finn fingered his earlobe suggestively.

"Thanks, but I like my ears the way they are. In one piece." I turned at last to Miranda, who was watching me intently. "Well, Captain? Do I blend in with your crew now?"

"You are my crew," she said. Her eyes locked onto mine. "You look good, Rose."

"A toast!" Finn declared, sparing me from responding to Miranda. She still held my eyes, her look full of promises I hoped to Neptune she planned to keep.

"A toast to what?" I asked, not breaking eye contact with my captain.

189

"To the liberation of your scalp."

"It wasn't that bad," Miranda said.

My free will drained out of me and I had the presence of mind to be grateful that Miranda had not, in fact, suggested I get a tattoo, because I would have broken my principles faster than I could say "Davy Jones." *Miranda Stillwater*, I reminded myself. Queen of renegades, the captain that turned the waters around Gemini station into bloodstained foam—hardly a person to trust with my life, let alone my heart.

Jeanine was right. I was in deep.

"How about we toast to our first visit to the fabled Archipelago mines?" Jeanine offered.

Finn raised his flask. "Sounds good to me. Now why aren't we all drinking?"

"Some of us have to stay sober," Miranda said. "We're deep in Ching's territory."

"I don't see you volunteering to take that hit," Finn said.

"Actually, it's my watch, which you should know, Finnegan. Drink up for me." She saluted us as she walked out of the room, leaving me struggling with the urge to trail after her.

Jeanine took pity on me.

"You gonna let her take that watch alone, navigator? Here. Take this." She tossed me a full flask and waved me out of the common area. "We can't talk about you behind your back if you're sitting right in front of us."

I shut the door. The sound of their laughter faded, leaving me to absorb the silence of the corridor.

Did I really want to be alone with Miranda? *Stupid question.* Of course I did. The real issue was *should* I be alone with Miranda, knowing what would probably happen. We'd registered three pirate ships in the distance today, which was three too many, in my opinion. It would take more data to get a clear picture of the pattern, but the size of the ships told me all I needed to know about what the Archipelago was up against. I couldn't afford to let Miranda distract me any more than she already had.

My feet ignored my brain and set off down the hallway, taking a pull of liquid courage for good measure.

"Hey there, navigator," Miranda said. I set the flask down on the empty chair and stood before her, words failing me. She reached out her hand. I took it, letting her pull me onto her lap and praying that our ship passed unnoticed over the deeps, because I sure as hell was not paying attention.

Chapter Thirteen

"Rose."

I woke up to Jeanine shaking my shoulder.

"Your watch."

"Ugh," I said, pushing back the blanket and squinting up into Jeanine's yawning face. She pushed a mug of hot tea into my fumbling fingers and crawled into her own bunk, leaving the trawler in my hands for the last hours until dawn.

The helm was quiet, with only the faint sounds of the ocean popping and whirring around me. I chugged down some of the scalding tea to wake myself up, then checked our position. We were deep beneath the waves, but even down here I could feel the hurricane exploding into the Gulf with a vengeance.

Stifling a yawn of my own, I scanned the sonar. If *Man o' War* kept up on her current trajectory, she should be due north of us, just outside of our sonar's range. I paused. There was a large swarm of jellyfish moving in that direction. If I was careful, I might be able to hide in the swarm long enough to get the main ship into range without revealing our coordinates to anyone else.

Nothing wakes you up like a sense of purpose. I forgot about my tea and brought the trawler to life, reeling in the nets and setting my sights on the swarm ahead.

Dark shapes flared occasionally in bursts of brilliant luminescence, illuminating the vast field of jellyfish in a cascade of blues, purples, and pinks. The lights from the trawler would pass unnoticed by any observer, hidden in the larger light show, and the sonar pinged back at me in irritation. Our pings could not penetrate the swarm.

Not that it mattered. I knew where we were headed, and after an hour or two the jellies began to dwindle and I turned my attention back to the screen.

There. About a mile or two northeast was a ship, her readings unmistakable to my desperate eyes. We had found *Man o' War*. My elation dwindled as I took in the rest of the scene.

She was not alone.

"Neptune's balls," I swore, sounding disturbingly like Finn. Three vessels surrounded her, in a formation that did not look entirely friendly.

By the time I roused the rest of the crew, the swarm had brought us closer, and the situation was unpleasantly clear. Three large pirate raiders had *Man o' War* effectively cut off from any chance of escape—and any chance we might have of contacting her.

"That doesn't look like a parley," I said, resisting the urge to turn the trawler around and return to safer waters.

"It most certainly does not." Miranda consulted the sonar. "What did Orca get herself into?"

"Whatever it is, you're better off out of it," said Kraken.

"Rose, can you get us there?" Miranda asked, ignoring Kraken.

"To the ship?" My voice squeaked a little at the prospect. I eyed the sonar with apprehension. In theory, I could. If we waited for the swarm to bring us close enough, we might be able get a message to *Man o' War*, drifting unnoticed between the ships. They would be too busy recalculating their depth to escape the swarm.

It might work, if luck sided with us and the night shift was sleepy.

"What if it is a trap?" Jeanine asked.

"Of course it's a trap." Miranda loosened her knife in its sheath. "That doesn't change anything. I should have known Ching would pull something like this. Of all the goddamn fish in the sea . . ." she trailed off, staring out at the water. Jellyfish pulsed around us, illuminating the worried faces crammed into the helm.

"Ching Shih?" I asked, hoping I had misheard.

"That's her ship." Miranda pointed to one of the blobs on the sonar. "I never should have let *Mercy* go. Those sons of bitches must have reported directly to her."

"We could hardly have sunk them with a trawler," Finn said.

"You'd be surprised what you can do with the element of surprise." Miranda turned her attention back to me. "So, Rose. Can you get us in?"

"I can get us close," I said, "but we will still need someone on *Man o' War* to open the docking bay."

"Don't worry about that. Finn has the codes."

"Then yes, I can get us to the ship." I didn't bother laying out the risks. They were obvious to anyone with eyes.

The swarm moved inexorably closer, until we could see the lights of *Man o' War* through the pulsing bodies. The dark shapes of the raiders lurked amid the jellyfish, circling like sharks. Three raiders seemed excessive, now that I thought about it. Two would be sufficient to subdue a mercenary ship under ordinary conditions. I thought about Orca's garbled message a few days earlier, urging us to stay away a little while longer. Something wasn't right.

"Finn. Codes. Now."

Finn fiddled with an oddly shaped handheld device, muttering to himself as he punched numbers into the system. A few meters away, the door began to open.

"That's enough! Any wider and the lights will come on."

Miranda grabbed the wheel and took the trawler into a higher gear, aiming for the small gap ahead. I clutched the seat of my chair and hoped she had judged the distance accurately. There was no room for error.

We shot into the first dock, nearly colliding with the wall as Miranda threw the trawler into reverse and then into a sputtering neutral while we waited for the sea door to close.

"Rose, I want you to stay with the trawler," she said, checking her weapons. "Until I know what's going on out there, you're safer here."

I bristled.

"I can take care of myself, Captain," I said.

"You're staying."

I opened my mouth to protest just as the door to the docking bay opened, releasing us into the hold in a wet rush. The words died in my throat.

Standing on the pier, surrounded by heavily armed sailors, was Orca. Her back was straight, and her eyes were full of suppressed rage. As the trawler slid into the dock, she dropped slowly to her knees, yielding to the pressure of the sword point resting in the small of her back.

Behind her was a woman I had never seen before, and never wanted to see again. Her black hair framed a plain face lined with the first hints of age, but there was nothing plain about the way she carried her short sword, or about the layer of command she wore wrapped around herself like a cloak.

"On second thought," Miranda said, her eyes glued to the pier, "you better come with me after all."

There was no graceful way to exit the trawler, but Miranda did her best, leaping down to the dock with a cat's thoughtless agility. The rest of us followed, Kraken's fists clenched and my heart pressing up against my teeth. The sailors on the dock were not familiar to me, and they wore dark shirts slashed with red over dark pants, instead of the astounding array of patched trousers I had gotten used to seeing on *Man o' War*. They watched us disembark with hungry eyes.

"Miranda." The woman's voice was calm and measured, a direct contrast to Orca's silent outrage.

"Ching," Miranda said. "What are you doing with my first mate?"

"That depends. What are you doing in the Gulf?"

"Looking for opportunities, as usual. Release her, and we'll talk." Miranda stepped away from us, blocking Ching Shih from my view.

"Very well." I heard the sound of a sword entering a sheath, and then Orca was at my side, eyes blazing.

"I told you to stay away," she hissed at me. "What the hell kind of navigator are you?"

"The kind that follows orders from the captain, not the first mate. What happened?"

"What does it look like? We were overrun." She glared at the pirates surrounding us. "Your brilliant idea didn't work. They were on to us the minute—"

Kraken held up a giant hand to silence us.

"Can I offer you a drink, or is this still my ship?" Miranda asked Ching.

"Don't insult me, Mere. I would never take back a gift. Consider this a precaution, nothing more."

A gift? I glanced at Orca. Her face was twisted with hatred, an expression that, for once, was not directed at me.

"Gift my ass," she said under her breath. "Everyone knows Miranda took it from you, you slippery bitch of an eel."

"Please," Miranda said, extending her arm in a gesture of mock courtesy. "This way. Will you be bringing your army, or are we going to be civilized?"

"Stand down," Ching said to the sailors around us. They moved a fraction of an inch away. "And will you be bringing your pets?" Ching cast her gaze in our direction, her eyes lingering on mine for a split second.

"Jeanine, Rose, Finn, you're dismissed," Miranda said.

I made to follow, but Ching's voice reached around me like a whiplash.

"Not you, sailor."

I stopped. I don't know what made me so sure she was talking about me, only that my legs obeyed before my mind caught up.

Miranda's eyes closed briefly at Ching's words, but her voice held steady as she called me back.

"Well then," she said, meeting my eyes as she addressed Ching. "Let's get this over with."

196

Miranda's council room looked different with Ching in it. Two pirates came with her, a woman whose spine looked as if it had been surgically replaced with an iron rod, and a slender man with eyes that dared onlookers to underestimate him.

"It's a little early for rum, even for me," Miranda said, taking a seat.

Orca sat at her right, and I sat next to Orca. Kraken remained standing behind us.

"Can I offer you some tea?"

"Rum is fine." Ching leaned back in her chair. "But if you want tea, go right ahead."

Miranda frowned, then nodded at a sailor at the door, who went to fetch the beverages.

"I forgot. You must have been up for a while, what with commandeering my ship and all."

"It did make me a touch thirsty," Ching said. Her tone was deadpan, but I had the distinct impression she was enjoying herself.

"I trust nobody died?" Miranda asked.

"Nobody you'll miss. How's Seamus?"

"Fat."

"So are his brothers."

Are they seriously talking about cats? I thought. I desperately wanted to ask Orca and Kraken what was going on, but that was impossible with Miranda and Ching sitting so close to us.

"How's Janelle?" Miranda's voice was guarded.

"Good. Pregnant, if you can believe it. The whole fleet is terrified of her."

"She's a good first mate," Miranda said.

"Almost the best I've ever had."

The meaning in Ching's words hung heavily over the table. I let out a small sigh of relief when the sailor returned, bearing a kettle, mugs, and a large flask.

"Tea?" Ching offered, taking control of the teapot so smoothly it took me a moment to realize it was a power play.

Miranda shrugged.

Ching poured the tea into cups, her hands neat and blunt. Her movements were efficient, calculated, as if waste of any sort repulsed her. I remembered, with a cold feeling in my gut, that Kraken had urged Miranda to avoid Ching. Of course, he had also urged her to avoid me, and she hadn't exactly listened to his advice then, either.

Ching filled her own mug with rum.

"You sure you don't want any?" she asked Miranda.

Miranda's jaw twitched.

"No."

"No you're not sure, or no you don't want any?"

"No, I don't want any rum," Miranda said. "Tea is fine."

It was the first time I had ever heard her turn down a drink.

"Suit yourself."

Orca shifted beside me. I shared her growing discomfort.

"So," Ching said, taking us in with a sweep of her eyes. "Your first mate comes to my territory looking to strike a deal without her captain. I might buy that from someone else, but not from you, Mere. What are you doing in the Gulf?"

"Last I checked, Ching, I didn't sail under you anymore. I don't owe you an explanation."

"Do you really want to talk about debts?" Ching raised one eyebrow very slightly, her voice still calm. "You owe me a great deal, Miranda."

"And when the time comes, I'll pay it." Miranda's face could have chipped steel. "But we both know you're not ready to collect."

"Your first mate says you have information to trade, in exchange for access to the mines," Ching said.

"Hardly grounds for taking my ship," said Miranda.

"You didn't answer my summons earlier this year, so I didn't know where your loyalties lay. I could have used your help, Miranda. We could have taken the mines with less bloodshed, instead of this mess. There are still sailors who would have rallied under Miranda Stillwater."

"Not if I sailed with you."

"Don't be so sure. The Archipelago is weak. The tyranny they've imposed on the rest of us ends now, if we play our cards right, which is why I have to question why you've chosen to appear at the eleventh hour with a Polarian Fleet navigator at your side."

I stiffened. Ching didn't bother to look at me again; her eyes were fixed intently on Miranda.

"You know my feelings about the Archipelago, Ching."

"Better than you, I think. Who is she, and what is she doing here?"

"She's my navigator."

"I can see that. Is she the source of your information?"

"Yes. If you know me as well as you claim, then you know I have a soft spot for fleet castoffs. Rose is mine. You have nothing to worry about."

"I'll be the judge of that. You still didn't answer my question. Why come to me now?" Ching took a measured sip of her rum.

"I was waiting to see how things panned out," Miranda said. "I had another contract."

"You're not a patient woman, Miranda. You waited for a reason, and I am not sure I like what I've been hearing from your crew."

"And I'm not sure I like that you've been talking to my crew, Ching. You come onto my ship, threaten my first mate, question my sailors, and then expect to sit down to parley?" Miranda's knuckles were white against her tea cup.

"We're at war, Miranda. I have to take extra precautions."

"War? Last I checked, you just had a few mines. You've got a long way to go before you can call this a war."

"Do I?" Ching asked, her voice mild. "All I have to do is cut the Archipelago off from the mines long enough to cripple them. Who is to say what will happen then? It is past time the ocean's wealth was redistributed. We were in agreement about that once. Who knows? You might get your mutiny after all, Stillwater."

I choked on my tea. Orca gave me a warning kick beneath the table, and I swallowed, trying to keep my composure.

"I've lost my taste for mutiny, Ching. Do I have a choice here?"

"Everyone has a choice. Work with me, and I can promise you plenty of trade in the future. Side with the Archipelago, and . . ." Ching trailed off with a shrug, the threat unspoken.

"I'm done with sides. You know that."

Ching let out a snort of derisive laughter.

"You can't be neutral. Not here. Make up your mind, Miranda, or I'll extract the coordinates and more from your little navigator, one way or another."

That didn't sound promising.

"Touch her and die." Miranda's lip curled in a snarl.

Orca swore almost inaudibly under her breath as Ching smiled, and I met the pirate captain's eyes with as much courage as I could muster.

"So it's like that, then. I thought as much. You've never been good at hiding your emotions, Mere. What will it be, cooperation or coercion?"

"Don't do it," Orca whispered, whether to Ching, or Miranda, or me, I couldn't be sure.

"I sent my first mate to you under the flag of parley, and you boarded my ship. I can't forgive that. Call off your raiders, get your crew off my decks, and then we'll talk."

"You're not in a position to set terms." Ching took another sip of rum, her dark eyes amused.

"You want my loyalty? Then get the hell off of my ship." Miranda slammed her fist on the table.

"I don't want your loyalty, Miranda Stillwater. It is too easily lost." Ching set her cup down with a decisive click.

Silence fell over the table. I risked a glance at Orca. Her face looked resigned, and when she met my eye a bone-deep chill passed over me. I was a navigator, and I knew when there was only one possible course.

Miranda did not look at any of us as she made her decision. She bit off her words, shaping each one with a vengeance.

"Then you have my cooperation."

"Good. Hand over the navigator, or I'll sink this ship and everyone on it."

My tea spilled across the table. Orca reached for her knife. Kraken rumbled deep in his chest, and Miranda stood, drawing her sword.

"Anyone ever tell you that you need to learn how to ask nicely?" Miranda said, pointing the tip at Ching.

"Wait," I said.

The pressure of Orca's hand on my thigh forced me back into my seat, and I realized with a hiccup of alarm that everyone was looking at me. I could feel Miranda silently urging me to shut up, but this was my ship, too—and my fight just as much as, if not more than, hers.

"Wait," I said again, hoping the rest of the words would fall into place.

"I'm waiting." Ching turned her attention to me, her eyes bright with curiosity.

"What do you want from me?" I asked her.

"Rose," Miranda said, the warning in her voice clear.

I ignored her. Ching was not like the bullies I'd grown up with; she was something far more dangerous. She would have me one way or another, and she had our ship surrounded. Miranda, for all her bravado, was heading in the wrong direction, and as her navigator I could not let her run us all aground.

"Proof that you are not a spy would be a good place to start."

"That's impossible," I said. "A good spy would have proof; I'm just a sailor, and all I can offer you is my word. Plus," I added, feeling a little shaky, "I'm pretty sure I would tell you whatever I thought you wanted to hear if you interrogated me."

"I am pretty sure you would too," Ching said, far too matter-of-factly for my liking. "But it could still be interesting."

"Why would the Archipelago work with Miranda Stillwater?" I asked. "I signed on with her because I wanted to get away from Polaris, not help them."

"Signed on?" Ching leaned forward.

I had her full attention now, and I held out my right hand with the mark sliced into it.

"A recent recruit," she pointed out. "That's quite a coincidence, don't you think?"

"Not really." I shrugged. "Archipelago hasn't done much to help my family or me. My dad's a drifter. He told me where to find Miranda. He said she might give me a better deal if I had something to trade. I can't speak for my captain, but she didn't have my information before. Maybe she was waiting to contact you until she had something worthwhile."

Ching's face looked skeptical.

"You really haven't sailed with Miranda for long if you believe that. How about this, Mere. I'll hear the information. If it's any good, I'll give you access to the Gulf, but there's a trade embargo on the Archipelago stations. You want something, you trade with my ships, and all trades with the mines get cleared with me. These are my waters now, and you'll play by my rules."

Miranda slowly resheathed her sword. I was not so quick to relax, nor was I fooled by her sudden change in tactic.

Our plans hung by a thread, and Ching Shih held the shears.

"Compass Rose. That's an interesting name," Ching said to me after everyone else had left the room.

I didn't know what to say. Things were happening too quickly. I had thought, for one brief, foolish second, that I would have time to talk to Miranda before Ching started her interrogation.

I could not have been more wrong.

Now, here I was, sitting at the deserted table with the most dangerous woman on the water.

"Is that your given name?" she asked, when it became clear to us both that I was incapable of an intelligent response.

"Yes. My mother chose it."

"I assumed, when I first heard it, that you had taken it for yourself. That's how most of us do it out here. Kraken. Orca. Miranda didn't, but she's stubborn."

"What about you?" I managed to ask, my voice coming out in something that was more than a squeak, but would not have qualified as a bold retort by any jury.

"My mother lacked your mother's foresight. Your Archipelago gave me my name, a long time ago. You know the legend of Ching Shih?"

"She was an ancient Chinese pirate queen."

"She was arguably the most powerful pirate in human history, Chinese or otherwise," Ching said, dismissing my explanation. "She was born a prostitute, but by the time she retired she commanded tens of thousands of pirates. I was not born a prostitute, in case you were wondering."

"I wasn't," I said.

"Nor did I have to marry anyone to get my first ship. Here's to progress." She raised her mug in a tiny toast. "But I suspect that my heritage, combined with my reputation, made Ching Shih a logical nickname. My given name is significantly less intimidating. Only my mother still uses it."

"Oh."

Why is she telling me this? My unease deepened.

"If you had chosen your name for yourself, I might have more faith in your abilities. That level of arrogance would have to be backed by competence for you to still be alive today. The fact that your mother gambled with your life, giving you a name like that, is less reassuring. Are you as good as they say?"

As who says?

"I'm good."

"Then why are you here? The Archipelago is not in the habit of letting valuable tools slip out of their hands."

"I deserted."

"You left Polaris for *this*?" she said, disbelief written across her face.

"Not everyone on the Archipelago is happy with the status quo."

"And yet most of them still prefer grumbling from the comfort of their stations. What made you different?"

"Do you want my coordinates or not?" I crossed my arms over my chest. "Does it matter why I'm here?"

"I hope your sense of direction is better than your ability to lie. Of course it matters why you're here. Why would I trust coordinates given to me by an Archipelagean loyalist?"

"I'm not a loyalist."

"But you are. If you weren't, Miranda would not have tried to keep you out of my sight."

"My mother is an eel farmer on Cassiopeia. My father was a drifter. Polaris barely tolerated me, and the council has not done anything to defend my home station. I am not a loyalist."

"Miranda's crew thinks you were sent for a reason. You don't seem to be very well tolerated here, either."

"I was picked up by Miranda's sailors after my captain tried to place me off ship. I should have been promoted. Instead, she sent me to work on a fucking trawler, like a drifter. I was the best navigator in my class. Maybe the best Polaris had ever seen, and she threw me away. So yes. I deserted. I found a drifter who could take me to Miranda, and now I'm here. I don't care who Miranda sides with or what she does. This is my ship, and I follow her orders."

The best lies were always composed of half-truths.

"And what are her orders?"

"To keep off the radar," I said.

"Even from me?"

"Even from you."

"I don't suppose she told you why?" she asked.

"No. And I didn't ask."

A tight pause followed my words. The other woman looked at me, and it occurred to me that conversation was just one of many options for her. There were other, more persuasive ways she could get information out of me. The thought sent a shudder of nausea through me.

"Do you know how Miranda got her scars?" Ching Shih held out her forearm.

I leaned in, against my better judgment, to get a better look.

Faint, long, tendrils of scars curled from her fingers up to her elbow. They were not as pronounced as Miranda's, but the marks were disconcertingly familiar.

"No," I admitted.

"Four years ago, I was sailing on some business along the Northern Equatorial Current. We were surprised by a large swarm of man o' war. I kept us topside, as we were having trouble with the bilge pumps. My lookout spotted something in the water. We didn't know it was human at first, and once we discovered that it was we almost left it. It should have been a corpse. Have you ever been stung by a man o' war, Rose?"

Her question echoed something Miranda had said to me.

"No," I said.

"It's excruciating. I know. I pulled her out of the water myself. She was hardly recognizable beneath all of the stings, and I got stung in the process."

She glanced at her arm.

"This was right around the same time as that nasty business with Gemini station. I'd had some dealings with the drifters near there, and even I was horrified by what I heard about the Council's retaliation. It made me look positively friendly. When they told me the woman in the swarm was alive, I was curious. I went out in the skiff myself. She'd wrapped sargassum around her body, although how she managed to stay conscious long enough for that has puzzled me for years. It did give her some protection, but she'd been stung so many times by then that her skin was more laceration than flesh. She'd been out there for days. It was the man o' war themselves that kept her afloat toward the end. I think they shocked her back to life each time her body died."

Bile rose in my throat.

"What struck me most, though, were her eyes. She has incredible eyes, doesn't she? Enough to spark a rebellion, and enough to convince me to haul what was left of her into my boat."

My mind trembled, looking for a way out. Ching went on, ruthless.

"She couldn't speak coherently for the first few weeks. The shock of everything was quite literal—I believe the pain drove her insane for some time—but I was curious about what kind of person survives days at sea in a swarm. When I found out who she was, I offered her a place on my ship. Even I had to admire that kind of resilience."

You knew she sailed with her, I reminded myself. *And you were an idiot not to find out more.*

"It took her a week to remember she was human. I nursed her myself, captain to captain. My contact, the drifter, showed up a few days later, asking to sign on to my ship. He couldn't stomach the Archipelago after he saw how they treated the rebels. You know him, too, I believe. He was the only one who could get through to her, when she finally stopped screaming. Told her the only monster in the room was him. He's been Kraken ever since."

Kraken had left that particular detail out of his story.

"I made her my first mate after six months. She was a gift from Neptune himself, with her broken ideals and her thirst for revenge. I learned more about your Archipelago in that year than I had from a decade of raiding."

Ching's eyes never left my face.

"She was your first mate?" I repeated.

"She helped me raise the Red Flag Fleet."

The room spun.

"Why are you telling me this?" I asked.

"I made Miranda. Whatever little plot you think you can hatch, remember that. Your people broke her and threw away the pieces, and I put them back together. She owes who she is now to me."

"I'm just a navigator," I said, in a voice that barely made it above a whisper.

"Which is funny," Ching said, "because I have never met anyone less sure of where she was headed."

"Well, that went better than I anticipated," Orca said as she towed me away from the room.

"How so?" I drooped with exhaustion.

Numbed by Ching's revelation, I had sat, stunned, while she

206

grilled me for several hours about fleet coordinates, pulling far more out of me than I had intended to give. If she launched a full-scale attack against the Archipelago, I would bear a significant brunt of responsibility for her success.

Me, and Miranda.

"She helped me raise the Red Flag fleet."

I clenched my fists to get her voice out of my head, bringing me back to the present. I could not afford to think about Miranda. Not now. Possibly not ever again.

"We're all alive, for starters," Orca said.

"Ching still has control of the ship, and now she'll be watching us." I leaned on Orca, too tired to care what the first mate thought.

"Don't be an idiot. She was always going to be watching us. That's why it would have been convenient if she had just parleyed with me, instead of the captain. Having the two of them together in the same room is a recipe for disaster. Good news, though. You've got your own quarters, now."

"What? Why?"

"Thanks to you, there was a little unrest while you were gone. I had to relieve a few sailors of their berths."

"Where are they now?"

"Davy Jones's."

Orca's face had a grim cast about it, and for a moment I almost felt a touch of pity for the first mate. She had not had an easy few days. Then the rest of her words registered.

"Thanks to me? What the hell did I do?"

"You're here. That's bad enough." She stopped at a door and opened it, revealing a small room with a hammock and a wash basin.

"I didn't ask to be here," I said, more tired than I could ever remember being.

Orca spoke low and fiercely into my face, forcing me to stare into her eyes. They looked like twin hurricanes.

"Before you came, Miranda took my advice. The crew respected me. Now she takes your advice, and they want to know why. They don't see any gain in helping you and your kind. They

207

liked it better, most of them, when she sailed with Ching. And me? I have to deal with all of you. Less than a week, and I had to put down a mutiny. I know why Miranda's doing this, but that sort of logic doesn't mean shit to sailors who have never known the luxury of security."

She grabbed the front of my shirt and pulled me closer, until I could see the shadows of her eyelashes on her cheeks.

"Keep your distance from the captain, jelly, if you know what's good for you. And her."

With a shove, she pushed me away from her into the room and slammed the door in my face, leaving me out of breath and dizzy. I heard the sound of her boots as she stormed away.

A mutiny. The fact that I had suspected as much was no comfort. I sank to the floor with my back to the door and stared at the hammock.

People had died while Miranda had kissed me. People had died because Miranda had kissed me. Kraken's warning came back to me. "The main crew won't like it. She's dangerous, Mere."

You should have listened to him, I thought.

I should have listened to him. I was a threat to everything and everyone I loved. Not only had I just revealed much of the Archipelago's patrols and positions to the greatest enemy the Archipelago had ever faced, but I had foolishly allowed myself to put my happiness before all else, placing my mission, my people, and even Miranda at risk.

Miranda, who had survived days at sea in excruciating pain. Miranda, who had more reason to hate the Archipelago than I had thought possible.

Ching was right. I didn't know my captain, not like she did. I did not know what Miranda was capable of, and I did not know what drove her. My heart ached for her suffering even as it clenched in fear.

What made Comita so sure Miranda was on our side?

For that matter, what made me so sure I could trust Miranda?

As long as my body overrode my mind, I could not keep a

clear heading. Miranda was a distraction. A dangerous distraction. If I wasn't careful, I was going to get everyone killed.

Including her.

No more. Ching Shih was here, and I would do what I had to do to bring her down, even if that meant turning my back on the one person besides Harper who had ever made me feel wanted, valuable, and human. As the Archipelago had four years ago, I would throw Miranda away.

Chapter Fourteen

"Change of plans."

Miranda had called another council, this time without Ching Shih. The pirate captain had retreated to her own ship, for the moment, but we followed in her wake. Orca, Kraken, Miranda, and I stared at her empty chair.

"I need to call a full council soon, once I replace a few sailors," she continued, her eyes hard, "and what I say to you I cannot say to them."

She had taken the news of the mutiny better than I'd expected, not that she had shared her thoughts with me. I had steered clear of her, too many conflicting emotions jockeying for my attention.

"This was always a possible outcome. We sprang a leak, and Orca patched it, but not before Ching got wind of things."

Orca wove thunderheads between her braids.

"It is unfortunate that Ching knows about our trawler, and even more unfortunate that she has facial recognition on Rose, but that doesn't change things. Leaving the mines in Ching's hands will lead to disaster. The crew can't see that, clearly, but they don't know her like I do. She's just as bad as the worst parts of the Archipelago, if not worse, and the only equality they'll get from her is an equally bad deal. Ching is in it for herself."

There was a bitterness in her voice I had never heard before.

"So," she continued, "it is time to fall back on plan B. I stay here, and keep Ching occupied. Orca, it's your turn to trawl."

Orca's eyebrows raised. "What about your navigator?" she asked.

Not even Miranda could miss the poison in Orca's words.

"She stays with me. I need her to track Ching's movements, and the best way to do that is by keeping her close to Ching."

"Close to you, you mean." Orca crossed her arms over her chest.

"First mate," Miranda began, but I cut her off.

"She's right. Not about that part, maybe," I backtracked, trying not to blush at the implications in Orca's accusation, "but I shouldn't be on this ship. I should be on the trawler. I am your best shot at navigating undetected."

And I need to stay far, far away from you, Captain. I met her eyes and felt my resolve waver. I pasted a mental image of Harper's face, bludgeoned and bloody from a pirate raid, and Miranda, lying unconscious in the helm of the trawler after putting her life before mine.

"And when Ching discovers you're not on this ship? She'll kill you, when she finds you," said my captain.

"She won't find me."

"No, she won't, because you'll stay here, where I can guarantee your safety. Too much is riding on you." Miranda dismissed me with a look, and turned back toward Orca.

I took a deep breath.

"Captain, I promised to serve you and obey you, but I am your navigator. You cannot guarantee my safety, no matter where I am. Let me do what I came here for. Let me navigate the coast."

Miranda's shoulders straightened, and she turned toward me slowly, blue eyes snapping.

"I'll go with her, Mere," Kraken said, placing a hand on her shoulder. "She's right."

"I'm the only monster here," he'd told Miranda. How many of Ching's words were true, and how many were chosen to unsettle me?

The three of us watched her. Captains and officers, in my experience, did not enjoy being overruled, especially in front of others. Miranda's scars stood out against her rage-white face as she surveyed us, and I suspected our words came too close on the heels of a near mutiny to merit forgiveness.

"If that is the best course, then there is no discussion," she said, and my heart broke at the coldness in her eyes.

Ching's escort took us close to the coast, so close that I could see flocks of birds if I climbed to the crow's nest. It was the only part of our ship that breached the surface; the air above the water was foul with hydrogen sulfide and the surface thick with algae. What sunlight managed to filter through had a dank, dappled, green quality that did not bode well for the ship's hydrofarm or solar cells.

As thick as the surface was with algae, the depths were thicker still with pirates. The scope of Ching's force was breathtaking. She'd pulled an armada out of floating scrap, transforming half-rigged tubs and salvaged, decommissioned fleet ships into flotillas of raiders—but the real threat lay in the sleek, dark ships that sailed just out of sight, similar in size to the ones that had escorted us into the heart of her territory. This was the Red Flag Fleet, and while the Archipelago still far outnumbered them, I had a sneaking suspicion that the materials in the mines were being put to good use by Ching in the coastal shipyards.

This was why I had to go. I had to know if she was building more ships, and how long it would take before starving the Archipelago of resources became mere entertainment, and she could take the stations by force.

First, however, I had to find a way past her fleet.

"There." Crow's Eye pointed, breaking my concentration. "Land."

I scrambled past him, pressing myself against the plastic and heedless of the bottle of piss at my feet. There was a slight haze against the northern horizon, but nothing more.

"Look through this." He pulled out a pair of binoculars and handed them to me.

I pressed them to my eyes and gasped.

These were no islands. As far as I could see, the coast stretched on and on, a low lumpy mass of solid ground that looked as endless as the ocean itself. It sent a thrill of hope and fear through me.

"It's something, isn't it?" Crow's Eye tone was reverent.

"It's beautiful."

It wasn't, not really, not this far away, but the thought of it was the most beautiful thing in the world—and the most appalling. A place where ships could not sail, where you could not escape the storms by diving beneath the waves, and where water was a scarcity, not a given.

"I wonder if I could navigate on land," I said, voicing a curiosity best left unspoken.

"About as well as I could walk, Compass Rose." He slapped the stumps of his legs with a laugh. "We've no immunity now to their pestilences. We've lost the way of it."

"How close have you sailed?"

"Close enough to smell it." He closed his eyes, as if remembering.

"How close could a small craft get?"

"How small are we talking?" He opened one eye. "Say, a trawler?"

"Hypothetically, yes."

"Pretty close, if she had a good skipper and knew the waters."

"How about Ching's ships? You know more about them than I do. Any pirate craft small enough to follow?"

"Sure, a few. Scouts. But no sailor alive would risk it. Waters are too treacherous. They say there are sunken cities there that flood the sonar with the cries of the damned and drag them to the bottom. More like run them aground, but there you have it."

"Interesting," I said, an idea forming in my mind.

"Interesting gets you killed, kid," he told me with a pointed pat on the hand.

I handed back the binoculars.

"Thanks, Crow's Eye."

"One more thing." He swiveled around. "There are sailors on

213

this ship who would like to see you dead for what you represent. I'm not one of them."

I blushed, unsure how to express how much his words meant to me.

"If you take the coastal route, remember this, kid. The most dangerous thing in the ocean will always be other people. And watch out for squid."

Squid? As I descended, I wondered if Crow's Eye was missing more than just his legs.

"Rose."

I froze on the last few rungs of ladder. The chart room had been empty when I entered, but it was occupied now by the last person on this ship I wanted to see.

"Captain," I said, dropping to the ground.

"I should order you to stay here," she said, her face only slightly less livid than it had been the last time I saw her.

"Why? It doesn't make sense." I kept my hands clasped behind my back, resisting the urge to touch her.

"I need you on this ship. Stay, and I'll make you second mate."

I tried not to focus on how the first three words had sounded. Then the gravity of her last statement sank in.

Second mate? I wavered. Harper's words came back to me.

"Wouldn't it be worth it, if you could be a navigator in your own right?"

Being second mate to Miranda was too much. I couldn't think. It was everything I had ever wanted, and accepting was the last thing I could do. I watched, as if I were in a dream, as a series of images paraded themselves before me.

Me, at the helm, with Miranda at my side. Miranda, Kraken, and I sitting down for a drink in the ship's bar. Waking up next to Miranda, day after day. Even sparring with Orca had become part of the fabric of my life.

I wavered.

Even if Miranda hadn't been Miranda Stillwater, I still had a duty to Admiral Comita, and unlike a mercenary I was not free to make my own choices.

"You need me to find out what else Ching is doing, more," I said, my head still spinning. "You were happy enough sending Orca, and she's your first mate. You have other people who can navigate."

"Orca is prepared. Orca is . . ." She trailed off, and I was glad Orca was not here. For all that I hated the first mate, Miranda's blindness to Orca's jealousy seemed unnecessarily cruel.

"Orca is what?" I asked.

"Replaceable."

I stared at her, and I didn't need to hold my hands back anymore. For the first time since I'd laid eyes on her, Miranda Stillwater repulsed me. I tried to cling to the feeling.

"How can you say that?"

"I didn't realize you cared so much for her," Miranda said, her face still a mask of carefully controlled anger.

"I don't, but she—"

"She is one of mine, and I would lay my life down for her in a heartbeat, but first mates can be trained. What you have cannot."

"So I'm a tool."

"Neptune's balls, Rose, we're all tools." She looked up at the ceiling.

I hoped she found inspiration there, because I had nothing for her.

"Then let me do my job."

"Fine. If that's the way you want it, fine. But if you get yourself killed it's not just your Admiral you have yourself to answer to. I'll drag your ass out of Davy Jones's myself."

She closed the distance between us and the momentary repulsion passed.

"No point in flogging a corpse, Captain. The Archipelago will be fine. You'll be fine. There are other navigators. Look hard enough, and you might even find one half as good as me." I gave her a weak smile.

"Don't be an ass, Rose," she said, and for a moment I was back in the helm of the trawler with my arms around her neck, losing myself and my sense of purpose beneath her. I shook my head to clear it.

"I can't do this," I said in a half-whisper that cut through me.

"You don't have to. Stay here. I'll send someone else out." She took my shoulders in her hands.

"Not that. This."

I gestured at her, then at myself, and her face froze.

"Remember what I told you, Rose? I don't care who my crew fucks, as long as it doesn't distract them from their duties. I over-estimated you. If you can't stay focused, then you're right. You can't do this."

The injustice of her words felt like a slap to the face, complete with the involuntary, hot prick of tears.

"You think I'm distracted? What about you, Miranda? You just tried to keep me from doing my job." My voice shook.

"You're not a distraction." Miranda's voice chilled by degrees. "You're a compass, and I'm a captain. Forgive me for wanting to keep my tools close at hand."

"What was all that about guaranteeing my safety then?" I was shouting, and I didn't care.

"I've got a lot riding on you, Rose. But you're right. This, this right here, is distracting me. I can't afford to waste my time listening to this bullshit with Ching on my ass. You think you'll be of more use to me out there? Then go. But whatever you think is going on between us is over when you come back. You are my tool. Nothing more."

"Okay," I said, swallowing the words. They settled like stones.

"Okay what?"

"Okay, Captain."

She slammed the door behind her, my last word echoing around the empty chart room. I swallowed that emptiness, too, and it came to rest beside the stones, as lifeless and barren as the bottom of the sea.

❄ ✦ ⚓ ✑ ✿

I probably would not have risked it, if it had not been for my encounter with Miranda, but later that day I tracked down Orca to finalize our departure. Her mood didn't look much better than mine, which was something of a small comfort.

"We're leaving tomorrow morning," I said to her, cutting her off mid-tirade as she yelled at a group of passing sailors.

"And how the hell do you plan on doing that?" she asked.

My plan was simple, if a little crazy. *Man o' War* was in need of supplies from the mines, and our trawler was just the sort of vessel suited for making a short delivery run, not to mention the fact that we carried a load of salvaged parts and supplies in our hold that the mines certainly could use. As long as I stayed out of sight and Miranda came up with a decent excuse for my absence from her ship, I thought we stood a chance, at least for a little while.

How I would stay out of sight during Ching's inspection was another matter entirely, and one that held little appeal. I decided not to think about that just yet, and filled Orca in on the details of my plan.

"Huh," she said, in a voice that suggested that just because she couldn't find fault with my plan now did not mean she would not blame me later if things went wrong. "What happens once we've finished trading?"

"We hide along the coast and see what else Ching is up to."

"The coast." Orca stopped walking and stared at me. "Do you have a death wish, jelly?"

"I might, after a day or two sailing with you," I said.

To my surprise, Orca gave a short laugh.

"I could always kill you myself and spare the rest of us," she said.

"So much less satisfying that way for me, though."

"You really think there's enough space in Davy Jones's for the two of us?" she asked.

"Well," I said, continuing down the hallway, "it wouldn't be hell without you."

We inspected the vessel together; Orca didn't trust the launching crew, and I didn't want to be alone with my thoughts. Hating Orca was a welcome distraction.

"You ever been in a trawler before?" I asked, watching her run her hands over the controls in the helm. The contrast between the unpleasant tension between me and Orca and the memory of the far more pleasant, if equally destructive, tension between me and Miranda grated on my nerves. I wouldn't even be allowed to keep those memories pure.

Stop thinking about her, I scolded myself. *She made herself clear. You're done.*

North, south, east, west. I would not cry over Miranda Stillwater. Especially not in front of Orca.

"I have standards," she said. It took me a moment to remember what I'd asked her, and another moment to realize that she'd insulted me.

"Your mother didn't," I said, and just like that the brief respite I'd had while trawling with Miranda, Kraken, Finnegan, and Jeanine might as well have never happened. At least Orca and I were just trading insults, for now, instead of blows.

"I hope you sail better than you fight," she said.

It was an uncharacteristically weak comeback, and I glanced at her, almost concerned. She was staring out the helm, one hand absentmindedly touching the wheel. There was nothing beyond the glass worth looking at.

"Well," I said, deciding I didn't care, "I'm going to go see what's in the hold for the inventory."

"You do that," she said, still lost.

I paused at the doorway.

"Orca," I said, not really sure why I bothered. "You want to grab a drink?"

"Not really."

"Suit yourself." I turned to go.

"I'd rather beat the shit out of someone. You game?"

We sized each other up.

Now that she mentioned it, punching Orca sounded like exactly what I wanted to do.

We walked to the training room in silence. It was empty, which suited my mood, and I wrapped my hands with vengeful precision.

"Whatever you think is going on between us is over."

That was what I'd wanted, wasn't it? To keep the chain of command clear? To end any entanglements that would make it impossible for me to do my job, and to eliminate the conflict of interest that was part and parcel of Miranda's identity?

That didn't make it hurt any less.

Orca stretched, her lithe body warming up to do what it did best: bruise.

Maybe it was just fun for her, I thought, jumping up and down on my toes to loosen my legs. *Emotions were overrated anyway.*

I did not fool myself. I was not Harper, who had mastered the casual fling by seventeen, nor was I capable of that level of self-denial.

I sized up Orca. It had been a week, at least, since we'd sparred, and I felt oddly calm. She couldn't hurt me any more than I'd already hurt myself, and she looked less intimidating, now that I'd seen pirates and dead bodies, and sold my people to Ching Shih.

We danced around each other for a few steps. I knew Orca's pattern. She always made the first move, and she struck low and hard.

This time, I struck first.

It threw her off, and she took a step back. I struck again, getting past her guard and landing a blow on her upper arm.

It felt good.

I moved in again, and again, forcing her back across the mat until she let out a growl of frustration and launched herself at me in a flurry of feet and fists. I edged away, smiling. Whatever was bothering Orca clearly had thrown her off her game.

"What," I taunted, "losing your touch?"

I was rewarded with a kick to the side that sent me staggering backward.

"Don't get cocky, fleeter."

I grunted in pain and lashed out with a left hook that took her in the jaw.

The look on her face as she caught her balance was almost worth the agony inside my chest, compounded now with pain from what felt like several ruptured organs.

Pure and unadulterated shock flitted across her features, sending ripples through her gray eyes.

"You hit me."

I hit her again.

The anger that felt like it had been boiling inside me for as long as I could remember erupted. I kept my core tight and my muscles loose, and I rained blows down on Orca like a cat o' nine tails.

She fought with all her strength, but she didn't have despair riding her like a whitecap, and I brought her to the ground in a tangle of sweat and blood.

"Fuck you," she said, as I pinned her arms over her head.

I had busted open her cheek, and a trickle of blood ran down her face onto the mat, but her nose and perfect teeth, which I had at one point vowed to break, remained intact.

Her eyes had flecks of green in them, like islands lost in fog. Her skin shone with sweat.

I didn't say anything. Her braids fanned out around her head, the tiny shells white against the stained mat and her black hair. I remembered the panic in her eyes after she'd beaten me, lifting my shirt over my head in the shower, snarling as she walked me in front of her, keeping the discontented mercenaries at bay.

I didn't feel panicked. I didn't know what I felt.

"Don't have anything to say?"

Orca's taunt bounced off me. It was fragile, like her, and brittle as glass.

I looked at her. Really looked at her, and the girl beneath me looked back.

"God damn you, Compass Rose," she said.

My hands tightened on her wrists. Something dark and force-ful pulled me toward her, like filaments to a lodestone, and I let my anger and betrayal guide me as the cardinal points fell silent.

I kissed her, surprising us both, and then her body surged beneath me and she met me with a passion that matched me grief for grief, despair opening up a hunger that went bone deep. I couldn't get enough of her lips, but she turned her head, her eyes closed and her breath coming quickly, and when I hesitated she broke one hand free from my grasp and pulled me down toward her, the roughness of the gesture breaking down the last of my inhibitions. I kissed her neck, her skin smooth and yielding beneath my lips and teeth, and Orca wrapped her hand in my hair and begged me with her body not to stop.

Her hips pressed against mine, and she moved beneath me with an urgency that quickened my blood, her breath warm against my ear.

I moved down her throat and toward her shoulder, tasting the clean sweat on her skin, and then she slid her leg between mine and I gasped, following the motion of her hips as she drove all conscious thought from my grateful mind.

This is what I needed. Violence. Oblivion. Lust.

"When you're finished here," said a voice that poured over me like a bucket of ice water, "we have work to do."

Orca and I broke apart, and if I had thought I was heartbroken before, it was nothing compared to the look on Miranda's face.

She turned her back on us and walked back out of the training room, her shoulders stiff and my insides trailing after her.

Orca and I exchanged an agonized look, united, at last, in guilt.

The knock on my door disrupted the slow swing of my hammock. I rolled out, not caring that my eyes were bloodshot and my clothes rumpled.

Please be Miranda, I thought, even as my heart pounded with dread.

Kraken filled the doorway.

"Are you here to drown me?" I asked, shoving my hands in my pockets to hide their spasm of disappointment.

"I thought about it," he said, looking me up and down.

I squinted up at his face. It was hard to tell when he was joking with those damned tattoos.

"Here," he said, tossing me a flask. "You look like you need this."

Rum. Rum sounded nice.

"So you're not going to kill me?" I asked as he stepped around me, filling the room with his bulk.

"I'm a cook, not an executioner."

Something about his tone warned me that beneath his casual words was a layer of very real anger.

"Miranda," I said, making her name both a question and an explanation.

He sank into the chair, and I climbed back into the hammock, rocking myself back and forth with one foot.

"Why'd you do it, Rose?"

"I don't know," I said. So many things had seemed clear only a few hours ago.

"Calling it off was the right decision. She should have done that herself before she got back to the ship. Orca, though." He shook his head.

I took a drink and offered the flask back to him to avoid meeting his eyes.

"Is she okay?"

"Miranda? She'll be fine, or as fine as she needs to be."

"Shouldn't you be getting her drunk?" I asked.

"She's more than capable of doing that alone. Besides," he said, taking a swig, "someone's got to make sure nobody kills you before you get on that trawler tomorrow."

"Let me guess. You drew the short straw?"

"I volunteered. Wanted to make sure you hadn't cracked. I don't want to deal with any squidshit from my navigator while we're near the coast."

"I'll be fine," I said.

222

"You damn well better be."

"Yes sir," I said before I could stop myself.

He laughed.

"I'm drifter trash, kid. Don't call me sir."

"Yes, Kraken."

"That's better. Enjoying Andre's quarters?"

"Andre?" I flinched at the thought of the sailor with the blood-stained whip who'd made his dislike of me so clear when I first arrived.

"He led the mutiny while Miranda was off ship. Orca walked him."

Making him the second person to die because of me. I reached for the rum.

"Maybe he was right," I said. "Not to mutiny, but about the Archipelago. They wouldn't even allow him on a station, let alone thank him. Why help a nation that would rather see you dead than benefit from their technology?"

"You're Polaris's prodigy, kid. You tell me."

"Why is Miranda really helping the Archipelago, anyway?" I asked him, ignoring his comment.

"That's Miranda's business."

"Ching told me what happened."

Kraken look pierced through the rum.

"Do you really want to know?"

I nodded.

Kraken took a long pull of the rum, nearly emptying the flask.

"I told you my family trawled near Gemini. I met Miranda shortly after she was made captain. She should never have been appointed that young, but Gemini station couldn't resist her."

There was a familiar bitterness in his words.

"I hated her, the first time I met her. She seemed too good to be true. She wanted to open a medical center for drifters, and she came down to the quarantine docks to talk to us. This was right after I'd lost my family. I gave her a piece of my mind."

He shook his head a little, as if remembering.

"She listened. That's what surprised me. Called me Kraken,

because all I wanted to do at that time was pull everyone around me down to Davy Jones's. She came back to talk to me a few times. Gave me that pair of dice, and promised they were lucky. Said she always won with them.

"There were a lot of raids that year. Ching had just moved into Archipelago territory, and Gemini didn't have a large enough fleet to hold them off. The Council refused to send in reinforcements. One of Miranda's brothers was a captain on a ship Ching's sailors sacked, and she snapped a little when he died. Started talking about seceding from the Archipelago if they didn't start intervening. She wasn't the only one who felt that way, but she was the loudest. She sent her demands to the Council, threatening secession if they didn't provide more ships. In response, they shut down the mutiny and destroyed half the station. You've never seen so much blood, Rose."

"Pirates attacked Gemini," I said, wishing there was more rum. Kraken's story directly contradicted the official report.

"Pirates were there, but no pirate ship at that time could do what the Council did. They threatened to sink the station if Gemini didn't stand down and give up the ringleaders. Miranda chose to walk herself, rather than face the Council. When they couldn't get her, they executed the others, but they named it the Stillwater Mutiny for a reason, and her family paid the price."

"What do you mean?"

"They executed her parents, and her surviving siblings were stripped of all rank."

This was too much information to absorb. Kraken's voice continued to flow around me, while my mind struggled to keep up with the changing coordinates.

"I joined up with Ching right after the mutiny. I couldn't stay near Gemini after that, and I was tired of trawling anyway. When I heard that Ching had pulled a woman out of the water, I identified her. I was the one who told her about her family. You could say we bonded over our mutual hatred of the Council. Ching fueled that hatred, and Miranda used what she'd learned as a fleet captain to help Ching rally the Red Flag Fleet and hit the Archipelago where they were weakest."

This was not what I wanted to hear.

"Why did she change?"

"She won a ship in a game of Crown and Anchor from one of Ching's captains. Changed the name to *Man o' War*, can't imagine why. She was a different person when she was away from Ching. Ching knew it, too, but she also knew keeping Miranda on a tight leash would only piss her off."

"What's the debt Ching was talking about?"

"Miranda owes Ching her life. That's a serious debt out here."

"Is that why Miranda hates her?"

"She doesn't hate Ching. She just doesn't agree with her. Ching's vision of the future is not that different from your Council's, only Ching would put herself in charge, and kick the Archipelago citizens to the seven seas and call it justice. Miranda has been fighting for a middle ground her whole life. She doesn't want to trade one tyrant for another."

"But the crew thinks Ching Shih has the right of it, don't they?" I asked.

"Some of them. Not as many as you think."

"What do you think?"

"Me? I think people fuck up power, no matter who they are. You?"

"I think I'm drunk."

"There are worse things to be, kid."

I rolled out of bed with a hangover the size of the Pacific and a hole in my chest that wasn't much smaller. I seriously contemplated drowning myself in the shower rather than eating breakfast. Jeanine took one look at me and rolled her eyes, muttering something under her breath that I did not care to decipher as I took my seat at the captain's table for what might be the last time. Orca and I sat ourselves on opposite sides, and Miranda ignored both of us. I tried not to look at Andre's empty chair.

We all departed from the mess hall separately. Miranda's cover for my absence was all too believable; there was just too much work to do. It would be easy enough to claim that I was working through meals, and if things went according to my plan, we would be back before anyone grew too suspicious.

Kraken arrived at the vessel bay first. He was alone. I wondered how he had managed to dismiss the usual bay crew, but didn't ask as I slipped down the hatch. He had done it, which was the important thing, and now all I had to do was hide until we were past Ching's ships.

This was the part I had been dreading, although this morning I was past caring. There was only one place to hide on the trawler where I was sure I was not going to be found, and it was the last place on earth I wanted to be.

Well, second to last. The first was definitely inside my own head.

I wanted to take back yesterday. I wanted to expunge it from the record, and I really, really didn't want to be on a trawler with Orca.

"Are you ready?" Kraken asked from behind me.

I swallowed hard and nodded as he handed me an oxygen tank and mask. Memories of my near fatal squidding expedition flashed through my mind.

Kraken led the way to the port side bulkhead and opened the maintenance hatch.

"It won't be for long," he promised, patting me on the shoulder.

"If I drown," I said, looking at the salt-stained walls, "tell . . ." I trailed off. Tell who, what? I had nothing to say that could be said out loud, and no way of getting a message back to Polaris. "Tell Orca I'll save her a place in the locker."

That should be reason enough to live, I figured as I climbed inside. If I drowned, my last words would be delivered to Orca, instead of to the people I loved.

Air hissed as the ocean flooded in. I was grateful for the diving suit I found stowed inside, courtesy of Kraken, and pulled it on over my clothes in the darkness as the trawler took on water and sank through the first airlock.

226

I had no idea how long I would be stuck in here. This oxygen tank was much larger than the one I'd used with Annie, and in theory should last me at least twelve hours. If it took longer than that, I would start wishing I was dead, anyway.

The total blackness was disorienting. I hung on to the hatch handle as water flooded in around me, rising past my ankles, then my knees, then my waist, and finally over my head. I had to force myself to listen to my inner compass. Every instinct in my body screamed that I was trapped, with no way to tell up or down, only the crushing pressure of the ocean pressing all around me.

Hours passed, giving me too much time to think. I could not hear anything, and despite the suit and the warmth of the water I grew chilled and huddled up around the door like a piece of lonely flotsam while the tears I had not spilled the night before flowed freely.

Sobbing while on an oxygen tank takes a special kind of skill. I nearly drowned before I calmed myself down, but not before my mask fogged up and the tears pooled at the bottom, stinging my cheeks. I tried not to think about my nose and what might have gathered in my air tube.

Miranda and I were finished before we had even had a chance to become something. I was not naive enough to believe that I had been simple entertainment for her, not with Kraken's warning to her still ringing in my head, but I didn't think her pride would let her acknowledge that now, and what Orca and I had done was unforgivable. There might have been hope before that, but I had seen Miranda's face.

At least you know, now, that she was lying, I thought. *She cares.*

The knowledge came at too high a price, and too late.

With it came another realization: I wanted to stay here, with this crew, despite the attempts on my life, the crappy food, and the murky origins of the captain.

Fat chance of that now.

This was supposed to be a good thing. The right decision. The only decision I could make, really, when I thought about it. Falling in love with a mercenary captain was about as smart as surfacing in a storm, and with similar consequences. Not only was it a violation of my training, but there was no future in it. I would return to Polaris and my fleet, and she would remain a mercenary. Miranda Stillwater would never be welcomed with open arms in the Archipelago, even if she spared us a war. And even if she wanted me, too, I couldn't stay here.

Knowing that didn't make it any easier. Part of me wished it had been Miranda who broke things off, as that would have followed chains of command I was used to. I could follow orders. Making the rules myself was a hell of a lot harder.

Another part of me wished she had fought me. It would not have taken much to make me change my mind. A kiss. A few words. A small declaration of caring.

Then I remembered how cold her voice had sounded as she'd explained why Orca was replaceable, and shuddered.

Orca.

I repressed a vivid memory of the first mate. For someone who jockeyed continually for domination in the ring and on the deck, she had certainly been quick to give it up the minute things got heated.

I had never been as thankful for anything as I was when I heard the hiss of compressed air forcing the water in the bulkhead back out again, freeing me from darkness and my thoughts. I pulled off the mask and scrubbed my face as soon as there was enough airspace, hoping my eyes were not as red as they felt. When the water stabilized a foot or so below the hatch, I floated by the ladder and waited.

"Ready to eat something?" Kraken asked, swinging the hatch open and spilling beautiful, blessed light into the bulkhead.

I clambered out to drip on the floor before him.

"You have no idea." I stripped out of the suit and took the offered towel, then followed him to the common room.

It looked the same as before, only with Orca sitting in Miranda's seat. The comparison did not boost my mood.

"You look like a drowned rat," she said, making a courageous attempt at returning to how things had been before.

And you look as miserable as I feel.

"How did the inspection go?" I asked instead.

Orca was the first mate, and as such the acting captain on this vessel. I would follow her lead.

"We hid most of the grain in the other bulkhead," Orca said. "Good thing, too, because they took what we didn't hide."

"Even our supplies?"

"Kraken switched those out into some old drifter grain sacks. Nobody touched them."

She glanced down at the food cooking on the stove, and I hoped Kraken had sterilized the sacks, first. There was a reason not even a pirate would touch drifter foodstuffs.

"So we're good, then?" I wanted to get out of my wet clothes and into something clean and dry.

"For now."

I tried not to dwell on the ominous note in her voice.

Chapter Fifteen

Our trawler bobbed in the murky water, the headlights illuminating the debris field left by the roving Archipelago miners. The central mining station hung suspended over the operation base, a massive ball of bioluminescence in the distance, and a warning ping registered on the sonar, reminding us this was controlled territory.

Finn pinged something back that seemed to satisfy them.

"All right," he said with a grim smile. "We're in."

"In?" I asked.

"These mines have been cut off from supplies for months. Ching occasionally sells the metals back to the Archipelago in exchange for goods she needs, but you can bet your ass these miners haven't seen decent Archipelago grain in weeks. They'll let us on."

The injustice of the trade galled. These were Archipelago mines. We didn't need to buy our own materials, and our miners deserved a decent diet.

"What are we asking for in exchange?"

"Discarded ore and low-grade phosphorous for the trawler. And information," Orca said as she fiddled with the instruments on the panel.

Finn leaned in between us to double-check the helm sonar. I wished he would stay like that indefinitely, a friendly shield between me and the first mate.

"How many pirates do you think will be on the mining station?" I asked.

"Enough to maintain control. Pirates don't like working this deep."

"No one likes working this deep," Finn said with a shudder.

This was where the remnants of the ocean's population lived, bottom-feeders tricked out with glowing eyes and mangled teeth, color rioting around the ocean vents in temperatures hot enough to melt flesh from the bone. My ancestors had spent many generations on the ocean's surface, but down here we were all still strangers.

I did not want to get left behind in the trawler while the rest of the crew did business with the mine. My accent would mark me as Archipelago born and raised, and my eyes were noticeable enough that anyone tracking us would eventually pick up our trail, but that logic didn't make the inevitable any easier.

"Who's boarding?" I got the question out without too much hesitation.

"Not you," Orca said, raising my hackles. "Ching catches wind of you asking questions, and we're all dead."

She was right, of course, but there was one problem with her logic.

"You'll never pass for a drifter," I said, trying to keep my voice neutral. We were much more likely to get reliable information out of the station master if he thought we were drifter scum, too beneath his notice to question, and I didn't think any Archipelagean would open up to mercenaries or pirates, given the current situation.

Orca was a warrior, through and through. Kraken, for his part, may have drifted once, but his tattoos told the story of his more recent past too well, as did Jeanine's. That left me and Finn.

Orca glared at me.

"It's too risky," she said. "And you're too recognizable with those damned creepy eyes of yours."

You didn't seem to mind them the other day.

231

She scowled at me, a hint of color in her cheeks, as if she could read my thoughts.

"Nobody looks a drifter in the eye."

"I should have left you in the bulkhead," she said.

I stifled a triumphant smile at her resigned look.

"Let's get this over with." She turned away from me, and I felt an absurd urge to cry.

"Orca is the best friend you have on this ship," Annie had told me.

I had been so fucking blind.

The docking bay airlock opened for us like a hungry mouth. I tensed as the bay pressurized, leaving us bobbing in the dark while we waited for the station master to send out an inspector. It was too much like my earlier stay in the bulkhead, and I distracted myself by wondering if my father had ever traded with the mines.

I didn't have long to ponder questions I'd never know the answer to. Finn and I clambered out onto the deck, leaving Orca to pace the trawler with Kraken and Jeanine, and stepped over the body of a grotesquely long sea creature that had wrapped itself around the railing. Long tentacles came unstuck from the deck with morbid pops as the creature died.

A light flared into life above us, the cold blue of burning methane. I shielded my eyes with my arm.

"Declare yourselves," said a voice.

"Finnegan, from the *Sea Cat*, here to trade for minerals, and my cousin."

"How many onboard?"

"Three more. No sickness to report."

"How about rats?"

"Can't say as I've seen any," Finn said, "but you know how things are down here. Can't see shit half the time anyway."

"What do you have to trade?" The voice did not sound amused at Finn's joke.

"Foodstuffs and scrap."

"I'll send the inspector over." The voice vanished, leaving me and Finn squinting in the brightness.

"How are we going to get onto the station?" I asked him.

"You'll see."

The inspector was a heavyset man who looked as if he had recently lost a lot of weight. His skin hung loosely on his frame, clad in a poorly fitting Archipelago uniform, and his jowls quivered as he looked us over. His eyes held a mixture of hope and distaste.

"You said you had foodstuffs?"

"Grains and dried fruit. Took it off a wreck. Gotta love those storage pods, eh?"

"A wreck?" The inspector's gaze sharpened.

"Nasty one, mouth of the Gulf. Fleet ship. Good fleet supplies, if you're interested."

"What kind of ship?"

"Wasn't much left by the time we got to it. Warship, maybe, but well supplied."

There was no denying the gleam of hope in the inspector's eyes at Finn's words.

"Did you see any other ships?"

"Mostly the sort my crew and I try to avoid. You cut off or something?" Finn asked, playing dumb.

"What's it to you?" the inspector shifted his stance.

"Might be I could fetch a better price. Any chance I could get a visit with your station's physician?"

"I thought you said there was no sickness onboard."

"I didn't say anything about sickness. It's my cousin here. She's . . ." he paused and gestured at his stomach, miming pregnancy. The inspector gave me a cursory inspection. I kept my eyes downcast.

"Let's see what you got, then," he said.

He glanced over his shoulder at the bay doors, and I shared his unease. Somewhere behind those doors were pirates, and I suspected it was only a matter of time before they made their presence known.

We had removed most of our personal supplies from the cargo bay, leaving only a few bags of grain and dried produce. The prudence of the decision became clear the minute the inspector laid eyes on the goods.

"Is this all you have?" he asked, the hunger in his voice unmistakable.

"For now," Finn said. "Why, you in short supply?"

"Where have you been, drifter?" the inspector asked with a humorless laugh. "We haven't seen a fleet supply ship in months. We've had malnutrition on some of the rigs. Malnutrition, on an Archipelago mining station." He shook his head in disbelief. It was a mark of his desperation that he spoke to us at all.

I grunted under the weight of the grain, following Finn and the inspector across the narrow ramp and through the doors to the weigh station. The inspector logged our vessel and goods, although I noticed that he had a creative way of spelling "grain." His careful scrawl looked a lot more like "plastic sludge."

The omission told me more than his recent weight loss about conditions on the station. The pirates were intentionally depriving the miners. Finn picked up on it, too.

"It's that bad, then?" he asked.

"Keep your eyes where they belong, drifter." He rang a distant bell, and in another minute two men appeared to spirit the food away. Neither bothered sparing me and Finn a glance.

Their timing couldn't have been better. Almost as soon as they departed, the door slammed open again, and a tall woman shouldered into the room with a thunderous expression.

"You're slow to report a vessel, inspector." She drew out the last word, making a mockery of the title. Her clothes were dark, almost black, crossed with Ching's crimson slash. I kept my eyes glued to the ground and my ears pricked.

"It's just a drifter tub, ma'am."

"How did a drifter tub make it into my bay without my knowledge?"

"My apologies, ma'am. I thought it was beneath your interest." The inspector's voice trembled with forced humility and suppressed rage.

"Nothing on this mine is beneath my interest, or beneath the interest of Ching Shih. Remember that, inspector. Now, what do we have here?"

She stepped toward me.

"Ching Shih?" Finn said, distracting the woman before she got too close to me. "I thought this was Archipelago territory, ma'am, or I would never have dared—"

"Shut up." She dismissed him with a curl of her lip and turned back to the inspector. "Consider this your last warning, inspector."

All three of us released our breaths when the woman left the room, and the station master slumped in his seat.

"She's a real piece of work," Finn said.

"She's a Red Flag Fleet officer. They're all like that." He paused. "Did you really not know that Ching controls these waters?"

"Nobody sees a drifter, inspector, so it's best that drifters see as little as possible. Noticing things gets you noticed. However," Finn paused, as if weighing something in his mind, "I might have exaggerated the degree of my ignorance."

"I'll take you to the physician, then," the inspector said.

"How many of those Red Flag sailors do you have on your station?" Finn asked as we navigated tight corridors with oppressively low ceilings.

"Fifteen, but it's enough. Their raiders are never far off."

"How many of those are there?"

"Hell if I know. Too many, and they're building new ships, too, using Archipelago supplies, not that the Archipelago is doing much to stop them." He spat.

My skin crawled at the thought of more of those sleek black vessels preying on the fleets.

We passed a few miners on the way, beaten-looking men and women who stared at us with dull eyes. The ship's doctor didn't look much better. Her black hair was disheveled, and her office offered little in the way of comfort.

"What's this?" she asked the inspector. "You know we don't have any supplies to spare."

"They brought grain, Dr. Torres, and dried fruit."

She let out a sigh of relief that nearly deflated her, and I worried that she might collapse then and there.

"Well then. What's the problem?"

"She's pregnant," the inspector said, much in the same tone of voice he might have used to describe a growing rat infestation.

"And I suppose you want me to do something about it?" The doctor sounded tired.

"No," I said, trying to sound meek and ashamed. "Just want to see if everything's okay this time."

Finn winked at me when the other two weren't looking.

"All right then," the inspector said. "We'll be right outside."

The doctor smiled at me once the door was shut, and I sat on the examination table, my heart beating too fast. Doctors kept careful records. If anyone knew the condition of the miners and the pirates, it would be her.

"Lie back for me," she said.

"What station are you from?" I asked as she pressed on my abdomen.

"Andromeda." She continued her examination, and I tried not to flinch as her cold hands touched my breasts. "You're not pregnant."

"What?" I feigned surprise. "I just hadn't had a period in a few months, so I assumed . . ."

"Could be malnutrition," she said, looking me up and down with a crease between her tired eyes, "although you look healthy enough."

I could hear the unspoken words as clearly as if she had spoken out loud. *But you're a drifter, so you must be deprived of something.*

"As long as I am not pregnant, I don't care."

"Bad time to bring new life into the world, anyway," she said, and the bitterness dripped through.

"My family trades with Andromeda sometimes. If—" I paused for effect, adopting an even more hesitant tone. "I've heard what's going on. Nobody looks at drifters. If there is anything I can do, any message I could send, I don't think anyone would mind."

236

I avoided looking directly in her eyes, but I could feel the sharpness in her gaze. She stopped her examination.

"That could be dangerous for you," she said. "If you're caught with a message, people might think you were a spy." Again the undercurrent surfaced.

Are you a spy? Her thoughts echoed in the cool, white room.

"Just something small. You wouldn't have to write it down or anything. Do you have family there?"

"I do." Her breathing changed. It was subtle, but I guessed that her heart rate was significantly higher now than it had been when she started the exam.

"I can't read anyway, at least not very well," I added.

"I suppose it wouldn't hurt." She paused, clearly thinking hard. "If you go back soon, tell the station master that Doctor Torres has a message for her sister. Tell him to tell her that I am safe, for now, but that she . . ." She paused again. "That she should be prepared for the worst. And tell him to tell my husband that I love him and the boys very much, and that I will miss them." Her voice broke.

"I will do it," I promised.

My heart ached for her, even as her words chilled my blood. *Be prepared for the worst.* The worst what? That Dr. Torres might die, or that the Archipelago was in even more danger than I realized? I did not dare ask. She would be a fool not to suspect me already, but she seemed willing to take a small risk for the sake of hope. Pushing her further could jeopardize everything.

"Thank you. Do you know how to avoid pregnancy?" she asked, her voice now brisk and businesslike.

I allowed her to give me a lecture on contraceptives and tried to glance around the room.

It had been ransacked thoroughly and put back together, judging by hastily repaired cabinet doors and cracked jars. Meticulously labeled shelves stood empty, and I would have bet my dinner that her supply of antibiotics and medications was similarly depleted.

Medicines would be the first thing pirates would go after, of course. Medicine, food, weapons, and the materials to make more weapons.

Finn greeted me cheerfully enough when I finished up my visit with the doctor. The glint in his eye told me that he, too, had learned a few useful things during my appointment. My heart beat uncomfortably fast. I had never been good at acting, and the past few minutes' performance was taking its toll on my nerves.

I hid behind Finn as we walked back to the bay. A burly miner with a pinched face had just finished depositing our newly purchased supplies in the *Sea Cat's* cargo hold, and two others stood guard by the door.

"Not like we're going to cause you trouble, mate," Finn said to the inspector.

"It's not you I'm worried about. Check your ship for stowaways before you sub."

My jaw dropped. It would take a lot for an Archipelagean to stow away on a drifter vessel.

"They won't get far," Finn promised, and I pictured Orca dispatching any miner who dared slip aboard her ship without a flicker of pity.

Despite the precariousness of our position, I was curious. I had never seen a mining station before, and so far this one was looking a little too much like a regular fleet station for my liking. I wanted to see the mines themselves, a wish that I had the sense to hope was not fulfilled, as the only way I was likely to see the mines now was as a slave to Ching Shih.

Finn and I helped load the rest of the cargo, and I watched the inspector's face as we shut the trawler's hold door. Hope faded from it, and I had a feeling that he truly believed he was going to die here.

"Next time you're feeling down," Finn said as we made our way back to the common room to report, "just be grateful that you're not a miner."

Finn's report corroborated mine. Ching Shih had stripped the mining station of anything valuable, and was giving her crews what they were apparently calling the "Archipelago treatment." Good food, medicine, and the means to get more of both.

"She can't make up for a lifetime of depravity," Finn said with a dark look in his eyes, "but she sure as hell is trying, and it shows. Your Archipelago isn't going to be dealing with the usual buccaneer scum. She wants her crews to be well-rested, well-fed, and well-armed."

"All at the expense of the miners."

"You really think they were treated all that well before?" Orca asked.

She looked pissed at having to wait around. Luckily for her, her favorite punching bag had just returned, although I didn't think either of us was willing to risk another physical bout anytime soon.

"Better than this," I said.

"Second-rate grain, second-rate drugs, second-rate doctors. I've been raiding these supply lines since I was a kid. The mines get shafted."

"Nice one," Finn said, nodding at the pun.

Jeanine elbowed him in the ribs and he shut up.

"It's a high-risk job," Kraken said. "No use putting resources into something that isn't going to last. I'd do the same. What I wouldn't do is abandon them to Ching Shih."

I kept my mouth shut. Defending the Archipelago's somewhat questionable human rights record was not my job, even if it was my first instinct.

Orca took the first shift at the helm. I knew I needed to rest. We would be nearing the coasts soon, and there would be no time for sleep for me then, but I walked past my bunk and toward the helm anyway.

"What do you want, jelly?" she said, looking up as I slumped into the chair beside her.

"I don't know."

"That is pretty obvious."

I recoiled at the sharpness in her words.

"Well what do you want, then?" I asked.

She had the lights dimmed, and I could only make out parts of her face.

"Not this."

In that, at least, we were in agreement.

"About what happened," I began, because that was what you said in situations like this, even if you had no idea what had happened or why.

"I don't really want to talk about it."

I wanted her to yell at me, or at least insult me. I wanted to forget how her lips tasted, and I didn't want to think about how her body had betrayed her, at the end, all of her harsh words like fog over the water, boiling away beneath the heat of the sun.

She, at least, didn't deny it.

"Good. Neither do I."

Silence filled the helm.

"It's your fault," she said, beginning to sound a little more like herself.

"How exactly do you figure that?" I swear I could hear her eyes rolling.

"You show up, and everything falls apart."

"Orca," I said, reaching out to touch her arm.

She flinched. "What?"

"I—" I stopped, fumbling for the right words.

"She wants you, okay? Is that what you want to hear? She chose you, not me, and I fucking hate it. I hate you. I hate her. And I hate this goddamn trawler and this goddamn fucking ocean."

She slammed the dash, and I saw tears slide down her face in the bow lights.

My hand was still on her arm. I should have been prepared, after kissing her, for things to be different between us, but I wasn't ready for the rush of sympathy. I stood, and Orca—my tormentor, protector, and unlikely ally—collapsed into sobs in my arms.

"You tell anyone about this," she said, working through a bout of hiccups. "And I will kill you."

"Sure thing, first mate."

She wiped her eyes on her sleeve and straightened, her face inches from mine.

"You know what the worst part is?" she asked, shooting me an evil smile. "It would have been good."

"You think?" I had a vivid image of Miranda's face, sharp with pain.

She looked me up and down, then sighed.

"Maybe not. You're still too much of a pushover." She punched my shoulder, catching me off-guard, and I fell back into my chair.

"Hey Orca," I said, looking up at her.

"If you get all mushy on me now, I will stab you in the throat."

"Does that mean we're all right?" I asked, holding out my hand.

"Yeah," she said, squeezing my forearm in the mercenary style. "We're good. Just about everything else is fucked, though."

Orca woke me for my shift with her usual charm, which was a relief.

"Get the hell up, jelly."

I rolled out of bed. She had not brought me hot tea. I made a mental note to make some for Jeanine when I woke her next, in the hopes that Orca would get the hint.

First, though, I made some for myself. The water steamed on the stove in the salt-rimed kettle, wreathing my hands and face. I breathed it in and fumbled for the tea in the cupboard. With luck, my watch would be uneventful.

As I walked down the hall to the helm, cradling the tea in my hands, I heard a thump. I stopped, spilling near boiling liquid down my front in the process, and listened.

Silence strung itself out around me. Then the thump came again.

I backtracked my steps until I stood outside the door to the cargo bay. This time, I heard a slither, followed by a very low, very strained curse.

Stowaways.

I latched the cargo bay door and walked as swiftly and silently as I could back to the common room. The helm would have to wait a few more moments.

Orca was still awake when I returned, and after one look at my face she woke the others. I explained the situation as quickly as I could. Orca's expression faded from worry to irritation.

"I thought you checked the cargo bay," she hissed through clenched teeth.

"I did," Finn said. "But clearly not well enough. What do you want to do with them?"

"As much as it pains me to say this, we want them alive. The last thing we need is Ching's sailors after us for harbored fugitives. We go in there, we subdue them, and we take them back. Got it?"

I didn't much like the idea of returning the desperate miners to the station, but Orca's reasoning was sound. We couldn't afford to attract attention to ourselves. I had the greater good to think about.

Orca, Kraken, and Jeanine were the best fighters, so we decided they would go in first. Finn and I would guard the door in case there were more of them than we expected, for which I was secretly grateful; I didn't want to fight, and I really didn't want to fight my own people.

Kraken unlocked the hatch slowly. It swung inward, switching on the automatic lights in the hold and temporarily blinding our uninvited guests. I couldn't see much from my vantage point, but from what I could hear of the skirmish, the stowaways had not been expecting a band of fully armed Mercs.

Kraken fought silently. Jeanine laughed, once, as if something had surprised her, and after a few moments Orca let out an explosive curse. Whoever she was fighting grunted in satisfaction.

242

My hand spasmed on my knife. I knew that grunt. I tripped over my feet in my haste to rise and stumbled into the room, ignoring Finn's startled look.

Standing before me, giving Orca as good as she got, was Harper Comita.

"Wait," I shouted, stunning my crew, Harper, and the lanky SHARK with her into temporary stillness.

"Rose?" Harper asked, sounding as incredulous as I felt.

"You know her?" Orca rubbed her shoulder, staring at Harper with a mixture of respect and frustration.

"Yeah, I know her," I said, and then Harper jumped into my arms and hugged my head so tightly I worried it might implode. When she was done squeezing the life out of me, she dropped to the ground, leaving bruises on my hips from the force of her grip.

"What the hell happened to your hair?" She reached up and touched my curls, and I got my first good look at her in weeks.

Someone, or several someones, hadn't been treating her very nicely. She sported faded bruises on her cheeks and arms, and her wrists were ringed with red marks that looked like rope abrasions.

That still didn't explain what Admiral Comita's daughter was doing in the middle of the Gulf of Mexico, fleeing an Archipelago mining station in a drifter tub.

"What are you doing here?" I asked.

The SHARK did not look nearly as overjoyed to see me as Harper. I didn't recognize him, which wasn't surprising, and at any rate his attention was fixed on Kraken.

Not that I could blame him. Kraken's shirt was off and his tattoos writhed in the light, an effect that was disturbing enough even if you were used to it.

"It's a long story," she said, running a hand through her tangled hair. "You got any rum on this thing?"

"Hold up," Orca said, taking a menacing step toward us.

Harper stepped in front of me, her familiar shoulders shielding me from harm, as she had so many times before.

Orca stopped her advance, more surprised than anything at Harper's protective snarl.

"I've known Harper since I was a kid," I said. "She's all right."

"Like hell she's all right. She's a goddamn stowaway."

"Well, now she's our stowaway. Just hear her out. Please."

The word hung between us.

Orca's scowl deepened.

"You were offering me rum," Harper prompted, shifting her posture from Ready to Kill to Casually Gorgeous.

There was no way Orca could have prepared herself for Harper Comita, I reflected, biting back a smirk. Harper's charm, when she chose to employ it, was just as vicious as her right hook.

"I should have let Annie drown you," Orca said, shaking her head as she gave in.

I didn't miss the sideways glance she shot at Harper.

For her part, Harper clung to me as we escorted her to the common room, but not before Orca bound the SHARK's hands behind his back. Courtesy did not outweigh precaution.

My body objected to the idea of rum so soon after waking up. I stuck with my tea as Orca poured a measure for herself and Harper. I couldn't take my eyes off my best friend. Seeing her here, in the midst of the once alien surroundings I had grown to love, was more confusing than I cared to admit. I saw them through Harper's eyes—cramped, rough, and more than a little grungy. The familiar feeling of displacement I had felt on *North Star* over-whelmed me, and I clutched to the scarred table for support.

Harper seemed totally at her ease, lounging in her chair and knocking back drinks with her usual enthusiasm. Questions queued in the back of my throat. Orca was acting captain, however, and so she got to call the shots.

"Who are you, and how do you know my navigator?" she asked Harper.

My navigator? I thought irritably. *Like hell.*

"I'm a fleet engineer," Harper answered. "I served on *North Star* with Rose." I took note of her caution. She did not mention her mother.

"What are you doing on my ship?"

"I thought you were drifters. We'd been waiting for a chance to get out of the mines. You seemed like our best bet."

"Any chance they'll realize that you're missing?" Orca gestured to Finn, who vanished, probably to check the sonar.

"Not any time soon," Harper said. Her eyes flickered toward me very briefly, and my stomach clenched. She was lying. "Rose, what are you doing here?"

"It's a long story, too. This is Orca, first mate, and Kraken, Jeanine, and Finn. Jeanine's the ship mechanic, Finn handles communications, and Kraken . . ."

"I'm the cook," he said with a smile that, to Harper's credit, did not seem to faze her. I tried not to roll my eyes.

"You're really sailing with them?" Harper looked incredulous.

"I'm navigator for Captain Miranda, of the *Man o' War*."

I emphasized Miranda's name very slightly, hoping Orca would notice. The memory of Miranda's face sent a stab of pain through my chest, and I regretted my petty impulse.

"That's not—" Harper broke off her thought, but I was pretty sure I could fill in the blanks. That was not what Comita had told her.

"Does your mother know where you are?" I asked her, changing the subject.

"Specifically? No. But by now she'll have an idea. I was on a routine jump to *Ursa Minor* to fill in for their engineer when we were intercepted." Her face darkened at the memory.

I hesitated. I could not let Orca return Harper to the station and Ching Shih for two reasons. One, she was my best friend. Two, she was Admiral Comita's daughter, and a valuable hostage. I didn't want to think about what that would do to Comita's plans.

I knew very well what it would do to ours. If Ching's sailors had even the slightest idea who Harper was, then they would go to great lengths to keep her captive and alive. That was bad news for us. We needed to get away from the mine, and fast, and to do that I needed Orca on my side. I had to hope the truce we'd drawn between us counted for something.

I weighed my options. If I told Orca the truth about Harper's heritage, she would rightly overrule me, and return Harper or risk blowing not only our cover, but Miranda's as well. If I kept with Harper's story, on the other hand, I would need to come up with a very good reason to get us out of Dodge, fast.

"Orca, can I talk with you?" I asked.

Orca sighed and followed me out of the room, leaving the more than capable Kraken and Jeanine to keep our unexpected visitors subdued.

"We're taking them back." She crossed her arms over her chest, anticipating a struggle. "Your little friend jeopardizes everything."

"Not necessarily," I said, thinking quickly. "Harper isn't a high-value hostage. They'll search the station first, which will buy us some time, and we can't have been the only ship to dock there in the last few days. If anything—" I paused, not quite able to believe what I was about to say. "If anything, we can give them the guy and stow Harper in the bulkhead, like you did me."

"Or I give them you and your fleet friends and call it a day. You would risk your Archipelago for one engineer?" She stared at me, evidently surprised.

"Yes," I said, blinking back tears of frustration. "I honestly don't give a shit about the rest of them."

Orca opened her mouth, then shut it.

"What about Miranda?" she asked. "Do you give a shit about her? What do you think Ching would do if she finds out Miranda's navigator and first mate went rogue?"

Her choice of words made us both wince.

"Mayday."

"What?"

I grabbed Orca's arm, bringing her close enough that I could see the green flecks in the gray of her irises.

"We send out a mayday. We're close enough to the coast that I can keep us hidden. If they think we've sunk, they won't come looking, and they won't find anything even if they do."

"I am not sending out a mayday—"

"Orca!" Finn's shout drew us both back into the common room. Finn's face was white. "We've got trouble coming in hot."

"What kind of trouble?" Orca asked, giving me a baleful glare.

"The kind with lots and lots of tentacles."

"What?"

"Shoal of giant ass squid heading straight for us."

"Neptune's balls. Rose, get us the hell out of here." Orca shoved me toward the helm, leaving Harper's fate to chance.

Giant squid were a submersible's worst nightmare. Their numbers, unlike the rest of the ocean, had risen over the past few hundred years as they adapted to the changing fisheries and rising toxins. They had also developed a species-wide hatred of smaller submersible vessels, and a shoal of angry squid could wreak havoc on a trawler like ours. Mostly, they avoided vessels, which made the instances where they didn't sound like the stuff of legend.

That didn't make those ships any less sunk.

I flung myself into my seat and felt for the currents. We could move faster than the squid, thanks to the W5000 engine I hoped Jeanine was engaging right that second, and we were close to the shallows, where they would not want to follow. Even so, it would be a near thing.

The sonar blinked steadily at me as more and more shapes jetted up from the deeps. The trawler's bow lights flickered as the first few squirted jets of blinding ink. Luckily for everyone on board, I did not need sonar or a line of sight to navigate. I turned the trawler toward the drowned shores of Florida and tried not to flinch every time I felt the thud of a soft body colliding with the trawler.

I engaged the other engine. Nothing happened. More ink exploded outside, and tentacles slapped across the plastic. They couldn't do much to a heavily built trawler besides damage the trawl itself, but they could throw us off course, which was deadly enough in these waters.

They were also just plain terrifying. A beak scraped across the plastic window, appearing through the inky cloud like an avenging angel. I closed my eyes and held our course, mentally cursing Jeanine's slowness.

The trawler bucked and rolled as the engine fired into life, spurting us forward and plastering the body of a squid across the helm. Its huge eye stared at me, unblinking as I wrestled with the trawler, veering toward the coastal shelf at speeds no sane skipper would knowingly condone.

Orca joined me shortly after we broke free of the shoal with a strange look on her face.

"Your friend just saved our asses," she said, sitting down more heavily than usual. "Damn W5000 wouldn't start for Jeanine."

"Harper loves that model," I said, putting the trawler in a slight spin to dislodge our external passenger.

"I sent the mayday."

"What?" I overcorrected in shock, sending several objects sliding around the helm.

"I said I sent the mayday. Anyone coming to rescue us will find these bastards and assume the worst." She curled her lip at a passing squid. "Are these mines really worth it?"

"Thank you," I said, ignoring her last comment.

"Don't thank me; thank your friend. She's useful. Decent fighter, too. How long have you known her?"

"Most of my life."

"And you still can't fight for shit?" Orca shook her head in disgust. "You are a constant disappointment."

"And to think, for a moment there, I was actually starting to like you," I said, steering us toward the hidden perils of the coast.

West

Captain's Log
First Mate Orca
Sea Cat
August 12, 2513
26.2, -91.4°

First mate here. The mission has been compromised. We have two stowaways on board, an Archipelago fugitive who knows the navigator, and a Polarian SHARK with a death wish. The only reason he is still alive is that I think we might be able to use him as bait, but if he thinks I will let him get away with his untouchable superiority for much longer, he's got another think coming.

The fugitive, I have to admit, is useful. She is some sort of fleet engineer, and she got us out of a bind with the retrofitted W5000.

Not that any of this matters, since we are all going to die.

Captain, if you find this log, I want it stated on the record that I have serious misgivings about sailing this close to the coast. Your navigator is good, but everyone makes mistakes, and one mistake out here and we're squid food. That's if Ching Shih doesn't get us first.

Speaking of squid, a school of them nearly took us out. They shouldn't even be this close to the shelf. Nasty fuckers. See attached official report for details.

Remember the day we met?

I know this is an official log, and a breach in protocol, but I put our odds of survival at thirty to one, and the chances of you finding this log even slimmer, as if I do survive the first thing I will do is destroy it myself.

It was January, and cold. When the ship surfaced for too long, the deck iced over, but you still preferred to take Ching's readings topside.

I never told you that I asked Janel to switch her shift with mine that day. She was happy to stay below. I think it was sleeting. Anyway, I wanted to meet you. I wanted to see why Ching Shih had made you first mate, when there were plenty of other sailors who wanted the job badly enough to kill for it.

Did I ever tell you that I had to knife Nicolai? He recovered, but he didn't wait outside your room anymore, after that. You're welcome.

You weren't what I expected. You were rude, for starters, but not like the Archipelago captives I'd seen before. You just didn't care. I could have been Davy Jones himself and you wouldn't have looked twice at me while you were topside. The crew were all full of how promising you were, this Archipelago rebel warrior goddess with your stupid blue eyes.

I just thought you were a bitch. You didn't even ask my name.

I didn't push you. I swear to Neptune it was the wind. You shouldn't have been that close to the edge, not with a Nor'easter ripping toward us and the ship waiting for your skinny ass to get below deck so she could sub.

You caught yourself on the guard rail, which was covered in ice and sharp enough to make you bleed, but too slick to haul yourself back up with.

I could have let you fall. I might have even if I hadn't looked into your eyes and realized that a part of you wanted it. It would have been quick, in the winter ocean, not like the swarm we pulled you out of. It might have finally stopped the stings from burning. You were always itching at them, making the scarring worse, so I knew they still bothered you.

I asked if I should help you. I really don't think either of us knew what you were going to say.

252

Do you remember what you said?

"You tell me, Orca."

I told you that wasn't my name.

"It should be. You're the best raider on this ship."

I was so shocked that you'd paid enough attention to me to know my stats that I didn't answer your question, just left you hanging there.

"So is that a no?" you said.

"If you were meant to drown, you'd already be dead," I told you. "And I don't want to spend the next hour explaining to the captain why I lost you overboard."

I've never been that good with words.

The ice had cut your hand pretty badly by the time I got you back on deck. It was an odd cut. I told you it looked a little bit like a Portuguese man o' war, and you laughed while the spray froze on our faces.

If I die, I want you to know something. Ching thinks she made you, but she didn't. You made yourself. You owe Ching nothing. You owe me nothing. We live by these stupid debts out here because there isn't anything else to hold on to, but now that Davy Jones is knocking on the bridge door I'm beginning to see how stupid, just how fucking stupid, it all is.

If anyone made us, it's the ocean.

I've had too much rum. Those fucking squid.

If we die, I'm sorry I failed you. You're a good captain. You have horrible taste in women, but I guess that's a bit hypocritical, all things considered, so I'll try and keep your navigator safe.

You're a real bastard, Miranda Stillwater, but I wouldn't serve under anyone else.

I guess I just thought you should know that.

Chapter Sixteen

"Sweet mother of pearl." Harper pointed out the helm window. "What is that?"

A school of tiny fish parted around the nose of the trawler. Behind them, crusted with algae and toxic shellfish, loomed the shattered remains of structures rendered unrecognizable by time and waves. Turrets of twisted metal and stone writhed from the ocean floor like jagged fragments of broken bones. Kelp waved, concealing more of the ruined behemoths.

"I think it used to be a city," I said, awe overwhelming caution.

I brought the trawler down a few meters to get a better view. Tumbled stone and steel rusted beneath a carpet of sand and ocean life. Rising seas and storms had done their best to flatten what they could, but the remnants remained, towering around us through the billowing curtains of seaweed.

This was the kind of water that got people killed. One chance encounter with a jagged piece of metal and we could spring a leak, taking on water and toxins faster than we could patch things up.

Orca had deemed Harper trustworthy enough to roam the ship, a courtesy she had not extended to the SHARK, who was kept under constant guard and was also an increasing liability to our sleep cycles. This was the first real chunk of time I'd had alone with my friend. What she had told me was more disturbing than the miles and miles of abandoned coastline.

According to Comita, I had been recalled to Polaris for reassignment to another ship. The recall had been sudden, and as I'd suspected, Harper had been furious with me for not saying goodbye. Comita had done nothing to allay her anger.

My absence was overshadowed by a more pressing reality. Even though my reassignment had been fabricated, the need for trained navigators and engineers was very real. Ching had launched a series of successful raids, crippling several of our warships and coming dangerously close to some of the outlying stations themselves. Polaris had lost two crews, and resources had gone from plentiful to thin in a matter of weeks.

And still the council dragged their feet, unwilling to risk a confrontation out of fear of losing the mines completely.

If Ching Shih wasn't stopped soon, there would be no stopping her.

Skulking along the coast no longer seemed like the right thing to do. We needed a plan, some way of putting a hole in her hull before her fleet grew large enough to outmaneuver ours. But what could one ship of half-loyal mercenaries, a former Archipelagean navigator, and the admiral's daughter do against the Red Flag Fleet? Counting Ching's forces, which had seemed so important only a few days ago, now seemed fruitless. We knew how many ships she had—too many. Now, here we were, with a fugitive onboard and no way of communicating with Miranda.

Miranda. I had not told Harper about that particular mess, nor did I know what Miranda would do when she found out we had allowed stowaways on board her ship. Everything had gotten so complicated.

I dodged more towers, steering us ever farther inland.

"So what's up with you and Orca?" Harper asked, breaking the silence.

"Nothing a long walk off a short pier wouldn't fix," I said.

"She doesn't seem too bad to me. I would have thought she was your type."

I choked, coughed, and came up sputtering.

"Orca?"

"Why not? She's pretty, edgy, and clearly has mixed feelings about you."

"Harper," I said, taking a deep breath. "If Orca and I were the last two people on earth, we would divide the globe down the center and stay at opposite poles. The only thing mixed about her feelings for me is whether or not she wants to kill me quickly or slowly."

Harper laughed, and I smiled despite myself, glad she had accepted the white lie. I had missed her.

"What did you do to piss her off so much?"

"It's complicated," I said, just barely keeping us clear of a reaching spire.

"Uh huh. There's a woman in this story somewhere, and I am going to find her. I know you."

"That's what I'm worried about," I said.

Harper slapped my shoulder playfully.

"Well, if you're not interested in Orca, don't say I didn't give you first dibs."

I choked again.

"How can you seriously be thinking about sex at a time like this?" I asked her.

The idea of Harper and Orca was unsettling. I had no right to be jealous, I reminded myself.

"I've been held in a pirate's brig, locked away on a goddamn mining station, shoved in a container of algae and smuggled onto what I thought was a drifter trawler, all in the space of a week. I have never deserved to get laid more."

"While that thought sickens me more than I can possibly explain, that's not a bad idea. Orca won't sell you out if she's sleeping with you."

"Who said anything about sleeping?"

"There's something in the air on this tub," I muttered to myself as I brought the trawler around to sail parallel to the sunken continent.

Maybe this was exactly what both Orca and I needed. Harper

256

was a handful. She would keep Orca more than entertained, and I . . . and I would have to deal with my ruinous feelings for Miranda.

"This means nothing."

Go to hell, Miranda Stillwater.

The morning passed. Toward noon, I brought the trawler closer to the edge, back through the drowned cities until we floated between a cluster of tall structures that overlooked the open ocean.

Finn was messing with our sonar. The display screen in the helm flickered occasionally as he adjusted the frequency, probing the depths for signs of life. A few days of this, and we would have a decent idea of the number of ships directly surrounding the mines. The rest lay in the middle of the Gulf, where Miranda would have to take her own inventory.

"Harp," I said as casually as possible, "what do you know about the Stillwater mutiny?"

"Do you never pay attention in class? It was a nasty piece of work. My mother was angry about it for months. She couldn't believe that they would react like that. I overheard her talking to Admiral Gonzalez about it, once."

"The rebels?"

"The rebels? No. The Council. They threatened to sink the whole station if the leaders didn't turn themselves in, and once they turned themselves in, the Council killed them, and some of their families, too, just to make a statement."

I flinched.

"Why do you ask?"

"No reason." My heart stuttered in my chest. "What about Stillwater's family? Where are they now?"

"They killed some of them for sure, but I think there's a sister left alive somewhere. Rumor says she married off station before that, so she got off lightly."

The helm spun around me. I hadn't wanted to believe Kraken. I hadn't wanted to accept that the commanders I served could justify that level of brutality. The thoughts I had pushed down,

257

or chalked up to too much rum and a faulty memory, rose up around me like wraiths.

I had grown up on a border station like Gemini. I knew what a raid could do. If someone like Miranda had galvanized Cassiopeia, would I have gone along with it, assuming, of course, that my mother hadn't done everything in her power to get me off the station at a young age? I had a feeling I knew the answer.

And yet I had accepted the official story, hook, line, and sinker, without a single hesitation. Even when I had confronted Miranda, it had never occurred to me to ask why she'd done what she did. I had assumed I knew her and her motives, and been so preoccupied with what her identity meant for me that I hadn't stopped for a second to think about what it meant for her.

Miranda was not just a bloodthirsty mercenary out for a profit, who had seduced me to suit her own ends. She was a woman who was willing to put herself on the line again and again to defend her home, even when that home had cast her out, and even if it meant going against the very people who had saved her.

Although, I reflected as my clenched right fist ached at the pressure on the scar tissue, there was definitely a thirst for blood in there somewhere. Normal captains didn't mutilate their sailors to make a point.

Then again, maybe I would if I found out that after the Council had tried to kill me, they had killed my family.

"Are you okay, Rose?"

I was not okay. If what Harper said was true, I had misjudged Miranda. Badly.

The cold prick of the knife against my throat was a reminder that letting down my guard had deadly consequences. I edged up in my seat, obeying the insistent pressure of the blade, and turned to face a stricken Harper.

"John," she said, "what are you doing?"

I froze. John was the name of the SHARK who'd accompanied

258

her. I hadn't given him a second thought since we'd locked him in the cargo hold, something I suspected I was about to regret.

"All right, Merc scum," he said to me, unaware of the irony in his words. "You're going to get us the hell out of here and back to the Atlantic, or I will kill you and everyone else on board."

He reeked of fresh blood, a coppery raw smell that flooded my nostrils.

Fear stabbed my chest. Who had he hurt? I couldn't remember who was on guard duty.

"John!"

"Shut up. I told you I'd get you back to your mother, and that's what I'm going to do. We don't have time to waste playing nice with Mercs and pirates. This lot will turn you in faster than you can say 'parley.' Trust me. I've met their type before."

John had been left in the dark about our true purpose. It was a strategy that had seemed wise at the time, in the event he was recaptured, but there was one major drawback: he didn't know we were on the same side.

Listening to the venom in his voice, I wasn't sure it would have mattered either way.

"Okay," I said, trying to buy myself time. "I'll take you back. Is anyone else hurt?"

"That's not your problem." The knife pressed closer, stinging as it parted the first layer of skin.

"It's not as simple as just leaving the Gulf. There are patrols—"

"Just. Do. It."

I swallowed carefully and sat back down in my chair. It seemed unlikely that John had managed to subdue the entire crew. If I stalled long enough, one of them would act.

"You don't understand," Harper began again, but she stopped as I cried out in sudden pain.

The SHARK's knife bit deeper, and blood ran freely down my neck to pool between my breasts. Stars danced in the corner of my vision.

"Oh, I do, and your mother will be getting a full report, you can bet on that," he said.

I could feel the hatred radiating from his body. It enfolded me in its sticky miasma, familiar and cloying. I knew that kind of hate. Nothing Harper could say or do now would change his mind, even if the evidence was overwhelming. He'd staked soul, pride, and life on it.

I knew what I had to do.

The trawler creaked as I turned her toward the Gulf. I needed my concentration on John, not an impending impact.

"Okay," I said, my voice oddly calm despite the searing pain in my throat. "I'm taking us back out. I'm going to have to hug the coast, but I should be able to get us to the straits in two days."

"Two days?"

"It's a trawler, not a fleet sub." I hoped he hadn't noticed the acceleration we'd used to escape the shoal of squid.

His knife slipped as he cursed. It was all I needed.

Drilling with Orca hadn't been a total waste of time. I ducked out of his reach, earning myself another graze, and reached for my own knife. I was no match for a SHARK, but I had the element of surprise on my side for the next few seconds and I sliced at his legs from beneath the shelter of the chair.

"Harper, run!" I shouted.

She didn't listen. Her fist collided with his face, and I heard her grunt as he retaliated. I lashed out again, taking him in the thigh, and ducked just in time to avoid his knife as it whistled past my ear.

Harper was unarmed. I didn't think he would kill her, but I was not willing to risk it. I charged him headfirst, knocking his knife out of his hand and sending us crashing into the wall.

He didn't stay down for long. His arm whipped around my throat, squeezing hard, and I forgot about the knife in my hand as I fought for air.

Go for the legs. Miranda's voice drifted through the rising veil. I kicked his knee, colliding with his kneecap and earning me a split second of release. I drove my knife into his other thigh and shoved Harper toward the door.

She took the hint this time, and ran. I followed, wheezing, and nearly collided with a bloodstained and wild-eyed Orca.

I heard the knife whistle again. If he hadn't already tried to decapitate me once, I might not have reacted as quickly, but my body remembered that sound. Orca's eyes widened as I flung myself into her, sending us tumbling to the ground. The knife quivered in the wall where her face had been a moment before, and then Harper's hand was on the blade and my heart broke as I heard it whistle for a third and final time, thrumming straight into the throat of the Polarian SHARK. The life gurgled out of him as he hit the floor, and I forgot myself just long enough to rest my head against Orca's shoulder to block out the sound.

"Hey there, fleeter," she said, patting me on the back. She helped me up, keeping an arm around my shoulder with the same awkward tenderness she'd shown me in the showers after beating me to a pulp.

Harper stood still as stone. She stared at the dead man on the floor, her hand still half outstretched in testimony to the fatally accurate throw.

"Harp."

She turned to look at me, eyes empty and staring.

"I got this." Orca squeezed my shoulder once and stepped toward Harper, helping her lower her arm. "Rose, close his eyes."

I obeyed, kneeling next to the growing pool of blood. His eyes were green and bloodshot in his lined face. I touched the still warm skin and recoiled. Bile rose in my throat. Only the thought of Harper behind me kept me from spewing all over his corpse. I gagged and deposited a small pile of vomit out of her line of sight.

"You're here," Orca was saying to her when I finished. "You've got your feet on the floor, sailor, and calm seas ahead. Look at me. There. That's better. It's like that the first time. It's supposed to hurt. You're paying the blood price. Only thing worse than killing someone is getting killed yourself, or watching someone you love die when you could have done something to stop it."

I let her words wash over me as I stood behind my best friend and the woman I'd once fantasized about stabbing. I had saved her life, forcing Harper's hand. That there had been only one course was not a comfort.

Orca led Harper and me to the common room where she sat Harper in a chair and turned to me.

"Finn's hurt. I need you with me."

I nodded, steeling myself under her gaze.

"Bastard got the jump on him. Sealed off the hold, locking Jeanine and Kraken in the engine compartment and took me by surprise."

"It wasn't your watch," I pointed out. "We all need to sleep at some point."

Finn lay on the floor in the cargo hold, his body slack and his chest rising and falling slowly. I didn't see any marks on his body, but I didn't like the color of his cheeks.

"Head shot," Orca said, kneeling beside him. "Looks like he got hit in the temple." She pressed her fingers to his throat. "Slow, but steady. Not a good place to get hit. Grab me a blanket."

"Should we move him?" I asked when I returned.

"No. He might be hurt somewhere else. You sit with him and shout if he wakes up. I need to go unlock Kraken and Jeanine from the hold. Jeanine can relieve you once she's out, and then I need you at the helm."

I nodded, squatting by Finn on the cold floor.

"Oh, and Rose?"

I looked up at her. Her thin braids framed her face, casting a bar of shadow across her eyes.

"Thank you."

"I didn't do it for you. I did it for the captain," I said, not feeling quite noble enough to give her the satisfaction of settling her debt that easily. The hurt on her face was worth it, despite the twinge of guilt. I stood up, feeling the wound on my neck gape open again, and grasped her forearm.

"Neptune's balls, Orca, you Mercs have no sense of humor."

She glared at me, and then her lips twitched and she squeezed my arm back, breaking into the first genuine smile I'd put on her face.

"You had me there, fleeter."

"Had to happen eventually."

"You know," she said, giving my arm a little shake. "You're like a barnacle."

"How so?"

"You're a pain in my ass, but you've grown on me."

I sat back down next to Finn with an odd feeling in my chest. A man was dead, Finn was badly injured, Harper was in shock, and I was lightheaded from blood loss and adrenaline, but the strange little smile on my lips was not a product of hysteria. I didn't know what was more unexpected—that I had finally won Orca's respect, or that she had won mine.

Maybe something good had come out of our ill-fated tryst after all.

"Finn!" Jeanine burst into the cargo hold and collapsed next to him, running her hands over his face. "Finnegan, baby, Davy Jones don't need you like I do. Wake up, baby, wake up."

"He hears you talking to him like that, he will," I said, mostly to myself.

"Damn straight I will." Finn's speech was slurred, but coherent. "Took you long enough to figure out you can't live without me, woman."

"Don't make me knock you back out, now," Jeanine said, stroking his hair. I patted Finn's other arm and stood to go.

"Not so fast, jelly." Jeanine peeled her eyes away from Finn long enough to look at me. "You need to get a bandage on that. Make sure Orca patches herself up too."

"I will," I promised.

It was a promise that was easy to keep. Orca thrust a bottle of rum and a clean bandage at me as soon as I entered the common room. Harper looked a little better, if grim, and she snatched the medical supplies out of my hands and proceeded to pour alcohol over the wound with an efficiency that brooked no argument. I hissed in pain and squirmed until she swatted me.

"Make sure she gets taken care of too," I told her, pointing at Orca when I finally escaped her less-than-tender ministrations.

I found Kraken in the hallway to the helm, mopping up the blood and vomit. He measured me with his dark eyes and leaned on the mop. It looked like a toothpick in his grasp. Something about his gaze undid the composure I'd managed to cling to.

"It's my fault," I said, wondering and not wanting to know where he had put the body. He grew up trawling, and there were stories about drifter dead that I didn't like thinking about, even if I didn't believe they were true. Especially because he was the cook.

"How is this your fault?"

"If I hadn't let them stay—"

"Compass Rose, you're a navigator. Orca is the skipper, and she let them stay. Finn let his guard down. Jeanine and I got ourselves locked in the engine room. Your friend Harper killed him. Not much blame left over for you."

"It could have been one of us dead, instead of him."

"Yes. Would you do it differently? Would you send them back to the mines to be interrogated? Tortured? They would have killed him anyway. They might have spared the admiral's daughter, but there is a big difference between 'alive' and 'unharmed.'"

"You know who she is?" I asked, stunned.

"I do now." He gave me his kraken's smile and moved to let me pass.

"Kraken," I said, turning back. The floor was slick with diluted blood. "Why did you warn Miranda about me?"

"You mean besides the obvious reasons?"

"Yeah."

"Only one thing that woman hadn't had broken, before she met you." He went back to mopping.

I tried to absorb that piece of information. I felt like a saturated sponge, and more than a little like a piece of garbage for thinking about myself while the body of another person cooled somewhere on the ship. First Annie, then Andre, now John.

"Is there any way . . ." I trailed off, then tried again, blurting out my words all at once. "Do you think she could forgive me? Do you think—"

"I'm not the one you need to ask. Out here, you want something, you make it work. Anyone who accepts anything less deserves it."

I settled in at the helm. Less than an hour had passed since the SHARK first pressed his knife to my throat. So much was different now. It was too much to think about, so I didn't.

North, east, south, west. I named the cardinal directions, checking each quadrant for signs of movement. North was clear, as was the eastern coastal quadrant. South lay wide open ahead of us, and to the west, moving steadily toward us, was a ship.

"You've got to be kidding me," I said to the universe at large. I pulled down the intercom. "Raider, incoming."

Our brief foray into the open had cost us. I steadied myself and analyzed the sonar. There was nothing else in our vicinity, and there was no good reason for a raider to show interest in a drifter vessel—unless, of course, that vessel harbored a valuable hostage. I bit my lip. So far we had not been hailed. If we could get back to the coast before they recognized our vessel, we might be able to evade them without directly disobeying Ching Shih's orders.

I turned the trawler around and gunned it.

Orca thrust herself through the doorway as the first of the drowned buildings came back into sight.

"Take the wheel," I said, moving to let her in.

Her gray eyes scanned the water.

"How far in do we need to go?" she asked.

"Farther than we want," I said, feeling grim. The sea churned around us, a disturbance on the surface rippling down to where we sputtered and churned.

"Hard to port," I said, closing my eyes. The currents ripped through the water here with a force that took my breath away. We were only a few miles further south, but the difference in oceanic conditions defied explanation.

"She's pulling hard," Orca said, mirroring my thoughts.

"I know." My eyes felt grainy behind my eyelids. "We need to get out of the riptide."

"That's all on you, navigator."

"Ride it." The certainty rose in me and I opened my eyes to stare at the ruins around us.

"What? Are you fucking crazy?"

"We need all the speed we can get. The current gives us an edge."

"And could run us right into one of these—whatever they are." The jagged remains of something large passed beneath us, illustrating her point.

"That's all on you, skipper."

She glared at me.

I was right. The current added wings to our clumsy trawler, and we wove through the ancient debris at a speed that was frankly quite terrifying. Jellyfish passed by us, not enough to qualify as a swarm, but enough to occasionally clog up the sonar and block the raider from view. I didn't dare hope that it would also block us from theirs.

Orca swore in a steady stream, obeying my commands with gratifying alacrity. I concentrated, trying to make sense of what my inner compass was telling me.

"Break us out," I said, forcing Orca to pull the trawler around more suddenly than was good for it.

"It's shallow," she said, staring out at the blue water.

It was shallow. Too shallow for a raider, which was a good thing, because one glance at the sonar showed me we now had not just one, but two on our tail.

"Take us in."

"In to where? The coast is right there. We'll run aground."

"No we won't." I laid out a rapid series of coordinates, trying not to think about the lives in my hands.

"This is suicide."

"Then give me the wheel."

Our eyes locked.

"Can't do that, navigator."

266

"Orca. What exactly is going to happen when they catch us?" She looked at the sonar, then back at me.

"Depends on why they are after us. You said your friend wasn't valuable." I heard the accusation in her voice.

"I lied."

"Of course you did." Orca shook her head in disgust.

"She's the Polarian Admiral's daughter."

"Wait." Orca's jaw dropped. "Harper is Comita's daughter? That cold bitch reproduced?"

"Yes. Not that it will matter if we don't get the hell out of here now." I tapped the sonar. The raiders were closing fast.

"Miranda will have your hide for this," Orca said, moving out of the way of the wheel.

"Yours too, first mate."

"Admiral's daughter. Send me to Davy fucking Jones, Rose. You might have said something sooner."

I tuned out her protests. She was right about the coast. The water would only grow shallower, and if I could not find a way through it, we were trapped.

"And they're firing at us. Great. This is really great, Rose." Orca slammed the dash.

"Actually," I said, noting the bubbles rising to starboard, "it is."

I pulled the trawler into a lower dive, coming dangerously close to the bottom, and pointed at the bubbles to the starboard side.

"Do we have anything combustible in the arsenal?" I asked Orca. Her face lit with a disturbingly enthusiastic smile.

"I mean, I tried to pack light, but there might be something. You do realize that if we blow a methane deposit, not only could we all die, but we'll have even more ships after us?"

"Not if these ones don't make it back."

She looked as surprised by my words as I felt.

"I've been a better influence on you than I thought," she said. "I might have a few low-grade explosives."

"Why are there low-grade explosives on a trawler?"

"Ask Kraken."

I checked the progress of our tail.

"There's just one small problem," Orca said, crossing her arms over her chest. "We need to lure them in."

I shivered in the helm, alone, as Orca went to prep the explosives for drop and set up the detonators. A man had already died today, and here we were, planning to kill who knows how many more. Harper's hand on my shoulder made me jump when she sat down in Orca's empty seat.

She didn't say anything. We waited, and when the time was right, I sent out the sonar blast.

"Don't shoot. Parley."

Short and sweet. The ships, cautious in the shallows, slowed their advance.

"Now," Orca shouted over the intercom.

I revved up our engine and turned us east, heading straight for the coastal inlet I hoped was ahead.

With the helm facing away from the blast, all we could see was the ocean floor ripple and writhe like some monstrous sea creature rising from an unnatural slumber as the shock wave rocked the trawler. I was prepared this time, and kept us on an even keel as the detonation sent us hurtling through the water toward an even more uncertain future.

Chapter Seventeen

"I can't believe I'm seeing this." I leaned forward, the depth readings blinking out of the corner of my eye. Ahead, obscured by the clouded water, lay the inlet, but this was not the inlet detailed on the coastal maps I'd memorized. This had the depth readings of a channel.

Orca frowned. "I can't see anything," she said.

"Exactly. We're twenty meters deep. We should be seeing bottom, and I've got open water as far as the sonar can see ahead."

"That's impossible." She leaned over to scan the sonar, then sat back, looking nonplussed.

I couldn't agree more. We were well over the border of the drowned continent, and maximum depth should have been less than twenty meters, not twenty and counting.

A small swarm of jellyfish emerged from the gloom, passing us with their usual aimless purpose. I watched them. Something about their movements tickled the back of my mind.

"How far does this go?" Orca asked.

"Hell if I know, but we might as well find out."

The detonation had taken its toll on our trawler, too. Harper, Jeanine, and Kraken were ensconced in the engine room, trying to repair what they could. From the sounds filtering up through the floor in frustrated bursts, things were not going well, and until they got us back in working order, we were in no shape to face more raiders.

"Fucking jellyfish," Orca said, watching another swarm pass us by.

I thought instantly of Miranda, and my chest constricted.

The trawler edged along the channel. Orca kept it slow at my insistence. The water was clogged with algae at the surface and sunlight filtered through in stray beams, shining through the tattered swarms.

Swarms.

Moving with us.

I tapped the dash, my inner compass whirring as the filaments aligned. Swarms followed the current. These were on a definite trajectory.

"Move us a few degrees starboard," I said to Orca.

She obliged. I felt the current pluck at us, a hesitant touch that tightened as we neared its embrace. An incredulous laugh bubbled up in my throat.

"You all right, jelly?" Orca gave me a wary look.

"We're in the Gulf stream."

"What?" It took Orca a moment to register my words. "That's impossible. The Gulf stream is farther south."

"Some of it is," I allowed, but the current was weak. Weak enough, maybe, that a small offshoot might have found a way through the submerged marshlands, carving out a new route for itself in the loose bedrock.

"What are you saying?"

"I could be wrong," I said, staring at the sonar, "but I think we just found a way out of the Gulf."

I had never wanted to be topside more in my life. The crew of the *Sea Cat* sat around the table in the common room, and all of them were looking at me.

"We're in the Atlantic," I said, forcing myself to look each of them in the eye in turn.

270

Over the past six hours, the trawler had drifted along a twisting channel, outpacing the current as we followed the impossible: an unmapped channel, a literal back door into the Gulf of Mexico and the answer to the Archipelago's prayers.

"Neptune's big old hairy balls," Finn swore.

I met Kraken's and Harper's eyes last. Harper's expression was full of hope; Kraken's was somber.

He knew.

"In case you haven't put two and two together, we have a problem," Orca said. "Rose."

"The channel is deep enough for raiders to follow us. It's also deep enough for the Archipelagean fleets. Right now, we are the only six people who know about it, but we can't count on that lasting, and we can't afford for Ching to find out."

If she did, she could come at the stations from a whole new direction, taking them by surprise. The same applied to the Archipelago. If Admiral Comita could rouse the other fleets, she could turn the tables on Ching.

The discovery could not have come at a better time, nor at a higher price.

"I don't understand the problem," Harper said. "Rose, we have to alert Polaris."

"What about the captain?" asked Jeanine. Her eyes held me accountable.

"There is a good chance Ching thinks we've sunk," Orca said, answering for me. "But she's too careful to make assumptions. If we leave the Gulf, we've as good as abandoned Miranda."

"If we go back, then Ching wins." Harper looked to me for support. "Right, Rose?"

"Yes." The word felt like one of Ching's raiders, lined with jagged knives. I'd left Miranda behind once, and it had felt like the hardest thing I'd ever have to do.

I was wrong.

Stars would be out by now. On the deck, I would be able to hear the soft sounds of dusk settling over the water. On the deck, I would be able to scream, the memory of Miranda all around me.

271

It was Orca's decision. To return to our captain, and lose what might be the only chance of ousting Ching, or to abandon her to an almost certainly bloody fate in the name of the greater good.

I knew what I wanted to do, and avoided Harper's eye.

They were all looking at me. Even Orca.

"It's your call, first mate," I said. My voice sounded far away.

"Is it?" She had an odd little half smile on her face. "This is your course, navigator."

You bitch, I thought. *Don't make me do this.*

I had been right to place distance between myself and Miranda. I could see that now, all too plainly. Orca would never had discovered the channel, had she been lucky enough to get that far in the first place. Miranda had clouded my judgment, and I had clouded hers.

I had been right, and now I was paying the price.

There was only one possible course.

"We make for Polaris," I said, turning away from the crew and making for the door. If I couldn't be on deck, I could at least be at the helm.

Orca grabbed my arm as I passed her, swinging me around to face the watching eyes. I don't know what she saw on my face, but the furrow on her brow softened.

"Get us there fast," she said as I pulled away.

I heard Harper's footsteps behind me.

"Leave me alone, Harp," I said once we were in the privacy of the hallway.

"When have I ever done that?"

I walked to the helm, trying to steady my breathing. Harper dogged my heels.

"Wanna tell me what that was all about?" she asked.

"I just need a minute." I sat, my head falling into my hands. My knuckles tightened on my shorn hair, and I remembered Miranda's words.

"It is just a preference."

"This is a good thing, Rose." Harper placed a comforting hand on my shoulder. "I'm sure your captain would have agreed." There was a question in her words.

"I don't know what she would have wanted," I said, my breath catching on barely suppressed sobs. "And now I never will."

"My mother—"

"Your mother sent me out here, Harper," I said, unable to contain the building torrent. "You have no idea what has happened to me since I left *North Star*. These people, this crew, even goddamn fucking Orca, mean more to me than anyone on your mother's ship."

Her face whitened, and she withdrew her hand.

"Except you," I added.

"You're a Polarian navigator."

"Am I? Then what am I doing here, on a drifter trawler, under the orders of Miranda fucking Stillwater?"

Harper's face froze. She, at least, knew enough history to immediately place the name.

"You're kidding."

"Do I look like I'm kidding? Do you know how many times I've almost died since I last saw you? How many people have died because of me? And Miranda—" My voice broke again, and I could feel the muscles in my face spasming with the effort of retaining control.

"It hasn't been exactly easy for me either, Rose," she said, her own temper flaring. "In case you've forgotten, I'm trapped on this piece of shit, too."

"You don't get it. If we leave, Miranda and Crow's Eye and the rest of the crew could die."

"Like John?"

A black silence fell between us.

"I can't believe you," Harper said eventually.

I didn't answer.

"When you figure out where you're going, navigator, let me know."

I let her walk away, and when Kraken showed up with a flask of rum an hour later, I didn't protest.

"You're not much for company," he said, plopping down in the vacated chair, "but it beats listening to Orca and your friend screwing like a couple of cats in the engine room."

I held my hand out for the flask.

Progress was slow. Harper and Jeanine were still making repairs on the engine, and I chafed at the helm as we chuffed along the submerged coast, doing my best to keep us off the sonar of any passing ships.

"What happens when we get to your admiral?" Orca lounged next to me, looking pleased with herself.

I was less pleased, but hardly in a position to say anything. Besides—out of Orca, Miranda, and Harper, Orca was the only one still speaking to me.

"I don't know," I said. I hadn't gotten that far in the planning process.

"It's a perfect trap." I tuned Orca out as she laid out the best strategy for catching Ching unawares. I'd heard it already.

". . . will you stay with your fleet?"

"What?"

"Will you stay with your fleet, or will you come back with us to *Man o' War*?"

"Try not to sound so hopeful."

Orca shrugged.

I hadn't thought about that, either.

"It's not really my decision," I said.

Gray eyes rolled skyward.

"Whatever you need to tell yourself."

"Hey, skipper," Harper said, saving me from a reply. "Engine's up and running." She leaned in the doorway, ignoring me.

"Let's get out of here, then. And you," Orca said, pointing at me, "owe me a real Archipelago meal, bath, and bunk."

Polaris station didn't just fill the helm, it eclipsed it. The curved outer walls of the station stretched on in every direction as the trawler approached the docking bay, and even Orca looked impressed.

The bright lights and portholes were achingly familiar. From an outward approach, the station resembled a toy top, with a spindly point at both ends, and like a top, it spun ever so slightly, powered by massive wave turbines, solar panels, and simple physics.

It was the internal workings of power that frightened me.

"Are you sure your mother is here?" I asked Harper.

The look she gave me was a little less frosty. Harper's temper flared hot and cooled quickly.

"It's the most likely place, given what's happened, and if not, they'll know where *North Star* is. You and I should get to the hatch."

I left Orca to navigate the docking and followed Harper to the exit. We didn't know what kind of reception Polaris would give a mercenary crew, and I didn't want any accidents. To be safe, Harper would go first, and I would follow.

"Harp," I said into the tight space in the hatch. "I'm sorry."

"I know," she said, letting out a sigh. "Miranda Stillwater? Really?"

I shrugged and looked away.

"You have terrible taste." She shook her head.

"You haven't met her yet."

"I don't need to." Her face was serious. "Why do you always have to go getting yourself hurt?"

"It's not like I choose it. How is it so goddamn easy for you? Orca? Really?"

"Why not?" Harper grinned.

"You don't even like women!"

"I never said that."

"Well you never said you did, either," I pointed out.

"You overthink things."

The trawler rode up against the dock. I heard the distant sounds of machinery grumbling, clamping us in place.

"Did Orca tell you that she regularly beats the shit out of me?"

"So do I."

My lips twitched in a traitorous smile.

"I'm sorry about John," I said.

"Me too."

The tension between us dissipated as the hatch sprang open, and the commanding voice of a fleet sailor shouted down.

"Send up the Admiral's daughter."

"Catch you on the other side," Harper said, swinging up the ladder.

Kraken appeared at my shoulder as Harper vanished.

"Keep your head out there," he said. "Remember who they are, and who we are."

Who we are.

Where did I belong?

Harper was busy explaining the situation to the waiting sailors.

"Who are you?" one of them asked me.

"Compass Rose, quartermaster for Admiral Comita."

"What are you doing off-ship?"

This was Polaris, but Comita had sworn me to secrecy.

"I have to make that report to the Admiral, sir," I said, hoping that would suffice.

He didn't look satisfied, but he nodded. I wondered what would have happened had we arrived without Harper, and shuddered.

"The crew of that trawler saved my life," Harper was saying. "They deserve sanctuary."

"That's not for you to decide."

"You're right. It's the Admiral's decision. Is she here?"

I held my breath. The sailor, who had the universal bad temper of most docking masters, nodded in curt assent.

276

"I'll let her know you've arrived. Until then, the rest of the crew stays onboard. Do you understand?"

I relayed the information down the hatch. Kraken did not look surprised, but I heard Orca mutter something from behind him.

The docking master himself escorted us to the Admiral. After weeks spent with mercenaries and a longer deployment than usual on *North Star* prior, the luxury of Polaris overwhelmed me.

Wide hallways lined with artwork and living walls of greenery gave way to open courtyards. Trees towered up through tiered lobbies, and pools sparkled in the distance, part of a living biosphere that only the biologists seemed to fully understand. Massive tubes of bio-light lined the ceilings, and I watched the water circulating through them as we followed the docking master. I didn't see any jellyfish.

We were in the command level, but we passed a group of schoolchildren with sufficiently awed expressions on a tour. Several of them stared at me, with my strange haircut and ragged clothes. Harper, at least, still wore her uniform, even if it was looking the worse for wear. The scrutiny hurt.

Will I ever learn to stop caring? I thought as the curious brown eyes of the children followed me.

Comita was in her office. The docking master ushered us into the waiting room, which was more refined than the quarters Comita kept on *North Star*. A side table offered refreshments, and there were even carpets on the floor, arranged around several low couches.

We didn't have to wait long. Comita opened the door and pulled her daughter into a tight embrace. I watched, fascinated, as Comita stroked Harper's hair and her gray eyes squeezed tightly shut over the tears flowing down her lined cheeks. Harper's shoulders shook, too, and I felt a pang of homesickness for Cassiopeia and my own mother.

Comita eventually regained enough composure to greet me.

"Compass Rose," she said, her voice grave. I could hear the unasked questions.

"Admiral." I gave her a salute. "Four crew members are with us."

277

"They will be treated with every courtesy." She turned toward the perplexed docking master. "Prepare a private reception for our guests. I will address them when I can. In the meantime, it would be best if we treat this delicately. Are any of the crew ranking officers, Rose?"

"Only the first mate. Her name is Orca."

Comita nodded, and while she showed no outward sign of relief, I knew that I had answered her unspoken question. Miranda Stillwater was not with me.

She dismissed our escort with a nod, shutting the doors to her office with shaking hands.

Harper gave her report first. I listened again to the story of her capture, and reached out to squeeze her hand when she explained what had happened to John.

"We will deal with that later," Comita said. "You are alive, and that is what matters to me."

It was the only time I had ever heard her say anything motherly in my presence.

When she turned to me, I hesitated.

"Admiral," I began, "on *North Star* you forbade me to speak of my mission with Harper. I have not been able to keep that promise."

"I hardly foresaw these circumstances when I gave you those instructions. You may continue. Harper, your absolute secrecy will be expected until I say otherwise."

Harper nodded.

I started from the beginning, leaving out the personal details of my journey and focusing on the relevant events. I explained how I had gotten us into the Gulf, and I gave a detailed analysis of all the encounters I had had with the pirates since then. When I got to the discovery of the channel, Comita's eyes lit up.

"You have exceeded my wildest hopes," she said, rising to her feet. I stood, too, and she clasped me by the shoulders. "The Archipelago thanks you for your service, Rose."

My cheeks burned and, despite the tangled mess around me, I allowed myself a small measure of pride.

"What now?" Harper asked.

"Now the rest of us risk our lives. Can you plot out those coordinates for us?" Comita asked me.

I nodded.

"Good. I'll need you to testify before the Council. I don't want to move without their support, although I will if necessary. We don't have time for their deliberations." She paused, clearly strategizing.

"What about the rest of my crew?" I asked. I noticed my slip-up too late, but Comita didn't seem to catch it.

"They will be given safe passage back to their captain, after we've secured the Gulf."

"What about Rose?" Harper gave her mother a curious glance.

"You will of course be promoted, Compass Rose. I will see that you are made second mate. Any ship in my fleet would be lucky to have you."

I need you on this ship. I could use a second mate. Miranda's words haunted me.

Comita turned towards the door, her usual efficiency taking over as she girded herself to face the Council and rouse the fleets.

Everything I had ever wanted had just been handed to me. A new ship would mean new crew members, people who didn't know me or my history. It would be a chance to start over fresh, away from Maddox, away from my memories of Miranda. As second mate, I would command respect even from those who resented me.

North. My inner compass trembled, aligning with the poles. I didn't want it.

Harper was watching my face. I looked at her, years of late night conversations and sweaty training sessions offering us the luxury of transparency.

Do what you need to do, her eyes said. *I'm here for you.*

"Admiral." My voice held firm.

"Yes?" Comita's eyebrows rose a fraction of an inch.

"Thank you for your generous offer, but I have to decline."

"Decline?"

"I can't accept your promotion."

"Is there something else you want?"

Sailors didn't question their admiral, but I had returned her daughter to her, alive and in one piece. I figured that bought me a little leeway.

"We should have known about that channel," I said. "With all due respect, we've neglected the coasts for too long. Our maps are no longer accurate, and it opens us up to new threats."

Comita leaned against her desk. I took her silence as permission to continue.

"The Archipelago is losing the surface, but we can't afford to let that blind us. I think it is time for a new survey."

"That's dangerous work. I am not sure I can spare a ship for that," she said. Her eyes weighed me.

"I think I know a captain who might be willing to take the risk."

"This shit is unreal."

Jeanine leaned back on one of the low couches in the courtyard where Comita had arranged for the crew of the *Sea Cat*, Harper, and myself to dine. What Comita thought of her daughter in such company, I didn't dare dwell on, but I was happy to have her there.

"Catch." Finn plucked a grape from the trellised vines behind him and tossed it toward Jeanine. She caught it in her mouth.

"Do you ever get used to this?" Orca asked me and Harper. She eyed the garden and the table loaded with food and drink suspiciously.

"Yes," Harper said, taking a long swig of some sort of sweet drink.

"No," I said simultaneously.

Orca glanced between the two of us.

"Stick around and find out." Harper gave Orca a suggestive wink.

"Doesn't look like I have much choice." Orca swirled her drink experimentally.

Comita had given me detailed orders to relay to Miranda's first mate. The *Sea Cat* was dry docked until Comita had the Council and the other fleets behind her. She could not risk word of the channel getting to Ching, and I didn't really blame her for not trusting Miranda's sailors, no matter how much they had sacrificed to get here. You didn't get appointed Admiral of the Polarian Fleet by being warm and fuzzy.

Despite the relaxed atmosphere, there was a palpable tension running through our group. The longer it took us to get back to Miranda, the longer she stayed in Ching's reach.

"Do you think your admiral has the balls to handle Ching Shih?"

"That's my mother you're talking about," Harper reminded Orca.

"If anyone does, it's Comita." I picked at the food on my plate.

"Why the long face, jelly?"

"What if we're too late?" I asked. "What if Ching has Miranda killed?"

"Ching won't kill her." Kraken stirred from his seat on the ground. He had his back to a young tree, and I thought it sagged in relief when he moved. "Ching and Miranda go too far back."

"Miranda couldn't kill Ching, either," Finn said.

"She didn't seem to have a problem going behind her back, though." Harper looked confused.

"Backstabbing is how pirates show affection," Finn explained. "Actual stabbing is acceptable, too, as long as it's not fatal."

"What, do you have some sort of code?" Harper asked.

"Of course we do. We're not savages."

"And we're not pirates," Orca said, finally finishing her drink. "We're mercenaries, thanks to the Caps."

"Moving on up in the world, aren't we?" Finn swept his arm around the room. "Soon we'll be dining in station restaurants across the Archipelago."

"You could, if you wanted to," I said. Five pairs of eyes latched on to me.

"The admiral issued you all full pardons. You'll be allowed entry onto Polaris station anytime you want."

In the silence that followed I could hear the water in the fountain tumble over the smooth stones at its base.

"And the captain?" Kraken asked.

"Full pardon," I said. I didn't tell them the rest of Comita's offer. I had to see if Miranda was interested first.

"She'll be happy to hear that," Kraken said. "I'll tell her you made sure we were treated well."

"Actually," I said, hesitating, "I was thinking I might tell her myself."

"You're fucking kidding me." Orca shook her head, making her braids swing around her face. "I thought we were getting rid of you."

"I'm like a barnacle, Orca. Remember?"

Finn let out a celebratory whoop and began collecting our glasses for refills. Jeanine shook her head, a knowing smile on her lips.

"I told you that you were in deep, kid," she said.

My laughter was cut off by a massive pair of arms, and then I was lifted into the air and crushed in a muscular embrace. Tentacles obscured my view as the sea monster enveloped me.

"Out here, you want something, you make it work. Anyone who accepts anything less deserves it."

"I'm gonna make it work," I said as he put me down.

"Good."

Harper pulled me aside a little while later, after we had all had too much to eat and drink.

"I'll miss you," I said, gently tugging on one of her curls.

"You're not going anywhere yet. You still have to face the Council."

"The Council has nothing on Ching Shih," I said, feeling perhaps a little overconfident.

"I still can't believe you're leaving me for Miranda Stillwater."

"Well," I said darkly, "I haven't told you everything. There's a good chance she wants nothing to do with me now."

"Then why the hell are you going back?"

I looked around the courtyard at the motley crew of merce-naries passed out on the couches. She followed my gaze and slung an arm around my shoulder.

"You really do have terrible taste," she said. "But I get it."

Good, I thought, *because I don't.*

North

Captain's Log
Admiral Josephine Comita
North Star, Polarian Fleet
August 16, 2513
36.9, -62.8°

Compass Rose's return could not have occurred at a more fortuitous time. The Council will convene in two days for an emergency session, giving us an opportunity to solidify Archipelago opinion in our favor. We must act.

As for Captain Stillwater, her fate may yet resolve itself.

Chapter Eighteen

The ride to the Council headquarters on Libra Station was the longest of my life. Harper and I fidgeted in the passenger cabin while Comita drilled me on my presentation and Harper on her corroborating evidence. I was all too aware that every passing moment brought me closer to the Council and farther away from Miranda, and that every minute wasted in inaction was a minute for Ching to act.

When the scales of Libra Station finally filled the porthole, the sigh of relief that left my body raised Comita's eyebrows.

Libra Station was, if anything, more opulent than Polaris. This was where the Archipelago elite ensconced themselves while the fleets patrolled the perimeters, content to bask in the glory of their positions and the luxury that accompanied them. Or at least, that was the general impression most of us had of our government.

Keeping the Archipelago unified was not easy. Each station functioned as its own city state, and the cultures that had evolved within their walls were unique and inclined to disagreement about tariffs, production, and goods allotments, not to mention which station's boxing and basketball teams were destined to pound the others into oblivion. The politics surrounding the Council were equally heated.

As we disembarked into the overly appointed landing bay, I could not shake the irony. The Archipelago had been founded over four hundred years ago to relocate displaced coastal populations too impoverished to move elsewhere; now, here we were, comparatively rich and eager to lord it over anyone less fortunate.

An obsequious docking master met us with a plastered smile. I was gratified to see that Comita did not return it.

"Are the other admirals here yet?" she asked him.

"A few." He hemmed and hawed for a moment before breaking underneath her stare. "Gemini, Andromeda, Orion, and Aries arrived a few hours ago."

"Aries," Comita said under her breath. "Well, that's one piece of good news."

The stations had been named for their location in the Archipelago, relative to the night sky, but a few defining characteristics of the zodiac had seeped in. The Aries Fleet was always primed for battle.

Gemini, on the other hand, could pose a problem.

"Please, let me show you to your quarters," the docking master said.

The rooms Harper and I shared could have housed half of *Man o' War*. Harper, following Comita's orders, set about running hot showers for us both. I emerged to find her laying out clean uniforms and a few cosmetics. The garments gleamed on the bedspread.

"Nothing we can do about your hair," Harper said, frowning at me, "but I've got some makeup to soften your look."

"I don't need to be softened."

"You look like a pirate."

"It's just a haircut. Once I put the uniform on I'll look exactly like I used to."

Harper frowned at me and adjusted my curls.

"Maybe it's not your hair," she said.

"What's that supposed to mean?"

"You look different. I don't know how to describe it, but I bet Maddox would think twice about yanking your chain if he saw you right now."

I glanced down at my body.

"I'm wearing a towel, Harp. Hardly intimidating."

"Yeah, about that. You need to get dressed."

I turned my back to her and pulled on a pair of pants and a bra.

"What is that?" Harper grabbed my arm as I reached for my shirt. I followed her eyes to the scar on my stomach.

"A lash."

"Who the hell lashed you?"

"It's a long story."

Harper's hackles were still up when I finished my tale.

"I'm going to give this Miranda of yours a piece of my mind," she said.

"Your friend Orca did worse."

"That's not the point."

A knock on the door interrupted our conversation, and I dragged the rest of the uniform over my head. We were respectably dressed by the time Admiral Comita beckoned for us to follow her.

Libra's hallways were mostly empty, occupied exclusively by richly dressed staff members walking with purpose and arrogance from appointment to appointment. A few gave us sideways looks, gossip brewing beneath their sleek exteriors.

The Council chambers crouched in the middle of the station, through a pair of huge, wooden doors with the Archipelago seal emblazoned on them. The seal of Libra hung beneath, the scales of justice resting in a perpetual balance that I found a little hard to swallow, in light of what I now knew about the Gemini mutiny.

We entered to a polite cacophony. Admirals milled in the lower Council seats while the high seats' occupants shuffled about, shaking hands and exchanging what I assumed were pointless pleasantries. Each station had a set number of seats, determined largely by population. My home station, Cassiopeia, had only two; both of them were empty.

I hadn't paid much attention to the actual procedures that determined government function in Fleet Prep, but I had memorized the chain of command. I knew enough to know that I was on the bottom rung in this room.

Comita led us to the Polarian sector, where we sat through the next hour as the Council came to order. I couldn't focus on most of what they were saying through the ringing in my ears. In the cabin of the transport ship, drilling with Comita had seemed like a repetitive exercise. I appreciated it now as my hands shook and sweat crept down my sides.

"The council calls Compass Rose to the podium."

I tried and failed to take deep, steadying breaths as I approached the center and took the stand.

"Under the orders of Admiral Comita of the Polarian Fleet, I infiltrated the Gulf of Mexico to gain intelligence on the movements of the pirate Ching Shih," I said, my hands shaking.

I paused to catch my breath. It was funny how speaking even a few words to an audience of this size left me more winded than swimming a mile.

Comita gave me a barely perceptible nod. At no point during this report was I to mention Miranda Stillwater. I swallowed and continued.

"I was part of a small crew of carefully selected men and women with diverse backgrounds and skills. Using a drifter vessel as cover, we were able to gain access to the Gulf. The coordinates you have before you detail what I learned of Ching's forces and their approximate locations.

"While at a mining station, our trawler picked up Harper Comita and a Polarian SHARK. The SHARK, Jonathan Flynn, sustained fatal injuries during a skirmish with Ching's raiders and is not available for testimony."

The formal words felt stiff in my mouth.

"We were targeted, but managed to elude the raiders along the coast, where we discovered a channel through Florida deep enough for Archipelago vessels. To the best of my knowledge, Ching is not aware of this passage and has set no patrols."

Chaos erupted after my words. It took a good five minutes for the council to settle down enough to come to the next order of business. Harper stood and swore that the words I spoke were true, and then Comita took the stand.

"My fellow Admirals, councilpersons, and citizens." Her voice carried around the room. "We have been given an unlooked-for opportunity. Many of you have urged caution over the past

291

months, but the time for caution is past. We can now safely assume that Ching Shih plans to launch a full-scale assault on the Archipelago, and we know that our mining stations are suffering under her unlawful seizure. I have additional information regarding Ching Shih herself, which I will clarify shortly, convincing me that allowing her an ounce of civility will end with the destruction of our entire way of life. We have to act, and we have to act now."

This time, the shouts did not surprise me.

Comita raised her hand for silence.

"A year ago, I received a message from an unknown sailor, warning me of a growing force of pirates outside of our patrols. You are all familiar with my reports from that time frame.

"Six months ago, I received another message, this time warning me that Ching was moving on the mines. As you are all aware, it was again Polarian intelligence that led the Council to send a probe into the Gulf.

"The third time the sailor contacted me, I arranged a parley. In exchange for continued intelligence, I offered the sailor a full Archipelago pardon for any perceived misdemeanors, and citizenship. It is through these efforts that Compass Rose was able to access the Gulf, and it is through these efforts that I can say to you, with certainty, that Ching has no intention of stopping at the mines. It should not come as a surprise. In fact, it should come as a warning. The more things continue to destabilize, the stronger the opposition will be.

"You think *we* are struggling to deal with rising toxicity and deeper waters? How do you think the rest of the ocean is faring? Humanity has always been divided between those who have and those who have not, and if you read the histories, which I assume everyone in this room has had the privilege of so doing," there was a pause, here, in which Comita's cutting words drew blood, "then you know that the balance of power can shift. Ching Shih is intent on upsetting the Atlantic order, and our failure to act has given her the means to achieve it."

Comita let this sink in for a moment. It was an uncharacteristically impassioned speech, and I saw shades of her daughter in her voice, if not her words.

"My third party knows Ching, and we have one more thing to pin our hopes on if all else fails. In addition to providing information and access, the sailor made a promise. If the opportunity arises, they will neutralize Ching Shih. I ask that the Council recognize my authority on this matter and prepare the pardon immediately following the closure of this meeting."

A full pardon?

Heads on the high seats conferred.

"The Council asks for disclosure of the party's name."

"The party does not wish to be disclosed until the pardon is signed, out of legitimate fear for their personal safety."

I paid little heed to the details of the debate that followed. A full pardon and citizenship for Miranda Stillwater was unthinkable, and yet Comita looked like she was about to pull it off. I bit my lip against the wave of hope.

The rest of Comita's words sank in a little more slowly.

I wanted to ask the admiral what she meant by neutralize. I remembered how keen Miranda had been to avoid Ching Shih, and now that I knew that Ching had saved Miranda's life, I thought I understood why. Neutralization would come at an incredible cost for Miranda, and for all her resolve I could not see her paying it.

And if she did? If she attempted to assassinate the legendary pirate queen, what would happen? Kraken was not with her. Orca was not with her. It would be suicide.

She doesn't want to die, I told myself. *Not with a pardon so close.*

Unless the pardon wasn't for her. If Comita did know the whereabouts of her sister, then it was possible that Miranda's deepest desire was to clear her name and her conscience, but not necessarily to live to enjoy the benefits.

My heart pounded, then subsided.

I didn't think she was quite that noble.

Harper fidgeted at my side, muttering something that I didn't hear over the sounds of the chamber and my own fears.

"The Council approves your request, Admiral. We will now open the floor to discuss moving on the Gulf, beginning with Admiral Gonzalez of Aries Station."

"This is going to take all night," Harper said, this time loud enough for me to hear as she sank into her seat.

It was worse than Harper feared. It took all of that night and into the next morning for the council to make its decision. I was called on again and again to discuss the channel, questioned about details that, in my view, had no bearing on the decision, and enjoyed the singular experience of having almost every answer interrupted by at least one belligerent councilperson.

The Aries admiral, Leticia Gonzalez, conferred with Comita on several occasions. She had a broad, plain face and a quick laugh. Harper greeted her warmly. I hung back. One admiral was enough for me.

"You must be the navigator," Leticia said, giving me a look that managed to be both casual and piercing at the same time, so that I was not sure if I had been dismissed or interrogated by the time her eyes moved on.

Comita nodded at her daughter, and Harper steered me back toward our seats and away from the Aries admiral's scrutiny.

"She's intense," I said, grateful for the hard chair.

"She's from Aries; what did you expect?"

I shrugged, but I could not help watching the way Comita spoke to her. Formal, but with a level of familiarity that sent a prickle down my spine. It occurred to me for the first time in a while that Polaris had a very large fleet. So did Aries Station, and the Aries admiral had a reputation for running hot. The sight of the two of them together, ice and fire, did not go unnoticed.

From the high seats, a few of the immaculately groomed heads turned slightly toward each other, and I was relieved when Comita returned to her seat.

The vote came down to Gemini Station. Their Admiral was a tired-looking man named Hiro Patel. He approached me and Comita during the next recess, his brown eyes grave.

Were you there for the mutiny? I wondered.

He nodded politely at Harper and me, then turned to Comita.

"Gemini acted hastily under my predecessor. You understand that I cannot make the same mistake."

It was not a question.

"I trust you will act in your station's best interest," Comita said.

I noticed she did not try to sway him.

"Sending such a young navigator into the Gulf, for instance, seems hasty. May I ask why you acted without consulting the council, Admiral Comita?"

Coming from this soft-spoken man, it did not sound like a reprimand, but more like honest curiosity.

"Sometimes you have to act on instinct, Hiro."

He weighed this behind brown eyes, his expression neutral. Comita introduced me in the silence that followed.

"This is Compass Rose."

"You are a credit to your station," he said to me, extending his hand.

I shook it.

North, east, south, west. My compass spun as I realized my mistake. There were too many directions, and I felt them pulling me apart as Patel's hand tightened on mine. I saw the stillness of shock creep over his features.

He did not turn my palm over. He did not shout. He simply knew.

His slip in composure lasted less than a second. With a nod to me, Comita, and Harper, he returned to his seat and did not look at me again, but I could feel the scar on my palm burning.

How does he know Miranda is alive? I wondered as we sat down for the final vote. Sweat poured down my face. Had I just destroyed everything I had worked toward?

"Those against swift and decisive action?"

Half of the room punched the dissenting button at their seats.

"Those for it?"

The other half stirred, making a much more vigorous display of voting. The Aries admiral was among the first to punch in her answer.

Admiral Hiro Patel and the rest of Gemini's representatives were the last. His fellow Gemini waited on him, and I watched him while the directions swirled and eddied around me.

Patel was now the only thing standing between me and Miranda. The tie was called with a hint of impatience, and still Patel sat there, weighing his options.

As he moved his hand to the button, his eyes flickered once to me.

Of course.

If he confessed that he knew Miranda was alive, then he would have to explain why he had not taken action against her. I had just given him a much larger dilemma than simply saving the Archipelago. Either way, he lost. If he voted no, the chances of the Archipelago discovering his negligence were slim, but only because we would have far bigger fish to fry with Ching beating on our portholes.

If he assented, if he voted to go after Ching in the Gulf on the advice of a known compatriot of Miranda Stillwater, he stood a good chance of losing his position the minute news of her pardon reached the Council.

He had to choose between his people and his career, and the higher in the ranks you rose in the Archipelago, the more you valued pride above all else.

Admiral Hiro Patel voted with the same reserve with which he'd shook my hand.

I met his eyes as he folded his hands in his lap, and tried not to show the relief ripping like a headwind through my body.

We would strike.

Blood smeared the wall.

"Let her be," Kraken said, thrusting his arm in front of me.

Orca hit the wall again, her arms slick with sweat and her teeth bared. Behind her, Finn sat with his head in his hands, and Jeanine stood with her back to us, staring out the window into the garden beyond.

"I. Will. Not. Stay. Here." Orca punctuated each of her words with another strike, her knuckles raw and weeping.

"She's going to fracture her hand," I said to Kraken, my throat tightening as I watched Orca break herself against the smooth, unfeeling plastic of Polaris.

"Let her," he said, and when he saw the look on my face he gripped my shoulder. "Better the wall than your admiral, Rose."

Orca looked over at me, and I shuddered at the murder in her eyes. She hit the wall one more time, spraying drops of blood over the gray floor.

"You will tell Admiral Comita that the *Sea Cat* departs when I say she does."

I flinched.

"If you're caught," I began, but she cut me off.

"You put on a real good show, didn't you?" She took a step toward me, shaking with rage.

"What?"

"You had me fooled, for a moment, there. I thought you actually cared about us." She shook her head. "I thought you cared about the captain. And now we're dry docked until your fucking admiral is done blowing up the Gulf."

"If we try to get back into the Gulf and Ching's sailors find us, she'll kill us and she'll kill Miranda."

"Don't talk like you're one of us."

"If I could change this, don't you think I would?" I shouted, trying to shove past Kraken's arm. I might as well have tried to move the ship itself.

"Then *do* something. *Man o' War* has no idea your entire fucking Archipelago is coming for her, and your admiral's pardon isn't going to do her much good in the locker, is it? What is she supposed to do, put up a flag of truce when she sees them coming? They'll kill her, and if they don't, Ching will. We have to warn her."

"If we take the *Sea Cat*, Comita will torpedo us out of the water," I said.

"Torpedos didn't stop you from picking up Harper, though, did they?" Her voice went quiet, and I glared at her over Kraken's arm.

"There is a big difference between a few raiders and an entire fleet."

Orca shook her head, an incredulous smile twisting her mouth. "You're a fucking coward, Compass Rose."

Kraken's arm kept me upright as I reeled from the insult.

"That's enough," he said.

"Whose side are you on?" Orca asked him, turning her bloodshot eyes away from me.

Kraken moved faster than an eel. He grabbed Orca by the collar and shoved her up against the bloody wall. Her feet dangled off the floor, and she hung there, shocked into silence.

"You listen to me, first mate," he said, and his voice filled the room like thunder, sending reverberations through the soles of my feet. The tattoos on his skin moved as his muscles rippled, and the only thing more terrifying than the inked horror was the look in his eyes.

"There are no goddamn sides. Do you know the reason we are here? On this boat? In this ocean, fighting for our lives like fucking bilge rats? It's because people like us turned on each other when the waters started rising. You are the first mate. You have a responsibility to your captain and your crew. Rose is your crew. Now start acting like a goddamn officer or I will flog you myself."

He let her slide to the floor.

I stood rooted to the spot. He filled the room, a vengeful giant with one too many arms.

Orca rubbed her collarbone and straightened her shirt.

"Thanks," she said, and I let my jaw hang open as she clasped his forearm.

"Don't make me do it again anytime soon," he said.

"What just happened?" I asked Finn, who had left off staring at his knees to observe.

"Orca released the Kraken."

"What?"

"That's what we call it, anyway. Takes a lot to get him riled up, but when he does . . ." Finn trailed off.

"Now," Kraken said, his voice subsiding back to its normal rumble. "Let's go over this again."

I took a deep breath, trying not to let Orca's words sink in, and laid out the Council's verdict and Comita's orders.

"It is a classic bait-and-trap maneuver. Aries will attack from the mouth of the Gulf while Andromeda strikes from the Caribbean Sea. That should distract Ching Shih long enough for Polaris and Orion to come in through the channel. Polaris will close the Red Flag Fleet in from behind while Orion takes back the mines, and the remainder of the Archipelago fleets will patrol the exits to keep any ships from escaping. That should also prevent any of Ching's patrols from coming to her aid. Without the mines, Ching will have nothing to hold hostage."

"And she will be penned in the middle of the Gulf while you sink her ships, one by one," Orca said.

"Yes." The word hurt.

I remembered those last few hours in the Council chambers, listening with mounting horror as they coldly ordered the execution of any pirate sailing under Ching. There would be no parley or surrender. The Gulf would run as red as Ching's flag.

Somewhere in the midst of the closing trap, *Man o' War* floated unaware.

Coward.

My own fists clenched, and I longed to hit the wall.

"Comita gave me her word that Miranda would not be harmed," I said. The words sounded hollow after Kraken's storm.

"Comita gave you her word, huh?" Orca kept her tone level, glancing sideways at Kraken, but I could see the anger quickening again.

"She'll send a message to Miranda once we get closer. *Man o' War* is the only ship that has clearance past our lines."

"Rose." Orca walked towards me slowly, nodding at Kraken to keep him placated, and put her ruined hands on my shoulders. "I know she's your admiral. I know you trust her. But think about it for a moment. How convenient would it be if that message got lost in translation or, better yet, was never sent? How very fucking convenient would it be for Miranda Stillwater to die in the Gulf, sparing your Admiral the difficulty of explaining to the Council how she tricked them into pardoning a known mutineer? And even if your admiral does her best to warn Miranda, there are still a million ways things could go wrong. Do you trust Comita enough to put Miranda's life in her hands?"

"I—" My voice strangled in my throat.

How very fucking convenient would it be for Miranda Stillwater to die in the Gulf.

Orca squeezed my shoulder gently. It was that, more than anything else, that unraveled me.

"I have to go."

I fled the room, running down the hallway with my eyes blind with unshed tears. I ran, heedless of the perplexed faces I passed, until I came at last to the North garden.

It was empty. It was always empty, only the pine and the boulder standing sentinel at the center. There was a spot behind the boulder hidden from view and soft with pine needles. I scraped my shoulder against the rock as I stumbled to my knees, sending a flurry of lichen to the ground.

The pain felt good.

I curled into a ball with my back against the rough stone. The garden, despite its austerity, reminded me of Miranda.

"Where we're going, I am going to need more than a borrowed fleet navigator. I need a navigator I can trust, and who does not question my decisions. I need your loyalty."

Loyalty, obedience, love. Miranda asked for it, Comita expected it, and I delivered it, because that was what I did. I pointed my commanders in the right direction.

I watched the needles blur in front of me.

I had been so ready to distrust Miranda—so eager, in a way, to be disappointed that I had not even thought to question Comita.

Comita was my admiral, but she was more than that. She was Harper's mother. She was the iron filling, the lodestone of Polaris, the point I set my compass by. She would not betray me.

She is your admiral, first.

Admirals had more than their navigators to think about. They had entire fleets to govern and a station to protect. Miranda was just one captain, and if Comita thought that Miranda jeopardized Polaris, or jeopardized Comita's legitimacy as admiral, could I really trust that she would keep her word?

I knew the answer. I knew it by the pit in my stomach, and by the heaviness of my limbs. I knew it by the cold, clear clarity of the constellations somewhere far above the ship.

"You're a navigator, Rose. You see several possible courses and you take the one that makes the most sense. Politics are different."

Only they were not that different. If I could distance myself enough, I could see the brilliance of the plan. Eliminating Miranda tied up loose ends. It might not have been Comita's plan in the beginning, any more than Annie had planned on drowning me beneath the ship when she first invited me to sit with her, but, like Annie, Comita was an opportunist. She saw several possible courses, and she chose the one that made the most sense at the time.

Even if she wasn't planning on deliberately abandoning Miranda to chance, Orca was right. There was still the possibility that things could go wrong. Sonar pings were notoriously unreliable over long distances.

I'm just a navigator, I thought to myself, but the thought was not comforting.

There was only one person who could help me now.

Chapter Nineteen

I found Harper in the baths. Her face was flushed from the heat, and a few curls escaped the towel piled on her head. She gave me a cat's smile, stretching her arms over her head and threatening to burst free from the second towel wrapped tightly around her chest.

I didn't have time for her games.

"I need to talk to you," I said, pitching my voice low.

Her smile vanished.

"Let me get dressed."

Back in our station quarters, I laid out my concerns, watching her face tighten.

"My mother wouldn't do that," she said, tapping her fingers on the table.

I poured her a drink.

"Even if she doesn't, it's still a huge risk."

"She wouldn't do that," Harper repeated. Her hair, hastily dried, spilled over one shoulder and she gave it a savage tug.

"I know, Harp," I said, but I had the feeling my words were not reaching her.

"She wouldn't. Would she?"

Harper turned wide, brown eyes on me. The bruises from her stint as a prisoner were almost gone, but a ghost of greenish yellow still stained her left cheek. It made her look older.

"She's the admiral. She will do whatever she needs to do to keep Polaris safe," I said, treading carefully.

"She sent you into the Gulf alone with a mercenary traitor." Harper's eyes welled, and it occurred to me that this was the first downtime either of us had had since our ill-fated adventure.

"If she could do that to my best friend, what else would she do?"

"We're at war, Harp. And I could have said no."

Harper's knuckles tightened on her hair, squeezing the last of the water out of it. I nudged her drink closer to her.

"Maybe you should have," she said.

I traced the scar on my palm.

"Rose," Harper began, then stopped herself and knocked back her drink. "There's something you should know."

I didn't need to be a psychic to know I wasn't going to like what I was about to hear.

"What?"

"My mother and Leticia, the Aries admiral, have been friends for a long time. Aries was one of the few stations that actually listened to my mother's warnings about Ching Shih."

She took another drink.

"The thing is, Leticia and Octavius Grant, the admiral of Andromeda, have always worked closely together, too."

"So?" The pit in my stomach yawned wider.

"Octavius has a cousin on the High Council."

I waited, bile rising.

"Do you remember who proposed the "no parley" policy?"

The "no parley" policy was what the Council was calling their decision to take no prisoners. I swallowed and took a guess.

"Octavius's cousin?"

Harper nodded.

I poured Harper another drink, downed it myself, then refilled the glass for her.

"What are you saying?" I asked.

"I don't know." Her voice cracked, and she rubbed her palms across her eyes to dash away the tears. "I don't know, but if my mother wanted to get rid of Miranda, she wouldn't do it herself. She would have someone else do it, someone who nobody could trace back to her. Someone like that councilman."

I was glad of the drink. The streak of heat it burned down my throat stopped the scream.

"We could be wrong," I said. Voicing the hope diminished it further.

"We could."

We stared at each other.

"She's my mother," Harper said through her tears.

I took her hand and held it tightly.

"I am so sorry, Harp."

She took a deep breath before putting into words the question in both of our heads.

"What do we do?"

"I don't know. If we try to leave, she might sink us. She'd have to, if we disobeyed direct orders."

Harper frowned.

"She wouldn't if I was onboard."

My chest ached.

"No. Absolutely not. We could all die, and she could accuse me of trying to kidnap you on top of that."

"Do you see an alternative? You'll never get out of our range any other way. If I'm onboard, she'll come up with an excuse. She won't want you taken captive, because you and your crew could ruin everything for her if you tell anyone who you're sailing under. She could try and sweep it under the rug, but it is risky. She'll fall back on her original promise and pardon Miranda."

"Harper, I can't let you do that."

"Why?"

"Because this is my problem, not yours. I have to warn Miranda, but you don't owe her anything."

"My mother wants to wipe ten thousand souls from the face of the earth." Her voice was thick with scorn. "I know that they are pirates. I know that they would probably have killed me if I hadn't stowed away on your trawler, but that doesn't make it right. That's not war, Rose, that's genocide."

"What are you saying?"

"I'm saying that I am not going to sit here waiting for my mother to kill the woman who saved all our asses. We'll have to wait until we're through the channel, though. If we leave before that, we risk sabotaging the attack. They need you to help navigate."

"I get Miranda. You stay here."

"And do what? Watch as my mother blows you out of the water?"

"We'll think of something."

"This is the most logical course, Rose," Harper said. "Besides. You would do it for me."

"It's not the same. You're the admiral's daughter. You're—"

"I did not ask to be the admiral's daughter, but I am an engineer. And if you want that tub of yours to outdistance my mother's advance guard, you're going to need me."

"But—"

Harper slammed her fist on the table, spilling her glass.

"Goddamn it, Compass Rose. Let. Me. Help. You."

"Yes, captain," I said without thinking, the authority in her voice overriding all else.

"That's more like it. Now come on. We've got work to do."

She stood, leaving the drink to drip down the side of the table, and strode out of the room with enough confidence to put Poseidon to shame.

The channel crept into view of *North Star's* portholes. Dead trees stuck out of the shoreline, pointing accusing fingers at our ships.

I stood beside Admiral Comita on the bridge, awed despite myself.

I had not had the luxury of sightseeing the last time I had sailed these waters. I had been too focused on getting us out alive.

I stared now.

Patches of green showed through the dead wood, and something brown, furry, and cat-sized darted up a distant trunk.

Ahead of us, swarms of insects rose off the water, and Comita shuddered.

"Make sure all hatches remain locked and guarded at all times, and the ventilation systems completely sealed," she instructed a nearby officer. "Anyone who breaks protocol is to be quarantined and docked two weeks' pay."

When she saw my startled look, she gave me a grim smile.

"It's not taught in the ranks, as there is little cause for it, but those insects out there are vectors for diseases that could wipe out an entire station. We do not have the necessary immunity, and there is only so much that our doctors can do. One outbreak could decimate us, and then Ching Shih would not have to raise a finger."

The swarms outside took on a more sinister meaning. They were similar to swarms of jellyfish, in the way they clung together, but they moved much faster—more like schooling fish than a swarm.

Mist rose off the morning waters through the haze of insects. We kept the ships to the center of the channel, but it was tight, and the bridge was full of nervous sailors taking sonar readings and shouting out depths. A smaller ship ranged ahead of us, reporting back every few minutes. If the worst came to pass, they would place a few explosives to clear the way.

"You have brought great honor to this fleet, Compass Rose," Comita said as she surveyed the buzzing bridge.

"Thank you, Admiral."

I tore my eyes away from her before she could see the anguish written clearly in the amber.

I could be wrong, I reminded myself.

A few birds took wing along the banks. I was not alone in watching them soar away, and Comita cleared her throat pointedly.

A ruined structure jutted out from the bank a few meters ahead. Comita slowed the ship, giving it as wide a berth as the channel allowed.

"There is a stretch of these," I cautioned as the rotting, gray stone stared at us through eyes of empty windows. Another one of the brown shapes scuttled on a ledge, and a sailor with a spyglass let out a shout.

"It's a rat. Neptune's balls, it's a goddamn giant rat."

"Language on the bridge," Comita said, but she gave the port-hole a curious glance.

I, for one, was perfectly content to keep as much distance as possible between myself and giant rodents. The rats in the bowels of Cassiopeia Station grew to an alarming size, and they were notoriously vicious. I had no desire to speculate about the nature of these terrestrial relatives.

More dead trees slipped by.

I felt useless, standing there, making only a few minor corrections. This was the easy part and, without the threat of a raider behind me, it was almost boring.

That left me time to worry about the plan Harper and Orca had come up with. Sweat ran down my sides, and I hoped Comita chalked up my nerves to the impending attack.

As I guided us through the channel, pausing now and then to wait for a detonation to clear some of the bigger debris aside, somewhere in the docking bay Harper inspected the *Sea Cat* on the pretense of following her mother's orders. The trawler had been transferred out of Polaris's hold to the *North Star*, which was a small miracle in itself, and Harper was supremely confident that no one would question her. She may not have asked to be the admiral's daughter, but the arrogance that came with the title had its uses.

The ship was not entirely as we'd left it. Polaris had removed the bulk of the weapons on *Sea Cat* as a precaution, which had reduced both Orca and Kraken to simmering fury.

Not that weapons would do us much good where we were going. We would be outgunned at every quarter. Our best hope lay in the anonymity of the drifter vessel. As long as we were perceived as harmless flotsam, we stood half a chance, and only a few of Ching's sailors had a visual identification on our vessel.

The rising sun splintered off the smooth water, and I shielded my eyes with my hand. The current moved slowly here, but it moved, a sinuous passage through the winding channel.

"There's a large thing ahead," I said, unsure of what to call the long wreckage I remembered. Sand and water had reduced the front of it to rubble, but the curved tiers of the structure reflected sonar waves back in bizarre geometric shapes. Most of it was below water, which made it harder still to identify from the surface.

"Hard to port," Comita said, not bothering with degrees.

I chewed on my lip.

"Are you all right, Rose?" Comita asked.

I nodded, not trusting my voice. I had plenty of legitimate reasons for concern without adding treason into the mix.

Among them was the disconcerting realization that I did not even know how Miranda would react when she saw me again. My heart constricted in my chest.

"It narrows up here," I said, my brain following the course despite my heart's defection.

North Star rounded a bend and her hull scraped sand. Alarms rang around the bridge, followed by shouts.

"Press forward," I told Comita, who was in the process of ordering a complete halt.

She frowned.

"It opens up in another few meters, but if we stop here, we'll need a tow."

I had grown used to the informality of Miranda's crew. Comita did not look like she appreciated the authority in my tone.

"With all due respect, Admiral," I added.

"Full speed ahead," Comita said, correcting the course. Her eyes warned me that this concession was not absolution.

It was evening by the time we reached the mouth of the channel. I felt it in the eddying current, and in the gradual influx of jellyfish. They blurred the sonar readings, tiny pricks of light on the screens as we left the shoals for deeper water.

"Go get yourself something to eat," Comita told me.

I forced myself to walk out of the helm. My legs wanted to sprint, and I ate alone in the mess hall, methodically shoveling food into my mouth.

"Well, look who it is," said a familiar voice.

I set my fork down deliberately and looked up. Maddox loomed above me, wasting oxygen with every breath.

308

"Get the hell out of my face, Maddox," I said.

His eyes gleamed with predatory interest as he stepped closer to my seat. The heat from his body invaded my senses, and I snarled, rising to my feet to glare up at him.

"I said get the hell out of my face." I kept my voice low and even.

"Watch your tone, drifter," he said.

"Get. Out. Of. My. Face."

His face purpled in the most gratifying display of shock I had ever seen. Between us, hidden from view, the knife Miranda had given me pressed against his groin.

"You're pathetic," I said. "Get back to work before you piss yourself."

I sat back down, not bothering to see if he had anything to say in response. The sound of his retreating footsteps restored some of my appetite, and I smiled grimly down at my plate.

"I've been looking for you," Harper said, dropping into the empty seat next to me. "We're ready. When will your shift be over?"

My food, which had looked tempting for such a brief, shining moment, might as well have been bilge sludge after that. I looked around to make sure no one could hear me before answering.

"Comita wants to launch the attack tonight. It will take a few hours to get the bulk of Polaris and Orion through the channel, and that's a few hours for Ching's scouts to discover us. The faster we strike, the less prepared Ching will be. That means I need to be on the bridge."

Harper shook her head.

"We need to get ahead of them. We won't last a second under heavy fire."

"I'm due back in a few minutes," I said, feeling the tides turn.

"Rose."

"What?"

"If we're going to do this, we need to do it now. Have you given Comita the coordinates?"

"Yes."

"She's been admiral for fifteen years, and she was a captain long before we were born. She can take it from here. You have done your duty."

"I—"

"She won't try you for treason," Harper said, shoving a satchel into my lap.

I looked inside. A thick envelope poked out, stamped with Comita's seal and the scales of Libra Station.

"What is this?"

"The pardon. I took it from my mother's desk. It pardons Miranda, her crew, and you."

"Me?"

"For serving under a known traitor."

"She never told me I would need a pardon," I said, my voice rising in anger.

Harper kicked me under the table.

"She also didn't tell you who you were sailing under, and none of this will matter anyway if we don't get out of here now. You said yourself that it will take a little while for the fleets to sort themselves out. We won't get a better opportunity."

"I know, I know."

"Break the damn rules, Rose. Everyone else does." Harper slung the bag over her shoulder, smiled at the table behind us, and made for the door. I followed, feeling significantly less at ease. This was worse, somehow, than facing off with pirates. These were people who trusted me—and if I failed, Miranda sank with me.

North Star gleamed under the healthy bio-lights, a stark contrast to the ships I'd grown accustomed to. If we got out of this alive, I vowed, I would do something about *Man o' War's* infrastructure.

"How are we getting out of the dock?" I asked. Harper had been intentionally vague about the details of her plan, in the event it fell through and I was questioned, and the uncertainty set my teeth on edge.

"Jessie is on duty, and she's scared out of her mind of pirates." Harper rolled her eyes. "I slipped her some of Jonah's brew before

I came here to help her calm her down. She won't give us any trouble. It's an extra-special batch."

"You drugged her?"

"I would never do something like that," she said, grinning, "but I can guarantee she'll be too worried about standing up straight to question my orders. Go get the others and meet me at the ship."

Without Harper, I felt exposed. It would not be long before Comita started wondering what had become of her navigator. I quickened my pace.

"About time," Orca said when I opened the door to the joint living quarters the mercenary crew had been assigned.

Harper had obviously tipped them off. The four of them were dressed in the clothes they had arrived in, and Finn had a suspiciously heavy bag over one shoulder.

"What?" he asked, taking the defensive when he caught me staring. "It's fruit. You know when the last time was I had fruit?"

I ignored him.

"We can do this," Orca said to me. Her knuckles were scabbed and her hands were bruised, but she clasped my forearm firmly.

The dock where *Sea Cat* was laid up beneath the shipping bay was only half lit. Most of the berths were empty. This was the quarantine and repair dock, and all of its remotely seaworthy previous occupants had been hastily patched up in preparation for the coming battle.

Harper chatted with a dazed-looking sailor I took to be Jessie. The other woman smiled and nodded, her eyes struggling to focus as she read over the sheet of paper Harper handed her.

"Calm seas," she said, stringing the words together so that they sounded more like "calmsies."

"Double-check for me?" Harper asked, shoving the paper in my face.

It was an engine checklist, and had nothing whatsoever to do with docking regulations. Jessie gave another wobbly smile. I forced one back, the risk Harper had just taken grating on my nerves.

311

"Looks good to me," I said, faking enthusiasm. "Will she even be able to open the bay doors?" I asked when she was out of earshot.

"If we hurry."

Harper followed Jeanine to the engine room, and Kraken popped out of one of the bulkheads with a smug expression.

"Still got a few explosives," he said before vanishing again.

"Oh, good," I said, feeling sick.

Orca joined me in the helm after a final sweep of the vessel. The rush of water sluicing into the berth soothed my anxiety. This was where I belonged, for all that the next phase of our plan was entirely up to chance.

"What if Kraken's wrong?" she asked, reading my mind.

"Then we're screwed," I said, wondering if death by missile would be preferable to Kraken's plan.

"How long did he say to wait?" Orca guided the trawler into the water lock, turning off the running lights once the hatch sealed.

"He said it would not take long, but we're so far from the shelf, here. I don't know." I paused as the second hatch opened and we purred into the deepening water. "Stay close to the ship. If we can stay in her shadow, we'll stay off the radar."

Orca hovered the trawler against the belly of *North Star*. Our lights were off, but the rest of the fleet had their running lights on, illuminating the jellyfish glinting in the murky water.

More sweat trickled down my sides. At this rate, my uniform would be drenched.

"Sweet mother of pearl," Orca said, leaning toward the glass.

I squinted, a shudder of primal fear rippling through me.

Large shapes emerged from the murk.

The first squid jettisoned past us, heading straight for the lights. I thought of Annie, and our later flight from the mines, and was glad that Orca had the wheel because I would have turned back toward the hatch in a heartbeat.

"They use light to find their prey," Kraken had explained back on Polaris. "The lights from all of your ships will draw them out."

"I thought they preferred deep water," I asked him. Squid were not a problem around the stations, and I did not know much about their habits.

"They do, but new lights in a new place will be too much to resist, and they do not like ships."

I could attest to that.

The squid attached themselves to the boats, long tentacles groping for purchase. Archipelago vessels were far too large to be bothered by squid this size, for all that they measured in at several meters, but they would confuse the sonar just enough to let us escape unnoticed, if all went well.

"Move slowly," I said, remembering Kraken's instructions.

Squid this size *were* a problem for us.

"Slowly my ass. I hate these fuckers," Orca said through gritted teeth.

"Keep straight. It is open from here on out, give or take a few dead reefs."

"Great. Reefs. This is why I stick to the open ocean." Orca drummed her fingers on the dash as she guided the trawler through the darkness.

"Current will pick up in a few miles. Until then it should stay shallow."

"Even better."

Something slammed into the back of the trawler, sending me sideways in my chair.

"That better be a squid," Orca said.

We didn't dare send out sonar readings, in case they were intercepted, and so there was only one way to find out.

"I'll go check the stern porthole," I said.

"Hurry back. I refuse to die alone, covered in fucking tentacles. If I die, you're coming with me."

I ducked out of the helm and hurried down the hall, past the fading bloodstains where the SHARK had met his messy end, around the narrow galley kitchen, and through the dark hallway to the stern, where the trawling doors waited in the ceiling, sealed but for the occasional drip. At the back of the wall was a porthole, and I stumbled as the ship shuddered under another impact.

Kraken and Finn arrived at a dead run, skidding to a stop in front of me.

"If it was a missile, we'd be dead already," Finn said, nodding toward the porthole. "So what is it?"

The three of us crammed our faces against the glass. Black water stared back.

"Helpful," Finn quipped.

He was tossed into me by another slam and an ominous creaking.

"That sounded like . . ."

"The trawl," Kraken finished for him.

"The squid we saw were not big enough to damage the trawl," I said, narrowing my eyes at the hatch doors. Was I imagining that the drips had increased in volume?

"Those were just the squid you saw." Kraken flexed his shoulder muscles, looking like a boxer preparing to step into the ring. "Do you know what squid's favorite meal is?"

"No."

"Squid. And where there are little squid, there will be big squid."

"What are you saying?" Finn asked.

A sucker planted itself over the porthole window, obscuring half of it with pale, palpitating flesh.

"I am saying that we have a monster on our hands."

"Squid never attack fleet trawlers." I backed away from the porthole as I spoke.

"That's because you shoot them. Drifters don't have that luxury, and the fuckers know it. They are smarter than they look."

The tentacle contracted, releasing its grip on the porthole with an inaudible pop. Above us, metal and plastic screeched.

"Is it—" I did not want to complete my sentence.

"Trying to open the hatch?" Kraken finished for me.

"Yeah . . ." my voice trailed off.

"Intentionally or not, that is what is happening," Finn said, pointing to the steady trickle of seawater.

"How do we lose it?" I asked, turning to our resident tentacle expert.

"With great difficulty."

This was not what either Finn or I wanted to hear.

"We can't blow it off us without giving away our coordinates, and unless one of us wants to go out there with a harpoon and a diving suit, we'll have to think of something else," Kraken said.

"The trawl," Finn said, his face brightening. "Can you try to dislodge it with that?"

"Might work," Kraken said, heading for the control panel.

A nasty wrenching sound pierced our ears, followed by a snap.

"Was that the trawl?" I asked in a decidedly faint voice.

Finn, who had remained by the porthole, shrugged.

"Whatever it was, it just got a lot darker out there."

"Ink." Kraken eyed the hatch.

Sure enough, some of the droplets coming in fell blackly against the basin.

An idea formed in an equally shadowy corner of my mind. It was a bad idea. A very, very bad idea.

"Kraken," I said, thinking of Miranda. "What if we didn't have to go out with a harpoon?"

"I'm listening, kid."

"What if we opened the hatch?"

Finn choked on an inhale.

"Are you out of your mind? We'd flood the ship."

"This room seals off." All the compartments on the trawler did. "If we can get it in the hatch—"

"—assuming it fits," Kraken said.

"—then we can close it in, open the bay doors in here, and . . ." I trailed off.

"Cut it to pieces?" Kraken supplied.

"Something like that."

"You ever done battle with a kraken? This isn't like chopping up calamari," Kraken said.

"Would it work?"

"Chopping it up like calamari?"

"Any of it."

Kraken ran his hand over his smooth scalp.

"You've got more drifter in you than I gave you credit for, wolf pup," he said as the trawler groaned again. "Get back to the helm. Finn and I will handle this."

"It was my idea," I said, wishing that it wasn't. "I can't just let you put yourself at risk."

"Someone needs to keep Orca on track."

"If this thing sinks us, it won't matter." I squared my shoulders.

"Fine. But stay on the other side of the hatch and keep watch. You better be ready to open that door for us."

I nodded, secretly relieved to be on the other side of a sturdy door.

Kraken and Finn drew their curved swords, and Kraken grabbed a few of the long poles drifters used to pluck valuable flotsam out of the holding tank.

"Release the kraken!" Finn roared as Kraken cranked the outer doors open and I ran to the hatch, slamming the door behind me. The window cut off some of the view and most of the sound, but I could see their mouths open as they shouted down the predator.

I didn't need to see or hear to know that the squid was not happy. Loud thumps came from the hatch, and water sprayed through as the creature beat at the walls, the pressure change forcing it into the cavernous space where the trawl nets normally coiled.

Kraken reversed the doors, his muscles and the tendons in his neck bulging with the effort.

Finn pressed himself up against the wall, holding on to a nearby ladder rung for support.

Kraken nodded once in my direction, and then chaos flooded the hold.

The squid's mantle took up most of the room, judging by the raw, red tint of the boiling waters, and its fins beat at the walls, shaking the vessel. I could not see Kraken or Finn past the flailing tentacles.

Shouts from behind me warned me that the rest of the crew was on their way.

"Get back to your stations," I said, mustering as much authority as I could. "We can't help them."

"Help them with what?" Jeanine pushed past me to stare through the hatch window. She swore more violently than I had ever heard her, and that was saying something.

"I have to open the door to let them out, and that could jeopardize the ship if the compartment doesn't seal." My voice sounded dead. "So you all need to be at your stations, preparing for the worst."

"Is there anything worse than a fucking squid *inside my ship?*" Orca said, aiming a kick at the hatch door.

We all jumped as something slammed back in a spray of water.

"How much water is getting in?" Orca asked.

"I don't know," I said, straining to see past the red flesh to where Kraken hacked at the squid's tentacles. Finn was nowhere to be seen.

"Let me in there." Orca pulled out her sword and tucked a throwing knife in her teeth.

"No," Harper, Jeanine and I said in unison.

"As acting captain of this vessel, I order you to open that goddamn door and seal it shut behind me."

I placed myself between her and the hatch.

"No."

"Any one of you can sail this tub without me. Now move, Rose, or I will make you move."

I hesitated, adrenaline obliterating conscious thought.

"If you go, I go."

Orca looked almost as surprised by my words as I felt.

"That thing will eat you alive," she said.

I opened the hatch and stepped into hell.

Orca screamed at Jeanine to shut the door behind her. I didn't look to see if she obeyed.

Water poured into the holding tank from the doors above. They were unable to fully shut with the better half of a few tentacles lodged between them, and we were going to be in serious trouble once the tank overflowed.

Kraken's roars filled the room. The squid, whether by luck or design, had managed to place the bulk of its body in the tank, leaving its tentacles free to grasp at the enemy.

The enemy in question was busy hacking at the tentacle wrapped around his waist, and black ink mingled with the churning water as the squid flailed.

Finn lay unconscious a few feet away.

"Get Finn," Orca said, launching herself at the monster.

I scrabbled across the slick floor, whimpering as I ducked beneath a red limb, and crouched beside Finn.

A nasty lump covered his temple, and I remembered with a jolt that this was the second time he had been hit in the head. I checked his pulse. It was strong, which I took as a good sign, but there was no way of moving him safely. I would have to drag him to the hatch.

There was only one problem with that scenario, and that was the rogue calamari between me and the door.

Orca, true to her namesake, dove into the fray. The squid shuddered as she used her knife to climb up onto its mantle, stabbing the blade into its flesh for purchase, and it released Kraken with what remained of its tentacle.

"The body. You have to go for the body. That's where the fucker's organs are." Finn's voice snapped my attention back to him.

"You all right?"

He raised his eyebrows, then winced.

"I'm seeing three of you, but you're easy on the eyes, so it's okay." His speech was slightly slurred. "Why do they keep aiming for my head?"

"I don't know. Finn, do you think you can walk?"

"I don't know about walking, but I can crawl. Where's my knife?"

"You need to get out of here, not—"

Orca screamed.

I turned away from Finn and was halfway across the deck, my

318

small knife in my hand, before I realized I had no idea what I was planning on doing. The squid had dislodged Orca, who had fallen into the water. Kraken dove in after her, leaving me face to face with the nightmare.

Time froze. The squid's eyes rolled towards me, huge and wide and not quite as empty of recognizable emotion as I would have liked. I had a faint impression of fear, compounded by the rank, fishy stench of the creature, and confusion.

Then it opened its beak, and any stirrings of creature sympathy fled.

Kraken shoved me aside just as one of the squid's remaining tentacles swept toward me. He was soaking wet and covered in wounds from the suckers, but grinning like a madman.

"Now," he shouted, and Orca made another leap for the creature's back. Water poured over her from the leak above, flinging off her braids in droplets as she drove her blade into the squid's back. The squid tried to pull itself up with the tentacles trapped in the door. Orca clung to the blade, and her weight, combined with the sharp edge, was enough to open a four-foot-long slice in the animal. White flesh puckered beneath the red of the mantle, and the squid released another jet of ink as it shuddered beneath the sundering.

"Get clear," Kraken shouted at Orca.

She slid off the squid and tried to leap for the rim of the holding tank, but the distance was too great. The squid writhed and flailed, submerging her in the inky water.

I dove.

I might be Archipelago fleet scum, but I had grown up on Cassiopeia station, swimming in the eel beds. I could hold my breath for five minutes at a time, and I always knew which way the surface lay.

The shock of the cold water hit me like a tentacle. There were none of those underwater, thankfully, but the bulk of the squid's massive body was much more dangerous. If it struck me, I could, at best, hope to lose consciousness and drown, and be crushed to death at worst.

319

I could not see Orca in the black water. I struck towards the bottom, feeling the vibrations in the churning froth. The squid felt like it was everywhere, its agony palpable in its savage death throes.

Orca, where are you?

Beneath the water, the absurdity of the situation cost me a precious bubble of air. Ching was out there somewhere, preparing to take down the Archipelago. Comita, my Admiral, was up to her elbows in pirate blood, the fate of the *Man o' War* in her fists. Meanwhile, Miranda, my captain—my infuriating, arrogant, and intoxicating captain—was trapped between the two of them, and here we were, battling a giant squid in the bowels of our own ship.

This goddamn ocean has a sick sense of humor.

There, to the left. I felt a shift in the water. It was smaller than the struggling cephalopod, and just as desperate. I kicked out towards it, my cupped hands slicing cleanly through the murk, and felt skin brush the tips of my fingers.

I circled around her.

We were deep in the tank, and I could tell from the frantic ripples that she was almost out of air.

I dove deeper, searching for the bottom. There was nothing more dangerous than a drowning person, I reminded myself as I released a stream of bubbles in order to sink onto the soles of my feet, and then I pushed off with all of my strength.

I collided into Orca on the way to the surface, wrapping an arm around her waist. She reached for me, but I kept my other arm free. My legs and lungs burned. Orca struggled, slowing our ascent, and I wished, for a moment, that she'd had the good grace to pass out like Finn.

Instead, she fought me as she fought every waking moment of her life.

I gulped my first breath of air quickly, anticipating her reaction. She was stronger than me, and she broke free of my grip the minute I relaxed enough to breathe. Her hands grabbed at my shoulders, pushing me back under as she coughed and spluttered.

I forced myself to relax, letting her breathe, until my lungs began to burn again. This was the tricky part. Some people calmed down with air, but most panicked until they were fully out of the water.

Orca seemed determined to remain in the latter category. When I breached again, she wrapped her arms around my neck, making it impossible to keep us both afloat.

"Kraken," I managed to shout.

Ripples and a splash preceded him, and then the giant propelled us towards the edge of the overflowing tank. There was almost a foot of water on the ground, and I coughed on my hands and knees.

Orca vomited black water beside me, the tattoo on her bicep glaring at me with its red eyes, as if daring me to point out the discrepancy between her name and her affinity for water.

"We need to get that shut," Kraken said, his voice grim.

I looked up at the doors. They were jammed with more than tentacles. Part of the trawl was snagged as well, the metal twisted and jagged. There was no way we were going to fix it.

"Wait." I wiped water from my eyes, staring at the bit of net dripping through.

"We don't have time to wait, unless we want to seal this compartment off."

"If you engage the trawl, and we open those doors, can you net this thing in our wake?" I asked.

"Why would we want to do that?"

"Can you?"

"Maybe."

"What better way to throw off sonar than to tie a giant squid to our stern?"

Kraken thought about this for a moment, rubbing one of the sucker wounds on his arm.

"You're crazy, you know that?" he said.

I shrugged.

"Get Orca out of here. When I open those doors, I'm going to have three seconds to get to the hatch. You be ready, and tell Jeanine to seal off the hallway just in case."

"Is it dead?" I nodded toward the twitching squid.

"You let me worry about that. Go."

I helped Orca to her feet. She spat out the last mouthful of brine, glared at me, and slogged through the rising water toward Finn. He had made it to the hatch, but judging by the look on his face, the effort had cost him.

Jeanine opened the door for us with a rush of water. I helped her slam it shut again, my face pressed against the window.

"Do you all have a death wish?" Harper said.

I ignored her.

Kraken pulled the last lever and bolted toward us. Behind and above him, the doors began to open, unleashing the full fury of the ocean.

"Get out of here and seal the hallway," I ordered.

The others scrambled to obey, too cowed by the sound of rushing water to argue.

"One, two, three," I counted to myself, my hand shaking on the latch.

North, south, east, west.

The force of the flood knocked me back as Kraken exploded through the hatch. I scrambled to my feet and threw myself at the door for the second time in as many minutes, my feet slipping on the slick floor.

Kraken let out a sound that might have been a curse or a roar, and the door clicked shut. He wound the lock and sank to the floor beside me.

"Well, wolf pup, there's a first for everything," he said, clapping me on the shoulder.

"You mean you've never done battle with a kraken?" I asked, the rush of adrenaline making me giddy.

"That wasn't a kraken, kid. That was just a piece of oversized sushi."

I let out a long sigh. The water pounded against the door at my back, a savage massage that imitated the rush of blood in my ears. I hoped Jeanine and Harper were keeping us stable.

"No one on my old ship would believe me if I told them what just happened," I said.

"Anybody on your old ship worth telling that story to?"

I thought of Comita, and the years I'd spent desperate to earn her approval.

"No, I guess not."

"Then I guess you better learn to tell it like a Merc."

"How do I do that?"

"Easy," he said, leaning his head back against the door. "Add a few more tentacles each time."

"Kraken?" Thinking about the dying squid reminded me of something Comita had said during the council. "Can I ask you something?"

"Is there anything I can do to stop you asking?"

"Is Miranda going to kill Ching?"

He gave me a sideways glance.

"What gave you that idea?"

"Comita said Miranda was going to neutralize Ching Shih."

He closed his eyes and let his face relax into exhaustion.

"There is nothing neutral about death, kid."

Chapter Twenty

Orca stared out at the water, her face illuminated by the occasional flash of distant torpedo fire.

"I suppose this is as good a time as any to thank you," she said, not meeting my eyes.

Looking at her was easier than watching the destruction of the world I knew, and so I noticed her lip twitch upward ever so slightly.

"First mate."

"What, jelly?"

"Accept it."

"I accept nothing," she said, shooting me a mock glare.

"You're glad I stuck around."

"I—" Orca cut herself off. "Yes."

"Yes?"

"Yes, I'm glad you stuck around. Don't let it go to your head."

My smile faded as reality imposed itself in another flash of light.

"That must be the Aries Fleet," I said. Only a few fleets still manufactured warheads with that kind of power. Aries was one of them.

Polaris was another.

"Ching's holding her own, though."

I watched the sonar. It was a mess of ships and flotsam. Ching's raiders darted around the larger fleet vessels, peppering them with smaller missiles and ripping into hulls when they got the chance.

"How the hell are we supposed to find *Man o' War* in the middle of this?" I asked.

We only had a few hours before Comita and the rest of Polaris snapped the jaws of the trap shut. A few hours to track down one ship in the entire Gulf of Mexico, without getting blown up, captured, or boarded in the process.

The last option seemed unlikely, given our mangled passenger. The squid trailed us, a dark shadow that attracted hordes of smaller squid. The feeding frenzy clouded the sonar, making us look more like a swarm than a trawler.

"Isn't that your department, navigator?"

I rubbed the hilt of my knife, feeling the cardinal directions beneath my thumb. If I was being honest with myself, I was afraid.

I was afraid of getting any closer to the battle ahead.

I was afraid of running into Ching Shih.

And most of all, I was afraid of Miranda. If she rejected me now, I was worse off than the lowest drifter, with no ship or harbor to my name.

"This thing handles like a pregnant cat," Orca said under her breath as she messed with the controls. "If someone shoots us, we're squid shit."

"I don't know how to find her," I admitted, pretending not to hear her.

"Aren't you supposed to have some sort of magical ability?"

"It's not magic, and no. I don't get lost. That doesn't mean I can find anyone else."

"You found me in that tank."

"That was different. You were close. I just had to sort through the wavelengths until I found one that matched a human, not a squid. There are thousands of ships out there."

"So find *Man o' War*. You've sailed on her, and you know the captain."

"Do I?" Now it was my turn to mutter.

Orca made a show of ignoring me.

"We'll be hitting the first flotsam, soon," she said. "You're not going to get sick again, are you?"

"I've seen wreckage before."

I didn't want to think about the fleet ship I'd seen destroyed with Miranda, or the raiders Orca and I had blown with a methane deposit.

"Not like this, you haven't."

"Have you?"

"I sail under Miranda Stillwater."

I took that for a yes and closed my eyes, trying to align my compass to a moving point. I might as well have tried to touch the North Star itself.

"Incoming," Orca said. "Open your eyes, jelly."

I blinked as the torpedo streaked past, missing us by only a few meters.

"Must have been aiming for someone else," I said.

"Do you have coordinates for me, or not?"

"I—" I didn't. "Isn't there a call we can use?"

"Like she'd hear it in that mess?"

"Do you have any better ideas?"

"Yes. And all of them involve me standing over your lifeless body if you don't get us to the goddamn ship."

"Just try it."

Orca let out a huff and fiddled with the sonar until she found the prerecorded track she wanted.

"It's a pod call. Orcas used to use them. She'll know it's me."

"Shit," I said, jumping.

A raider ghosted past us, jagged fins primed for battle with a gleaming edge. It paid us no heed, but our proximity to the battle-field set my teeth chattering.

"You sound like a rat," Orca said, keeping the trawler in low gear.

"Sorry." I clenched my jaw.

"It is probably a bad time to ask, but is the only weapon you have that knife?"

"Yes."

"I swear that woman makes me earn every cent. She didn't give you anything else?"

I remembered the way Miranda had presented the knife to me. The rush of emotion that followed was at odds with the fear gripping my body.

Just imagine how she would have presented a sword, I thought.

"She wasn't exactly in the best mood when we left," I said.

Both of us were quiet for a moment.

"Well, if anything happens, stay behind me."

"Sure thing, first mate. Just try not to drown me again."

"Whatever. Hey, listen to this."

She turned up the receiver. Inane whistles and clicks flooded the helm, sounds of a long dead sea still echoing beneath the waves.

"Remember these coordinates." She closed her eyes to listen more intently, then named a location only a few miles south of us.

My heart ricocheted off my chest.

We were close.

So close.

The squid milled around us, passing in front of the trawler as they tore chunks from their vanquished brethren.

Get to the ship, I told myself. *And then get the ship out of the Gulf. Everything else is secondary.*

There was only one problem. The coordinates Orca named were right in the thick of the fighting.

"How do we get in there without taking crossfire?" Orca asked.

I reached for the ship's intercom.

"Harper," I said into the mouthpiece, "is she ready to fly?"

There was a crackling pause.

"As ready as she'll ever be," came the reply.

"Give me the wheel," I said, fixing the coordinates in my mind's eye.

"You're the navigator. I'm the skipper."

"Do you want to be a dead skipper?" I asked.

"Fine, but I'm having you flogged for insubordinate behavior."

She sounded like Miranda.

"Go for it," I said, taking the wheel and a deep breath. "And hold on."

I brought the W500 to life and tuned out everything but the ocean.

The raiders were fast, and the missiles were faster. I felt for them, knowing we only had seconds to adjust course, and circled around until I felt an opening ahead.

"Are you a whale or something?" Orca asked, breaking my concentration.

"No."

"Then how are you seeing this shit?"

"I don't know. I just am."

"Echolocating freak," she muttered, but there was respect in the insult.

"Okay, here we go," I said, and turned us head on into the fray.

Orca sent out another whale call, alerting Miranda's crew to our approach, and then I lost track of what she was doing as every ounce of my being focused on maneuvering our bulky trawler through the tangle of watery death.

Directly ahead of us a raider tore a jagged rent through a smaller fleet submersible, and I jerked us clear before the raider could swing around for another pass.

Several hundred meters past the raider, in the intermittent light of the battle, I saw bodies striking out for the surface from a sinking vessel.

"Holy shit," Orca said, and I followed her gaze for a perilous second.

The surface was on fire.

"It's the bloom." Her words were hushed with awe. "The fucking algae bloom is on fire."

"The swimmers—"

"There is nothing we can do for them, Rose, and unless you want to join them, get us to Miranda."

I obeyed, clutching the controls with white knuckles.

The sleek, heavy bodies of the Archipelago ships cut through the black water, illuminated by the flashes of the explosions and the eerie glow from the flames above. I tried not to wonder how we looked to them. We were losing our entourage of squid as we pressed deeper into the fray, and I did not think there was much left of our passenger after the ravages of the journey.

How am I going to find Man o' War *in the middle of this, even with coordinates?*

"Shit," Orca shouted as something hit us.

I did not have time to think about the implications of the impact. Ships clustered above us, black shapes against the unhealthy red surface, and the water was thick with debris. It was impossible to tell which side had the upper hand. Ching's raiders darted about like eels, quick and slippery compared to the imposing might of the Archipelago, and in the darkness, all I knew for sure was that people were dying whichever way I looked.

"We're fine," Jeanine said over the intercom. "Took out one of the smaller port-side bulkheads, but we stabilized her."

"Good. Keep us that way," Orca replied.

There. The certainty locked in like due north. *Man o' War* sailed close by, 30 degrees starboard, taking on water.

"I found her," I said, disbelief lacing my voice.

"About time—"

The second impact cut her off, and we both clutched at our seats as the boat tilted.

"Dammit, Rose."

"She's dead ahead. I can get us in," I said, gritting my teeth as the trawler bucked against me. The nose wanted to drop, no matter how much power I gave it. "Let her know we're coming."

Orca send out one last sonar blast, and I locked in on *Man o' War*. Even in the dark, I knew her shape.

The docking bay opened, revealing a wash of traitorous light before the crew extinguished it. I focused on the coordinates, bringing us out of our death spiral just long enough to sputter into the hold.

"By all that is holy, let's never do that again," Harper said as she emerged from the engine bay. Both she and Jeanine were soaked with brine and stained with grease, and Kraken, when he limped in from trying to patch up the hole from the missile strike I'd failed to avoid, looked equally grim.

"That was damn close," he said, leaning his large bulk against the common room counter and rubbing his leg. "This little beauty won't be getting back in the water any time soon."

His words chilled me.

There was no way out. I was on this ship, for better or for worse, and so was Harper. I felt the side of my uniform, where Comita's pardon was shoved deep into a damp inside pocket, and let out a very small whimper.

Orca was right. A pardon was a very flimsy thing indeed.

"I need to get to the engine room," Jeanine said, breaking into my tide of worry. "And you're coming with me. Those bilge rats won't know what hit them, and nobody sinks this ship without my say-so." She patted Finn on the shoulder and seized Harper's arm, towing her toward the hatch.

Harper shot one slightly confused look back at me, and then she was gone, off to hold her own against an alien crew.

I figured her odds were infinitely better than mine had ever been, for all that she was the Admiral's daughter.

That left me, Orca, Kraken, and Finn, who was looking decidedly ill.

"We need to get him to the doctor," I said, shifting my weight from foot to foot.

"I can carry this sack of shit on my own, kid," Kraken said. "You two go find the captain." The grim expression on his face had lifted, and he was looking faintly amused at my discomfort.

Orca cleared her throat.

I fiddled with the hem of my shirt sleeve.

"Come on, jelly," Orca said. "In case you forgot, we're in the middle of a war."

"Right."

330

Kraken lifted Finn gently, cradling the smaller man's head against his shoulder, and climbed out of the hatch one-handed.

"Where do you think she will be?" I asked Orca.

"How the hell should I know?"

I decided not to remind her that, as first mate, her guess was better than mine and followed her out of the *Sea Cat*.

Nobody greeted us in the landing bay, and judging by the echoing shouts from elsewhere in the ship, that was because everyone had significantly larger worries on their hands.

"Think you can keep up this time?" Orca asked, reminding me of the first time I'd set foot on this dock.

"Screw you." I jogged a half step to catch up with her as we waded into the warren of hallways that made up the *Man o' War*. The ship creaked around us, and I heard the distant rush of water, punctuated every few seconds by another shout.

"There's fighting on the decks," Orca said, unsheathing her short blade.

I followed suit, trying not to compare the size of my little knife to her sword.

"Who do you think it is?"

"Either a mutiny, or the ship's been boarded."

We rounded a corner and got our answer. A man in Ching's uniform fled before a bellowing *Man o' War* crew member, clutching at a partially severed arm.

Bile rose in my throat and I fixated on the directions, reminding myself that I did not have time to feel.

Orca grabbed me roughly and pulled me tighter into her shadow, grumbling under her breath about soft, rice-fed fleet scum who could not be trusted to hold their own against an infant with a toothpick.

"Where's the captain?" Orca demanded of the next sailor we saw. This one was wrapping a length of cloth around a gash in her thigh, and did not even bother looking up to answer.

"Bridge," she said, tightening her tourniquet with a savage tug.

331

Orca took off at a dead run, which seemed a little risky to me, considering the number of blind corners we turned, but I followed.

"Motherfuckers." Orca's curse came at the same moment she skidded to a halt at the doors to the bridge, where a heavily armed group of Red Flag Fleet pirates held their ground.

"I'm the first mate," she said, lowering her weapon in a decidedly temporary manner. "Let me in."

"Your captain's gone soft, girl," said one of the sailors. "Till she remembers who she serves, Ching wants her kept docile."

"So you've locked her in the command center?" Orca asked, stating the obvious flaw in the pirate's logic.

"Kill them," the woman in charge snarled.

We're doomed, I thought, doing a quick head count. There were at least ten of them, and two of us.

A roar came from somewhere down the hallway.

Three of us, I added to myself as Kraken exploded past me, swinging a length of knotted rope in one hand and his sword in the other. Orca was a step behind him, and I was swept up in their wake, a cry on my lips as I raised my small knife to inflict what damage I could.

"Rose."

I looked up as something soared through the air toward me over the heads of the pirates. Behind them, leaning out of the bridge door, was Miranda.

My hand reached out to catch the length of pipe she'd thrown at me just as a pirate ducked around Orca, forcing my eyes away from my captain.

The adrenaline that had been keeping me going for days threatened to give out. The pirate wasn't very big, but he had clearly been nursed from an iron teat, and he eyed me with confident scorn as he raised a weapon that looked like the discarded offspring of a cudgel and a butcher knife.

I blocked it with the pipe. My arm buzzed with the impact, but I didn't have time to think about the pain. He struck again, and again, and it was all I could do to keep the pipe between us.

332

"Like this," Orca said, appearing beside me in a mist of blood. A silver blur whipped past my ear and sprouted from the man's throat.

"Don't look," Orca advised, but it was too late.

The pirate's blood bubbled up around the knife hilt, and his eyes went wide as he clawed at it, streaking blood up and down his neck.

"Get to the captain and get us out of here," Orca said, pulling me away.

Miranda had her back to the door and her sword drawn. Three pirates ranged warily around her, trying to get past her and into the bridge.

Orca engaged with a new foe with a grunt, and Kraken had two more pirates circling him, treading carefully around the bodies of their fellows.

Get to the captain, I thought, my heart hammering. *Easier said than done.*

The pirates were all occupied with my deadlier companions. This was my chance. I raised the pipe and brought it down on the head of one of pirates between me and Miranda. The sensation sent shockwaves up my arm as his skull gave under the pressure, and he staggered into the fighter next to him.

"Now," Miranda commanded, and I ducked behind her as she stepped away from the door.

The bridge lacked the chaos of the hallways. Here, Miranda's sailors stood glued to the instruments, and their shouts were ordered instead of bloodthirsty.

I turned back to Miranda, but she was still half in the doorway, the muscles in her back shifting as she swung her blade in the tight space.

"You, navigator."

I'd been spotted.

A burly sailor I vaguely recognized waved me over to the navigation panel, rubbing the back of his neck.

"We've managed to patch up the portside aft bulkhead for

now, but we're not as quick as we used to be and we won't be able to get topside till we can pump her out."

I stared at the sonar screen before us, my mind momentarily blank. It was a wash of color, rendered nearly useless by the conflict around us.

"We can't surface anyway," I said. "It's on fire."

"Where to, then?"

"We drop further." I paused, thinking. "As deep as she'll go. That will give us a little more warning for any incoming fire, and then we make for the coast."

"The coast?"

"The coast," I repeated. Sailing toward Aries or Andromeda amounted to a death sentence, and so I had to hope that Comita was so worried about her daughter that she had put out a ceasefire on all ships that fit the *Man o' War's* description.

"And put out this sonar blast when we get down there," I added, illustrating a sequence of pings that Comita's sailors could not fail to recognize.

He gave me a long look, presumably taking in the fleet uniform I still wore and the blood spattered across my arms—*when had that gotten there?*—before nodding. I wondered if he was one of the ones who had wanted me dead.

Not that it mattered. We would all be dead in the next few minutes if we weren't very, very lucky.

Thuds sounded from behind me, and I jerked around in time to see more of the crew re-forming the barricade that had clearly been hastily disassembled to let Miranda out and me in.

The captain was nowhere in sight.

"Where—?"

"That's the captain's business," he said, throwing the levers and switches that would open the rest of the bulkheads, allowing us to submerse further.

"But—" I cut myself off, feeling closer to drowning than I had even with Orca's arms around my neck, pushing me under. "Right. I'm just a navigator," I said to myself, and I turned my face toward the cardinal directions and took the ship into the deep.

We almost made it out.

I felt Ching Shih's ship break away to follow us, and in the strange, red light of the ragged dawn, I raised the inevitable alarm.

"Brace for impact."

The ships collided with enough force to knock me into the dash.

"Where the hell is the captain?" I asked. Miranda had not returned to the bridge, and neither had Orca nor Kraken.

Nobody answered me. The remaining crew checked the barricade at the door and prepared to be boarded. I slumped in my seat and listened, feeling the boat grind beneath me as it struggled to stay on course.

"Remember, we don't surrender unless we hear the order from the captain herself," one of the sailors instructed the rest.

"Fuck them all," said another, wiping her hand across her forehead in a gesture that I recognized as the pure exhaustion I felt.

I had failed. We were almost in range of the Polarian Fleet, and I had failed to get us there before Ching found us.

Minutes turned into what felt like hours as the shouting grew louder, ebbing and flowing as the conflict raged throughout the ship. On the bridge, we focused on what we could, closing off flooded compartments and trying to keep the ship upright and on course.

The ship shuddered again. I didn't look up. We couldn't afford to take on any more water.

"Seas save us," said the burly navigator.

I gave my silent agreement before I realized he was laughing.

I didn't see anything funny about it. I had returned to Miranda, only to condemn her, myself, Harper, and the rest of the crew to death.

"Open your eyes, navigator," he said.

When I obeyed, he pointed out the window.

Ching's ship drifted away from us, fire burning through her hull from the force of the detonation that had ripped her nearly in half.

"Who—?" I asked.

"Us? The Archipelago? A rogue missile? Hell if I know, and hell if I care. We're clear."

He was right. *Man o' War* lurched free, gaining speed as we cleared the wreckage.

A few seconds later, we picked up a sonar reading that sent a thrill of hope and fear through me. It was a Polarian sequence, and it only had one use—to welcome home sailors presumed lost at sea. We had made it out of the battle, and into the dubious protection of the Archipelago.

Now I just had to hope that Comita would hold up her end of the bargain.

"That's Archipelago Fleet clearance right there," I explained, jotting down the sonar code and fighting the hysterical laughter bubbling up in my throat. "It worked."

"What worked?" he asked, but I didn't bother answering. Our gamble had paid off.

"I need to find the captain," I said. "Hold her steady at these coordinates."

"You sure?" he asked, pointing once again at the lightening sea.

Circling our vessel was a small silver ship, and I recognized the gray head I could just make out through the glass of the helm.

Admiral Comita.

I opened my mouth to curse. Nothing came out.

"Looks like they're trying to get us to open the landing bay," he said.

"I guess we open the landing bay, then." My voice wavered. "And I better get down there."

The sounds of fighting still echoed through the walls.

"Think you can make it alone?" he asked.

"Yes."

No.

He helped me clear the barricade, and I stood in the carnage outside the door as they piled the crates back in front of it.

My eyes jumped from body to body, my heart pounding in fear until I was sure that none of them belonged to anyone I knew.

Harper, I thought. I had to find Harper.

I ran along hallways I halfway remembered, doing my best to avoid any lingering scuffles.

Ching's sailors fought bitterly, now that their ship was gone. They knew as well as I did that they would not receive mercy from the victors. I passed one as he fled, though whether he was looking for his fellows or a place to hide, I could not tell, but when I did not make a move toward him he kept running.

I had never been to the engine compartment of the ship. I knew where it was, but nothing prepared me for the gout of steam that billowed out of the hatch when I opened the door, or the massive pipes that twisted through it. Two people could have crawled through them abreast, a fact I was able to affirm when a sailor hopped down out of one of the pipes and called something back up to the man still inside.

"Have you seen Jeanine?" I asked the man on the ground.

He grunted and pointed deeper into the steam.

I stepped carefully, not wanting to fall into any of the poorly marked holes in the walkway that opened onto ladders and, in one memorable case, a vat of coolant.

"Jeanine? Harper?" I called out.

"Rose?" Harper's voice drifted out of the fog, followed by the rest of her.

"The Admiral is here."

Her eyes widened slightly, and then she set her face in an expression of grim determination. Jeanine materialized beside her, wiping grease-stained hands on her trousers.

"Can you find the captain and tell her to come to the landing bay?" I told her after I explained the situation.

Jeanine looked around at the hissing engine with a long-suffering look.

"Not much more I can do here anyway."

"What do you think she's going to say?" I asked Harper when we were back in the comparatively fresh air of the corridor.

"Nothing we're going to like. Let me handle her, Rose, and follow my lead."

337

"Don't I always?"

"No."

We jogged on in silence. I hoped Jeanine found Miranda, and quickly. I did not want to be alone with Harper, the Admiral, and any forces Comita had brought with her.

The hatch to the landing bay loomed at the end of the next hallway, partially buried beneath a pile of bodies.

"Should we wait for the captain?" I asked.

"If we make my mother wait too long, she'll storm the ship," Harper said. "Help me move these?"

Together we hauled the corpses away from the door. A few were Ching's, but I recognized some of the others from my time on *Man o' War*. I flinched when I touched their cooling flesh. Neither Harper nor I said anything.

"Together, then," she said, putting her hand on the hatch.

I glanced down the hallway, but Miranda was nowhere in sight.

"Together."

Harper put her other hand in her pocket and opened the door.

Comita's crew ranged protectively about their small ship, and there were a few bodies that looked suspiciously fresh on the ground before them. I hoped they were Ching's.

Comita herself stood on the streaming deck, her hands firmly planted on her hips. She didn't waver when her eyes fell on Harper.

"Retrieve Harper Comita," she ordered.

"No," Harper said, pulling her hand out of her pocket.

I took an involuntary step away from her as the detonator glowed ominously in the blue light. Comita's sailors froze.

"Put it down, Harper." Comita's voice was calm. Cool, even, unlike the bead of sweat that trickled down my throat.

"I will put it down when you acknowledge the pardon you had me deliver to Captain Stillwater."

I could tell by the puzzled reaction of Comita's crew that this did not match with the official story.

"Harper," Comita said, the warning in her voice unmistakable.

"Acknowledge the pardon, mother."

"Take her; she won't detonate the ship," Comita said.

"It's not my ship you need worry about."

Comita's sailors hesitated.

"The explosive is on the dock, mother."

Comita's lips thinned into a pale scar.

"Admiral Comita," I said, hoping to dissipate the tension between mother and daughter. I had no way of knowing if Harper was bluffing, but knowing Harper the odds were even either way.

"Compass Rose," Comita said. There was no warmth in her voice.

"Harper's expertise has been instrumental in keeping our craft afloat. Perhaps, as a gesture of faith, she could stay on until repairs are made."

As Comita's face changed, I realized that I had never truly seen her angry.

She was angry now.

"Polaris does not require gestures of faith. A pardon is a pardon, and now that it has been delivered, Harper Comita will return to her post."

I swallowed.

The minute Harper left this ship, the only thing I had to go on was Comita's word, which at the moment wasn't something I was comfortable settling with.

"Rose," Jeanine said, stepping into the bay and setting the Polarian sailors on edge. "Miranda isn't coming."

Her face was carefully neutral.

"We need her here," I said, pitching my voice low.

"She said that, I quote, 'Rose can damn well get us out of this herself, her Admiral and the entire Archipelago be damned.'"

"Oh."

"This was after she put a knife to my throat and demanded to know if you were alive," she added.

"Oh," I said again. There was a strange buzzing in my head.

The hatch opened again, and we both jumped as an exceptionally bloodstained Miranda Stillwater pushed through it to stand between us. She gave Harper a quick glance, ignored me and Jeanine, who looked as confused as I felt, and addressed Comita.

"Admiral Comita. Is it you I have to thank for getting the scum off my back?"

Comita's face froze, then changed, erasing its earlier rage as the mask of Admiral slipped back into place.

"You looked like you needed the help," Comita said.

"That wasn't just any ship." Miranda tossed the bloody sword she carried on the ground. It swung on its hilt, gleaming in the light, until the blade came to rest pointing directly at Comita.

My compass twitched. The blade was aligned directly with due north.

"That is Ching Shih's sword, as promised."

"She is dead?"

"There is only one way to take a sword from a woman like Ching."

The familiar way she said Ching's name turned my insides to ice. What had it been like for Miranda to kill the woman who had saved her life?

Comita stepped down off the deck and past her sailors to stand over the blade. The tip barely grazed her boot, and a hot, metallic taste filled my mouth.

It took me a moment to realize I had bitten my lip hard enough to draw blood. The filaments roared in my ears, and I clenched my fists to clear my head.

"Well, captain, the Archipelago owes you a great deal," Comita said.

There was a nasty silence, in which I suspected all of those assembled who knew Miranda's history were thinking the same thing: the Archipelago owed Miranda far more than a pardon.

"I keep my promises," Miranda said. "A bargain is a bargain."

The two women stared at each other, and I had the unsettling feeling that more passed in that look than I would ever know.

"I have sent an emissary with your pardon," Comita said, her eyes flicking toward her daughter. The sailors around her shifted

340

uncomfortably, but none were as poorly disciplined as I was, because they recovered from this change in tactic much more quickly than my stuttering heartbeat.

Miranda squared her shoulders and nodded.

"I appreciate the loan of your navigator. As you can see, she is unharmed. Mostly," Miranda added, her eyes taking in the blood on my clothes but avoiding my face.

"Loan?" Comita's voice betrayed a hint of confusion.

"I fulfilled my end of the parley. She is still alive."

"Keep her a little while longer," Comita said, and the chill in her voice made me shiver. I remembered with a pang of loss how I had felt in her study when she poured me that first glass of rum, bubbles of joy rising through me. I did not think I would ever feel that way again about Admiral Comita.

Miranda's hand twitched against her thigh, but that was the only thing that revealed the slightest hint of emotion.

"Thank you, Admiral. Do I have your leave to repair my ship?"

"I will send you supplies to assist you. Harper, let's go."

Harper stood her ground, her face thunderous.

"That was an order, sailor."

"With all due respect, Admiral, I will serve you much better if I stay here for the duration of the repair."

Comita's eyes glinted like knives.

"It was never my intention to spare you discipline, as my daughter. Now I see I should have heeded the advice of others, and sent you to serve on another ship. Your insubordinate behavior will not go unpunished."

"Mother," Harper said, and even Comita flinched at the venom in Harper's voice. "The greatest honor I could ever do you is to disobey you here today."

"Very well then," Comita said, deadly calm, "consider yourself stripped of your rank and position. Fair seas, daughter."

And with that, she turned to board her sleek silver ship, trailed by her crew, one of whom had the sense to grab Ching's sword, and they sank beneath the brackish water of the hold.

"Well," Harper said, forcing a laugh, "I hope you could use an

Archipelago engineer, Captain Stillwater, because I appear to be out of a job."

Miranda's back was to me, but I could hear the smile in her voice as she shook Harper's hand.

"As it just so happens, I could use an engineer right about now."

Jeanine slapped Harper on the back. I wrestled my lips into a smile and met my best friend's eyes. They looked as dead as I felt.

Miranda strode out of the room without a word to me, forcing Harper and Jeanine to follow.

I stood in their wake, tears blurring my eyes.

Would it have been too much for her to even look at me?

The emptiness of the hold pressed in around me. I knew there were a million things I should be doing, from helping to subdue Ching's sailors and checking the wounded to keeping us on course.

Instead, I knelt on the piece of ground where Ching's sword had lain and pressed my fingers against a drop of blood.

Ching Shih, the greatest living threat of our time, dead. It seemed surreal, and while I couldn't ever forgive the woman for the things she'd done to my people, I had known her, and now she was gone. Things like that were not supposed to happen.

I touched my forefinger to my thumb. The blood was growing tacky, and I rubbed it between my fingers as exhaustion swept over me. I had been awake for more hours than I could count. I had battled a giant squid, fought with pirates, and been ignored by the woman I wanted more than anything else in the world.

I needed a shower. I needed a meal. I needed a good night's sleep, and more than that, I needed to let go of Miranda Stillwater.

"Crow's Eye," I said, surprising myself with my croaking voice.

The thought of climbing to the crow's nest filled my limbs with lead, but I forced my legs to stand and make the journey back through the ship, turning a deaf ear to the cries of the wounded and the hiss of water.

He was still alive. I figured this out as his blade pricked the tender skin beneath my chin, and then he dropped it, letting out a long sigh.

"So you're still with us then, wolf pup," he said, leaning back in his swivel chair. The water around us was empty, the growing morning light sending shafts of splintered sunlight down even to our depth.

"I'm not a sea wolf," I said, dropping to the floor. "Miranda told me what they were, and I am anything but legendary."

Crow's Eye raised his grizzled eyebrows.

"Says the girl who found the channel."

I shrugged, then paused, my sluggish brain adding two and two together. In the midst of the fighting, none of the late *Sea Cat's* crew had had time to tell *Man o' War* about the channel.

"How did you know about the channel?" I asked, a dark suspicion rearing its head.

"I see things," he said.

"You knew." The accusation hung between us.

"Aye," he said, sighing again. "I knew."

"Did Miranda know?"

"No, the captain doesn't know. Nor does the rest of the crew, unless I'm mistaken, and Ching never could be bothered to send out scouts."

"Why didn't you tell me?"

"The channel is a legend, girl. I thought I found it, once, when I was a little younger than you. Sailed in deep enough to never want to go back before we ran aground. Lost one of my best mates to fever, digging ourselves out. When your Archipelago's ships came at us from behind, though, I knew you'd done it."

"You could have given me a hint."

"And told you to chase after a legend?" he said, mocking me. "It takes someone legendary to find a legend, kid."

"I'm not—" I broke off, a different question on my lips. "Are there other people like me out there?"

Crow's Eye smiled and patted his stump in an absentminded way.

"Hard to say." He winked. "Sea wolves are a legend, too, remember?"

"You're a real barnacle, you know that?" I said, feeling a little better despite myself.

"Oh, aye. And you're the saddest excuse for a sea wolf I ever saw. You made up with the captain yet?"

"She hates me."

"Don't be such a squid shit, kid. You disobeyed her orders. Ching's sailors have been on us like remora since you vanished, and the only reason the captain isn't dead is because Ching can't bear to kill her."

I did not correct his present tense. He clearly didn't know Ching had been killed, yet.

"She's madder than a spitting tom and, worse, she thought you all were dead. Cut her some slack. And eat this."

He tossed a rice cake at me, and I devoured it in two bites.

"Will she have me flogged?" I asked when I had licked the crumbs from my lips.

"Only if you want her to." Crow's Eye gave me a leer that made my skin crawl, even though I knew it was in jest.

"You're awful."

"Look, kid, you shouldn't take romantic advice from a single man who pisses in a jug, and I'm not saying the captain's even a good woman, but it seems to me like the only way this ship is going to run smoothly is if you take matters into your own hands, so to speak."

This time he spared me the leer.

"You can sleep when you're dead. Go wash the blood off your face and make things right with Miranda. The way things move around here, you might not get a second chance."

I found her in the bilges, up to her knees in black water, working one of the pumps and laughing at something Kraken was singing in his deep, gravelly, and wonderfully terrifying voice.

Her back was to me, and so Kraken saw me first. He paused. The stillness sent out ripples through the flooded space.

Miranda kept working the pump. I could see the new tightness in her shoulders, but she didn't break her pace.

Fine, I thought, double-checking that the pardon was still in my pocket as I descended the ladder. My boots filled with water, and my trousers wicked moisture up past the waterline at my knee, creeping like cold fingers up my thighs. I waded towards the captain with enough sense still left to me to be grateful for the shock of cold water. It made it easier not to run to her, damning pride and the consequences.

"Captain Stillwater," I said when I was a few wet feet from her.

She turned and leaned against the pump with an arrogant grace that made my mouth go dry, and looked at me, really looked at me, for the first time since my return.

"Compass Rose," she said. Her eyes traveled down and up my body, taking in my soaked knees and the fleet uniform with the North Star emblazoned on the jacket breast.

"I have the pardon," I said, wishing I had thought of a more compelling opening line.

"And I have a hole in my ship. A navigator, however, would have been useful a few days ago."

I glared at her. In the dank lighting, her eyes looked nearly black. I stripped out of my jacket and down to my undershirt and trousers, hanging the bloodstained uniform on a piece of broken pipe.

Miranda's knuckles whitened on the pump. Navigators might wear a looser style of uniform than engineers and mechanics, but there was nothing loose about the fleet-issued undershirts. They left little to the imagination.

"Looks like you could use a hand, Captain." I gave her a mocking salute.

"You ever worked a bilge pump?" she asked.

I could feel her eyes on my body.

"Nope." I braced myself for the full force of her gaze. "But I can find true north from the belly of a whale. Captain."

"Let's start with the bilge pump for now," she said, but her eyes lost a little of their cold disdain.

I shrugged, for all the world as if my heart was not battering its way out of my chest, and stepped past her to take over the pump. Her scent, faint beneath the smells of blood and salt, nearly knocked me to my knees.

Kraken dropped a heavy hand on my shoulder as I worked the handle, then resumed a bawdy drifter ballad about the many ways the ocean tried to fuck a plucky and impossibly proportioned crew of sailors. I listened in amused horror while my inner compass followed Miranda. The tune, for all its bawdiness, had an underlying, mournful note that fitted the loss of life and limb around us.

When the water level had receded to below my ankles and my undershirt was drenched in sweat and bilge water, Miranda called it quits.

"A word, navigator," she said, her hand brushing the small of my back.

I shivered and grabbed my jacket.

O captain, my captain, went the old poem.

My boots squelched up the ladder and through the ship, coming at last to a soggy halt outside the door to her private quarters. I stood in my little puddle, frozen to the spot.

There was a reason captains rarely summoned crew to their quarters. Comita had done it, and, like the summons, her request had breached many layers of protocol. No matter what happened behind these doors, I knew with a firm certainty that I would not emerge unscathed.

North, east, south, west.

I walked through the door and let it shut behind me.

Miranda sat in one of the low chairs in her receiving room, her boots crossed at the ankle. She didn't seem to mind that her clothes were soaked. At least the water had rinsed out some of the bloodstains.

"You have the pardon?"

I handed her the envelope.

Miranda brushed her thumb with its Gemini ring across the paper once, then set it on the side table next to her chair, unopened. I straightened beneath her scrutiny.

"Nice uniform," she said.

"The rest of my clothes are on your ship."

"I'll have them packed for you."

Any lingering, desperate hope that she might have forgiven me in my absence crumbled.

"Is that a dismissal?" I asked. My voice trembled, and I hardened my tone to hide it.

"You directly contradict my orders, vanish without a trace, and then walk onto my ship wearing a fleet uniform after taking my oath, and you have the balls to ask about dismissal? I have walked crew for less." She let out a cruel laugh and shook her head.

I dropped the jacket to the floor. Her face didn't change. We both knew there were things between us far worse than a uniform.

"I chose the only course available to me, Miranda, and I came back. You know who I am and who I serve, which is more than I can say for you."

"I serve the same thing I've always served."

"Yourself?" I said, crossing my arms over my chest. I had forgotten, in my anguish, how infuriating she could be.

"This fucked-up, poisonous, beautiful ocean."

Of all the things she could have said, that was the last thing I expected. I bit my lower lip and spoke the words I wished I had spoken sooner, sparing myself the pain of everything that had happened since.

"Then you're going to need a second mate."

Miranda stood, slowly. There was a distant ringing, like a bell, only deeper. It echoed through me, filling up the empty, sore places with a sound that nearly broke me.

"Second mate?"

She was so close to me. Her shirt, like mine, was soaked, and it clung to her body.

"If you'll have me," I said.

I can take you any way I want," she had told me on the day she'd flogged Annie. Had she known then, just how true her words would prove to be?

Several different strong emotions crossed her face, leaving minute wakes behind.

347

The absurdity of my guilt washed over me while Miranda weighed her options. So what if something had happened between me and Orca? This woman had rejected me, had flat out told me I meant nothing to her. If she had really wanted me, she should have fought a little harder. And at the end of the day, I was a navigator. A damn good navigator. She should be asking me to stay, not the other way around.

I regretted my words. I regretted my soaking wet pants, and all that I had given up to be standing in front of this callous, two-faced, selfish mercenary. More than that, I wanted to fall to my knees and take her hands, begging her to let me stay. As the silence between us stretched thin, my heart plunged into the next trough, battered by waves ninety feet tall and growing.

I could have sailed on any ship on the ocean, I thought. *And I hate that I only want whatever one you're on.*

"Rose."

It was half question, half plea, and then her hands were on my face and her lips were pressed to mine, more real than anything I'd felt over the past week. Her fingers cupped my jaw, tilting my head up toward her, and I wrapped my hands in her shirt collar and pulled her to me.

The urgency in her kiss struck me like due north.

I kept one hand on her shirt while the other ran down her side, feeling her body move against me, and when I found her belt I clung to it with all my strength. The fatigue of the past twenty-four hours blurred into a delirium of longing. Her breath came faster as my fingers brushed the delicate skin beneath, and I shivered as she pulled me hard against her, the heat from her palms leaving red-hot brands along my back and up my sides.

Her lips paused on my jaw, and her fingers dug fiercely into my hips as she broke away enough to whisper in my ear.

"If you ever leave me like that again, Rose—"

I tangled a hand in her hair and pulled her lips back to mine. She responded with an intensity that made us both stumble, and she caught me as we fell back into the chair behind her.

I landed on top, my hands braced on her shoulders and my

hips pressed against hers. Every molecule of open space between us felt like a crime.

Miranda's eyes trailed down my body and paused at the hem of my shirt.

"You want to be my second mate?" she asked, her breath coming as quickly as mine. "Then lose the uniform."

She tugged the undershirt over my head. Cool air hit my flushed skin as Miranda traced the scar on my stomach, and I shuddered uncontrollably beneath her touch. When her lips brushed my collarbone, the collar of her shirt brushed against me and I pushed her away, fumbling at the buttons. I wanted to feel her skin against mine, not the rough weave of damp fabric.

Her lips were flushed a deep red, and the desire in her eyes was shattering. Ignoring my desperate fingers, she ripped the shirt over her head and undid both of our bras with the sort of efficiency one expected from a captain who could mobilize an entire Archipelago station into mutiny, survive a swarm of man o' war, serve beneath the most ruthless pirate on the waters, and still end up the captain of her own ship.

I stilled her with a hand on her chest. I wanted to see her.

The scars on her skin did nothing to lessen its perfection. The firm line of muscle that ran down her stomach softened at her hips, and above it her breasts rose and fell with her unsteady breathing. A scar crossed her left nipple, a pale tracery of remembered pain.

She let me look. Her eyes were several shades darker as she sprawled in the chair beneath me, and she couldn't keep the arrogance out of her posture any more than I could have stood and walked out of the room. Her body had molded itself to command, and even shirtless she radiated power.

"I never wanted to go," I said, the truth coming easily, and then her skin lay hot against mine and she lifted me into the air, her lips on my breasts as she tumbled me onto her bed.

Like any good navigator, I let my captain take the wheel while I kept my eyes on the stars.

"Rose," she said, her words vibrating against me as she brought me to the brink.

"What?" I cursed her mentally for stopping. No matter how good my name sounded on her lips, it didn't feel as good as the way her lips felt on me, stripping away doubt and betrayal and death and bringing me perilously close to a place that felt like home.

"Now."

I blame it on years of conditioning, and on the innate human desire to follow commands. Despite my intentions, as her mouth closed over me and she slid her hand inside me, I obeyed.

"For a pardon, this has a lot of demands," Miranda said.

I opened my eyes. There were several pages of official-looking writing in her hands, and I recognized Comita's signature.

The last thing I wanted to think about was Admiral Comita. I adjusted my head, pillowing it deeper into Miranda's arm.

"She wants you to scout for her," I said, my lips brushing her skin with each word.

"An official mercenary?"

"And full citizen. You could go home, if you wanted." I traced the scars on her chest.

"No," she said, putting the pages down and leaning back.

I weighted her down with more limbs.

"No?"

"I can't go back to Gemini. I made my peace with that a long time ago."

"What about your family?"

Miranda rolled me onto my back and looked down at me, her hair falling in a tangle over her shoulder. It smelled like the strange flowers that grew in her garden, and salt water.

"I made my peace with them, too."

"What about your sister?"

Her eyes clouded.

"Shouldn't you try to see her?" I pressed.

Miranda shook her head, placing a finger over my lips.

"I took everything away from her. It's a lot easier to forgive the dead than the living."

Her words reminded me of something.

"What happened with Ching Shih, Miranda?"

"You," Miranda said, giving me a look that effectively shut down further rational thought, "have way too many questions."

My body rose to meet hers, and I let Ching Shih go. The pirate's memory would haunt me later, I knew, but right now I had no time for ghosts.

The next time I opened my eyes, Miranda was watching me, her eyes full of a desperate tenderness that vanished almost as soon as I saw it, making me doubt what I'd seen.

"As much as it pains me to say this, I'm still the captain of this ship, and we have work to do."

I glowered at her. I was no longer convinced my limbs were all connected to each other, let alone that they could support my weight, and I was still exhausted from a full trawl's worth of near death experiences.

"Are you accepting Comita's offer?" I asked, forcing myself to sit up.

"It seems to be the only way to keep you around." She winked at me, stood, and stretched. I couldn't keep my eyes off her.

"Do you want to keep me around?"

Miranda walked back over to where I lay and extended her hand. I let her pull me up, but she didn't release me. She turned my palm over and kissed it, once.

The mark she'd left was fading, blending in with the other lines on my hand. It looked natural now, an extension of my life, head, and heart lines.

"I never regretted marking my sailors, until you." Her voice was rough.

"It's all right," I said.

"It's not. I knew what I was taking away from you."

For an instant, I could see her, younger and unmarred, standing at the helm of a Gemini ship. I liked her better this way, naked, scarred, and holding my hand.

I closed my fingers around hers.

"Miranda," I began, unsure of how to put my feelings into words. "I was an idiot. I never meant—"

She waited, letting me stutter over my explanation.

"About what happened with Orca. It didn't mean anything."

"Of course it meant something."

"Well, it didn't mean what you think it means," I said.

"It meant I was an idiot, and you were confused. And you were right. You were a distraction."

I could hardly deny that.

"I'm not confused now."

"Good." Her fingers tightened around mine. "Because I've known Orca for four years, Rose. She followed me here from Ching's ship, and she's saved my life more times than I can count. I really, really don't want to have to kill her."

"That's a pretty bold statement, coming from the woman who told me she didn't give a rat's ass about me."

Miranda didn't flinch.

"I wasn't sure I did, until you left."

"You are an ass." I snatched my hand away from hers.

"I'm from Gemini," she said. "We're all like that."

"Well, where I'm from, people like you tend to die alone."

She raised an eyebrow.

"Is that a threat, second mate?" she asked.

"Depends."

"On what?"

"On if you care about me now."

She kissed me, and I could taste the anger and the fear and the longing on her lips.

It was all the answer I needed.

Center

Captain's Log
Captain Miranda Stillwater
Man o' War
September 11, 2513
13, -59.5°

This goddamn ocean. Finally escaped the anoxic bloom we've been riding for days. Three days, six hours, and twenty-seven minutes, to be exact. I took the surface reading myself this morning, against the sound advice of both the first and second mate, who wanted their objections noted.

It is my official opinion that the only good thing that will come out of mapping the coasts is the distance it puts between *Man o' War* and Admiral Comita. The southern wind itches, and I'm beginning to think Kraken might have the right of it, after all. We'd be better off rounding the horn and taking our chances in the Pacific. Rose could get us there.

Compass Rose, who still hasn't figured out that beneath her heading lies something far more dangerous than anything methane hydrate can throw at us.

Strip away the uniform, and Josephine Comita, Ching Shih, and Miranda Stillwater are all the same, ambition poured into identical molds.

I have not told my navigator about the second half of the bargain I struck with her Admiral. The Council's pardon is paper, and will disintegrate as soon as it gets wet, and even if it wasn't false hope, that life is gone. My home is this ship, and Gemini might as well be inland Antarctica. I would not have put either at risk for a pardon.

I know why Comita has agreed to have us map the coasts, and it is not to search for further passages. It keeps us off the radar. It lets people forget, for a while, that Admiral Comita dealt with revolutionaries to claim her victory. It prevents the Council from connecting any dots that would be better off left in isolation.

For my part, I am trying to enjoy this fleeting peace. I am trying hard to lose myself in the amber center of the compass, ignoring where it points, but Comita's promise is like a cardinal direction.

"You'll get your mutiny, Miranda Stillwater."

Epilogue

The repairs took the better part of a week. Harper was instrumental in refitting some of the systems that had been damaged beyond repair, and Comita stayed true to her word. The supplies Harper requested arrived, signed by the admiral herself. It was the only communication that took place between mother and daughter.

Harper handled it with a stoicism that was far more worrying to me than rage.

"I've always said I wanted to serve off ship from her," she said when I asked her how she was doing.

"Do you think she'll let you stay?"

"I don't plan on giving her a choice."

I let the subject drop after that.

Man o' War remained on the outskirts of the Polarian Fleet while the battle for the Gulf raged on for another three days. Word of Ching's demise had not so much as demoralized her sailors as invigorated them. Driven by the reckless knowledge of their own deaths, and the fate of the few ships that did try to surrender, they fought with a viciousness that defied the limitations of violence.

I was more than happy to stay out of the battle, and with Harper on board, Comita made sure none of the Archipelago ships mistook us for the enemy. Her anger with her daughter did not extend to murder.

We did not speak about her possible betrayal. There was no proof that she had ever intended to go back on her word to Miranda, and Miranda herself seemed unconcerned by the prospect the only time I brought it up.

"What did I tell you when you first signed on? Deals at sea are rarely weathertight. She gave me what I wanted, and I gave her what she needed. There was always the risk that one of us would fall short, for one reason or another. We each had our contingency plans."

I did not ask her what hers had been. There was still a great deal about what had happened in my absence that I didn't know. Ching's sailors had not been hospitable guards, and Miranda's surviving crew no longer harbored any sympathetic leanings for the pirate cause. As for what else may have passed between Miranda and Ching, I didn't ask. Miranda's face closed at the mention of the pirate's name, and I remembered what Kraken had said.

"There is nothing neutral about death."

We were given clearance to leave the Gulf a full week and a half after my arrival. I did not blame Comita for wanting us gone. As the carnage settled and the squid fed on the bodies of the drowned, the attention of the Archipelago fleets was bound to turn to the inevitable speculation surrounding the pardon of a certain, presumed dead mutineer.

We set sail with a subdued Harper still onboard for a set of coordinates that Miranda laid before me without explanation and a promise to wait for any further instructions from Comita.

I, for one, was shocked that the admiral had allowed Harper to remain with us, but Harper did not share my confusion.

"You don't know my mother as well as I do," she said. "She doesn't like mess, and I have created a mess. She will tidy up her other loose ends before she deals with me."

I was thinking about what those other loose ends might be as I closed in, at last, on Miranda's coordinates.

"We're here," I said, staring out of the helm at the island in the distance with a touch of trepidation. Crow's Eye's warning about

358

fever was still fresh in my mind. "Are you going to tell me *why* we're here?"

Miranda stared at the mottled mass of green and brown.

"Starbuck." She brought the ship in closer, and I watched in mild alarm as the water turned from dark blue to turquoise.

"Your tortoise?"

"I need to pick up some new seeds for him, and drop off a shipment for someone else."

I followed her out of the bridge with a growing sense of unease. We were miles from anywhere and too close to land for comfort.

"Climb aboard, Captain," Finn said, waiting outside the parley vessel that had picked me up from *Man o' War*, back when both my palms were smooth and my dreams limited. He was looking a little better, but he walked with a limp now, and his left hand shook when he used it.

Orca offered me a hand up onto the deck, and I shared her eye roll as Miranda hauled herself up effortlessly after. I stood at the helm while more crew loaded the parley vessel's small hold, and swallowed a faintly bitter taste of fear as we drifted out of the docking bay into a brilliantly blue morning.

I could see the sand on the shore and the mountain reaching up into a bank of low clouds, rain falling on its green slopes. Miranda steered us straight toward it.

"Do you need me to navigate?" I said, unable to keep the apprehension from my voice.

"I've been here before." Her eyes lingered on me just long enough to bring a blush to my cheeks. I forced myself to look away, and my jaw dropped as we passed between two cliffs and into a wide harbor.

"Neptune's . . ." I said, leaving the curse unfinished. Ships lay at anchor in the bay. Drifter trawls bobbed alongside pirate raiders, and there were some more ships I could not identify. My eyes jumped from deck to deck, distracted at last by the structures I could see built along the shore.

"Welcome to Paradise," Miranda said, guiding us through the

ships and toward a finger of broken wood jutting out into the water.

"Where did you think drifter scum pick up yellow fever?" Finn asked with a wink. "Don't worry. We won't be here long enough for anything to bite you."

"Bite me?" My voice faded to a ragged whisper as I stared around me at the trees on the shore and the people walking toward us down the wharf.

Miranda wrapped an arm around my waist and I sagged against her for support, too stunned to do more than stare. I wished Harper had come along, but she was busy retrofitting the ship's hydrofarm to grow something more appetizing than algae.

Kraken, Orca, and Finn vanished below, and then reappeared on the wharf, escorting a fourth person. Whoever they were had a hood over their head, and their clothes were dark and stained with salt. There was something vaguely familiar about the way they carried themselves, but then Kraken's large bulk blocked them from my view and my eyes drifted back to the crowd.

"This is neutral territory," Miranda added, pointing at the gathered ships. "Pirates and drifters come here for repairs and to escape Archipelago patrols. It's worth the risk, for them."

Neutral territory.

"Miranda," I said, pointing at the prisoner with an impossible idea forming in my overloaded mind. "Who is that?"

She leaned against the rail, her blue eyes reflecting the water and the sky.

"A settled debt."

The prisoner vanished from sight amid the gathering crowd, and our crew returned carrying several large sacks.

I breathed in the smell of land and made a mental note to leave this particular island out of any correspondence with Comita. Some things were better off left uncharted.

Behind us, *Man o' War* waited, fully repaired and ready for her first voyage under official Archipelago contract. Her holds were stocked with decent food, and her crew, while a little bemused at their sudden change of fortune, were more than happy to resume their betting on my abysmal boxing outside the hearing of the captain.

I smiled into the wind, letting my doubts blow away while Miranda ran her thumb over the knife on my belt, tracing the cardinal points in the hilt. This was where I belonged.

Beyond the ship, underneath a darkening winter sky, the currents pulled us farther south. We could ride them around the South Atlantic gyre, swept south, then west, until we crossed over the equatorials and the Brazilian current flung us toward the pole.

North, east, south, west.

I looked up at my captain. Ching Shih had been wrong about me. I was born facing due north, and I knew exactly where I was going.

About the Author

When she is not writing, Anna Burke is an overly ambitious gardener with a penchant for terrible puns. Even though she wrote her debut novel, the high seas adventure *Compass Rose*, while living on a small island in the West Indies, she currently lives in Massachusetts with her wife and their two dogs. You can visit Anna at www.annahburke.com.

Acknowledgments

I got lost many times writing this book. To the people who helped get me and Rose back on track, thank you, especially those of you who joined me in agonizing over plot twists while drinking rum on a Caribbean beach. It was a tough job, but someone had to do it.

Many thanks to the folks at Bywater Books, who believed in this project from the beginning, and a special shout-out to my mentor, Ann McMan, whose sense of humor and sound advice helped keep me afloat toward the end there.

This book would still be foundering without the early readers who braved rough drafts, especially Alessandra Amin, Stefani Deoul, Karelia Stetz-Waters, and my fellow islanders. Your enthusiasm, honesty, and witty commentary helped me keep things in perspective. Thanks also go out to the experts who let me pick their brains about biology and submarines—the crew of "The Vegetable Boat," who unwittingly inspired this novel—and to my parents, whose belief that there was "always money for books" (and library fines) led to this whole writing thing in the first place.

Writing is easier with a supportive spouse. Thank you, Tiffany, for believing in me, for always laughing at my nautical puns, and for helping me navigate life's perilous straits. I couldn't have asked for a better first mate.

THORN

On a cold day deep in the heart of winter, Rowan's father returns from an ill-fated hunting trip bearing a single, white rose. The rose is followed by the Huntress, a figure out of legend. Tall, cruel, and achingly beautiful, she brings Rowan back with her to a mountain fastness populated solely by the creatures of the hunt. Rowan, who once scorned the villagers for their superstitions, now finds herself at the heart of a curse with roots as deep as the mountains, ruled by an old magic that is as insidious as the touch of the winter rose. Torn between her family loyalties, her guilty relief at escaping her betrothal to the charming but arrogant Avery Lockland, and her complicated feelings for the Huntress, Rowan must find a way to break the curse before it destroys everything she loves. There is only one problem—if she can find a way to lift the curse, she will have to return to the life she left behind. And the only thing more unbearable than an endless winter is facing a lifetime of springs without the Huntress.

Thorn

Paperback 978-1-61294-143-1
eBook 978-1-61294-144-8

Bywater
BOOKS

www.bywaterbooks.com

Bywater BOOKS

At Bywater Books we love good books about lesbians just like you do, and we're committed to bringing the best of contemporary lesbian writing to our avid readers. Our editorial team is dedicated to finding and developing outstanding writers who create books you won't want to put down.

We sponsor the Bywater Prize for Fiction to help with this quest. Each prize winner receives $1,000 and publication of their novel. We have already discovered amazing writers like Jill Malone, Sally Bellerose, and Hilary Sloin through the Bywater Prize. Which exciting new writer will we find next?

For more information about Bywater Books and the annual Bywater Prize for Fiction, please visit our website.

www.bywaterbooks.com

CPSIA information can be obtained
at www.ICGtesting.com
Printed in the USA
JSHW040218211022
31955JS00001B/5